STORMWOLFE

A MEDIEVAL ROMANCE

BY KATHRYN LE VEQUE

A SONS OF DE WOLFE NOVEL

KATHRYN LE VEQUE NOVELS

The Dragonblade Series:
Fragments of Grace
Dragonblade
Island of Glass
The Savage Curtain
The Fallen One

Great Marcher Lords of de Lara
Lord of the Shadows
Dragonblade

House of St. Hever
Fragments of Grace
Island of Glass
Queen of Lost Stars

Lords of Pembury:
The Savage Curtain

Lords of Thunder: The de Shera Brotherhood Trilogy
The Thunder Lord
The Thunder Warrior
The Thunder Knight

The Great Knights of de Moray:
Shield of Kronos
The Gorgon

The House of De Nerra:
The Promise
The Falls of Erith
Vestiges of Valor
Realm of Angels

Highland Warriors of Munro:
The Red Lion
Deep Into Darkness

The House of de Garr:
Lord of Light
Realm of Angels

Saxon Lords of Hage:
The Crusader

Kingdom Come

High Warriors of Rohan:
High Warrior

The House of Ashbourne:
Upon a Midnight Dream

The House of D'Aurilliac:
Valiant Chaos

The House of De Dere:
Of Love and Legend

St. John and de Gare Clans:
The Warrior Poet

The House of de Bretagne:
The Questing

The House of Summerlin:
The Legend

The Kingdom of Hendocia:
Kingdom by the Sea

The Executioner Knights:
By the Unholy Hand
The Promise (also Noble Knights of de Nerra)
The Mountain Dark
Starless
A Time of End

Contemporary Romance:

Kathlyn Trent/Marcus Burton Series:
Valley of the Shadow
The Eden Factor
Canyon of the Sphinx

The American Heroes Anthology Series:
The Lucius Robe
Fires of Autumn
Evenshade

Sea of Dreams

Purgatory

Sons of Poseidon:

The Immortal Sea

Other non-connected Contemporary Romance:

Lady of Heaven

Darkling, I Listen

In the Dreaming Hour

River's End

The Fountain

Pirates of Britannia Series (with Eliza Knight):

Savage of the Sea by Eliza Knight

Leader of Titans by Kathryn Le Veque

The Sea Devil by Eliza Knight

Sea Wolfe by Kathryn Le Veque

Note: All Kathryn's novels are designed to be read as stand-alones, although many have cross-over characters or cross-over family groups. Novels that are grouped together have related characters or family groups. You will notice that some series have the same books; that is because they are cross-overs. A hero in one book may be the secondary character in another.

There is NO reading order except by chronology, but even in that case, you can still read the books as stand-alones. No novel is connected to another by a cliff hanger, and every book has an HEA.

Series are clearly marked. All series contain the same characters or family groups except the American Heroes Series, which is an anthology with unrelated characters.

For more information, find it in **A Reader's Guide to the Medieval World of Le Veque**.

THE NEXT GENERATION DE WOLFE PACK

(Issue = children)

Scott (Wife #1 Lady Athena de Norville, has issue. Wife #2, Lady Avrielle Huntley du Rennic, has issue.)

Troy (Wife #1 Lady Helene de Norville, has issue. Wife #2 Lady Rhoswyn Kerr, has issue.)

Patrick (married to Lady Brighton de Favereux, has issue)

James (known as Blayth) – (Wife #1 Lady Rose Hage, has issue. Wife #2 Asmara ferch Cader, has issue)

Katheryn (James' twin) – (Married Sir Alec Hage, has issue)

Evelyn (married to Sir Hector de Norville, has issue)

Baby de Wolfe – died same day. Christened Madeleine.

Edward (married to Lady Cassiopeia de Norville, has issue)

Thomas (married Maitland "Mae" de Ryes Bowlin, has issue)

Penelope (married to Bhrodi de Shera, hereditary King of Anglesey and Earl of Coventry, has issue)

Kieran and Jemma Scott Hage

Mary Alys (adopted) – (married, has issue)

Baby Hage, died same day. Christened Bridget.

Alec (married to Lady Katheryn de Wolfe, has issue)

Christian (died Holy Land 1269 A.D.) no issue

Moira (married to Sir Apollo de Norville, has issue)

Kevin (married to Lady Annavieve de Ferrers, has issue)

Rose (widow of Sir James de Wolfe, has issue)

Nathaniel

Paris and Caladora Scott de Norville

Hector (married to Lady Evelyn de Wolfe, has issue)

Apollo (married to Lady Moira Hage, has issue)

Helene (married to Sir Troy de Wolfe, has issue)

Athena (married to Sir Scott de Wolfe, has issue)

Adonis

Cassiopeia (married to Sir Edward de Wolfe, has issue)

Author's Note

Welcome to Thomas de Wolfe's story!

We first met Thomas in *SERPENT*, where he had a fairly large secondary role. He also had a major secondary role in *SCORPION*, freshly back from fighting the Turk and Mongol invaders in the Holy Land. In *SERPENT*, we were introduced to a passionate, very sensitive young knight who fell for the hero's very young and pregnant sister, who was a widow. Though the sister didn't survive the birth, Thomas' father, William de Wolfe, took the baby back with him to Castle Questing to raise. The child's name, originally Tacey after her mother, was changed for her protection. As a full-blooded Welsh princess, William and Thomas wanted to protect the baby. Baby Tacey, eight years later, has become Caria de Wolfe (her name changed to hide her from King Edward), raised by William and Jordan.

Meanwhile, Thomas had gone to The Levant with Kevin Hage, both of them essentially for the same reasons – to forget about the women they had loved. Thomas' angst for Tacey wasn't really mentioned in *SCORPION*, but now in *STORMWOLFE*, we can address it.

What fun it was to write about Scott and Troy and Patrick and Blayth after *A Wolfe Among Dragons*. But to tell the truth, the guys are getting kind of… old. Old*er*, anyway. We're two years after Kieran's death, post-*Scorpion*, so this is the de Wolfe Pack and the new generation of de Wolfe cubs coming up. You'll get to meet some of them!

A few things to note –

Something called a *tempestarii* is mentioned in this novel, and it really is a thing. In Medieval folklore, it was, literally, a storm witch, stemming from pre-Christian beliefs.

Also mentioned in the tale is knitting, which wasn't widely known – but not *un*known – around this time. And the method for making goat's milk cheese is authentic.

The Earldom of Northumbria is a title used in this tale, and it was an actual title, though very old, and reverted to the crown by the time this novel takes place. I have given it to a descendant of the Duke of

Normandy, through very plausible lineage. More than likely, a descendant of the duke stole it from the original holder, or married into the family. In any case, the Normans took it from the Angles.

And something else to note – I have had something interesting come up with this book: William's age. Believe it or not, I was kind of ambiguous about it in *The Wolfe*, but there is a part of the novel where Jordan says that William is about ten years older than she is – and she was twenty years old in *The Wolfe*. So, that makes William born in 1201 A.D., meaning by the time we hit *STORMWOLFE*, our beloved William is 89 years old. Yes, that's very old (especially in Medieval times), but not "completely" unheard of. William is spry and active, so for him, age is just a number. He's truly ageless. But that also means, all things considered, that William and Jordan had their youngest children – Thomas and Penelope – when Jordan was well into her forties. I have made mention that they were "late babies". That's pretty late!

The last thing of mention – the names Edward and Thomas and William are much re-used in the House of de Wolfe because Edward was the name of William's father (he is a secondary character in *Rise of the Defender*), Thomas is the name of Jordan's father (*The Wolfe*), and, of course, William. You'll see those names popping up a lot as the children of William and Jordan have children and name them to honor their ancestors. I mention this because Scott de Wolfe's two eldest sons are William (Will) and Thomas, both of whom make an appearance and/or are mentioned in this book. Young Thomas (Scott's son) is not to be confused with the hero!

Now, without further ado, enjoy Thomas and Maitland's story because it's a powerful one – and I have three words for you: Helm of Shame. Watch for it!

Love,

DE WOLFE PACK CASTLES AND LOCATIONS
C.1289 A.D.

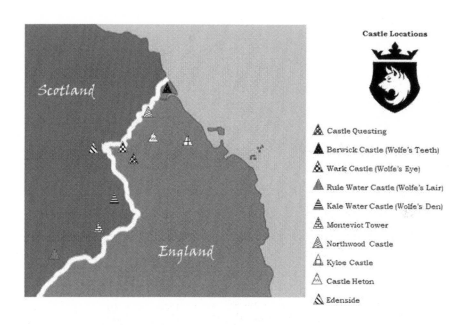

Castle Locations

- Castle Questing
- Berwick Castle (Wolfe's Teeth)
- Wark Castle (Wolfe's Eye)
- Rule Water Castle (Wolfe's Lair)
- Kale Water Castle (Wolfe's Den)
- Monteviot Tower
- Northwood Castle
- Kyloe Castle
- Castle Heton
- Edenside

Wark Castle (Wolfe's Eye):

Larger outpost for the Earl of Warenton, William de Wolfe. Literally sits on the border between England and Scotland.

- Thomas de Wolfe, commander
- Desmond de Ryes, second

Berwick Castle (Wolfe's Teeth):

Massive border castle, strategically important, de Wolfe holding.

- Patrick de Wolfe, commander
- Alec Hage, second

Castle Questing (Wolfe's Heart):

Massive fortress, seat of the Earl of Warenton, William de Wolfe

- William is technically in command, although Blayth (formerly James) de Wolfe is the active commander.
- Andreas de Wolfe, second. Son of Troy de Wolfe.
- Markus de Wolfe, senior commander, newly knighted. Son of Patrick de Wolfe.

Rule Water Castle (Wolfe's Lair):

The largest outpost in the de Wolfe empire, known as The Lair. Belongs to the heir apparent to the Earl of Warenton, Scott de Wolfe.

- Scott de Wolfe, Commander
- Willian "Will" de Wolfe, second. Will is Scott's eldest son. Married Lily de Lohr, great-granddaughter of Christopher de Lohr, in 1281. Daughter Athena was born in 1282.

Monteviot Tower (Wolfe's Shield)

Smaller outpost in Scotland, strategic. Holding of Troy de Wolfe.

- Brodie de Reyne, second

Kale Water Castle (Wolfe's Den):

Larger outpost, on the England side of the border, strategic.

- Troy de Wolfe, commander
- Cassius de Shera, second. Cassius is the son of Maximus de Shera (*The Thunder Warrior*).
- Troy also commands Sibbald's Hold, former home of Red Keith Kerr (his wife's father). A minor property.

Castle Canaan (Cumbria):

Scott de Wolfe's southernmost holding, not directly related to the Scottish border but a source of additional troops if needed. Inherited the property when he married the widow of Canaan.

- Milo Auclair, commander

Northwood Castle:

Massive border castle, very important and strategic. Belonging to Adam de Longley, Earl of Teviot. Not part of the de Wolfe empire, but strongly allied to de Wolfe by marriage and blood.

- Captain of the guard is Paris de Norville, though he no longer takes an active role. Michael de Bocage, his former second-in-command, is still alive, as is another old Northwood knight, Deinwald Ellsrod.
- Hector de Norville is serving with his father as the head of Northwood's army. Hector married Evelyn de Wolfe – sons Atreus and Hermes serve with their father at Northwood Castle, both newly knighted.
- Deinwald Ellsrod and wife, Aloria, have two sons also – Edric and Rhys Ellsrod serve at Northwood Castle along with Edric's two sons, Garr and Hugh.
  - o Garr is courting Lisbet de Norville, daughter of Hector, granddaughter of Paris.
  - o Rhys' son, Landry, will be knighted in the coming year. Also serves at Northwood.
- Michael de Bocage serves with his eldest son, Tobias, while his younger sons, Case and Corbin, have gone south to serve with the House of de Lohr and the House of de Winter, respectively.

Roxburgh Castle (in English hands at this time, royal acquisition)

- Garrison of Northwood Castle, manned by Tobias de Bocage
- Edric Ellsrod, second, along with son, Hugh

Earl of Northumbria (House of de Vauden) properties:

- Kyloe Castle (seat of the Earldom)
- Twizell Castle (border property). Guards strategic bridge over the River Tweed.
- Etal Castle (strategic border property, very close to de Wolfe lands)
- Guardian of Bamburgh Castle, a royal property and enormous economic and military center.

THE SONG OF THE STORM WOLFE

In days of old,

When knights so bold,

Would wield their sword of truth.

A tempest came,

A witch of shame,

A vessel of evil and youth.

Upon the wind, a storm arose,

Bearing a warrior abound,

The Storm Wolfe, they say,

His soul to lay,

In a cold and hollow ground.

Until the day of Mae,

It would forever lay,

In the cold and hollow ground.

~13th c. ballad, author unknown

(has been known to be sung at funerals as a lament)

PROLOGUE

December, 1291 A.D.
Castle Questing, Northumbria

T HEY WERE OUT to get him.

He knew these walls. God, he knew them so well. He'd been born here and had grown up here until the time he'd gone to foster, so the old stone walls of Castle Questing were like being in the embrace of his mother or his father. The walls loved him, protected him, and he was as fond of this place as if it were a member of his family.

For certain, it was.

But now, these comforting walls represented great peril.

He knew they were out to get him, perhaps waiting for him around the very next corner. There was danger everywhere and all he had to do was make it to the entry of the keep and beyond that, freedom.

He wasn't going to go down without a fight.

The trouble was that those stalking him were as clever as he was, born and bred for battle, so they would be thinking exactly as he was. Therein lay the key to surviving this; if he wanted to evade them, he had to think differently. He had to think in a way that they wouldn't.

But that wasn't so easy; he was a de Wolfe.

Still, he was younger, faster, and smarter, wasn't he? Those who were stalking him may have had the money and the titles and the reputations, the finest knights England had ever seen, but that didn't matter in the long run because *he* was going to defeat them. He knew the identities of his stalkers well.

Nighthawk...
ShadowWolfe...
DarkWolfe...
The Dragon Wolfe...
The Wolfe...

Some of the most powerful names on the Scottish borders, but they were little match for the man who brought a storm with him wherever he went. Where Thomas de Wolfe walked, thunder rolled. That's what those in the north said. Each de Wolfe knight had his own particular brand of power, but with Thomas, it had always been dangerous unpredictability. He was as fast as lightning and twice as deadly, but wildly unstable. Those were the rumors, anyway, but those who had witnessed such talent swore by it. The youngest son of the Wolfe of the Border brought his own individual type of death to any given situation.

There was no one else like him, anywhere.

Which was why he wasn't going to let them catch him. He had four older brothers and a father out for him at the moment, all of them elderly in his opinion. At thirty years and five, he was the baby of the de Wolfe brothers, who were at least fifteen or more years older than he was. Not that it made them any weaker or slower. In fact, even his eldest brothers, as old as they were, could outfight men half their age. It was a specific de Wolfe trait, because their father had been fighting battles well into his seventh decade of life. He was still fighting even now, at least whenever his wife would let him.

Old knights never died. They simply fought until their bones crumbled and their skin turned to dust.

And that was the unfortunate part in all of this – Thomas knew they were ready for him, stalking him, waiting for the moment to pounce. And it wasn't dealing with just one skilled knight, it was dealing with more than his brothers and father because he knew for a fact that others were in on this. His uncle, Paris, was here at Questing, and more still. All of them, hunting him down like an animal, an animal who had been lured to Questing yesterday under false pretenses. He thought he'd come for a conference on some unrest along the border, but it didn't take him long to figure out he'd been duped.

Damn them!

Now, he had to flee.

Castle Questing was a vast maze of chambers, corridors, servant's alcoves, and secret staircases. As a child, he'd found endless entertainment in the old castle, and now as an adult, he still remembered those hidden staircases and alcoves. He'd been moving from one to another for the past two hours, trying to evade capture. Now, he was closer than ever to that entry door.

He'd been hiding in a seldom used servant's staircase for the past twenty minutes but knowing that, at some point, his brothers would check it. He'd been one step ahead of them since this insane chase started and he didn't intend to relinquish that lead. Down to the bottom of the staircase, then about twenty feet down a small corridor, and he'd been at the foyer with the entry door ahead of him.

He could smell freedom.

But that vestige of hope would prove to be his downfall. His focus was on the door and not where it should be – in the shadows around it.

The wolves pounced.

"HE IS RECKLESS and mean," a big, blond man hissed to a collection of battled-scarred knights. "You know what happens when he fights; he has no restraint and no regard. If we are not careful, someone is going to come away missing an eye. No offense, Papa, but none of us want to end up like you, courtesy of our baby brother."

Scott de Wolfe was looking at his father, William, who had, in fact, lost an eye over forty years ago in a battle in Wales. Elderly, but still strong, competent, and intelligent, the legendary William de Wolfe shook his head at his eldest son.

"If you lose an eye to your brother, I will be ashamed of you," he said. "At least I lost mine in battle. You would be losing yours in a fist fight. That does not say much for your skills."

It was a serious situation they were all facing, but one with an odd undercurrent of humor. Ridiculousness, really. Thomas de Wolfe was running from his destiny like a child running from a physic's potion, but it was a concerning situation, nonetheless.

The youngest de Wolfe brother had grown up, matured, and become one of the fiercest knights England had ever seen. Not simply the borders – but in England as a whole. As a youth, he'd been reckless and silly, but blindingly brilliant. He was innovative and cunning, outsmarting his parents on more than one occasion. As a young man, he'd been dutiful but resentful of living in the shadows of his elder, and greater, brothers.

A young man with something to prove.

But then came the fateful trip to Wales to escort his youngest sister to her new husband, a man who also had a sister Thomas had fallen for. It was something they didn't really speak of any longer, mostly because it was in the past and wasn't something to be fondly recalled. It had been a moment in time that had shaped Thomas' entire life and he'd returned from Wales a different man.

Changed.

His father, William, had known he'd had to do something for his distressed son and that help had come in the form of a mission of mercy, of sorts. Kevin Hage, son of William's dearest friend, Kieran, was determined to go to The Levant to fight with the Christian armies against a new wave of Mamluks to escape the woman he'd lost. It had been the very sister Thomas had escorted to Wales, in fact, who had broken Kevin's heart, and Kieran Hage himself had begged Thomas to go with his son.

In truth, Thomas and Kevin had shared the loss of the women they had loved, one to death and one to another man, and in that sense, they were kindred spirits. They both needed to get away, to find a life for themselves that did not include their women. So, they had gone to The Levant and they'd learned warfare on an entirely different level, learning to fight against an enemy that was not English or Scottish or even Welsh, an enemy who hated them on a level they'd never seen before.

They had learned to be killers.

In fact, Kevin had learned that lesson so deeply that he'd become an English assassin known as the Scorpion, the knight with the deadly sting. Thomas, too, had learned the lesson so well that it had become ingrained into him, a man who thought like a hunter and hunted like a killer, who struck as fast as a bolt of lightning. *Dhiib aleasifa*, the Mamluks called him.

StormWolfe.

The hunter who brought the storms with him.

The Thomas who returned to England afterwards was not the same Thomas who had left them. Some thought that the time in The Levant might have done Thomas more harm than good, because the man who returned was a true hunter-killer in every sense of the phrase. He'd served the Duke of Dorset for a time after his return to England before heading home, where his father had given him command of Wark Castle. Scott had been correct when he'd said Thomas was mean; he could be quite mean when the mood struck him, and deadly in the blink of an eye.

Therefore, every man in that solar knew that Thomas would not be taken without a fight, which was why they were converging near the keep entry in a pack for safety. The postern gate from the keep that led into the kitchens had been barred and locked, so there was no chance he could go that way. Soldiers were covering the exterior in case he decided to drop from one of the windows, and one very capable knight was waiting in the stables in case he made it that far. Better still, the commander of Questing, James de Wolfe who was also known by Blayth, was standing just outside the entry door.

Every possible exit was covered, meaning Thomas was being driven to the entry where the majority would be waiting for him.

At the moment, however, they were simply anticipating his movements as best they could. He was somewhere in the keep, lurking. There was a small guard room, a solar, and then a main receiving chamber and a servant's corridor that comprised the access points of the foyer. But at the moment, the knights were gathered in the solar, planning for the inevitable. Waiting.

A storm was about to roll through.

"Uncle Thomas will strike to injure," a very tall, very large young man with big blue eyes and nearly black hair spoke. "I suggested the older knights wait here while the younger men attend to him. He will not escape us."

He had an eloquent way of speaking, one that made everyone look to him. Markus de Wolfe was the eldest son of Patrick de Wolfe, and he had his father's size and strength, but his manner was much as his grandfather's had been at that age – supremely confident in all things. It was a confidence borne of youth, but at only nineteen years of age, he was already a full-fledged knight, which fed into that pride. He also happened to be the grandson of a Viking king, and he looked every inch the powerful Viking prince.

But his father, who was standing a few feet away, shook his head at his arrogant son. "And you think he will escape *us*?" he said, incredulous. "Markus, either you think your uncles and I are going to collapse like brittle old women before your Uncle Thomas, or you are genuinely trying to protect us. I will choose to believe the latter because if it is the former, I will unleash your uncles, Troy and Scott, on you so that you can see just how weak they really are."

Patrick was referring to his older brothers, the eldest sons of William de Wolfe, twins by birth. Scott and Troy de Wolfe were, even at their age, remarkable warriors and seasoned commanders, so the threat was not an idle one. They were still quite tough and quite deadly. Markus knew that; he looked to his uncles, who were gazing at him in varying degrees of displeasure. Realizing his boast wasn't well met, he held up a quelling hand.

"I meant to say that it is good training for us to take Uncle Thomas ourselves," he said, backtracking. "It is not often we get the chance to go up against someone of his caliber who is not trying to kill us."

Over near the wide-mouthed hearth that was spitting out sparks into the stale solar air, William snorted at his grandson's statement.

"What makes you think he will not try and kill you?" he said, eyeing the proud, young knight. "The moment you truly believe that is the moment he will take your legs out from under you and you'll be lucky to come away with all of your teeth intact. He is desperate and he is angry, making for a volatile combination. So presume he will hurt you if he can, because he will. However, given that you believe this to be a challenge, then I suggest you take your cousins and go hide yourselves in the entry. If I know Thomas, he is looking for the right opportunity to make a break for that entry door. Make sure he does not reach it."

Markus nodded sharply at his grandfather, motioning to his cousins, who were standing grouped near their grandfather. Young knights who had all of the hunger of the de Wolfes and the skill of their powerful fathers and grandfathers. William de Wolfe, or Will as he was known to the family, was Scott's eldest son. At twenty years and nine, he was powerfully built and extremely talented. He was also far more level-headed than his arrogant cousin and the smirk on his face told William everything the young man was thinking. Following Will was Andreas de Wolfe, Troy's eldest son, at twenty years and eight. Andreas was taller than his father and built for battle, yet another gifted de Wolfe offspring.

Along with Markus, those three rounded out the eldest of the grandsons of William de Wolfe present in the solar, a legacy that any man would be proud of, but there were more grandsons waiting in the wings. Specifically, waiting on the fringes of the solar and practically gnashing their teeth to be involved in the ambush of their Uncle Thomas.

Young, foolish, eager lads.

William eyed the collection of them, who looked at him with great hope that they would be allowed on this endeavor. Rowan de Wolfe was the leader of the de Wolfe cubs at fifteen years, son of James de Wolfe. James, who went by his Welsh name of Blayth, was William's fourth son, a man believed killed in battle years ago but who had been found living amongst the Welsh, unaware of his true identity. But Blayth had eventually returned to England, bringing with him a Welsh wife, and he had reestablished a strong relationship with his firstborn son, a young man who was growing up to be much like his gentle, humorous, but fierce father.

Along with Rowan were his cousins Edward and Axel, at twelve years and ten years respectively, sons of Blayth's twin sister, Katheryn. Edward and Axel's father was Alec Hage, son of Kieran Hage, who had been William's close friend and second-in-command up until his death two years before. The boys had Kieran's immense size, even at their young age, and they were tough lads who were more than willing to jump into a fight, both a noble and foolish inclination. In this situation, William thought it was more foolish than noble, and he shook his head in resignation at his grandsons.

"You intend to help, do you?" he asked them, watching heads bob up and down eagerly. Suspecting it might do them good to get pummeled in a real fight, he held up his hands as if to surrender. "Then go. Will, watch out for the younger boys. Make sure Thomas does not bash their heads or kick in their teeth."

Will, standing over by the entry to the solar, fought off a grin. "No promises," he said, waving impatiently to the three younger cousins. "Get over here, you scabs. Stay behind us and move when we move. If your Uncle Thomas catches you alone, he will box your ears."

The boys scampered over to him, although the command was mostly geared towards Edward and Axel. Rowan was a very big lad for his age and could hold his own in a fight, but the younger two were aggressive and ludicrous at times. With a long look at William, Will grabbed Axel by the neck and yanked the boys out into the darkness of the entry where Andreas and Markus were already looking for a place to hide.

To wait.

With the six of them out in the entry somewhere, William motioned to Patrick and Scott, standing closest to the banks of fat tallow candles that were burning low and sooty.

"Douse those tapers," he instructed quietly, blowing out the ones at his table, the one he used to conduct Questing business. "Atty, shut the door but put your ear against it. We will wait in here until Thomas makes his move, but the second we hear sounds of a struggle, out we go to join it."

Atty was what the family called Patrick, even now that he was a middle-aged man. When he'd been very young, he'd been unable to pronounce his name and it had come out as *'atty*. Patrick moved quickly to do his father's bidding as Troy and Scott bunched up against the closed door in the darkened chamber, listening to the sounds in the entry outside.

The struggle wasn't long in coming.

It started with a blow, something heavy either being hit or falling, followed by the wail of a boy. Then, two boys. Patrick jerked open the door to find a mass of men writhing on the keep entry with the yelling coming from Edward and Axel. It was so dark in the entry that they couldn't see what was going on other than a dark, undulating blob of arms and legs, and Patrick, Scott, and Troy plunged into it, grabbing a hold of legs and trying to pull the younger boys from the top of the pile.

But that didn't work so well. Unfortunately, Edward and Axel had battle fever and when Scott grabbed Edward by the leg, the boy panicked and lashed out a foot, catching the man in the chin. As Scott stumbled back, Troy inserted himself into his place, grabbing at another leg that happened to belong to Axel. Thinking he was being attacked,

Axel screamed as if he'd been stabbed, momentarily startling everyone involved in the melee.

Believing the young boy must have been gored somehow, William came charging out of his solar with an iron bank of candles in his hand, lit up so he could see what the screaming was about only to notice Thomas at the bottom of a pile of men. He could see his youngest son's head and hands, but that was about it. Everything else had Will, Andreas, Markus, Edward, Axel, Patrick, and Troy all over it. Unfortunately, the surprise of Axel's scream had most everyone but Thomas pause in what they were doing, which allowed Thomas to shimmy out from underneath Will and Andreas.

But he didn't have a chance to escape. Realizing Thomas was using a frightened young boy to his advantage, Scott, Troy, and Patrick pounced on Thomas' upper body, wrestling him to the ground and keeping him there. With Will, Andreas, Markus, and the two young boys on his legs, Thomas was effectively trapped but he wasn't giving up easily. He continued to growl and strain against men who weren't going to let him escape.

With all of the noise and screaming, it was inevitable that the entry door opened. Blayth entered, enormous and blond and scarred, his eyes widening at the pile of men on the floor. He came to stand next to his father, looking rather incredulous.

"You caught him," he said to his father. "Excellent work."

But William wasn't feeling so proud. He thought this was all rather futile. He watched the mass, sighing heavily.

"Thomas," he said calmly. "Is this truly how you wish to end up? With your brothers holding you down like an animal? If your Uncle Kieran was here, you would be suffering his Helm of Shame for your actions. That is what he did to knights who shirked their duties."

Scott, Troy, and Patrick all fought off grins to varying degrees, knowing what the Helm of Shame was. They'd heard the stories from the old knights and, truth be told, Thomas was very lucky Kieran wasn't present. No one wanted the Helm of Shame. As it was, Thomas' face was pressed into the wooden floor of the entry by virtue of Patrick's hand on the back of his head. He tried to say something to his father but the words were muffled, so Patrick wrapped his enormous hand in Thomas' long, dark hair and pulled his head up by the strands. William bent over, trying to look his boy in the eye.

"Did you say something?" he said. "I hope it was an apology. I hope it was a plea for my mercy because it is only by the grace of God that I am not going to throttle you."

Thomas' lips were covered with dirt from the floor. "You lied to me," he said, spitting out the dirt. "You were not truthful when you told me that you were gathering your commanders to discuss increased border activity. You lied to me and expected me not to react."

William shook his head. "I did not lie to you," he said steadily. "I have never lied to you. What I told you was true; we *have* all gathered to discuss increased border activity with the border reivers. We have discussed it. Now it is on to other business."

It was that other business that had Thomas so enraged. He kept trying to push himself off the floor and dislodge his brothers, but it was impossible.

"Where is the Earl of Northumbria, Edmund de Vauden?" Thomas demanded. "I will tell him to his face what I think about his little scheme!"

Anger had him at least lifting his brothers up, who were starting to laugh because Thomas' unearthly strength was born of his fury. The younger knights weren't seeing any humor in it, but Scott and Troy and Patrick were having a difficult time keeping a straight face. Yet, William met his son's anger calmly.

"It is not Northumbria's scheme," he said. "At least, not completely. Thomas, you are acting like an idiot. With all of the recklessness of your youth and your unsavory reputation in The Levant, I was never ashamed of you, but if you keep this up, I will, indeed, be ashamed of your behavior. You ran off before I could fully explain the situation to you and now I must explain it to you as Scott and Troy are squeezing the breath from you and Atty has his hands in your hair. Is this truly how you want to behave? To have your brothers restrain you so that I may speak to you on the situation?"

Thomas was so angry that he was lifting his brothers up again and again, trying to dislodge them. Seeing this, Blayth moved from his father's side and straddled Thomas as much as he could, sitting down on the man's torso to force him down. Thomas went down to stay after that; not even he could dislodge four very large men from his upper body. As he lay there, head turned to one side, William crouched down beside his son so that he could see his face.

"Now," William said quietly. "You will listen carefully to me because it is important. You have had your entire life to do as you please, Thomas, but it is time you fulfill your destiny as a de Wolfe, and that means a strategic marriage. You owe that to your family and to the de Wolfe legacy. Do you understand me so far?"

Thomas refused to answer. He refused to look at his father, but William knew he heard him. He continued.

"Edmund de Vauden is a major landholder in the north and the man is wildly rich," he said. "He is related to the royal family from generations back, a direct descendant of a bastard of Robert Curthose, son of the Duke of Normandy, and by virtue of that relationship, holds the title Earl of the ancient kingdom of Northumbria. His only child and heiress, daughter Adelaide, is in need of a husband. Allow me to explain to you what this means even though I know you are already aware – Edmund owns Kyloe Castle and Twizell Castle, plus several others. His lands go from Warenford down to Rennington, and all the way out to the sea. Kyloe Castle itself is a massive fortress that holds more men than Berwick does. It has the largest standing army outside of Alnwick in the north, but more importantly, Edmund de Vauden is the governor of Bamburgh Castle, a royal estate. You know how important that castle is. It is that castle, that army, and that empire which needs a strong hand – *your* strong hand, Thomas. Marry Adelaide de Vauden and you shall know an empire bigger than any estate in the north, including mine."

Thomas was still staring off into space, refusing to answer, which perturbed William. His patience began to thin.

"I did not raise you to disrespect my will as blatantly as you are doing, so listen well," he growled. "I will tell your brothers to release you. If you run, it will not be back to Wark Castle. Wark belongs to me and if you disobey me, you are no longer my garrison commander. You may as well keep running because no one will take you in. You are the youngest of my sons but I have never known you to be disobedient. If you intend to start now by refusing this betrothal, then you should tell me now. I will have other arrangements to make."

Thomas' jaw was ticking angrily but the hazel eyes, a similar color as his mother's, moved to William, gazing at the man steadily. It was clear that he had something to say, but he never got the chance. A voice from behind them, from the great mural stairs that led to the upper level of the keep, rang out against the cold stone walls.

"Thomas, get up." Jordan de Wolfe was viewing the mass of men and grossly displeased about it. "Atty, Scott, Troy, Blayth – get off the man. Do ye hear me? All of ye, get up."

The heavy Scottish accent of Jordan was not to be trifled with. The mother of the enormous men wrestling on the floor, and more besides, she was a strong, ageless beauty, a tribute to her family and to woman-hood as a whole. They didn't come any finer, stronger, intelligent, or beautiful than William's wife of over fifty years.

More than any battle commander, her voice made men move.

Blayth was the first one to stand up, pulling Patrick up with him. Patrick pulled on Scott as Troy leapt to his feet, hissing at Markus and Andreas and Will. Those three got up, yanking Edward and Axel to their feet as Thomas, at the bottom of the pile, bolted to his feet, turning to look at his mother as she began to come down the stairs.

Jordan had a little girl with her, an eight-year-old child, one that she had not given birth to, but one she had raised since birth. The child looked like a porcelain doll, with curly dark hair and big, dark eyes, and the moment Jordan and the child came to the base of the stairs, the little girl yanked her hand from Jordan's grasp and ran to Thomas, who picked the child up and cradled her.

It was like throwing water on a fire.

It had been a strategic move on Jordan's part. Thomas could not become too angry with little Caria around, a child named after the Welsh word for *heart*. Though Thomas was not the father, Caria de Wolfe belonged to him.

She *was* his heart.

"Intae the solar," Jordan said quietly, pointing to the door and turning her son for it. "Go in and sit. Caria has been askin' for ye, so take her with ye."

What ten men couldn't accomplish, one small woman and a little girl could. As the men backed off, Thomas silently moved into the solar, followed by his father and mother. Slowly, Scott and Troy and Patrick and Blayth trickled in after them, allowing Will and Andreas and Markus in, but shutting the door in the face of Edward and Axel, who were visibly upset by the fact that they were not included in the group.

As the boys ran off to complain to their father, who was out in the stable guarding against Thomas stealing away on his horse, those settling into the solar under much calmer conditions were now left to deal with the crux of the situation.

This was what it all boiled down to...

An unwanted betrothal.

"Thomas, I realize a marriage between you and Lady Adelaide is unwanted, but I would not do it if I did not believe this was in your best interests," William said. Jordan came to him and he put his arm around her slender shoulders, presenting a unified front against their resistant son. "Your mother and I have kept silent on any matrimony where you were concerned for eight years, ever since..."

Thomas put up a hand, stopping his father from continuing. "I know," he said. The fight was out of him now as the reality of the situation settled, but it was also because of the child on his lap. He looked at Caria as the little girl affectionately tugged on his shoulder-length hair. "You do not have to say it. You have not mentioned any betrothals to me since we brought Caria back from Wales, and you have let me lead the life I have needed to lead. I have appreciated it."

Now, they were at the heart of the situation, the real reason Thomas had been kept clear of any betrothals for the past eight years. William watched the interaction between his youngest son and the little girl, the child of a young woman Thomas had loved.

The woman he'd fallen in love with in Wales had been a woman he'd lost.

She had been a Welsh princess, the sister of the husband of Penelope de Wolfe, Thomas' youngest sister. Penelope had married the hereditary king of Anglesey and when Thomas had ridden escort to her wedding, he had met Bhrodi de Shera's very young sister, Tacey, who was pregnant and recently widowed.

The young knight with the soft heart had fallen hard.

But it was a love not to be. Tacey had died in childbirth with Caria, and William had brought the baby back to Castle Questing to hide her from King Edward and his systematic destruction of the Welsh royal houses. Caria was a full-blooded Welsh princess, only she didn't know it. All she knew was that she was the youngest child of two people old enough to be her grandparents, and her brother Thomas adored her more than any of them. He'd spent years away from her and since his return home, seemed to be trying to make up for all of it. Little Caria was loved deeply and greatly spoiled.

It was what her mother would have wanted.

But the fact remained that Thomas had been resistant to any suggestion of marriage since the loss of Tacey. It was the whole reason he'd been sent away with Kevin, the whole reason he'd tried to find himself on the hot sands of The Levant. Caria was his link, his reminder of what he'd loved and lost, and since Thomas had assumed Wark's command, the child divided her time between Wark Castle, Thomas' outpost, and Castle Questing, home of William and Jordan. Thomas' mother wouldn't let the child out of her sight, and William didn't like her spending an over amount of time at Wark, so Caria went back and forth between the two fortresses frequently.

It wasn't an ideal situation.

Thomas knew that. Even now, as Caria tugged at his hair and hugged his neck enthusiastically, he couldn't imagine marrying anyone and leaving Caria behind, but he also couldn't imagine anyone but his mother or Tacey raising the little girl, and that was a problem.

One problem of many.

William wasn't unsympathetic. He knew what Thomas' issue was; he'd known for some time. The years that Thomas had spent in The Levant and beyond, broadening his experience and doing God-only-knew what else, had been a not-so-subtle way of purging the loss of Tacey from his mind. He'd fought, he'd whored, and he'd lived a life on the edge, but all of that adventure and death hadn't worked. Tacey was there as strongly as ever but, in William's opinion, it had gone on for too long. As he watched Caria snuggle with Thomas, he went to stand in front of his son.

He had to make the man understand that this was for his own good.

"Thomas, I know this betrothal is not something you want, but it is important that you not pass up this opportunity," he said. "De Vauden is offering you everything he has, and his riches are vast. Do you understand that?"

Thomas sighed heavily. "I do."

"If you remain here in my service, you will always only be my garrison commander for Wark," William stressed gently. "What de Vauden is offering you is so much more. Can you not see that?"

Thomas still refused to look at him. "Of course I can."

William eyed Jordan, who was looking at her son with some sorrow. She knew his heart was still wounded, eight years after Tacey's passing. But she also knew the situation with de Vauden might be just what he needed to get on with his life.

"Thomas," she said quietly. "Ye canna grieve forever. I know ye dunna want tae marry, but ye must understand that marryin' another willna push Tacey from yer heart. She'll always be there, love. Men have been known tae love again after loss. It has been eight years since Tacey's passin' and it is time tae move on with yer life while ye're still young. Ye've had yer adventures and ye've done things that ye've needed tae do, and now it is time tae settle down and accept responsibility. Yer father is offerin' ye a marriage that will secure yer legacy, and 'tis somethin' ye deserve. Tacey would want ye tae take it, I say. Will ye not give yerself that chance?"

Thomas shrugged as Caria slithered off his lap and ran to Patrick, who was the next brother most willing to play with her. Having several children of his own, Patrick picked her up and hung her by her ankles as she giggled. Thomas watched her as she played. As he watched Patrick gently swing Caria back and forth, Thomas ended up looking at Scott and Troy.

"You knew about this," he said to them. "You knew what Papa was going to do to me."

Scott cleared his throat softly, looking to his feet as he formulated his reply, but Troy didn't hesitate. "We knew," he said. "De Vauden is a great northern lord, Thomas. Any one of us would be pleased and proud to accept such an offer, but you act as if Papa is giving you a death sentence."

"Do you really have no ambition in life other than to be Papa's garrison commander for the rest of your life?" Scott lifted his head, speaking in a low voice. "I have multiple properties to call my own in addition to commanding the Wolfe's Lair. Troy also has multiple properties and still maintains Papa's outpost at Kale Castle, and Atty is the same. He commands mighty Berwick, for God's sake, and Blayth will command Castle Questing when Papa is gone in addition to his Welsh properties. We have all done very well for ourselves, Thomas, and we have married well. What makes you think you are any different from us?"

Thomas was starting to feel scolded. "And Edward serves the king," he said, turning around in his seat to face his parents. "My brother, Edward the diplomat, the great adviser to the king, who has been gifted a barony in Cumbria near Scott's holding of Castle Canaan. He's a great man; *all* of my brothers are great men. And then, there is me."

"Thomas, I am *trying* to gain you your legacy so that you will also be great, like your brothers," William stressed. "Marrying Adelaide de Vauden is not the end of your world. For all you know, it could be just the beginning."

"Enough," Jordan snapped softly. "Thomas, stop feelin' sorry for yerself. Ye'll marry the de Vauden lass and that will be the end of it. If ye dunna do it, ye'll always regret it, and I'll not have ye wallowin' in self-pity for the rest of yer life. Let this be the end of it."

She said it rather harshly, leaving no room for argument. Strangely enough, Thomas didn't seem to have one. He understood that his father was trying to do something great for him and, in truth, the man was correct. It wasn't the end of his world, but it was a major change. Truth be told, he wasn't sure he wanted any of it or was ready for any of it. Deep down, he was still as muddled and directionless as he had been when he'd first left for The Levant. The only thing fighting in the Holy Land had done was give him a chance to grow as a warrior. But as a man of flesh and emotion, there hadn't been much development. He'd purposely kept himself sealed off.

Now, here his father was trying to do something good for him, something that would bring him the responsibility and riches he wanted so that he could be as prestigious as the rest of his brothers. In time, he would come to appreciate what he would inherit. At least, he hoped so.

It wasn't as if he had a choice.

"Papa," he said quietly. "It is not that I do not appreciate what you are trying to do. I do not want you thinking that I am ungrateful. If I must be honest about it, I suppose... I suppose it is simply easier for me to remain in my world as it is than to take the chance of stepping out of it. With de Vauden's offer... what, other than the marriage, is expected of me?"

That sounded more like the Thomas that William had known before he'd gone off to The Levant, a reasonable man behind the sometimes-foolish façade. But the man who had returned from The Levant – that was the selfish Thomas, moody and unpredictable and far too arrogant for his own good. William had been dealing with that Thomas for the past few years. But hearing something sensible from Thomas' lips gave him hope that somewhere beneath that prideful exterior was a man he could reason with.

He considered the question carefully.

"De Vauden wants to send his daughter and her nurse to Wark Castle so you and the young woman can become acquainted," he said. "He does not expect the marriage right away, Tommy. In fact, Adelaide is quite young, so he prefers a delay of a year or two."

Thomas eyed him. "*How* young?"

"She has seen fifteen years."

Thomas rolled his eyes. "She is a child," he said, becoming agitated again. "You expect me to marry a girl of fifteen?"

William held his ground. "If you want a couple of years, she will be seventeen," he said. "That is an acceptable age."

"And I will be thirty years and seven."

"Age did not seem to bother you with Tacey. She was extremely young when you two met."

That comment shut Thomas up, mostly because his father was right. He'd never seen Tacey as very young; all he'd seen was the woman, a tiny woman with an old soul. Without an argument, he simply shrugged, sitting back in his chair as Patrick set Caria to her feet. The child ran back over to Thomas, her little hands tugging at his hair again. Thomas' focus was on the little girl as he spoke.

"When does de Vauden expect this to take place?" he asked.

"Soon," William said honestly. "The sooner you get to know the young woman, the better for us all. De Vauden is in the great hall; let us go and see the man. He is most anxious to speak to you."

Thomas shook his head, his dark hair lashing the sides of his face. "I am sure he is," he said sarcastically. "The man saw me bolt out of a conference when you told me about the contract. He knows that you and my brothers have had to hunt me down. I am sure he is *quite* eager to talk to a most anxious suitor for his daughter."

William fought off a grin. "Lie to him," he said, reaching over and pulling Thomas up from the chair. "We will lie to him together."

Thomas thought it was rather humorous that his always-truthful father should suggest such a thing, but he didn't contest the man. William always knew best. But that didn't stop his brothers from chiming in.

"Tell him that you ate something that did not agree with you," Blayth said helpfully. "Tell him that you were about to explode out of every orifice in your body if you did not make it to the garderobe in time."

In spite of himself, Thomas grinned. "Tell the man that his future son-in-law was about to soil himself, eh?"

The brothers were starting to laugh, the heady mood lightening considerably. "Is it better to tell him that you were running out of fear of the betrothal?" Scott asked. "Take your pick, Tommy – tell the man your guts were about to run over or tell him you are a coward. Those are your choices."

Thomas cocked an eyebrow. "They are terrible choices," he said, taking Caria's hand as William began to lead him away. "But I will be truthful with you – now that I have had time to think on it, there is only one reason I would be willing to accept this betrothal."

The brothers were interested. "Hell, if I was not already married, I would take this betrothal myself for the sheer wealth it would give me," Patrick said. "What is your particular pleasure?"

Thomas stopped at the solar door and turned to face them. "Knowing I have a bigger army than all of you," he said arrogantly. "For Atty pulling my hair in that dogpile in the entry, I shall march on Berwick and raze it. And for Scott and Troy sitting on me and someone, I swear, was pinching me, I shall send my army to burn down their homes and steal all of their ale and fine food. And Blayth – you big ox, I have a particular punishment planned for you."

By now, they were all starting to laugh, including Blayth. "You do?" he said. "I am very interested, Tommy."

Thomas pointed a finger at him. "I am going to send my wife to live with you and your lovely wife for eleven months out of the year," he said. "You can deal with the woman whilst I bask in the glory of the de Vauden estates all by myself. You wanted me to marry – very well. I will. But *you* can keep the woman company. There is no law that says I must live with her."

William snorted as the brothers chuckled, opening the entry door so they could all head back to the hall. All but Caria; Thomas hadn't taken two steps before his mother was there, taking the little girl from him.

"Go tae the great hall," she told her son as Caria whined. "Caria must go tae bed now. She doesna need tae be in that smoky hall with all those men. Bid her a good eve, Tommy."

The men were starting to filter out into the night, heading for the great hall, as Thomas lingered behind, kissing Caria's unhappy little face. She didn't want to go to bed, nor did she want to be separated from Thomas, but Jordan was insistent. The woman had nine children and nearly two dozen grandchildren, so she was the final word when it came to the care of any child under the Castle Questing roof.

Thomas never contested that; he'd always appreciated how much his mother had loved and nurtured Caria, so he didn't argue. But he did linger behind as the others drifted out into the cold bailey beyond.

"Mama," he said quietly. "I am sorry if I disappointed you. I was angry… angry at Papa, angry at the situation. I may have run, but I would not have gone far. I hope you know that."

Jordan smiled at her youngest son, reaching out to touch his face, which was bristly with stubble. The man didn't shave much these days, and with his long hair and scruffy beard, that made him look rather rough. Handsome, but rough. Since his return from his adventures in The Levant, she seemed to be the only one who truly understood the new Thomas. Or, at least, she was more patient with him.

"Ye've always been like a wild colt," she said. "Ye buck and ye fight, but eventually, ye calm. Ye know yer father wouldna do anythin' he dinna think was best for ye."

"I know."

"Do ye?"

"Truly, I do."

She pointed to the door. "Then tell him," she said. "Dunna make yer da feel as if ye're the one son he has that doesna trust his judgement."

Feeling ashamed of his behavior but not entirely sorry for it, Thomas knew what she meant. Nodding his head, he kissed her on the cheek before following his father and brothers and nephews out into the cold, heading out to speak with the father of his future bride.

His future everything.

Little did Thomas know, and little did William or the others know, that the final cold evening at Castle Questing before Thomas agreed to the contract would be the last night of peace for Thomas for a very long time.

Chaos was about to follow.

William would remember that night and wonder if he shouldn't have let Thomas escape, after all.

CHAPTER ONE

Six months later
Wark Castle

"**I** WANT TO see Tommy!"

Caria had her face pressed into the door of the cab that was carrying her and Jordan to Wark Castle. It was a fortified cab, with iron and wooden sides, and small holes cut out for ventilation and light. It looked like a box on wheels, painted with the de Wolfe colors of silver and black, and the door on the rear of the cab was of iron slats, like a portcullis.

It was that door that Caria was pressed against, seeing William riding behind the cab, surrounded by about a hundred soldiers and at least two knights. When traveling with his wife, even for a short distance, William always made sure to bring an overabundance of armed men. Being this close to the Scottish border, that was prudent practice.

"Poppy!" she cried to William, holding on to the grates like a prisoner in a cell. "Where is Tommy?"

William reined his horse closer to the cab, smiling at the eager little girl. "He is up ahead," he told her. "We shall be there soon."

Soon wasn't good enough for Caria. She made a face at him, sticking out her tongue, before rushing to the opposite side of the cab to try and see Wark Castle from the ventilation holes. Jordan, who was sitting towards the rear of the cab, shook her head at the excitable child.

"One would think she hasna seen him in months," she said, watching Caria climb up onto the bench of the wagon as her nurse tried to hold the child steady. "We were only here two weeks ago."

William's gaze moved from Caria's antics to the countryside. It was June and, so far, it had proven to be a pleasant month with little rain. But that was the only pleasant thing about it considering Thomas' situation.

With Adelaide de Vauden.

God, he couldn't even voice it because to voice it made it real. In fact, no one in the family had really voiced the reality of the situation for the very same reason, all of them praying that the situation would soon iron itself out. For William, it was his worst nightmare come to life. He, too, prayed daily that somehow, this terrible circumstance would come to a peaceful conclusion.

But six months into it, he'd seen little evidence that it would.

God help him.

Riding in the carriage, he knew Jordan had enough to say about it but, mercifully, she'd mostly kept silent on the matter. Perhaps she, too, was waiting for the situation to settle down. Or perhaps, she simply didn't want to admit guilt in all of this. She'd forced Thomas into the circumstances as much as William had, so it wasn't as if she could go blaming her husband. Nay, she knew she harbored much of the guilt, too.

But it was coming to the point where neither parent could keep quiet any longer.

Hence, the very reason they were heading to Wark on this fine day. William had invited de Vauden to join them for a feast and the man had accepted, but the invitation to the feast was really a ruse. William wanted to speak to de Vauden about his daughter because he was coming to think this contract was not such a good idea, no matter how wealthy the heiress.

A man's sanity was worth more than the money.

"Northumbria is goin' tae be present at Wark this night?" Jordan asked, breaking into his thoughts. "He promised tae come, did he not?"

William nodded. "Aye," he said. "He said he would come. We have much to discuss."

Jordan sighed faintly. "English," she said to her husband; her pet name for him since before they were married had always been *English*. "Ye know I've spent a good deal of time at Wark since Adelaide came tae live there, and ye know I've tried not tae give ye my opinion on what is goin' on."

William had suspected this would come up on their journey there. He could smell it in the wind, like the scent of the summer flowers. He knew his wife well and he knew her mind, and he knew this had been pulling at her. They'd spent so much time avoiding talking about it that, in truth, he felt some relief that she was bringing the subject up.

"I know," he said evenly. "It is Tommy's life and his situation. I had thought it was better if we did not involve ourselves."

Jordan looked at him through the slats in the door. "But ye dunna think that now, do ye?"

He hesitated a moment before shaking his head. "Nay."

"Good," she said. "Before we arrive, I feel as if I must say what is on my mind. We may not have another chance."

William nodded. "You have done remarkably well at keeping your thoughts to yourself," he said. "You do not need to give me your opinion, for I know it. It is my opinion as well."

Jordan held up a hand as if to beg his patience. "Let me say what I must," she insisted. "Do ye know what I think? This is de Vauden's fault, all of it. He knew that girl was mad when he brokered the contract with ye. What I have been witnessin' with Adelaide is not somethin' that simply happened over night. This is behavior she has indulged in all her life. Do ye know what else I think?"

"Probably, but you are going to tell me, anyway."

She pointed a finger at him. "I think he is tryin' to rid himself of that mad, skittish creature and with good riddance," she said. "I've not said it before, but I'll say it now – Adelaide de Vauden is a bizarre, unstable creature."

William puffed out his cheeks in a gesture of great regret. "I know, love."

But Jordan wasn't finished. She'd been holding back quite a bit all this time and once the dam that held her opinions back had cracked, the breach was only growing larger. "She's so desperate for Tommy's attention that she does things no reasonable lass should do," she said, throwing a thumb in Caria's direction. "The only reason I'm bringin' the wee lass is for Tommy's sake. He needs somethin' sweet and lovin' in that house, because Adelaide has made it a livin' hell for him. But Caria willna be around that madwoman, not at all! Do ye know what I heard her tell her nurse? That she thought babies and children were tasty!"

William nodded patiently. "I know," he repeated. "You told me that. But she could have meant figuratively. I am sure she does not want to eat Caria."

"How do ye know?"

He lifted his big shoulders. "I do not," he said. "Not for certain, of course. But let us be frank, Jordan; de Vauden isn't completely to blame for all of this. I accepted the contract without investigating Adelaide or anything about her."

Jordan shook her head firmly. "Ye shouldna have tae," she said. "De Vauden tricked ye with the promise of his riches for Tommy. He never told ye that his daughter was filled with insanity. It is *his* fault."

"And that is what I intend to talk to him about tonight," he said evenly. His attention was suddenly diverted as Wark came into view in the distance. He had a sick feeling in the pit of his stomach at the mere sight. "I *am* guilty, Jordan. I thrust this upon Tommy and convinced him it was for his legacy. Both Troy and Atty have visited Wark in the past six months and they both say the situation is intolerable. Atty's wife tried to be kind to Adelaide and talk to her, but the woman thought Bridey was trying to trick her somehow and put a curse on her. So she says, anyway. Atty says that if harm befalls his wife, he'll kill Adelaide and toss her body in the river."

Jordan growled. "And he'll do it, too," she said. "And then de Vauden will attack Berwick and the entire de Wolfe clan will be forced tae defend Atty. All because de Vauden lied about his lunatic of a daughter!"

Caria squealed at that point, distracting them, presumably because she caught a glimpse of Wark through one of the small windows. The little girl knew that castle and she was very excited to see her brother again.

"Matha!" she said happily to Jordan. "Matha" was a version of the Gaelic "*mathair*", which meant "mother". It was what all the de Wolfe grandchildren called Jordan. "I see Tommy's castle! Do you think he will be waiting for us?"

Jordan motioned to the nurse, who pulled Caria away from the window. "Sit down, lass," she said. "And he will be waitin' for us. He'll be very excited tae see ye again."

Caria may have been seated, but she still managed to wriggle and bounce around, so terribly happy to be seeing Thomas once again. As the nurse leaned over and quietly admonished Caria to sit quietly, Jordan turned to look at her husband once more.

In truth, she didn't have to say anything. Their eyes met and silent words passed between them, words of comfort and courage for what was to come. Aye, they knew that Thomas' situation was of their own doing and they finally intended to do something about it. Six months with Adelaide de Vauden was six months too long, and Thomas, oddly enough, had never once voiced his concern over the girl. Perhaps he thought it would have been futile, or perhaps he was simply learning to live with it.

Whatever the case, William and Jordan intended to come to their son's rescue.

It was time to do something about the witch from Kyloe.

HE COULD SMELL that stupid weed again.

She was burning it because she believed it warded off evil spirits, but as far as Thomas was concerned, the only demon in all of Wark was that woman he was slated to marry.

The mere smell of that weed made him sick to his stomach and it always, without fail, drove him out of the keep and into the great hall of Wark where she wasn't allowed to burn it. Thomas had to have one chamber that was dedicated for him alone, and the great hall was it. He'd surrendered the keep to Adelaide nearly the day she arrived.

Her arrival had been everything horrific he thought it would be and more.

For some reason, he could still smell it in the hall, so he wandered out into the warm summer day, heading for the wall walk of Wark Castle so he could at least breathe. He found that he couldn't breathe with Adelaide anywhere near him and that weed she burned simply wanted to make him get on his horse and start riding. He didn't care where he ended up, so long as she wasn't anywhere close by.

His beloved Wark had now become a prison.

His parents were coming on this day and they were bringing Caria, which was a bright spot in his otherwise dark day. He looked forward to seeing little Caria; he had some newborn goats to show her, little creatures that were just a few days old, bouncing and energetic little beasts that he knew Caria would love.

He'd never wished more in his life than he did now that he could take Caria and go away somewhere, living quietly where no one knew him or the House of de Wolfe. He could raise Caria as his daughter, as he'd wanted to before his parents told him he was too young and too inexperienced to do so. He could raise Caria in a way he thought Tacey would have wanted.

God, so much of his life had gone so very wrong, up to and including the denial to raise a little girl that belonged to his dead love.

And now… Adelaide.

Making his way up the narrow spiral staircase inside the great gatehouse of Wark, he found himself on the wall walk, mulling over what his life had become as he overlooked the green countryside and the river beyond, watching the sun glimmer off of the water. There were some kind of water fowl on the river's edge, swimming around, fishing for a meal. He watched them a moment, wishing his life were just as simple.

"There you are."

Thomas heard the voice, turning to see his second-in-command coming off the steps and onto the wall walk. Sir Desmond de Ryes was from an excellent Norman family, a dark-haired, dark-eyed man with a perpetually pale pallor. He could have looked sickly had he not been so handsome, but his comely looks made up for the sallowness. At least, that was what the maidens said about him, and he and Thomas had many adventures in the past involving multiple women and copious amounts of drink. They were friends to the bone. Thomas leaned against the wall, eyeing the man.

"And so you have found me," he said. "What do you want?"

Desmond grinned. "To console you," he jested, watching Thomas roll his eyes and return his attention to the landscape beyond the wall. "To offer you my shoulder to weep upon. Go ahead, Thomas; it will do you good. Cry on me. I demand it."

He came to stand next to Thomas, who refused to look at him. "Shut your lips, you idiot," he grumbled. "There is nothing to weep over and I do not need any consoling. Do you understand me?"

"I do."

"Good. My parents and Northumbria are to arrive at some point soon and you'll not mention anything about weeping or consoling in front of them. If you do, I will be forced to take measures."

Desmond fought off a grin. "What measures, may I ask?"

"You may not ask."

"I see," Desmond said, rubbing his chin and wiping the smile that threatened. "Then I will be left to imagine the worst. But in speaking of guests arriving, that is exactly why I was looking for you. I wanted to mention that I, too, shall have a guest this evening."

"Oh?" Thomas looked at him. "Who?"

Desmond dug into the pocket of his tunic and held up a yellowed piece of parchment. "I received this earlier today," he said, carefully unfolding it. "It seems that my sister will be stopping over on her way to Kelso Abbey. Well, not exactly Kelso, but their charity at Edenside."

Thomas was interested. "Edenside?" he repeated. "Isn't that the foundling home?"

Desmond nodded. "It is," he said. "Haven't I ever told you about my sister?"

Thomas shook his head. "Not really," he said. "I knew you had one, and a father, but not much more. Why is she coming to Edenside?"

Desmond leaned on the parapet. "Mae was married to a fine knight when she was sixteen years old," he said. "A fine knight who turned out to be rather poor and directionless. My father hasn't much money, you know, so he married my sister to the man in the hopes he would provide better for her. But he didn't. Poor Mae has had a time of it."

"Mae? Your sister?"

Desmond nodded. "Her name is Maitland, after my mother's family, but she has gone by Mae since she was an infant," he said. Then, he sighed heavily, with traces of regret in that gesture. "The House of de Ryes is a noble institution but the money started to fade with my grandfather, meaning Mae's chances of finding a good husband were slim from the start. My grandfather liked to gamble, so by the time my father inherited the lands and manse, there wasn't much left. Only on the strength of the de Ryes name did I foster at Alnwick, you know. My father subsequently lost what remained of the family land and money. I have had to earn everything I have."

Thomas knew the story with Desmond; an old and respectable

Norman family who lost their fortune through a careless ancestor. Thomas and Desmond had met many years ago, in fact, when Desmond was squiring for a great Alnwick knight. Both men shared the same sense of humor and the same qualities for the most part, and a quick friendship formed. Even when Thomas went on his travels to The Levant, he hadn't forgotten about Desmond and when he returned to assume his post at Wark, he had his father go to the lord of Alnwick, Lord de Vesci, and bargain for Desmond's services. The man had served Thomas ever since, a friend and confidant and cohort in crime.

"I know you have," Thomas replied to his statement. "And you have worked hard. But what about your sister? Why is she attached to Kelso Abbey?"

Desmond snorted ironically. "Because her stupid husband got himself killed," he said. "This was a couple of years ago. Somehow, he got mixed up with the sheriff from Ashington and the man killed him. The sheriff said that Henry charged him, but I do not believe it. Henry was a buffoon, but he was not reckless."

"Henry is the husband?"

Desmond nodded. "Henry Bowlin was the name of Mae's husband," he said. "In any case, the man was killed and Mae had no choice but to commit herself to a life of contemplation, as they call it. She is a Beguine."

Thomas understood. A Beguine was a widowed woman who, for lack of other opportunity, would pledge herself to the church for charitable work. It was perfectly acceptable for a noble woman to do so, finding solace in widowhood by serving the less fortunate. Now, the sister's destination of Edenside was making a great deal of sense.

"I see," Thomas said. "So she is going to manage the Edenside foundling home?"

"Exactly," Desmond said. "She was south in Newcastle, serving at a foundling's home there, but now she is to have a charity of her own. I've not seen Mae in a few years, but she was always such a sweet lass. I have missed her. When she married Bowlin, I was furious at my father, but I supposed he did what he thought was best for her. But sometimes those marriages do not turn out as one had hoped."

That very same thing could have meant the situation Thomas found himself in, and he and Desmond looked at each other a moment before realizing just how close to home that statement was. First Maitland, now Thomas. In fact, Thomas forgot about Maitland de Ryes Bowlin and returned his attention to the green landscape beyond. He puffed out his cheeks as his thoughts moved to his own situation.

"What am I going to do, Des," he muttered. It wasn't a question, but a rhetorical statement. "What to do, indeed."

Desmond eyed him as he grew serious. Thomas' predicament sobered them both. "I do not know," he replied. "Have you spoken to your father about it?"

Thomas was shaking his head even before Desmond finished the question. "You know I have not," he said. "I've not spoken to my mother or my brothers when they came to visit, either. There is nothing any of them can do, except for my father. He is the only one who could possibly do anything and I have a feeling that is why he invited Northumbria to join us for sup this evening."

"But you are not certain? Why not ask him?"

"I cannot bring myself to."

"Why not?"

Thomas shook his head. "I am not sure," he said. "Mayhap it is because if I do, it is admitting my father has made a mistake, and as we all know, The Wolfe does not make mistakes. He is always right, about everything, so my asking him to break the betrothal... he wanted this so badly for me. If he wants to break it, then let it be of his own accord. I suppose that I would rather endure a hellish marriage than have my father look like a fool."

"Even though you never wanted this betrothal?"

"Even though."

Desmond knew how much Thomas loved his father and how difficult this situation had been for them both. It was a noble attitude for the son to take, but one that would see his life ruined. Unable to think of a comforting reply, Desmond put his hand on the man's broad shoulder and gave him a pat. But as he did so, a harried-looking soldier suddenly appeared at the top of the turret stairs.

"My lord," the man said to Thomas, breathlessly. "It is the lady. You have been asked to come quickly."

Thomas moved away from the wall, but not quickly. He'd been summoned too many times in the past six months, for foolish reasons, to show any concern at yet one more summons with regard to Lady Adelaide.

"What now?" he asked.

The soldier shook his head. "I was not told," he said. "I was only told to fetch you quickly."

"Where is she?"

"In her chamber, my lord."

Thomas simply brushed past the man as he headed down the narrow spiral stairs and emerged out into the dusty bailey. Crossing the sloping outer ward at a normal pace, he realized about halfway across the bailey that Desmond was following him. Not that he cared. He simply kept walking, crossing into the inner ward and up the steep steps. But by the time he hit the keep, an oddly-shaped three-storied structure, he could hear the screaming.

More screaming.

In times past when he'd heard such sounds, Thomas' knightly instincts had kicked in and he'd run to the source, ready to do battle, or to help, or whatever was needed. But the truth was that Adelaide screamed so much that he'd grown numb to it, so he took the spiral stairs in the stairwell immediately to his left, up to the floor above where the screaming was coming from.

The first thing he saw was blood.

And it didn't even get a rise out of him.

Adelaide's nurse, a stout German woman, had blood on her hands and on her crisp, white apron. She was heavily-wimpled, with a white wrap around her neck as well as around her big head, and she stood there screaming in the doorway to Adelaide's chamber. She wasn't making any move to help; she simply stood there with blood on her hands and wailed. As Thomas came to the door, he shoved the woman out of the way only to see Adelaide sitting on the floor, leaning against her bed, as two stoic maids worked furiously to wrap the wrists that Adelaide had cut.

Again.

Thomas couldn't even muster the will to be concerned. This was at least the eighth time Adelaide had cut herself since she'd been at Wark Castle and he simply didn't care any longer. As he stood in the doorway, Adelaide happened to look over, catching sight of him.

"My lord!" she cried out weakly. "You have come! Praise to God, you have come!"

Dramatics were Adelaide's staple. She wielded her flair for the inane like a knight wielded a sword for battle. This was where she was most at home, seeking sympathy and attention from a man who had no interest in giving her any. The first two times Adelaide had cut herself, Thomas had shown the appropriate concern, but the third and fourth times, he began to suspect she was doing it just to gain his attention. The fifth and sixth times, he was sure of it, and that was when he began to see many small scars all up and down her arms. It would seem she had cut herself like that in the past, several times, not enough to truly kill herself, but enough to cause a good deal of blood, which she would melodramatically smear on the walls and bed.

This time, Thomas not only didn't care, but he found himself becoming quite irritated about it, struggling with his usually-quick temper. When she held out a bandaged hand to him, inviting him to take it, he simply stood by the door.

"Aye, I have come," he said, his patience gone with her. "In fact, you could have just as easily sent a servant for me rather than cut your flesh simply to gain my attention."

The hope and joy on her pale features turned into a grimace. "But...

but I *have* sent servants for you and you will not come," she said, instant tears in her eyes. "You never come when I send for you. You ignore me constantly and I can no longer take such disrespect. I want to die, I say! It would be better if I faded away!"

Thomas took a few steps into the chamber, reaching out to rip the careful bandages off the arm she still had outstretched. "There," he snapped. He gestured to the shocked servants who had been trying to bandage her. "Remove the other wrap. She wants to die, so let her die. Let her bleed to death if that is what she wants. What right do you have to stop the bleeding if Lady Adelaide truly wants to die?"

He said it so viciously that the two maids snatched their linen rolls and fled the chamber in terror. Thomas stood over Adelaide with his big fists resting on his narrow hips.

"There," he said. "You want to die? Now you can. Go right ahead. I'll not stop you."

Adelaide was beside herself with outrage and distress. "You want me to die!"

Thomas shrugged. "You have been trying to kill yourself since you came here," he said. "Go ahead; I will no longer stop you from doing what you truly wish to do. If you are going to do it, then get on with it."

Adelaide burst into loud wails of anguish, as did her nurse, still in the doorway. Pushed beyond his limit by two women screaming in his ear, Thomas went to the door and slammed it in the face of the nurse, turning his rage-filled expression to Adelaide, who was sitting on the floor trying to wrap her skirts around her bleeding arms.

"What are you doing that for?" he demanded. "You said you wanted to die. You will not wrap up your arms to stop the bleeding."

Adelaide rolled onto her knees, looking at him as if in complete and utter fear of the man. "You *want* me to die!" she screamed. "You cruel, vicious beast of a man! I am going to tell my father that you tried to kill me!"

Thomas lifted his hands in a resigned gesture. "Tell him," he said. "He is coming here tonight. In fact, and you can tell him everything.

Then, when he comes to accuse me of such things, I will produce a hundred witnesses who will tell him exactly the opposite. Why do you do this, my lady? Why do you create such chaos and dramatics?"

By now, Adelaide was on her feet, moving away from him, crossing the very fine carpet she'd brought with her from Kyloe Castle, moving to the window that was hung with damask curtains. Everything in her chamber was luxurious and fine, but that didn't matter to her. She was still unhappy, still wild with her behavior. She wept loudly as she shuffled away from Thomas, clearly nothing like the weak woman from moments earlier.

"I have done nothing," she sobbed. "All I want is for my betrothed to notice me, to spend time with me, and to be kind to me. Is that too much to ask?"

Thomas shook his head. "It is not," he said. "But I have tried to be kind. I have tried to notice you, but it is never enough or it is never the right kind of notice. What have you ever tried to do for me except bleed all over my walls or make demands of me? You have never once shown any of the kindness you profess to want in return."

Adelaide turned to look at him, frowning as she wiped her face. She wasn't an unattractive woman. In fact, she had pretty eyes and a nice smile. Her dark hair was always well-groomed and she dressed in fine clothes. But her behavior, from the very first day she arrived at Wark Castle, had been an abomination. Thomas knew, in hindsight, that he should have suspected something was wrong those months ago when Northumbria brought her to Wark and then left within the hour. He didn't even stay for supper.

Aye, Thomas should have known something was terribly wrong.

"No one understands me here," Adelaide said. "No one understands anything about me."

"What are we to understand, my lady?"

Her eyes flashed. "There is no respect for my skills or knowledge," she said. "I can do many things, my lord, but you have never respected anything I have done."

He folded his enormous arms across his chest. "What have you done?"

Adelaide was turning from tears to fury. She pointed to the bright day beyond the window. "I am *tempestarii*," she hissed. "I control the weather. The fine sky – *I* did this. But you do not believe me!"

Thomas could only shake his head. They'd had this conversation before. The woman believed she was a witch capable of controlling the weather – a *tempestarii*, as they were known. She was convinced that everything that happened with the sky was something she had brought forth with her divine spells. He'd discovered that belief about a week after she'd arrived, sometime around the first instance of her cutting herself. There was something in her blood, she said, that controlled the weather. Every time she cut herself in her dramatic, attention-seeking fashion, she expected the weather to change.

It didn't.

"I told you not to speak on such things," Thomas said. "There are superstitious people about and if they believe a storm witch lives at Wark Castle, they may blame you for failed crops and famines. You put yourself in danger every time you say that."

Adelaide was wiping at her bloodied arm with the long sleeve of her shift; the cuts had been shallow, just enough to smear blood and make the situation look dire. But now that Thomas was no longer reacting to them, Adelaide cleaned herself up.

"What do you care?" she said, sniffling. "You will not protect me."

He lifted those big shoulders again. "I do not want my castle razed simply to punish you," he said, watching her pale cheeks flush with rage. Before she could retort, he held up a hand. "I will say no more on the subject except for this – my parents as well as your father are coming to visit today and you will behave yourself. If you do not, I will send you back with your father and I do not care about the betrothal. I will take my chances with his anger. I will no longer tolerate your foolish, irrational behavior and I will not permit you to embarrass yourself in front of my family any more than you already have. Do you understand me?"

Adelaide was defiant. Having grown up with no one to deny her or set boundaries for her, she rebelled against anything of that nature that Thomas had ever tried to do. "I will not be silenced," she said. "Mayhap your parents would like to know that you want me dead. I will tell them, I swear it!"

Thomas had enough; one couldn't argue with a mad woman, and that was exactly what Adelaide was – mad. Without another word, he turned on his heel and marched from the chamber. The weeping nurse was still out in the hall, still smeared with blood, and he grabbed the woman by the arm, tossing her into the chamber where she fell to her knees. As her cries resumed in earnest, Thomas slammed the chamber door shut and bolted it from the outside.

"And that is how you cage a rabid beast," he hissed to Desmond, still standing outside the door. "Pass the word to all of the servants. No one opens that door and I do not care how much those two scream. I am at an end with my patience. I will have to release them when de Vauden arrives for tonight's feast, but not before."

Desmond was particularly approving of that order. "Aye, my lord," he said. "I will ensure they do not make it out alive."

He muttered the last word inaudibly and Thomas turned to look at him, curiously. "What did you say?"

Desmond shook his head quickly. "Nothing, my lord," he insisted. "I will ensure no one opens that door until you give the command."

Thomas' gaze lingered on the man a moment, still trying to figure out what he had said that he wouldn't repeat. He suspected what it was, but he didn't ask again.

It wasn't as if he didn't agree with the man.

Listening to the weeping and screaming on the other side of the chamber door, Thomas descended the stairs, mentally preparing for the arrival of his parents and Northumbria.

He had a feeling that tonight would be an interesting night.

CHAPTER TWO

I T WAS JUST at sunset and a warm stillness had settled over the land. The sun was kissing the horizon, turning the sky shades of pink and orange, and the trees were swaying gently in the breeze as the birds were settling in for the night. As the tiny, old palfrey plodded along the dirt road beneath the fluttering branches, dust and leaves scattered.

It was just another evening in a long line of evenings that had made up the unspectacular life of Maitland de Ryes Bowlin. Sitting atop the little gray palfrey, it was a rare time that she was actually riding the beast because it was so old. The little creature got tired easily if it had to carry Maitland's insignificant weight, but even so, she'd kept off the animal for the most part and had practically walked all the way from Newcastle.

But she hadn't minded, in truth. The weather had been excellent, so excellent that she and her traveling companion, Tibelda, had made excellent time between walking and riding the ancient palfreys that had been provided to them by the diocese in Newcastle. In fact, everything they had was donated – horses, clothing, traveling bag. All of it had come from church donations and had, at one time, been fine in their original states. The little horses had once been quite strong and pretty, the satchels had been excellently crafted, and the clothing had been draped across the frames of rich women.

But now, everything was worn and threadbare, yet serviceable. They were grateful for it.

The two Beguines had taken the road north from Newcastle, a smaller road that navigated between the larger road to the east along the coast, and the still-larger road further off to the west that carved through the middle of Northumberland and headed straight up into Scotland. The road Maitland and her companion had taken snaked up through some remote lands and through a chain of unremarkable villages until it reached the village of Coldstream, which was just to the east of Wark Castle.

Even now, as the colors of sunset deepened, Maitland could see the big walls of Wark Castle off to the west. In fact, as they drew closer, the gray stone walls were silhouetted against the sky, and with the shadows, the place appeared a lovely shade of purple. It was fascinating. The sun was sinking and the land was darkening, and Maitland and her companion pushed their little horses as fast as they could go, making their way to the castle just as an enormous party with hundreds of armed men and a big, fortified carriage entered the gatehouse.

The ladies waited until the entire party passed through the rather large gatehouse with a small portcullised opening. It meant that only two or three mounted men at a time could pass through. Having fostered at Alnwick years ago, Maitland knew something of castles, of their size and importance, and she'd always been fascinated by the military aspects of them. It was one of her many interests which her late husband had not appreciated. To him, a woman should only have womanly interests, one issue between them in a long line of issues that had gone from bad to worse before his untimely death.

She tried hard not to think of Henry these days.

The gate guards gave her their attention after the enormous party passed through, and she and her companion were taken to the guard chamber just inside the portcullis while someone took their palfreys to the stables and yet someone else went in search of her brother, Desmond. That was the entire reason Maitland had come to Wark

Castle – to see the brother she'd not seen in a couple of years, at least. Not since her husband's burial, where he'd tried not to show too much joy in it. But Maitland knew; she'd always known what Desmond thought of Henry Bowlin.

Death was his preference for the man.

In truth, Desmond was some time in coming because of the big party in the ward. He'd been needed to help settle them, but when he arrived at the guard room, the delight on his face was evident at the sight of his sister. Maitland was lifted right out of the chair and swung around until she ended up kicking a poor soldier who happened to be standing too close.

Desmond only laughed.

"Mae!" he cried, kissing her on the cheek as he set her down. "My God – little Mae! Is it really you? I am not dreaming?"

Maitland shook her head, patting her brother on the cheek. "It is no dream," she said, her eyes glimmering as she looked at her big, older brother. "Des, life has been good to you. Have you been well?"

He nodded firmly. "Well enough," he said. "And you? How has it been in Newcastle?"

Maitland shrugged, though she was still smiling. "I have had my work," she said. "I have led a busy and useful life."

"You must have if the church is giving you a charity of your own," he said. "I am very proud of you, Mae. I always knew you would do good for this world."

She laughed softly. "And just when did you know that?" she asked. "In between pulling my hair and trying to put frogs in my pockets?"

Desmond had a mischievous little grin. "It was fun," he said simply. "You screamed beautifully."

"I still do. But if you try your tricks now that I am a grown woman, you shall find that I will retaliate."

It was his turn to laugh. "I promise, no tricks," he said. "I am very glad to see you. How long can you stay?"

"Only for the night," she said. "We must be to Edenside by tomorrow. It is not far away, is it?"

Desmond shook his head. "Not at all," he said. "In fact, it will be a half-day's ride at most. I am very happy because now you will be close to me. We can see each other all of the time."

Maitland looped her arm through his. "You can come and visit me," she said. "But for now, we are weary and require something to eat. Do you have a place where my companion and I may rest?"

She was indicating Tibelda, who nodded shortly when Desmond glanced at her. She was older, rounder, and with a big, red nose. He returned his attention to the much more pleasant sight of his sister.

"Of course," he said. "Come with me now. I shall show you where you may sleep tonight."

With her satchel in one hand and her other hand gripping her brother's elbow, Maitland followed Desmond as he led her and Tibelda out of the guard room and into the bailey beyond. It was still crowded, but the majority of the large party had disbanded. Maitland looked at the men and their banners with interest.

"I have seen those red and yellow banners, I think," she said to her brother. "Who has come?"

Desmond eyed the escort. "The Earl of Northumbria, Edmund de Vauden, from Kyloe Castle," he said. "But some of the crowd in the bailey is still part of the de Wolfe escort that arrived about an hour ago. You did not see them on the road?"

Maitland shook her head. "We did not see anyone at all."

"Which way did you come?"

"Up the road that crossed through the village of Wooler."

At that point, the conversation faded a bit as Desmond led the two women through the remains of Northumbria's escort in the attempt to take them someplace that wasn't crawling with men and animals, someplace safe. Even so, Maitland was much more interested in everything around her, castle included, as her brother dragged her through the crowd.

Wark was an oddly-shaped castle with those big gray walls but, inside it, the dimensions were rather strange. The whole thing seemed to be built on a slope that angled up before coming to a crest and then sloping downward towards the River Tweed. As they walked, they were walking uphill, heading for the keep, which was another oddly-shaped but rather large structure atop a walled motte.

To Maitland's right, hidden behind the crowd of men and animals, was a great hall on the river side of the bailey. Cutting the bailey in half was another wall, creating an inner ward around the keep, and they had to pass through that to get to the keep itself. More hiking up the slope led them to steps that took them up to the big keep, high above the river and the countryside, with views for miles.

Before they entered, Desmond turned to her.

"We have several important guests here tonight," he said, "not the least of which are my liege's parents and the father of the woman he is to marry. My chamber is in the keep, right next to the entry door, and I am going to give you my chamber for the night so that you will be more comfortable."

Maitland smiled. "Thank you, Des," she said. "I am sure we will be very comfortable. And I promise we will not be any trouble at all. Just a little food and we shall go right to sleep."

Desmond frowned. "You shall eat in the hall tonight, with me," he said. "I have not seen you in years, Mae. Would you truly deny me some time to get reacquainted with my little sister?"

Maitland struggled to keep the smile on her face. She was exhausted and sitting in a hall of strangers wasn't exactly something she was eager to do. She would have been much happier with a meal brought to her chamber, but she could see from the expression on Desmond's face that such a request would not be well met. In resignation, she nodded.

"Of course not," she said. "But Tibelda need not join us. She can remain in the chamber while I join you. I hope that is acceptable."

"I should say so," Desmond said. "Come on, then. Let's get you settled. Then I am eager to introduce you to my liege. I have told you about him."

"Who is your liege?"

"Thomas de Wolfe."

"De Wolfe," Maitland said thoughtfully. "I know that name."

"You should. His family controls the entire northern section of Northumberland, up to the borders. You are on the border right now, in fact. Did you know that? Scotland is just over that river."

Maitland caught a glimpse of the river before Desmond took her inside the darkened keep, stopping at the very first door they came to and shoving it open. Beyond, it was almost pitch black until Desmond sparked a flint and stone, lighting a fat yellow taper on a table next to the door. Beyond, a tiny and rather crowded chamber came to life.

There was a narrow rope bed, a table and chair, a trunk, and little else. Maitland could see, already, that she and Tibelda were going to have trouble squeezing onto that tiny bed, but she made no mention of it. She simply set her satchel down on the table as her brother crouched down next to the dark hearth, trying to spark a blaze.

"Will you permit me to clean up a little before I join you in the hall?" she asked him. "We have been traveling for four days and I should like to wash my hands and face."

A flame flickered in the hearth and Desmond stirred it about, watching the blaze quickly grow. "I will have a servant bring you hot water," he said. "Hurry and wash. I will return for you shortly."

Maitland smiled at him as he brushed off his hands and quit the chamber, shutting the door quietly behind him. Once he was gone, Maitland gave off a little sigh of relief, happy that she had made her destination. Looking around the chamber, she once again saw how tiny it was, and the first thing her eyes fell on was Tibelda. The woman had fallen onto the small bed and was already sound asleep. Cocking an eyebrow at her traveling companion, Maitland could see that the best thing she could look forward to that night was a blanket on the floor.

Already, it was going to be a long night.

CHAPTER THREE

"**N**ORTHUMBRIA HAS SEEN his daughter," William said grimly. "The girl says that you have cut her arms and wish her to die."

Thomas stared at him a moment before lifting his eyebrows to display his complete and utter disbelief at what his father was telling him.

"Are you mad?" he hissed. "Papa, she cuts *herself*. She has done it since her arrival and I have an army of servants and soldiers to attest to this. The woman has upended my house and hold with her constant dramatics. Nothing she says is of my doing, I assure you."

William exhaled slowly, heavily, and plopped down into the nearest chair. He was weary, and frustrated, and far too old to be dealing with a situation like this.

It was worse than he had suspected.

Nothing could have prepared him for his conversation with Northumbria just a few moments ago. William and Jordan had arrived shortly before the earl's heavily-armed party, and when he greeted the man amiably, it had been in the presence of the man's daughter, who immediately held up her bandaged arms and declared that Thomas kept her locked in her chamber and abused her.

The earl, of course, had been shocked, turning accusing eyes to William, who assured the man that his son would have done no such thing. His response drove Adelaide to tears, and she wailed loudly as her father berated William for Thomas' behavior. Through it all, William knew it was a lie. He knew what Adelaide had been doing to his son these past six months, but he didn't say so. He let the man berate him, a man so blind to his daughter's treachery that, in truth, he probably genuinely believed her.

William's anger at the situation grew.

Now, he found himself facing his irate son, and the man had every reason to be irate. A madwoman was ruining his life and his reputation. At the moment, Northumbria was still in his daughter's chambers, still hearing her obvious lies, while William and Jordan were in Thomas' chambers, trying to figure this all out.

The entire circumstance was a nightmare.

"Your mother spoke to Adelaide briefly when we arrived," William said after a moment, rubbing his good eye wearily. "The girl sobbed and told your mother that you wished her dead, too. She has fresh cuts all over her arms."

Thomas nodded impatiently, trying to keep his voice quiet because his mother had managed to put Caria to sleep on his big bed. The woman lay beside the exhausted child, rubbing her back, and Thomas was trying very hard to keep quiet. With what his father was saying, however, it was difficult.

It was hell.

"She cut herself this morning and smeared blood over all of the walls of her chamber," Thomas said, becoming angrier as he spoke. "As always, the servants rushed to her aid and wrapped her arms. By the time I got to her chamber, she was telling me how glad she was to see me and acting as if she wanted to be affectionate with me."

William was listening to it all with disbelief and sorrow. "What did you do?"

Thomas lifted his big shoulders. "I went into the chamber, yanked off the bandages on her arms, and told her that I would not prevent her from killing herself if she wished to do so," he said, exasperated. "Papa, every time she has cut herself, she has told me she wishes to die. So this time, I told her I would no longer prevent her from taking her own life. If she wants to die, she can die. I do not care."

William put a hand over his face for a moment, struggling with the situation he found his son in. "And you told her that?"

"I told her I would not prevent her from doing as she wished. I never said I wished her to die."

"Anything else?"

Thomas rolled his eyes and turned away. "She told me she was a *tempestarii*," he said. "Again, she told me this. She has told me this before. She believes that something in her blood controls the weather, that she can make it rain or shine. She seems to genuinely believe she has the power."

William had heard that from him the last time he'd visited. A storm had rolled in and he had witnessed Adelaide claiming responsibility for it. "There *is* no such power," he muttered. "Something will be done about this, Thomas. This behavior your intended exhibits is why I have summoned Northumbria. Your mother and I are convinced that Adelaide has been this way her entire life, and her father knows it, which was why he was so eager to broker a betrothal with you. You will inherit absolutely everything when he dies, and it is a princely estate, but in order to get it, you have to marry his mad daughter. The man knew exactly what he was doing when he talked me into the contract."

Thomas hadn't expected that kind of confession from his father, not now. Perhaps not ever. He'd expected more fatherly pleas for patience, so this turn in William's attitude was a surprise. As Thomas had told Desmond, William de Wolfe didn't make bad decisions. He stood by every decision he'd ever made, and although he was standing by this one, it was clear he intended to do something about it. Thomas had to admit that he felt more relief than he thought he would at the realization.

But he didn't like seeing his father so defeated.

"You had no way of knowing his daughter was insane," he said. "It is Northumbria who bears the shame. He should have been honest about her."

William gave him an impatient glance. "As if I would agree to a marriage between you and a madwoman? Nay, Northumbria knew I would not, which is why he did not tell me. For not investigating Lady Adelaide more on your behalf, I am sorry, Thomas. It would seem that I have created an intolerable situation for you."

Thomas was feeling particularly magnanimous. In fact, he felt rather sorry for his father. "I do not blame you," he said. "You did not know. You thought you were doing what was best for me."

William snorted softly. "Is this the same man who tried to escape his brothers those months ago?" he said, a smile on his lips. "The same one who fought and kicked, and refused to be part of this contract?"

Thomas grinned, displaying his big, white teeth. "Would you feel better if I shouted at you?"

"Probably not," William said. "But you have every right to be angry about this."

"Yet, I am not," Thomas said. "I will reiterate that you did not know about Northumbria's deceit. It is not your fault."

William sighed heavily, one more time, before standing up from the chair. "I got you into this and I am going to try and get you out," he said with determination. "I will speak to Northumbria again and see if we can end this as painlessly as possible."

Thomas put his hand on his father's shoulder. "Everything will work out as it should," he said. "You are The Wolfe. You did not come by your reputation by being weak and ineffective."

William lifted his eyebrows, agreeing with the statement but knowing the hard work he'd put in to achieve such a thing. "Indeed, I did not," he said. He patted Thomas' hand. "Go, now; I will meet you in the hall after I have spoken with Northumbria."

Thomas nodded, turning to look at his mother, who was still laying on the bed with the snoring little girl. His mother silently waved him on, so he departed the chamber with his father, closing the door softly behind them. As his father went to Adelaide's chamber for an attempt at reason, Thomas took the narrow stairs down to the floor below.

He didn't want to be around when Northumbria realized his father was breaking the contract.

Even so, Thomas' mood had lifted. His father intended to help him and he felt a great deal of relief at that. Finally, there was hope on the horizon and he couldn't have been happier about it. Hope that when Northumbria left Wark this time, he would take that madwoman with him.

Taking the steps down to the bottom floor, which was the entry level with the vaults dug into the rock below, Thomas was about to quit the keep when he saw Desmond heading in his direction. Desmond lifted a hand, catching his attention.

"I have been looking for you, yet again," he said. "Are your parents adequately settled in?"

Pausing in the entry door, Thomas nodded. "Aye," he said. "My father is with Northumbria and Adelaide, while my mother is lying on the bed with Caria as she sleeps. I am not for certain my mother will be joining us in the hall. She and the child are weary from the journey."

Desmond put a hand on him, turning him around rather firmly. "I hope she can manage to attend," he said. "My sister has come and it would be good for her to have another woman to speak with at sup. Meanwhile, I am eager to introduce the two of you."

Thomas allowed the man to push him back inside. He followed Desmond a few short steps to his chamber door, just inside the entry, where Desmond pounded on the door a few times. After several moments, the door slowly creaked open.

It was so dark that Thomas really couldn't see much, but the one thing he did see was a petite woman emerging from the doorway. As she took a step out into the entry, she held a single tallow taper with her purely for light and, suddenly, Thomas could see her quite clearly.

A wave of surprise washed over him.

"Sir Thomas de Wolfe, this is my sister, Lady Bowlin," Desmond said, indicating the woman. "Her name is Maitland, but I am sure she would not mind if you called her Mae. Everyone does. Mae, this is Thomas de Wolfe, my liege and my friend. He is one of the finest men you shall ever meet."

Thomas found himself looking into light brown eyes that had a hint of orange to them. He'd never see that color in his entire life, and they were set within a remarkably beautiful face. Lady Bowlin had long, dark lashes, arched brows, and a sweetly oval face. Her skin was like cream and her lips were rather lush and soft-looking. She wore a wimple around her head, as befitting her widowhood status, but he could see bits of dark hair peeking out. Truly, Thomas was taken aback by what he saw and, for a moment, he simply stared at her.

This is Desmond's widowed sister?

"My lady," he said after a moment. "Welcome to Wark Castle. You have a very interesting name."

The woman smiled, revealing straight teeth that were quite lovely, like the rest of her. "Thank you, my lord," she said. "It is a family name; my mother's maiden name, in fact. It is very kind of you to allow my companion and me to stay here for the night on my way to Edenside. I am sure my brother has told you of our destination."

Thomas nodded; her voice was soft and sweet, melodic. It assaulted his ears in a most pleasurable way.

"He has told me," he said, suddenly very interested in Desmond's sister. Those pale brown eyes had his attention. "Surely you are joining us for supper in the hall. I should like to hear about your plans for the charity."

Maitland nodded eagerly. "I do have plans," she said. "I hope to make it one of the biggest and best in all the north. From what I understand, it is not a very big one right now, but I hope to change that. Do you get to Kelso very often?"

Thomas nodded as he held out his elbow to her, politely inviting her to take it. "Absolutely," he lied. He hadn't been to Kelso in months. He couldn't even remember the last time he had been there before that, but he suddenly saw himself visiting there much more often. "If you are ready to go to sup, I was just heading to the hall myself. I would be honored if you would permit me to escort you."

Maitland didn't even hesitate to take his arm. "It is my pleasure, my lord," she said. "Mayhap we can even discuss my charity, if you are interested. It is my intention to find a great patron for my charity and, mayhap, the House of de Wolfe would consider it. It is a great house with a great reputation."

Thomas all but shoved Desmond out of the way as he led Maitland from the keep. She was clutching his arm, already talking about money for a charity she wasn't even in charge of yet, but he didn't care. A pretty face had a way of making him listen quite attentively.

"You honor me by saying so," he said unpretentiously, a complete departure from the normally arrogant knight. "My father is a great man, mayhap one of the greatest men who has ever lived, and he has worked hard to establish our family in the north."

As Thomas lost himself in conversation with Maitland, Desmond watched the pair walk from the keep, listening to Thomas say things he wouldn't normally say. Had he been to Kelso often? Of course not. And since when did Thomas speak modestly about the greatness of de Wolfe? Something odd was afoot and Desmond found himself shuffling after the couple, listening to Thomas behave in a way that Desmond had seen before. The hard-fighting, hard-living knight with enough pride to sink an island under the sheer weight of his ego was behaving rather charmingly, and that always indicated his intentions.

Not good intentions, either.

Confused, and not at all amused, Desmond was going to have to keep an eye on the man. He'd been with Thomas on too many occasions when the man charmed his way into a woman's bed. It had, at times, started out like this – flattery, modesty, and charisma. Thomas had a wagonload of it when the mood struck him.

Or a woman appealed to him.

Desmond realized with chagrin that he was going to have to make sure his very own sister didn't end up in Thomas' bed this night. But he could already see it was going to be a hard fight. Like any wolf, when the animal was on a scent, it was difficult to shake it.

And Thomas de Wolfe was no different.

HE HAD BEEN nothing as she had expected.

In truth, Maitland hadn't known what to expect from her brother's liege, and a de Wolfe, but she found Thomas de Wolfe handsome, friendly, and intelligent.

So handsome.

He was a tall man, though she'd seen taller, but he had enormously broad shoulders and the biggest hands she'd ever seen, scarred and battle-worn. Everything about him was muscular and powerful, but it was his appearance that had her notice – he had long, dark hair that went past his shoulders, hair that glistened like a raven's wing in the light, and eyes that looked like dark, burnished gold. His square jaw was covered by the beginnings of a beard, but when he smiled, she could see an enormous dimple in his left cheek.

She rather liked that dimple.

Truly, he was a specimen the likes of which she'd never seen and although she wasn't one to become giddy over anyone, within the first few minutes of knowing Thomas, he seemed to have the ability to cause her stomach to quiver. The first time he'd smiled at her, flashing white teeth with big canines, it was enough to send her belly into a bit of a state.

Odder still, she didn't mind one bit.

Talk of her charity had been brief, as the conversation had turned to Wark Castle and the House of de Wolfe in general the moment they had entered the hall. Desmond seemed to be hovering over her, enough to be astonishingly annoying, and every time Thomas would try to speak to her, Desmond was there to insert his own opinion or knowledge into the conversation. It didn't take Maitland long to figure out that Desmond was more than likely feeling left out, as they hadn't seen each other in a couple of years, so she reluctantly turned her attention to her brother from time to time. If the poor man was so desperate to talk to her, then she would oblige him.

But Thomas didn't give up so easily. He didn't seem to like Desmond taking her attention away from him. After telling the servants not to wait the meal on his father and Lord de Vauden, he put himself back into the conversation between brother and sister. Maitland was quite happy to pay attention to him again, but Desmond wrangled her focus away with talk of their father, something Thomas didn't have much to say about because he didn't know the man. Feeling disappointed, Maitland begrudgingly focused on her brother again.

"One of the last times I saw you was before our father died, Mae," Desmond said as he poured her a measure of wine from the pitcher on the table. "Did he ever come see you in Newcastle before he passed?"

Maitland took a gulp of the sweet, rich wine. "I'd not had much to do with Normand de Ryes since my marriage to Henry," she said. "He made it clear that he wanted to be rid of me, so I obliged him."

Desmond could see the stiffness in her manner when she spoke of their father, which wasn't something he'd ever seen from her before. "I would like to think that he married you to Henry to provide a better life for you."

Maitland cast him a long glance. "He married me to Henry to be rid of me," she said. "Des, you and I have hardly had time to sit and talk to one another over the past five years, so permit me to tell you the truth behind Normand – you were away to foster from a young age, so you did not see how it was at home with him. He lamented your absence daily and cursed me that I was not born a male. Did I ever tell you that?"

Desmond was forced to shake his head. "You did not," he said, distressed. "You should have."

Maitland lifted her shoulders as she turned back to her wine. "It does not matter," she said. "It was not your fault. But you hated Henry; I know you did. I saw you berate Father for agreeing to the betrothal."

"Of course I did. Henry was a fool."

"Father did it simply to be rid of me."

The pleasant evening was taking a downturn. Desmond had always known that was his father's reason for marrying Maitland to a middle-aged knight with a less than stellar reputation, but he wasn't going to admit it. To do so would make it seem as if his sister wasn't worth anything, and she was. He had a great deal of respect for her. Maitland was educated and clever, and she was certainly worth far more than their father gave her credit for.

"And it was fortunate for you that he did," he said, trying to sound encouraging. "He married you to Henry and the man got himself killed, which has allowed you to commit yourself to a pious life of servitude. You are now going to Edenside to take over the foundling home and you will make an excellent life for the less fortunate. Mayhap, this is what God had in mind for you all along, Mae."

Maitland turned to him, a forced smile on her face. She didn't exactly look at it like that. All she'd ever wanted was to marry a man she at least liked and have a dozen children of her own. Now, she was relegated to taking care of children who had no parents. She would never have children of her own. If that was God's plan for her, she wasn't happy about it, but she had little choice in the matter.

"I am fortunate that the Bishop of Newcastle thinks so highly of me," she said. "When I first came to the church there, I was put in charge of the foundlings simply because they had no one else, but it was something I liked very much. I can educate them, you see, and I taught them how to draw letters and write their names. The bishop thought I did such an excellent job that he is sending me to Edenside because those children have no one at all. Scottish children, I am told."

Next to her, Thomas grunted. He had been listening to the conversation mostly because he was quite interested in Maitland, but also because he rather liked hearing her speak. But now she was veering onto a subject he had an opinion about.

Scots.

"If they're Scots children, they should be suitably unruly," he said. "My mother is Scots, the daughter of a clan chief that I am named for, but that does not mean I have any love for them. You said you were looking for a patron for the home?"

Maitland turned to him, her big eyes fixed on him, and he felt just the least bit quivery inside. He thought it rather humorous because he'd never experienced a reaction like that to any woman, not even to Tacey, but there was nothing about this woman he didn't find attractive. What had started out as sheer interest in a pretty lass was turning into something beyond the interest in her beauty.

She was a woman of substance.

"I hope to," she said, breaking into his thoughts. "As I said, having a de Wolfe as a patron would be a proud thing, indeed. Mayhap you will consider it after visiting the home once I have had a chance to organize it. You will see that I am very good at managing a home, and the children shall be cleaned and fed and educated. I have vowed this to the bishop."

"Who is this bishop?"

"Antony Buxton, the Bishop of St. John's Parish," she said. "But the diocese is allied with Kelso, which is why I have been sent here. They needed someone and Father Buxton recommended me because of my service to St. John's."

Thomas watched her mouth as she spoke, watching the ends of her mouth curl up. It was fascinating. "That sounds quite prestigious," he said, tearing his focus away from her mouth. "But you said the children shall be educated. I am assuming you are educated yourself?"

She nodded but before she could reply, Desmond chimed in. "You have no idea, Thomas," he said. "My sister is the most brilliant woman in England. She taught herself to read, write, do mathematics, and manage a house and hold when she was very young. It was out of necessity when my mother died, but she already knew a great deal when my father sent her to Alnwick to foster. I was already serving there, and the earl and his wife were most kind to take Mae. By the time she left to marry Bowlin, she was practically running the place. I do not believe the countess has ever gotten over losing her."

Thomas frowned. "She was at Alnwick?" he said. "I went there many times in my youth but I never saw her."

Maitland laughed softly. "I was probably not there when you visited," she said. "If you went in your youth, then I am sure I was still living at home with my father. He did not send me there until I had seen twelve years of age."

Thomas's attention was drawn to her. "How old are you now?"

"I have seen twenty years and three."

Thomas stroked his chin. "I see," he said. "In that case, you are probably right. I am a good many years older than you are."

Maitland was still smiling at him. "If you are, you do not look to be. I cannot imagine you being much more than thirty years or so. Am I wrong?"

Thomas cocked an eyebrow as he reached for his cup of wine. "Very," he said, disgruntled. "Add five years to that figure. And I am the baby of the family, no less. Christ, I'm feeling old."

Maitland giggled as she watched him drink, flushing madly when he caught her eye and winked at her. There was a bit of flirtation going on between them, but she was certain that he was only being kind to her because of Desmond. Still, she could swear there was something more to it… perhaps there was even a hint of warmth there.

Or perhaps it was just wishful thinking.

Maitland wasn't sure how to deal with it, to be truthful. She'd enjoyed gentle flirtation in her youth, before she'd married Henry, but those days were long gone. At least, she'd thought so until she was introduced to Thomas de Wolfe. In the brief time she'd spent with the man, she could feel that giddy heart coming back to life, the tender heart of her youth that she was certain had hardened over the years. Henry Bowlin had seen to that. As it turned out, she may have been wrong.

Something in her breast was stirring.

As Maitland sat there and pondered what was happening, a little girl with long, dark hair made a rather loud entrance. She came racing into the hall, well ahead of the elderly couple trailing her, running across the dirt floor and straight to the long table near the hearth where Maitland and Desmond and Thomas were sitting. The child ran at Thomas, leaping onto his lap and causing the man to grunt as she hit his rather tender gut with her elbow. He scooped her up under the arms and plopped her onto his knee.

"Tommy, I'm hungry!" the child declared. "I want meat!"

Thomas grinned. "And you shall have it," he said. "But first, let me introduce you to someone. Will you be a good lass and greet Lady Bowlin? Lady Bowlin, this is my... sister, Caria de Wolfe."

Maitland smiled at the pretty, vivacious child. "Greetings, Lady Caria," she said. "May I say that you have a very pretty dress on. I like the color."

Caria wasn't much interested in the strange woman sitting next to Thomas, but she did look down at her garment when the lady commented on it. "It's mine," she said simply, tugging at it for a moment, before her attention swiftly moved elsewhere. "I want *meat!*"

Thomas wriggled his eyebrows at the rude child. "Greet the lady, Caria," he told her. "Be courteous."

Caria was spoiled, but she wasn't insolent, and anything Thomas told her to do, she would do. She looked over at the woman, studying her for a moment, before speaking.

"Why are you dressed like that?" she asked. "Are you from a nunnery?"

Maitland glanced at her clothing. In addition to the linen wimple on her head, she was dressed in a rough woolen shift and an old woolen tunic that went to her ankles. Around her waist was a belt fashioned from leather, certainly not like the belts she used to wear when she was married to Henry. He liked to have his wife nicely dressed and she had three very nice surcoats to wear along with a collection of shifts, belts, scarves, and anything else fine ladies wore. Any meager money they had went to her clothing and appearance because Henry was convinced that men would see his well-dressed wife and think he was well-off.

She'd been a symbol for him and nothing more.

"Nay, I am not from a nunnery," she said after a moment. "But I do serve the church, which is why I dress modestly. Do you go to church and pray, Lady Caria?"

Caria nodded. "Sometimes," she said, her attention briefly diverted to Jordan and William as they sat on the opposite side of the table. "Matha gives me alms for the poor and I choose who gets the coin."

Across the table, Jordan heard her and she snorted softly. "I've told ye before that ye dunna pick and choose," she said, smiling apologetically at Maitland. "That lass doesna quite understand the concept of compassion, but she is tryin'."

Maitland smiled, a genuine gesture. "I see," she said, her attention returning to Caria. She really was a pretty little thing, with bright eyes and pale skin. "Caria, I want you to think on something I am about to tell you. Can you do that?"

Caria nodded, but it was clear that she was disinterested. "Think about what?"

"I want you to pretend you are very poor," she said. "I am sure you can pretend you are a poor girl. Now, imagine if you had no food and because you had no food, you went to church to hope that a fine lady would help you and give you a coin. But imagine that the fine lady decided to give someone else a coin over you, and now you have nothing to buy food with. Would that make you happy?"

Caria's brow furrowed. "I would *make* the fine lady give me a coin."

Maitland nodded. "Of course you would want her to," she said. "And if she did, that would mean she was showing you compassion. She would want to help you. But if she gave the coin to another, that would make you feel badly, wouldn't it?"

Caria was rather confused with the concept, but she was a bright girl. She understood what Maitland was saying, sort of. "But Matha only gives me one coin," she said. "I can only give it to one person and I must pick who that person is."

Maitland had a point to illustrate with the child who only seemed to see the power that the coin gave her when choosing a worthy recipient. Compassion was a strange concept for the entitled sometimes, and especially with children who hadn't seen much of the world and its problems.

Everyone was watching Maitland at this point and she knew it; perhaps she was hoping Thomas was watching her enough to be impressed with how she was communicating with the child. Everyone had always told her she was very good with children and she had no idea why she should want to impress Thomas, but she did. Perhaps impressing him might just get her the patronage for Edenside that she wanted. Or perhaps it would prove to her that the warmth she had been feeling from him wasn't simply her imagination. Whatever the case, she was determined to impress him.

Reaching out, she picked up a hunk of bread from a wooden plate on the table.

"But your coin can feed more than one person," she said, holding the bread up. She began to tear pieces away. "The next time your mother gives you a coin, remember that the coin can help many people at once. Find a baker and purchase all of the bread that coin will buy, and then give that bread to the poor. You will be looked upon as a great and generous benefactress."

Clearly, Caria had never even considered such a thing and she looked at Maitland, at the pieces of bread she had lined upon on the table, before finally looking to her mother.

"How much bread will a coin buy, Matha?" she asked. "Will it buy enough to feed many people?"

Jordan had a smile on her lips as she glanced at Maitland. "I think it will buy enough tae feed several," she said. "I like the lady's solution."

As Caria grinned and picked up one of the soft pieces Maitland had torn off, popping it into her mouth, Thomas looked at his mother over the child's head.

"This lovely and wise creature is Lady Bowlin, Mother," he said. "Forgive me for not introducing you earlier. She is Desmond's sister, on her way to take charge of a charity in Edenside."

"Edenside?" Jordan repeated as if surprised. "The foundlin' home?"

Maitland nodded eagerly, realizing the woman knew of it right away. "You have heard of it, then?"

"Aye," Jordan said hesitantly. "My husband and I are patrons of Kelso Abbey. The foundlin' home is part of that, although it recently became a point of contention between me and the abbot."

"Why a point of contention, my lady?"

Jordan thought a moment about how to phrase what she was about to say. Not knowing the lady, or her loyalties, she was careful about it. But more than that, it was a very sensitive subject she was about to speak on.

"The abbot's sister ran the foundlin' home," she said. "She was a very rich woman from Roxburgh and she felt it was her duty tae take care of the less than fortunate, as she would say, but the truth was that it was all for show. The woman dinna care about the bairns in her care."

Seated next to his wife, William put a hand on her arm. "Jordan," he said softly. "Not now."

But Jordan wouldn't be silenced. She was an opinionated woman and especially about things she didn't agree with, and she suspected Maitland truly had no idea what she would soon be facing with Edenside and its dark past.

She was doing the lass a favor.

"Lady Bowlin needs tae know, English," she shushed him, returning her attention to Maitland. "The woman had her servants manage the charity and she was the patroness in name only. There used tae be twenty-one children at the charity, all of them homeless waifs with no parentage, no hope. Rumor had it that one of the servants was sellin' the children tae whoever was willin' tae pay the price, for any purpose.

The abbot's sister was never the wiser until one of the children turned up dead in a field outside of Kelso. That was when the sky crashed down on the woman. I threatened tae pull our patronage if she wasna dealt with and the last I heard, she'd moved tae London and her servants with her. Her great house now sits empty."

Maitland was looking at Jordan in shock. "That is the most terrible thing I have ever heard," she breathed, genuinely disturbed. "My God… those poor children. But why were they sold? Who would do such a thing?"

Jordan lifted her slender shoulders. "Greed," she said, disgusted. "It was purely for the money. A greedy servant saw a commodity in the children, like cattle or sheep."

Maitland was beside herself. "Selling them like… like livestock," she breathed. "What a beastly thing to do. But you said there used to be twenty-one children? How many are there now?"

"Seven."

Maitland's jaw popped open. "Out of *twenty-one*?" she gasped. "My bishop never told me these stories, not even a hint of them. I have never heard anything about this."

Jordan accepted a cup of wine as a servant came to the table. "I am not surprised," she said. "It is possible he doesna even know. 'Tis not somethin' the abbot at Kelso wishes tae get around, for it would reflect very badly upon him."

"But *you* know," Maitland said, almost insistently. "Have you demanded justice for these children? Surely they must have someone defend them."

Jordan glanced at her husband, then, only to see that he was looking away, drinking his wine. It was clear from that glance that it was a distressing subject for the both of them. The de Wolfe name stood for honor and character, so for something like this to happen to a place they were supporting was clearly disturbing.

"The clans know," she said quietly. "My father was the chief of Clan Scott, years ago, and the clan from Lothian Castle is still my kin. They knew what happened and from their lips, other clans knew. They cornered the abbot one day and demanded tae know who the children had been sold tae. Some were found, some were not. Those who were found were taken in by the clans, so not tae face the terrible memories of Edenside again. Sorry tae tell ye such things, lass, but 'tis best ye know what ye are walkin' intae since no one has seen fit tae tell ye."

Maitland was almost in tears by that point. No one had told her any of this and she could only hope it was because they didn't know. She couldn't imagine Buxton sending her to a house of horrors and not even tell her about it.

No wonder Kelso had looked outside for someone to manage their charity.

"Thank you for telling me, my lady," she said, her voice tight. Then, she looked to her brother. "Did you hear any of this, Des?"

Desmond shook his head. "I have not," he said grimly. "I do not attend mass in Kelso, nor do I pay attention to gossip. It is possible someone might have muttered such things to me, but I surely cannot recall. I must admit that I feel rather stupid for being ignorant to all of this."

Inevitably, both Desmond and Maitland looked at Thomas, who was still sitting there with Caria on his lap. When he saw their attention upon him, he simply shook his head.

"Much like Des, I do not attend mass there," he said. "My parents attend, but I have not in many years. Although I have heard whispers that Edenside was poorly run, neither my mother nor my father have ever mentioned what my mother just told you. It simply never came up and, to be completely truthful, the only thing that concerns me is information pertaining to the safety of the border and the safety of my family. I am a warrior, not a crusader for lost children, as harsh as that sounds. What happened at Kelso is Kelso's problem, not mine."

"It happened very quickly," William finally spoke up, nearly cutting off his son. "Let me clarify this before you start believing your mother and I have been negligent when it comes to the welfare of foundlings.

Everyone believed the charity was being run quite ably until the dead child was found. Then, it all unraveled in a matter of a few days. When we found out and threatened to pull our support, the abbot's sister was already on her way to London. The abbot swore he had no knowledge of what was going on and because we have known and trusted the man for twenty years, we believed him, and you know I am not one to give my trust easily. Now that Lady Bowlin shall be heading up the charity, it seems to me that we must focus on ensuring the children that remain there, from now on, are given the best care possible. So, let this be the end of it."

It was both a command and a request. Given that this day had already been upsetting enough, William didn't want the tale of the missing children to take over the conversation when he had more important things on his mind. The disappearing children had happened several months before and, in truth, Kelso was still reeling from it. It had been a horrible situation that they were trying to overcome and that was the way it needed to be looked at – all they could do was move forward and not make the same mistake twice.

But it had been quite a revelation to Maitland, who was still sitting there in shock as the trenchers were brought forth from the kitchens. Big discs of stale bread were placed before the diners, filled with meat and gravy and vegetables. The smells of beef that rose up filled the nostrils and the focus was diverted away from the lost children of Edenside and on to the meal at hand.

At least, that was what they all pretended.

But Maitland couldn't shake what she'd been told. She'd always had the unfortunate problem of feeling too deeply for things and taking them personally. She ached for a fallen sparrow and wept for a lost child. That was simply her nature. But she pretended to move forward as the others were, spooning the delicious beef into her mouth as soft conversation went on around her.

But inside, she was filled with sorrow.

"What are your first plans once you reach Edenside, Mae?" Desmond asked, his mouth full of bread. "Do you have any grand plans for the place?"

Maitland looked at him. "Until I found out about the horror of its past, you mean?"

Desmond shook his head. "I assumed you had a plan when you came, regardless of what you have been told," he said. "My little sister always had a plan, for anything she ever did. What is your great plan for Edenside?"

Thinking about what she intended to do for the charity somehow made her feel better about the terrible things she'd heard about it. She knew for a fact that she would never permit the children in her charge to know fear or heartache or hunger. She was too determined and smart for that.

"Well," she said, swallowing the bite in her mouth. "I am hoping to make it a productive charity. The first thing I must find out is if the charity owns livestock, like sheep or cows."

"There are sheep," Jordan said. She had been listening in on the conversation between brother and sister. "I know there are sheep because when we discovered what had happened tae the children, sold as they were, I wondered why the greedy servant hadna sold the livestock instead. It was speculated that the livestock would have been missed more by the abbot's sister than the children themselves. The sheep are valuable tae the foundlin' home in that they give milk and wool."

They were back on that horrific subject, but Maitland focused on the advent of sheep. "Good," she said. "We can use the milk to produce cheese. I supervised the servants who made cheese at Alnwick, so I know how it is done. If we could get some goats, that would be even better. Do you know that you can make soap from goat's milk? An old fishwife from Newcastle showed me how. She could make soap from flax oil and seawater and ash and mixing a little goat's milk into it made it soft on the skin."

"We are a little far from the sea," Thomas said, his eyes glimmering at her when she turned to look at him. "You can use water from the River Tweed."

Maitland grinned. "It would not be the same," she said. When she continued speaking, it was for everyone's benefit. "If we cannot make soap or cheese to sell, then we can at least harvest the wool from the sheep and create caps."

Thomas' eyebrows lifted. "Caps? Like for a man's head?"

Maitland nodded firmly. "I can teach the children to knit the wool," she said. "Lady de Vesci knew how to knit and she taught me. I can make caps and capes and even a tunic. I can teach the children and we can sell the results, thereby making money for the charity. We must teach these children to be productive so that when they go out into the world, they know how to support themselves."

A faint smile crossed Thomas' lips. "Well said," he murmured. "And utterly brilliant. The lady has a head for business."

"Now do you see why Lady de Vesci was so devastated when Mae left Alnwick?" Desmond said, chewing on a knuckle of beef. "My sister is smarter than most men. If anyone can turn Edenside around, she can. I have the greatest faith in her."

While Thomas sat there and nodded his approval, unable to take his eyes from Maitland, Jordan spoke up again.

"The lass' mind is in the right place," she said firmly. "Are ye sure ye can make the charity productive with the right tools?"

Maitland nodded. "I know I can," she said passionately. "In fact, I was hoping to find a patron so we can obtain what we need – sheep, goats, and anything else. If I have these things, then I can teach the children the trade of knitting. I can teach them how to manage their caps and sell them. I know it sounds like a grand idea, but I know I can do it. I have done it before, at Newcastle. The children sold dried fish from the abbey's pond in the marketplace and made money for themselves."

Jordan genuinely hadn't touched much of her supper. She'd been so fascinated listening to Maitland speak that she hadn't thought much about her food. What she saw before her was a woman of great vision and skill, an impressive thing to see. If she could only do half the things she said, she would still be an accomplished woman, indeed. Already, she liked what she saw and from the way Thomas was looking at the woman, she suspected her youngest son did, as well.

Call it women's intuition.

"Say no more, lass," Jordan said. "Ye needna look any further for a patron. My husband and I will be happy tae supply Edenside with whatever ye need tae make it self-sufficient. I'll send word tae Castle Questing tomorrow tae send ye a herd of goats."

"Wait," Thomas suddenly piped up, looking at his mother almost accusingly. "The lady has asked that I be her patron, and I shall. It would be my pleasure."

Jordan's eyebrows lifted. "What did ye say not a few minutes ago?" she said. "Ye said that ye dunna pay attention to anythin' other than the safety of the border and yer family. Ye even said that ye werena a crusader for lost children."

Thomas pursed his lips at his mother. "And I cannot change my mind?" he said. "Lady Bowlin makes an excellent case. Why would I not want to support Edenside under her skilled management?"

Jordan thought it was more that he wanted to be seen as a hero to a pretty widow, but she didn't say so. Now that she realized Thomas had an eye for the lady, she was still trying to figure out what his game was without embarrassing him. Since Tacey's death, her son had led a rather wild life over the past eight years, and she'd heard her husband and sons whispering about Thomas' drinking and whoring behavior, so in a sense, her instinct to protect Lady Bowlin from her son's predatory ways was starting to kick in. She liked Lady Bowlin and didn't want to see her son toy with the woman.

The man had enough trouble on his hands.

"We'll talk about it later," she said, gesturing to Caria, who was eating most of Thomas' food. "Wipe her mouth, Tommy. She's makin' a mess of herself."

Distracted, Thomas leaned over to see that Caria did, indeed, have gravy all over her face, so he took the sleeve of her shift and wiped her face with it, causing her to howl. Now she was dirty, she cried, and she slithered off his lap and ran around the table to Jordan, who soothed her angry tears. Thomas simply shook his head at the fickle child, glancing over at Maitland only to see that she was grinning at him. He lifted his big shoulders.

"I wipe my face on my sleeves," he said. "What is wrong with that?"

Maitland started laughing. "Nothing if you are a man," she said. "But young ladies in pretty dresses do not like to get them dirty. Do you know nothing?"

Thomas was properly contrite. "Evidently not," he said. "It shall not happen again."

"See that it doesn't."

He grinned at her. He liked a lady who could verbally match him, and since meeting Maitland de Ryes Bowlin, Thomas was coming to see that there was nothing about her that he didn't like. Everything out of her mouth was a brilliant revelation from the mind of a woman who was clearly as sharp as she was beautiful. All he could think of was that it was a damned waste that she had chosen a life of religious servitude. A woman like that was a hell of a prize, for any man. She had been a pleasant surprise, and a welcome one, from the moment they'd been introduced.

The attraction he had for her was turning into something else.

Interest.

Thomas was rather startled to realize that. Certainly, he'd been attracted to women since Tacey's death, but only on a superficial level. What he was feeling at the moment seemed to go beyond that. He always thought that he'd never overcome Tacey's death, or the sadness of it, but at the moment, he wasn't quite so sure. He remembered his mother telling him, once, that the right lady could change his mind, but he'd never believed her. Until now.

Lady Bowlin might have just altered that belief.

Pondering that very strange turn of events, Thomas was about to continue the conversation, to explore whatever it was that Maitland seemed to stir in him, when the entry doors to the hall opened and two figures entered the dark, smoky hall.

Adelaide and her father had arrived.

CHAPTER FOUR

Caria wasn't paying any attention to the lady who had just entered the hall.

She knew who Adelaide was, at least distantly, because she had seen her in the past when she'd come to visit Thomas. But her glimpses of the lady had been brief, as Lady Adelaide didn't like children and made no attempt to speak with the child. Whenever Caria had come to Wark, Adelaide always made herself scarce.

Therefore, Caria didn't know the woman and didn't really care that she didn't know her. Now that Jordan had cleaned up the sleeve that Thomas had so grievously dirtied, the child was happy once more and darting back around the table to sit with Thomas. In doing so, however, she cut right in front of Adelaide as the woman made her grand entrance into the feast. Amidst the layer of smoke in the hall, the stale warmth, and the heady smells of steaming beef, Adelaide presented herself as a proper, demure lady until a child dashed in front of her and made her trip on the hem of her gown.

Then, the real Adelaide made a swift return.

"God's Teeth," she hissed, grabbing hold of her father to prevent herself from falling. "There are wild animals loose in the hall this night. Who is that little beast?"

As Jordan and William cringed, Thomas was on his feet. Caria came right up to him and he put his hands protectively on the child's shoulders as he faced Adelaide.

"This is my sister, Caria," he growled. "If you'd taken the time to come to know her, you might recognize her. As it is, you will not call her a beast again or my displeasure shall be known. Is this in any way unclear?"

Adelaide's eyes were wide as her father, Edmund, cleared his throat loudly to cover for his daughter's faux pas.

"It is dark enough in the hall that she might not have recognized her even if she knew her," he said, which wasn't much of an apology. "It is dangerous for children to run about. Dangerous for the child, I mean."

Thomas looked at Edmund. He was a tall man who had been muscular in his youth, but now he'd gone completely to fat. He was bald for the most part, with what hair he had long past his shoulders and gathered at the nape of his neck in a stringy tail. As Thomas knew when the betrothal to Adelaide had been broached, Edmund de Vauden, Earl of Northumbria, was a cousin to the king, descended from Robert Curthose, but that impressive lineage had worn thin the moment Thomas became acquainted with Adelaide. No lineage in the world could make up for what she lacked.

"This is a de Wolfe hall and as long as it is a de Wolfe hall, my sister may run about as she pleases," Thomas said. "She is welcome here and welcome to do anything she wishes."

William, seeing that Thomas was verging on serious disrespect for Northumbria, stood up and went to Edmund and his daughter.

"No harm done," he said, diverting Northumbria's attention. "Caria is well, Adelaide is well. Come, let us sit and feast. Sit next to me, Edmund, so that we may converse. Your lady daughter may sit on Thomas' right hand."

Thomas could have killed his father for that direction but, in truth, it was Adelaide's proper place at his table, as his betrothed. Without another word, he sat down, pulling Caria onto his lap as Adelaide came to sit next to him. He made no move to help her by pulling out her seat; he simply focused on Caria as the child reached for a bowl of fruit. Incensed that she was being ignored for a mere child, Adelaide sat down without any attention whatsoever from her intended.

And that set the mood for the rest of the meal.

Servants emerged from the shadows, bringing Adelaide a trencher of beef and vegetables. There was fresh bread and butter on the table, along with stewed apricots and other smaller dishes to choose from. Usually, it was both polite and customary for a man to serve a woman food at his table, especially if they were betrothed, but Thomas completely ignored Adelaide in favor of Caria, who was starting to chatter about the dogs that were milling around the hall and wanting to know if there were any puppies she could play with.

Unwilling to give Adelaide any attention, Thomas used Caria's dog-chatter as an excuse to leave the table. He stood up with the child and led her away from the table, over towards the hearth in search of puppies, leaving an open seat between Adelaide and Maitland.

It was a big, insulting gap, as Adelaide now sat all alone.

As Thomas wandered away with Caria in-hand, Maitland watched him go. In fact, she had witnessed the entire scene, from the brusque young woman entering the hall to Thomas' rather harsh words. Having no idea who the woman was, and having not been introduced to her, she leaned over to her brother.

"Who *is* that woman?" she whispered.

Desmond sighed heavily, leaning around his sister to see Adelaide there, sitting all alone, clearly unhappy that she had to butter her own bread.

"Lady Adelaide," he muttered. "Be careful of her. She is a nightmare."

The comment concerned Maitland, but not because she was concerned for Adelaide and what the woman was capable of. She was concerned that the woman was being treated poorly by Thomas and even Desmond, which didn't sit well with her. Even though she didn't know the woman, she didn't like the idea of her brother being nasty to her.

"The poor woman is all alone," she hissed to her brother. "Why are you not speaking with her?"

"She is a beast. I will *not* speak to her."

"Of course she is going to be a beast if everyone is being cruel to her."

Desmond rolled his eyes, seeing that his sister clearly didn't understand the situation. She hadn't met Adelaide before and therefore didn't know her for what she was. That being the case, Desmond took his life in his hands as he opened his mouth to speak to Adelaide. Perhaps if his sister had a demonstration of the woman's behavior, she might understand that Adelaide was nothing to be trifled with.

"Lady Adelaide," he said, leaning in front of his sister to catch Adelaide's attention. "I would like to introduce you to my sister, Lady Bowlin. She is on her way to Kelso to assume charge of their foundling home at Edenside."

Adelaide turned to look at Maitland as if only just seeing her for the first time. Her dark eyes appraised Maitland openly, looking her up and down as if determining if she was worthy to speak to.

"A foundling home?" she said, disdain in her voice. "What on earth for?"

Maitland remained polite. "I am a Beguine, my lady," she said. "My husband was killed two years ago and I have devoted myself to the service of the church. I seem to have some talent when it comes to children, so I am being sent to Edenside to tend the foundlings there. It is quite rewarding, I find."

Across the table, Jordan was watching the exchange very carefully. "Lady Bowlin has some very good ideas for teachin' the children a trade," she said. "She can teach them tae knit, or tae make cheese from sheep's milk, or even soap. I seem tae recall that ye sew very well, Lady Adelaide. Everyone should have a skill tae be useful."

Adelaide's brow seemed to be perpetually furrowed as her attention moved back and forth between Jordan and Maitland.

"Of course I can sew," she said. "But it is not a *trade.*"

There was great disgust in her tone as she said it. Maitland was coming to see even from the short conversation that the lady was somewhat disagreeable. "Did you sew the dress you are wearing?" she asked. "It is quite beautiful. It took great talent to make it."

Adelaide looked down at her surcoat, an elaborate creation made from blue silk and a good deal of colorful embroidery.

"My maids sewed this," she said. "I would never sew a dress for myself. Why should I when I have an army of women to do it? But you are correct; it is quite lovely. And expensive. I have many garments just like it."

Now, Maitland was coming to understand what her brother had been trying to tell her. Adelaide seemed quite disagreeable and unfriendly no matter what the subject, and she didn't see much use in continuing the conversation.

"You are quite fortunate, then," she said, turning back to her food. "It was very nice to make your acquaintance, my lady."

She picked up her spoon with the intention of finishing what was on her trencher, but Adelaide didn't seem to understand that the conversation had been ended. Her attention was fully on Maitland, even as the woman practically turned her back on her.

"Why did you commit yourself to the church when your husband died?" she asked. "I should think you would want to find another husband right away."

Maitland put her spoon down and politely faced her again. "I have no interest in marrying again," she said. "Moreover, my husband did not leave me with a great fortune and a prospective husband would require such a thing."

"What about your father? Surely he will provide for you."

"My father is dead, but he had even less than my husband did."

The conversation lagged as Adelaide seemed to take a second look at Maitland, dragging her gaze all over the Beguine, scrutinizing her worn clothing. It was clear that she was judging based solely on appearance. Then, she looked at Desmond.

"You should have brought her to me before you permitted her to feast in the hall of a de Wolfe," she said. "She is not appropriately dressed."

"She is wearin' the proper clothin' for her station," Jordan spoke up, her disapproving gaze on Adelaide. "If anyone has a right tae speak on improper clothin' in the hall of de Wolfe, 'tis me, and I say she is properly dressed."

It was a rebuke, turning Adelaide's pale cheeks a dull red. She was embarrassed. "I simply meant that I would have loaned her a dress, my lady."

"Did ye, now?"

The rapid response in a doubtful tone caused Adelaide's eyes to widen. It was clear that Lady de Wolfe, the matriarch of a very powerful family, was displeased, and even Adelaide wasn't stupid enough to provoke her.

"I did not mean anything by it, Lady de Wolfe, truly," she said, looking over to Maitland. "If... if I offended, I did not mean to."

Maitland nodded, but next to her, Desmond was holding back guffaws. Only Lady de Wolfe could put Adelaide in her proper place enough for the woman to stay there. But Maitland, still trying to be polite, spoke.

"I am sure you have a beautiful wardrobe and your offer is very kind," she said. "But for my life of piety and service, this is the best I am allowed. I am sure you understand."

Adelaide simply turned back to her food, fearful to say anything more lest she provoke the wrath of Lady de Wolfe. As she began to eat her bread and butter, Thomas returned to the table and resumed his seat.

"Caria found a litter of puppies over near the hearth," he told his mother. "She is very happy right now."

Jordan turned to the hearth, straining to catch a glimpse of Caria, laying on the warm stones and letting the puppies lick all over her. She grinned.

"Ye shouldna have done that," she said. "The lass will want tae take them all home with her."

Thomas grinned, reaching for his cup of wine and catching a glimpse of Maitland's trencher. It was nearly empty and he pointed to it.

"Are you satisfied, my lady?" he asked. "I can have more food brought forth if you are still hungry."

Maitland shook her head. "I have had my fill, thank you," she said. "It was delicious. Your cook is to be commended."

He grinned, taking the half-empty pitcher as he filled her cup. "The cook is an old man who is twice my size, but he knows well how to cook for an army," he said. "He served with my father back in the days when William de Wolfe would lead his armies."

Maitland's attention drifted over to the handsome elderly knight, deep in conversation with Adelaide's father. "He does not fight any longer?"

Thomas shook his head. "He is still capable for the most part, but my mother will not allow it. She says he has done his service for king and country and if he tries to go out with the army again, she'll break both of his legs."

Maitland laughed softly but before she could reply, Adelaide spoke. "When I am chatelaine of Wark Castle, I shall bring a cook all the way from France," she said. "We will need a more refined cook, as I intend to do much entertaining as Lady de Wolfe. It would not do for the fine nobility of England to return to their homes and spread gossip that we have a soldier doing our cooking for us."

Thomas heard her voice, grating on his nerves. He was certain she had said that to remind him of what her place would soon be and it only served to infuriate him.

"I am quite happy with my cook," he said. "I have no intention of changing."

Adelaide huffed sharply. "I was only suggesting…"

He cut her off. "I know what you were suggesting."

He glared at her, daring her to argue with him, but it occurred to him that it would be poor behavior to display in front of Maitland. Poor behavior on his part, at any rate. He had a temper, and especially with Adelaide, and for some reason, he didn't want Maitland to think he treated all women so shabbily.

He didn't want her to think ill of him.

Since when did he care what others thought of him?

Taking a deep breath, Thomas calmed his building annoyance at Adelaide and struggled to be civil.

"I simply meant we can discuss it at another time," he said evenly before returning his attention to Maitland. "Tonight, I simply wish to feast and enjoy the evening. I noticed there was a brilliant moon out tonight. The land looks as if it is bathed in silver."

As Thomas tried to pretend that there was no issue with Lady Adelaide, Maitland was starting to see that there was more to that relationship than met the eye. Maitland was very intuitive and what she first thought was merely a guest at Wark Castle was clearly much more than that.

When I am chatelaine of Wark Castle.

That told Maitland that Lady Adelaide was something more, indeed, and the truth was that the realization caused Maitland great disappointment. It shouldn't; she knew it shouldn't. Thomas was a de Wolfe and commander of his own outpost, and that made him a man most worthy of the best bride. Lady Adelaide seemed to be that bride, but it was clear that Thomas had no love for the woman. Neither did Desmond. If anything, there was a good deal of animosity there and Maitland could see why. The woman, though lovely in a pale sort of way, was as friendly as a shrew.

But, God… the foolish, giddy woman in Maitland wished that Thomas was not attached.

It wasn't as if she could have him, *but still…*

"'Tis as bright as the sun," Maitland said after a moment, trying to sound pleasant when the truth was that her protected heart was filled with disappointment. "I enjoy nights such as this when the weather is good. There is something soothing about them. They bring about an easy sleep."

Before Thomas could reply, somewhere on the other side of the hall, a soldier with a lute struck up a tune. It was a lively melody and men began clapping as a few drunken soldiers stood up to clumsily dance around. Seeing this, Jordan suddenly stood up from the table and headed over to the hearth where Caria was buried in puppies. Drunken dancing men were too close to the child, even though they were several feet away, so she moved Caria away from men who might step on her and not even see her.

Thomas watched his mother collect the little girl, and two of the puppies, but his attention was drawn to the music. It wasn't unusual to hear music in the hall of Wark. In fact, Thomas had a beautiful baritone singing voice and he liked to sing quite often, but since the arrival of Adelaide, he hadn't really sung at all. He hadn't felt like it. Singing, to him, was joyful, and he hadn't felt joyful since Adelaide had joined his household.

But looking at Maitland, the urge to sing again struck him.

"Do you know that tune, my lady?" he asked, holding up a finger as he caught the tune and hummed a few notes. "'Tis an old song, usually sung by soldiers after a victory."

Maitland turned her head in the direction of the playing, catching a glimpse of the man with the lute and soldiers as they danced about. She shook her head.

"I do not know if I have heard it," she said. "My father was not much of a warrior and even when I fostered at Alnwick, I was kept away from the men. All of Lady de Vesci's wards were."

More men were starting to sing the song now as the man with the lute played on. It was a low hum of words but soon grew in volume as the drunkards began to join in. Quickly, nearly half the hall was singing, and as Maitland tried to make out the words, she heard Thomas' deep voice in her ear.

We came to battle, for to see,

An enemy tide a'wait for me.

A song of bravery filled my soul,

I held my sword, I rushed to and fro.

The end of the battle, and still I stood,

Friends and warriors, men who could

Still face the enemy, soon fell away,

And in my glory, I now shall stay.

Fight on, men of iron,

Fight 'til the day has passed.

Glory awaits you,

Your honor shall last.

Maitland had turned to watch him as he sang, a twinkle in his hazel eyes as the melody came forth in a gorgeously rich voice. Across the table, William began to sing towards the end of the song, unable to carry much of a tune, grinning at his son across the table as fighting men joined in something that only fighting men were allowed to sing. It was a man's song, something that those who had faced death together understood.

"Astonishing," Maitland said, clapping her hands when the song was over. "You have a remarkable singing voice, my lord."

"He does," Jordan agreed from across the table. "I've not heard Tommy sing in quite some time. Ye did my heart good, lad."

Thomas grinned at his mother. "I've not had much to sing about," he said. "I don't just walk around, bursting into song, you know. That would look rather foolish. I have to feel the song in my heart before I can sing it."

Jordan opened her mouth to speak but was interrupted when the doors to the hall flew open, slamming back on their hinges. A burst of cold wind blew in, snuffing out half of the tapers that were lit near the tables, and smoke billowed out from the hearth. Thomas looked to the door with annoyance, only to see several soldiers rushing in. A couple of them were heading straight for him.

"My lord," one of the men shouted as he came near. "Trouble across the river. Coldstream is being raided."

Thomas, as well as William, moved to his feet. "How do you know?" Thomas demanded. "Is there a messenger?"

The village of Coldstream, a rather large burgh, was to the northeast just across the River Tweed. In fact, Wark Castle protected a bridge crossing over the river, one of the main crossings between Kelso and Berwick, so it was an important access point. The soldier, breathless from having run all the way from the gatehouse, spoke quickly.

"We don't need a messenger, my lord," he said. "The moon is so bright it might as well be day. We could see the torches coming from the north and entering the village, but we held station until we began to see people running for the bridge. Our sentries on the bridge returned to tell us that the Scots are in the village. 'Tis a night raid, my lord."

"How many?"

"I'd say a hundred, at the very least. The village is crawling with Scots."

Thomas was already on the move, with Desmond and William beside him. As he headed away from the table, he paused briefly to speak to his father. "You and your men remain here at Wark, Papa," he said. "You will have command of the fortress. I will take Desmond and most of my army to the village, but I need you to keep the castle secure. That is the most important thing."

He was trying to spare his father's pride as one of the greatest knights who had ever lived, who now, in his eight decade, was simply too old to ride to battle. Truthfully, it was difficult for William not to go. That had been his calling for over sixty years, but he'd made his wife a promise a few years back that he would no longer actively fight.

Whatever he did had to be from a command standpoint and not active engagement. He'd pushed the fighting aspect of his career for as long as he could, when he became so old that his sons were focusing on protecting him in a fight and little more. That was when he knew it was time to retire.

But he didn't go quietly.

Even now, William could feel his wife's gaze upon him, her critical eye. He knew she was watching him to see if he was going to go back on his word to her, but William had no intention of breaking a promise to his wife.

No matter how difficult it was.

Old knights never die…

"Aye," he said to his son. "Go muster your army and I'll put my men on the walls. Be careful, Tommy."

Thomas and Desmond fled, thundering out of the hall along with nearly every other man who, moments before, had been singing and even drunk in some cases. All of them rushing out into the cold, silvery night, doing what they'd always been doing at Wark Castle –

Protecting the border.

As William stood there, feeling rather useless and sad to watch the hall drain of men when he couldn't go with them, his wife with Caria in-hand came up beside him.

"How can I help?" she asked her husband quietly. "What do ye need me tae do?"

William turned to her, trying to keep the disappointment out of his eyes. "Assume we'll have wounded," he said. "Get Caria to her nurse and make sure the keep is secured. Then, have Adelaide and even Desmond's sister help you here in the hall to prepare for the wounded. This is nothing new for you, love. You know what to do."

Jordan did. Turning back to the table, she instructed Adelaide and Maitland to remain in the hall and wait for her to return, but as soon as she hustled out with Caria to take the child to the keep, Edmund decided that he didn't want his daughter to remain in the hall and escorted her to the keep personally. They stayed clear of Lady de Wolfe, because Jordan never saw them retreating to Adelaide's bower and bolting the door. And there they remained. When Jordan finally returned to the hall, only Maitland had waited for her. Jordan didn't even ask where Adelaide was, because she already knew.

Useless girl.

In little time, Jordan came to see just how smart and resourceful Maitland de Ryes Bowlin was when it came to organizing an infirmary, and Jordan came to like the woman even more than she already did. She never had to ask twice for something to be done and, as the evening went, Maitland seemed to know what Jordan was going to say before she said it. It became a symbiotic relationship of the best kind.

Now, all they could do was wait.

IN THOMAS' ESTIMATION, there had been more than one hundred men.

In truth, he had no idea where they'd all come from. A raid this size had been organized well in advance because he was positive there were Scots from other clans participating. As he'd charged into the heart of Coldstream, into the merchant district where the raiders seemed to be doing the most looting, he thought he caught sight of a Scotsman he'd seen before, months ago when his father had held a great gathering of sorts to speak to the clans along this stretch of the border about the *reivers* who had been hitting the villages rather hard on both sides of the borders.

Elliot, Kerr, Scott, Maxwell, Haye and Johnstone had all been at the gathering, with Gordon and Armstrong remaining standoffish. The border reivers were not from the clans, but rather a mix of Scots and English outlaws who had no regard for citizens on either side of the borders. They would raid the Scots as easily as the English, and along with the clan unrest, the rise of the reivers had been particularly taxing on those charged with border security.

That was why the great Wolfe of the Border had called the gathering, which had been moderately successful. William's goal had been to get a commitment from the clans to work in conjunction with the English to rid the borders of the reivers, and there had been instances of successful cooperation. That was why Thomas had been shocked to see a man he thought he recognized from one of those participating clans. It didn't make any sense to him.

But then, he saw the man again, this time heading right for him, and he unsheathed both his broadsword and a rather lovely wolf-head dagger that he always carried on his person. There was a good deal of fighting as the man in the long tunic and braies approached on a sturdy horse. He was holding up a hand to show he was unarmed and he informed Thomas that he and his men had followed a gang of reivers from the village of Duns, one step behind them as the group tore through the countryside.

It was then that Thomas realized that there were *two* factions in Coldstream – reivers as well as men from Clan Kerr, trying to stop them. He was just about to tell Desmond of his suspicions when the hut he was next to collapsed forward under the weight of a group of men fighting on the other side of it.

Thomas and his horse were shoved forward and the horse nearly fell over, unbalancing Thomas to the point of falling from the horse. He landed on his feet with his sword still in his hand, but the wolf-head dagger fell by the wayside as one of the reivers who had busted through the wall of the hut took a swipe at Thomas, catching the man on the shoulder near his neck, enough to carve through his mail and drive the blade into his shoulder.

But Thomas didn't falter. He leapt onto his horse again, weapon in hand, and went after the reiver with a vengeance. Three strokes of his blade later, the reiver was on the muddy ground, bleeding to death, and Thomas was furious with what was going on. Along with that fury came a storm of action and of behavior, a storm so fierce that Thomas liberated that anger and the fight turned vicious. The StormWolfe was unleashed.

Dhiib aleasifa had returned.

The reivers were clever, but they weren't any match for an enraged English knight. Thomas' sword cut down two men trying to pummel a hapless villager, a man who was holding on desperately to a ham that the reivers were trying to steal, and as the reivers fell in a bloodied heap, the man ran off with his precious ham.

But Thomas wasn't done.

His entire purpose was to kill at this point. It wasn't even to chase men away. He knew if he chased the reivers away, they would simply regroup and return. The only thing he could do was try to decimate their numbers, so he gave the order to kill on sight – not defend, not capture, but to kill.

His men took the order seriously.

When the clans who had chased the reivers realized what the better-armed English from Wark Castle were doing, they backed away, concerned they would be caught mixing with the reivers and be confused for the enemy. They didn't want to die in a hail of sharp blades and arrows. Thomas and Desmond and three hundred angry English soldiers drove the reivers east, past the tall bell tower of St. Cuthbert's, and towards the slick, green cliffs overlooking the River Tweed.

When Thomas had been a young boy, his father and uncles had taken him to this area of the river where they would fish for the massive salmon that populated the river. He hated to eat the fish, but his mother and father loved it, so there were nights he had been forced to eat the orange, oily fish. His Uncle Paris would tell him Irish folk tales of a fish called the Salmon of Knowledge, and whoever ate the fish would be very wise, but that still didn't make the stinky fish more palatable. Thomas didn't care how smart the fish made him; he simply didn't like it.

Odd how Thomas thought on those peaceful days when he was a boy, fishing with his family, as he wielded a sword and drove men to their deaths. He had a purpose for driving them to these cliffs, with a fairly serious drop to the river below, and his men began to form a net around the reivers, pushing them to the cliffs.

When the reivers realized what was happening, they tried to break free and some seriously heavy fighting occurred, but Thomas and his men held them off. It was not without casualties on their side, but the lines held. The wounded were moved to the rear of the fighting, and subsequently sent on ahead back to Wark, but Thomas and Desmond and those who were still capable of fighting drove about fifty or sixty reivers straight off of the cliff, watching them fall into the river below.

It was an impressive sight.

Men and horses tumbled over the cliff, rolling and rolling down into the water below with great splashes. There were some hysterical screams mingled with the sounds of fighting but, gradually, Thomas drove them all over the side. Even those who begged for their lives. Coldly, he either ran them through with his sword or kicked them over the side of the cliff.

The screams, the carnage, and the drowning went on for the rest of the night as the StormWolfe turned lethal.

CHAPTER FIVE

MEN HAD BEEN trickling into the great smoky hall of Wark Castle for most of the night, telling tales of the battle in Coldstream. There was a big clash going on between wily reivers and an English army, but Maitland and Jordan were ready for the results. At least, Jordan was. Maitland truly had no idea what to expect, but she faced it bravely.

So she thought.

The first men returning from the battle had fairly serious wounds, indicative of the brutal level of fighting. One man returned missing several fingers on his right hand and his companion had found those fingers, presenting them to Jordan to sew back on again, but she couldn't do it. No one could reattach fingers or limbs. Calmly, she had the man toss the fingers in the fire, and the smell of burning flesh began to fill the great hall where the wounded were gathering.

Maitland smelled the acrid, oily smell but she had no idea what it was until one of the soldiers told her. Sick to her stomach and trying not to think about burning fingers, she was focusing on cleaning and bandaging some of the less serious wounds. Truth be told, she didn't have any experience at all tending wounded, as she'd never been involved in an active siege or battle. This was all quite new to her, but rather than become fearful or upset at the bloodied men around her, she simply focused on what needed to be done. Men needed help and she was determined to render aid.

But then, more men started filtering in.

Now, there were about twenty men and only two women and a few servants to tend them. Maitland left the hall briefly to go rouse her companion, Tibelda, and brought the woman into the hall to help. Tibelda was calm and helpful, and it was she who began to oversee the boiling of linen strips, taken from servants who had stripped off some bed linens, to be dried before the fire and then used to bandage the myriad of battle wounds they were seeing.

Still, it was just three women and several servants for all of the wounded they had, and Maitland thought that Lady Adelaide should, indeed, be part of this. She'd been bold enough to announce that she would be chatelaine of Wark Castle someday, and part of those duties would include tending her husband's wounded.

Her husband.

Thinking of Thomas as the woman's husband brought disappointment anew to Maitland. She had no right to feel this way. It was foolish! She'd spent the better part of the night trying not to think about the union between Thomas and Adelaide, but the more she tried not to think of it, the more she couldn't seem to shake it.

Something inside her was changing.

Until she'd met Thomas de Wolfe, Maitland had never entertained the thought of marrying again much less marrying someone she could actually like. She hadn't liked Henry. In fact, towards the end of their marriage, she couldn't even stand the sight of him. When he would bed her, it was all she could do not to become physically ill and she thanked God that their union hadn't produced any children. But to actually be married to someone she liked and respected... well, she'd never allowed herself to entertain such a thought.

She never wanted to get her hopes up.

And now, she'd met a man she genuinely liked, but he was too far out of her reach. A de Wolfe, in fact. Maitland felt rather sorry for

Thomas, knowing he was about to marry a woman he couldn't stand. She could very much relate to that. But there was nothing she could do about it, though she was coming to wish she could.

Life was a cruel thing, sometimes.

Telling Lady de Wolfe she would return very shortly, Maitland fled the hall and rushed up the stairs to the keep, which was heavily manned. The soldiers allowed her to pass and the keep entry was unbolted for her. Inside the cold, dark entry, she had to ask the soldier stationed inside the keep where Lady Adelaide was but the man didn't know. He simply pointed to the top floor, assuming she was in the master's chamber, and Maitland made her way up the narrow spiral stairs until she reached the top floor.

It was dark and spooky on this floor, and there were two heavily-fortified doors, and she knocked on the first one, which was opened after a few knocks to reveal Caria and her nurse. Caria wanted to know where "Matha" and "Poppy" were, and Maitland pacified the child by telling her they would come to her shortly.

After the nurse shut the door again and bolted it, Maitland went to the second door and rapped on it several times. When a man demanded to know who had come, she answered truthfully. She expected the door to open, but it didn't. She had to knock several more times and invoke the name of Lady de Wolfe before the bolt was finally thrown.

Edmund de Vauden's sweaty face appeared in the cracked doorway.

"What does Lady de Wolfe want?" he asked suspiciously.

Though Edmund's face was filling up the doorway, Maitland caught a glimpse of the cowering lady in the background.

"Lady Adelaide's presence is required in the hall," she said evenly. "We have several wounded and Lady Jordan requests that Lady Adelaide join us."

Edmund was extremely hesitant as Adelaide came forward. "But I do not know anything about tending wounded," she said, sounding panicked. "I cannot stand the sight of blood."

Maitland fixed on her. "Being chatelaine of a great fortress is not only about selecting the proper cook or scheduling the right parties during the right season," she said. "Being the wife of a great warlord means that you must know something of the tending of the wounded of his army. If you do not know, then you should come and learn. You cannot fail Sir Thomas when he will need you the most. Now, come along, my lady. Time is wasting."

Adelaide looked at her with big, terrified eyes, turning to look at her father to see what his take was on all of this. Edmund continued to appear very hesitant, but there was truth in what Maitland said and he knew it.

"If Lady Jordan has summoned you, then you must go," he told her. "Go and do as you are told."

Adelaide panicked. "But Papa!"

Edmund opened the door wide. "You will not disobey," he said. "Go, child. The nun is correct. This is your duty."

Adelaide was beside herself as her father all but shoved her out of the chamber. She nearly crashed into Maitland who, in fact, had to put a hand out to stop her from tripping. The door slammed and was bolted from the inside, leaving Maitland and Adelaide out in the corridor.

"But… I know nothing of this," Adelaide was starting to get teary-eyed. "I am afraid!"

"Of what?" Maitland said, grabbing the woman by the arm and pulling her towards the stairwell. "There is nothing to be afraid of. All you have to do is follow instructions. You can do that, can't you?"

Adelaide was dragging her feet as Maitland practically yanked her down the stairs. "But what shall I do?"

"Anything Lady de Wolfe tells you to do," Maitland said, tugging her down the last few stairs. "You can sew. Mayhap you shall sew gashes. Lady de Wolfe said you were quite skilled. I am sure you will stitch them up quite nicely."

Adelaide turned a sickly shade of white and tried to grab on to the wall as Maitland pulled her down another flight of stairs.

"I shall vomit," she hissed. "I shall become ill if I have to sew a man's flesh."

Maitland didn't say anything until they came to the bottom of the stairs. Then, she paused, looking Adelaide in the eye.

"When your father pledged you to a great warlord, what did you think your life would be?" she asked. It wasn't a catty question, but an honest one. "Did you not think that you would have to help your husband at some point?"

For the first time since their association, Adelaide's guard seemed to be down. "Help him?" she repeated. "Of course I would help him. I would keep his house and hold, and ensure our visitors were graciously attended. Everyone would be greatly impressed. *That* is helping him."

Maitland nodded as she began to walk again, pulling Adelaide along. "Aye, that is helping," she agreed. "But he is a de Wolfe. Battle is what he knows, my lady. You cannot marry the man without marrying the part of him that is a warrior, too. Did you not realize that?"

Adelaide was less resistant at that point, or Maitland was simply pulling harder. In either case, Adelaide was walking a little faster, without dragging her feet. It was true that she had looked to the House of de Wolfe as something prestigious and nothing more. Certainly, she realized the de Wolfes were battle lords, but it had honestly never occurred to her that she would be expected to take part in anything related to battle.

But she wouldn't admit it.

"Was your husband a warrior, then?" she asked Maitland. "Is this something you have done before?"

Maitland shook her head. "My husband was a knight, but he never participated in a battle the entire time we were married," she said. "However, I fostered at Alnwick. I know what is expected of a military fortress. It is the nature of things."

They were heading down the stairs now beneath the cold, bright moon. "I fostered at Durham," Adelaide said. "I was under the care of the chatelaine, Lady de Salvin. She taught me everything fine that I should know. She did *not* teach me how to stick needles in men's wounds."

"Then you are about to learn."

Down in the inner bailey now, they were heading towards the outer bailey and the great hall when Adelaide suddenly yanked her arm from Maitland's grip and came to a halt.

"I will *not* do it," she declared. "I will not be expected to stick needles in men and wipe their bloodied noses. That is for physics and servants and soldiers to tend, but not me. I will not do it!"

Maitland faced off against Adelaide in the dark yard. They were about the same height, but Maitland had a few pounds on Adelaide, who had bony arms and hands. She knew she was stronger than Adelaide simply from the resistance the woman gave her whilst she dragged her from the keep and, at that moment, Maitland could have done one of two things – either fight with Adelaide and make demands, or try to reason with her.

For the moment, she chose the latter.

"My lady," she said patiently. "From what I have seen, it seems to me that your relationship with Sir Thomas is strained. Would that be a fair statement?"

Adelaide frowned and the vulnerable woman disappeared. "That does not concern you."

"I am trying to help you. Will you please answer the question?"

Adelaide almost refuted her again but she thought better of it. "If you are going to tell me that sewing up bloody gashes will please Thomas, then don't. I do not care if it pleases him."

Maitland cocked her head. "Don't you want your husband to be proud of you?"

Adelaide looked at her as if she had gone daft. "It does not matter if my husband is proud of me," she said, almost sarcastically. "We will be married and I will run his castle as I see fit. I will do as I please."

Maitland could sense either a very spoiled woman or one that was being inordinately defensive to cover up for the fact that, perhaps, she really did want her husband to like her but had no idea how to accomplish that.

"Is that all that matters to you?" she asked. "Doing as you please? My lady, I was married to a man I did not like and he didn't have any particular love for me, either. It was a miserable existence, I assure you, so it would be in your best interests – and in Sir Thomas' – for you to be a little more cooperative. I am sure if you were, he would be, too. Do you truly intend to go the rest of your life doing battle with a man whose children you are going to bear?"

Adelaide geared up for what was sure to be a sharp retort but she couldn't seem to bring it forth. Her jaw seemed to work angrily for a moment.

"None of this concerns you," she said. "And I am not going into the hall."

With that, she turned on her heel and headed back towards the keep as fast as she could walk. Maitland didn't follow, but she did call after her.

"Do you not understand that I am trying to help you?"

Adelaide paused and swung on her. "I do not need your help, you… you *nun!*"

As she turned back around, Maitland could feel her patience slipping. In fact, realizing that Adelaide had completely slapped her down, her annoyance got the better of her.

"Then I hope you like being miserable because you are going to have a miserable marriage and a miserable life," she called after her. "This is why no one likes you, Lady Adelaide. You are nasty and uncooperative, and the more you deal out those horrific traits, the more hatred you will find as a result. It will be you against the entire de Wolfe clan if you do not open your eyes and see what a worthless cow you are. Enjoy your unhappy life because if this is all you are, then you deserve it!"

Adelaide had come to a stop just short of the stairs to the keep, turning to Maitland in outrage, but Maitland didn't give her the opportunity to retort. She was already rushing back to the hall as fast as she could without running, angrier than she'd been in a very long while. She was also embarrassed that her frustration had caused her to say something she wouldn't have normally said.

Worthless cow.

Although she probably shouldn't have said it, she meant it. Every damned word.

Nearing the hall entry, she could see that the door was open and Jordan was standing there, wiping her hands on a linen towel. She looked at Maitland curiously as the woman swiftly approached.

"What was all the shoutin' about?" Jordan asked.

Maitland didn't want to tell the woman that she'd lost her temper, but she presumed she'd hear about it soon enough. She was quite certain Lady Adelaide would tell anyone who would listen how horribly the "nun" had treated her. Therefore, she knew she had to confess.

"I was trying to convince Lady Adelaide to come and help us," she said.

"*And?*"

"And she feels that it is beneath her."

Jordan simply nodded. "Oh," she said. Then, she sighed heavily. "Well, ye tried, lass. Ye're a good soul for at least tryin'."

Maitland shook her head. "Not such a good soul," she said. "I became angry with her. She's stubborn and foolish."

"Aye, she is that."

"Just so you are aware, I called her a worthless cow," she said reluctantly. "I will not apologize to her, for it is true, but you will not have to worry about me any longer. I shall be gone in the morning and you will not see me again. If my insult causes you any undue trouble, then I will gladly apologize to you for it. I would never knowingly cause you trouble."

Jordan stared at her a moment and Maitland was afraid she'd grossly insulted the woman. But after a few seconds, it became apparent that Jordan was fighting off a smile, with losing results. The smile broke through and she snorted, putting one hand over her mouth as she put her arm around Maitland's shoulders.

"Why couldna my Tommy marry a woman like ye?" she wanted to know. "Lass, ye're honest and I canna fault ye. I appreciate a woman who speaks her mind."

Because she was snorting, Maitland grinned reluctantly. It was rather funny, but she wasn't proud of it. "I should not have called her names, but I could not help it," she said. "The woman is frustrating."

Jordan nodded, pulling her back into the hall. "Ye're okay, lass," she said. "Ye and I are goin' tae get along just fine. And even after ye leave here tomorrow, I will make a point of seein' ye again. Ye've not gotten rid of me yet."

Maitland was coming to see that a well-placed, impulsive insult had gained her acceptance with Lady de Wolfe, perhaps the most respected matriarch on the border. She smiled at the woman and, putting her arm around Lady de Wolfe's waist, headed back into the hall with her.

They had work to do.

"WORTHLESS *COW?*"

Thomas broke down into soft laughter as his mother furiously shushed him. "Not so loud," she said. "Mae will hear ye. Aye, she called Adelaide a worthless cow. She said everythin' I've wanted tae say tae her all along."

Exhausted and bloodied from having just returned with the bulk of his army from Coldstream as dawn broke in the east, Thomas had to put a hand over his mouth to stifle the snorts.

"Bloody Christ," he hissed. "Did she really call her that? It almost makes this entire skirmish worth it just to have that come out in the open. And you called her Mae?"

Jordan nodded. "Of course I did," she said. "'Tis her name. I like the lass, Tommy. She has fire in her soul and the wisdom tae use it. She'll be a fine addition tae Edenside and help them recover from their troubles."

Hearing his mother speak well of Maitland made Thomas feel rather strange, mostly because he wanted to agree with her but he couldn't. He *wouldn't*. Whatever he was thinking about Maitland, he didn't want anyone else to know, especially his mother. Something about Maitland de Ryes Bowlin made his heart beat, just a little faster, and he was still trying to figure it all out.

"Des thinks a good deal of his sister," he said, the smile fading from his face. He realized he had to get off the subject of Lady Bowlin. "Where *is* Adelaide?"

Jordan threw a thumb towards the keep. "Where do ye think?" she said. "She's locked up in the keep with her father. It has been Mae and Tibelda and me tendin' tae the wounded all night long."

Thomas glanced at the keep as the gentle rays of morning warmed the gray stone. Shaking his head in disgust with the behavior Adelaide continued to display, he turned for the hall entry and held out a hand to his mother.

"Come along, my love," he said. "Let us see to my men."

Jordan stopped him. "Let me see tae ye," she said, noting his shoulder wound. "It looks as if ye took a blow there."

Thomas had nearly forgotten about it; the rush of battle had seen to that. It hadn't even hurt until his mother said something, and now it was suddenly stinging.

"It can wait," he said. "My men first, please."

Jordan didn't argue. He was much like his father in that respect, always concerned for his men first. Inside the hall, there were about two dozen wounded in total and perhaps the same number of those with small scrapes, cuts, and bruises.

Wounded were still trickling into the hall, as well as unwounded men who were simply looking for food after an exhausting night. While the wounded were segregated against the eastern wall of the hall, the able-bodied were gathering on the western end, being served stewed beef from the night before. The beef had been pulled off the bone and stewed with carrots and gravy, and Thomas grabbed a slab of bread soaked in the stew as he made his way towards the wounded. He wanted to check on his men but, more than that, he wanted to see a certain Beguine who had insulted his dreaded betrothed.

God help him, he shouldn't want to see her.

But he did.

The light from dawn was streaming in through the vents at the top of the hall and in through the door when it would open. A fire was blazing in the hearth and there were banks of fat tapers in the corners of the room, providing what light they could, and Thomas clearly saw Maitland as she bent over a man back in one of the corners. As he came closer, swallowing the last of the bread in his mouth, he realized that she was feeding the wounded man something out of a bowl.

For a moment, he simply watched her. She had fluid movements, so lovely and graceful, and it occurred to him that the sight of her lightened his spirit somehow. If he could come back from a battle to her sweet face for the rest of his life, he would be a happy man. Maybe his mother really had been correct; the right woman *would* change his mind. He didn't even really know Maitland, and he'd surely not spent an overly long amount of time with her, but his instincts told him that she was worth knowing.

But there was also the little matter of that unpleasant woman in the keep.

God, what a mess this all was.

"My lady?" he said, making his presence known. "My mother says you have been helping her with the wounded. I would like to personally thank you for your assistance."

Maitland turned her face to him. Even having been up all night, she still looked lovely. Somewhere during the night, she'd taken the wimple around her head and rolled it into a strip, using it to tie her hair back tightly, away from the wounds she was working on. She had dark, shiny hair, and he could see the curls at the end of it, dragging along the floor of the hall as she sat on her bottom.

"It is my pleasure, my lord," she said, a twinkle in her weary eyes. But that twinkle vanished when she saw the blood on his shoulder, near his neck, and the damaged mail. In fact, there was blood all in his hair and, quickly, she stood up. "You are wounded!"

Thomas put his hand up to the swipe on his shoulder and was about to brush her off as he had his mother, but the look in her eyes stopped the words on his lips. Maybe he wouldn't brush it off at all.

A little attention from a lovely young woman wouldn't be such a bad thing... *would it?*

"Aye," he said after a moment. "I should probably have it looked at. Can you spare the time?"

Maitland nodded, taking his arm as if he needed her help and directing him towards the hearth where there was an empty space against the wall.

"Sit there," she said, pointing to the bare wall. "I shall return quickly."

As she rushed off, Thomas did as he was told. He made his way over to the spot she had indicated, away from the other wounded but near the hearth so that it was warm and dry. Wearily, he unfastened his belt and sheath, setting his broadsword on the floor, and removed the assortment of daggers he always carried with him into battle, laying each and every one down as well.

The de Wolfe tunic came off, carefully draped on top of the weapons, but his mail coat was under that and with his shoulder increasingly painful, he knew he couldn't get it off without help. Just as he looked around to see which of his men around him were the least injured enough to help him with his mail, Maitland suddenly reappeared.

She had a wooden bowl of something steaming in one hand and things to tend the wound in the other. She set everything down against the wall before putting her hands upon Thomas with the intention of pushing him down into a sitting position.

"Please, sit," she said. "You are simply too tall for me to tend your wound standing up."

He held out his arms. "I cannot get my coat off without help," he said. "When I bend over, pull it off."

There had been rare occasions when Maitland had helped her husband dress, so she was somewhat familiar with the process. Taking hold of Thomas' mail sleeves as he bent over, she began to pull. As he shimmied a bit, she tugged on the sleeves, eventually pulling the mail right over his head. It was heavy and dirty, and he took it from her quickly, handing it off to a nearby servant to have it cleaned. The last thing to come off was his padded tunic, sweaty and bloody, and he tossed it on top of his de Wolfe tunic.

"There," he said, sitting heavily against the wall. "I surrender to your capable hands, my lady."

Maitland heard his words... sort of. The man had just stripped down to his naked torso and, for a moment, she was dumbstruck. Having been married once, she'd seen a man naked before. Henry wasn't shy about parading around with no clothing, but he'd had rather skinny legs and a large gut, which Maitland had never found attractive. In fact, she'd made a point of avoiding looking at Henry when he'd stripped off his clothing.

But with Thomas...

Looking at the man's bare chest made her feel faint and flushed. It wasn't just any bare chest; it was muscular and firm, with a few scars, and a soft matting of dark hair over it. His shoulders were enormous, including the muscles that adjoined his neck. It was into the muscle on the left side that the sword had carved into the flesh, and she could see the dark and caked blood around it. But with all of that staring, mesmerized by the sight, she suddenly realized she hadn't taken a breath and she gulped air like a landed fish.

Thomas looked up with concern when he heard her gasp. "Is anything wrong, my lady?" he asked.

Feeling embarrassed that she'd been caught studying the man, Maitland quickly shook her head and knelt down beside him, next to the steaming bowl and the other things she'd brought.

"Nay," she said. "I was just thinking of... your wound. It may be beyond my capabilities. I should send for your mother. Surely she has tended more of these than I have."

Thomas waved her off. "I have faith in you," he said. "Just clean out the debris and stitch it. I will heal."

"But you say this so casually. I can see that you have other scars, so is this usual for you? Wounds like this, I mean."

He nodded. "It is nothing," he said. "You can do this. I know you can."

Maitland appreciated his confidence in her, but she was rather worried. Timidly, she leaned in to his shoulder to get a better look, touching his flesh as she did so. His skin was hot and smooth, and the moment she touched him, she felt her stomach lurch in a most wonderful way. To gaze upon the man was one thing, but to touch him... it was entirely another.

Her fingers were warm and gentle as she touched the skin around the wound, inspecting the gash to see just how bad it was. All she could think about was his searing flesh beneath her hand, and so very near her face, and she resisted the urge to lick him. God, she would have liked nothing better at that moment than to lick him.

To taste him.

Long ago, when she first married Henry, he'd managed to arouse her once or twice before the dislike between them grew. She'd liked the feel of a man upon her, his body embedded within her. She thought she'd lost the ability to be aroused by a man but, clearly, she hadn't. Thomas had unwittingly brought it out in her.

It was a startling realization.

Taking a deep breath, she struggled to focus, turning to her steaming bowl, which was really a bowl containing boiled water with wine mixed with it. As Lady de Wolfe had told her, the wine kept away the poison, so Maitland went about washing out the wound with the hot water and wine, using a soaked rag to rinse it out and rinse it again. The mixture rolled down Thomas' chest and back as she cleaned, but he didn't move, nor did he complain. He simply sat there, as still as stone, and let her work.

"See?" he said. "You are doing an excellent job already. I have had a good many battle wounds, so I know. You are doing quite well."

Maitland smiled, a humorless gesture. "You are being kind," she said. "I will be truthful – up until this evening, I have never tended a wounded man."

"Your husband did not have an army?"

She shook her head, concentrating on removing a piece of mail that had been jabbed down into the wound. "Henry had a few soldiers, but nothing that could be considered an army," she said. "He came from an old and distinguished family, the House of de Bowland, but his father was a bastard."

"Is that so?"

She nodded. "He changed his name to Bowlin."

Thomas thought on that. "I know the House of de Bowland," he said. "From Lancashire."

"It is," she said, removing the offending piece of mail and dropping it on the ground. "Henry had very little and whatever he had, he inherited from his father."

"Then if he had so little, why did your father allow you to marry him?"

Maitland's movements slowed as she reached for a large pair of tweezers, debating just how much to tell him. "Several reasons," she said as she returned to picking out the last bits of debris from his shoulder. "Female children can become a burden if not married at the proper age."

"Did your father tell you that you were a burden?"

She plucked out a tiny piece of something, tossing it aside. "He cursed the fact that I was not born male," she said. "I suppose that meant I was a burden. When Henry made the offer for me, my father took it immediately. Mayhap he was afraid that I would never have another offer."

Thomas frowned. "You?" he said, incredulous. "With your beauty and accomplishments? Your father is a fool, Mae. He could have commanded a very high price for you had he only been patient."

She suddenly stopped and Thomas turned his head to look at her, to see why she had paused. She was simply sitting there, staring at him, a hint of warmth and delight flickering in her brick-brown eyes.

"What's wrong?" he asked.

Maitland shook her head. "Nothing," she said. "But you... you called me Mae."

Thomas thought she looked rather pleased that he had and it fed his boldness. "Did I?" he said. "Des said I could. You heard him. If you have issue with me addressing you as Mae, then you'll have to take it up with him."

Her smile broke through at his defiance. "I have no issue with it," she said. "You may call me Mae."

He grinned. "Good," he said. "Because I like the name. I shall call you it often."

She flushed, a pretty pink coming to her cheeks, as she returned her attention to his shoulder. This time, Thomas didn't turn his head around. He kept his gaze on her.

"Tell me something, Mae," he said softly.

She could feel his breath on her face, causing her heart to thump madly against her rib cage. "What shall I tell you?"

"Why would a woman like you commit yourself to a life of piety?"

Her gaze flicked up to him. "What do you mean?"

Thomas lifted his eyebrows. "I mean that you are lovely and intelligent," he said. "You would be a wife a man would be proud to have. Why must you waste all of this glory on the church?"

The flush in her cheeks deepened, flattered by his words even though she probably shouldn't be. They bordered on insulting, but she didn't care. It was still the nicest thing anyone had ever said to her.

"Lady Adelaide asked me that at supper," she said, picking the last of the debris from his wound. "You were with your little sister hunting puppies, so I will tell you what I told her. Any husband of merit would require a wife with a fortune, and I have none. My father had no money and neither did my husband, so I had little choice but to seek a life of service with the church."

Thomas watched her as she spoke, seeing that it was upsetting for her to tell him the truth. Hell, he was upset hearing it. It simply wasn't right that this magnificent woman should be handicapped by her circumstances when someone like Adelaide had the world laid out before her purely because of her wealth and breeding.

"A decent man worth his salt would not look for a woman of fortune," he murmured. "Any decent man, a man you should want to be married to, would simply look for a woman of brilliance and character and accomplishments. I think you did not give yourself enough time to find such a man before you decided on serving the church."

Maitland sighed faintly as she set the tweezers aside and picked up the rag soaked in the warm wine and water mixture. "I had little choice," she repeated. "My father did not want me to come home and I had nowhere to go, so the church was my only option."

"I wish I'd known."

She looked at him curiously. "Why?"

His eyes glimmered at her as he threw a thumb in the general direction of the keep. "Because I would have married you two years ago when your husband was killed and that misfit in my keep would have never happened."

Maitland stared at him a moment as his words sank in. Then, her eyes widened. "You would have *married* me?" she gasped. "But… why should you even want to? You are a de Wolfe and you can command the greatest bride in all of England. What on earth would you have wanted with a destitute widow?"

He grinned, the big teeth flashing. "You would have made a very fine Lady de Wolfe," he said. "I am rather perturbed to have lost you to the church. They do not deserve you. Mayhap I do not, either, but at least I could have offered you more than they could."

Maitland stared at him a moment longer and he swore he saw the pink in her cheeks go pale. She lowered her gaze and rinsed his wound one more time with the wet rag, dabbing at it to ensure there was no more debris. She didn't reply to his statement right away but he knew she was thinking on it. Her hands had started to quiver. Something inside of her was stirring as the result of what he'd said, and she seemed either nervous or agitated, but he couldn't tell which. Concerned, he spoke softly.

"Did I upset you?" he muttered. "I did not mean to. Forgive me. I should not have said what I did."

Maitland shook her head, picking up her needle and strong silk thread that Lady de Wolfe had provided. "I am not upset," she lied. "You simply do not understand my situation. It is so easy for you, not having known poverty or unhappiness, to assume I could have simply found another man who would have married a penniless widow. But I assure you, it is not that simple. Not in the least."

Her hands were still quivering as she lifted them to suture his wound, but he reached out and grasped her hand, stopping her. When she looked at him curiously, his expression was both gentle and kind.

"I *have* upset you," he whispered. "And I am very sorry. I was simply... I *have* known unhappiness, Mae. The woman I loved perished eight years ago in childbirth, and the life I have led since then has not eased that sorrow. My mother always told me that the right woman would bring me happiness again, but I never believed her until..."

"Until *what*?"

He squeezed her hand, gently. "Until I met you," he murmured. "Oh, I know it is foolish. I do not even know you, yet I am telling you I would have married you two years ago. It *is* foolish of me, and far too bold, but I was simply lamenting the misfortune not to have met you before that she-devil came into my life. Truth be told, I think my mother was right. I think you would have made me forget my grief. I would like to think so. I would like to think we could have built a good, stable life together. Had I known you after your husband perished, I would have pursued you and I am very sorry I did not know you then. But I am glad to have met you now."

With that, he kissed her hand and gently released it, leaving Maitland looking at him with an expression of complete and utter disappointment on her face. His words were like a dagger to her heart. Perhaps she shouldn't have believed him. Perhaps it was his exhaustion speaking, his emotions running high after a battle. But she swore that she had never heard more sincere words in her life.

Perhaps she believed them only because they were words she had dreamed of hearing.

Feeling elated and devastated at the same time, she returned her focus to his wound. "I am very sorry for your loss," she said. "Your lady must have been very grand, indeed."

"She was. You remind me of her in many ways; both caring and compassionate souls."

Maitland smiled faintly. "That is a very nice thing to say," she said. Then, she lowered her voice, for his ears only. "And you would not have had to pursue me. I would have let you catch me."

Thomas was facing forward at that point, breaking out into a massive grin and laughing softly, his head leaning back against the wall as she put the first of several quick stitches into his shoulder.

"You are a treasure, my lady," he said softly. "And I fear you may be my biggest regret. In fact, when I see Des next, I am going to punch him in the face for not having introduced us sooner."

"I will hold him for you."

Thomas continued laughing, even as she put stitch after careful stitch in his shoulder. He turned his head slightly, able to see the top of her head as she bent over him. "Are you truly going to leave me today to go to Edenside?"

"I must, my lord."

"You will call me Thomas. Or Tommy. Call me what you wish, Mae. I shall answer."

Maitland slowed her stitches, realizing that when she was done, their conversation would be over. It had been the most meaningful conversation of her life.

"I must go, Thomas," she murmured. "I am expected."

He sighed heavily. "I know," he said. "May I come and visit you, then?"

"For what purpose?"

"To see you, of course."

"As my friend?" she asked. "As my patron? Because those are the only capacities in which you can visit. Anything else would not be... proper. You are a betrothed man."

It was a stark reminder of the situation and Thomas was coming to see that she was much more level-headed than he was. He was impulsive, she wasn't. In truth, he wasn't surprised. She was a woman of character. He felt rather foolish for what he had said to her, but he wasn't sorry about it.

Not in the least.

"I wish that I was not," he mumbled. "I wish more than anything that I was not, but you are correct. It would not be proper. May I explain something to you?"

"Of course."

He thought carefully of what he wanted to say to her. It might be the only chance he ever had to explain the reality of the situation. "My father made this arrangement," he said quietly. "It was not of my doing. He thought he was doing what was best for me at the time, but it has since turned into a nightmare. Northumbria misrepresented his daughter, or at the very least, omitted the fact that she was... well, I suppose it does not matter. The fact remains that this is an unpleasant situation for us all, as you have guessed. But I want to make it clear to you that I am not a man of fickle loyalties. I do not treat contracts, women, or marriages with such disregard. But this is an unusual situation, and an unhappy one. I do not want you to think I am not a man of my word."

She glanced up at him. "I do not think that. I never have."

"That is good." He paused a moment before continuing. "Therefore, if you are agreeable, I will come to see you as both your friend and your patron. I should like to see this charity and all of the wonderful things you are going to do for it."

"Then you are welcome to visit."

"Thank you," he said sincerely, pleased that she hadn't denied him. "And this brings about another point. The battle tonight; it was border reivers, outlaws who have no loyalty to anyone but themselves. For safety's sake, Des and I will escort you to Edenside. I would feel better if you allowed it."

She looked up from the last of her stitching. "Do you believe it is necessary?" she asked. "Surely they would not attack women of the church."

He lifted his eyebrows. "They have been known to attack churches," he said. "Do not believe for one minute that they would grant you a reprieve. Even though you carry nothing of value, still, it would be a horrific experience for you. Please, let me escort you. It would make me feel better."

He didn't have to beg, truly. Maitland had already made up her mind to permit his escort. It would give her a little more time with the man, stolen moments to tuck away in her heart for the times when the loneliness of life overwhelmed her. That had happened a lot in her short lifetime already. Perhaps it was selfish of her, stealing moments with a man who was to marry another, but she couldn't help herself.

She wondered if, in the end, the sorrow of a man she could never have would be too much.

"Of course you and my brother may escort me," she said after a moment. "I am grateful for your concern."

Thomas' gaze lingered on her. "I will always show you such concern, Mae."

Maitland finished her last stitch. Instead of rising to his comment, which was something quite leading, she simply bit off the silk and set her needle down. Thomas' flirting had become something bold, something that could get out of hand should she let it, and given the situation, she simply couldn't let it become more than it already was. Therefore, it was best to simply change the subject, as much as she didn't want to.

It is safer this way.

"You are finished," she said. "Try to keep it dry and do not put any pressure on it, for at least a day. I heard your mother tell another man that with a similar wound, so I am telling you also."

He smiled at her, rather sweetly. "As you wish," he whispered.

For a moment, they simply looked at each other, a thousand words passing between them, words of hope and gratitude and interest, and eventually resignation. Resignation that he had his life to live and she had hers. It was a disappointment beyond words.

"How is yer wound, Tommy?"

Jordan was suddenly standing in front of them and they both turned to look at her as if startled by her appearance. They had been so wrapped up in each other that neither one of them had seen her approach. Maitland jumped up so that Jordan could take a close look at her handiwork.

"I cleansed it with the wine and hot water," Maitland said, perhaps a little too quickly. "Did I sew it correctly?"

Jordan passed a practiced eye over the wound; there were fifteen very neat stitches in her son's big shoulder. "Aye, lass," she said with approval. "Ye did a remarkable job. I dunna think I could have done better myself."

"She did a beautiful job," Thomas said, though he really couldn't see it. "I hardly felt a thing."

Maitland smiled proudly as Jordan took a final look and stood up. "Seek yer bed, Tommy," she said to her son. "Rest while ye can. I'll keep an eye on yer men and yer father is still on the walls. He's been there all night."

Thomas frowned. "You and Papa should get some sleep," he said. "I will stay here with my men."

Jordan frowned. "Since when does my son disobey me?"

Thomas knew he'd been licked before the battle really got started. There was no use in arguing with her, especially when she started throwing around words like "disobey". With a heavy sigh, he stood up, bending down to pick up his belongings as Maitland crouched down, handing him his padded tunic and collecting the de Wolfe tunic, which had been damaged in the fight. As Thomas collected his weapons, she noted the torn shoulder of the black and silver de Wolfe tunic.

"It has been torn," she said, showing it to Jordan. "I can mend it if you have thread of the same color."

Jordan fingered the tear, stained with her son's blood. "I have the thread in my sewin' kit," she said. "Take what ye need."

Thomas was on the move while the women talked sewing. "I will sleep only a short while," he said, looking at Maitland. "And you, my lady, should rest as well if you intend to go to Edenside today."

Maitland was rather tired, all things considered, but she looked around the hall. "I do not think I should sleep," she said. "I should help with the men, at least for the morning. I cannot leave it all to Lady de Wolfe."

But Jordan shook her head. "Rest, lass, and take yer companion with ye," she said, pointing to Tibelda on the other side of the hall. "The men have all been tended. There is no urgency any longer."

Maitland was still doubtful. "Are you sure you do not require my help?"

Jordan shook her head again. "Go," she said. "In fact, ye can leave me Tommy's tunic. I'll mend it."

But Maitland held the tunic close. "Nay, I can do it," she insisted. "It will only take a few minutes. I... I should like to earn my keep, my lady. Sir Thomas has been a gracious host and I should like to repay him."

Jordan cupped Maitland's face between her two hands and kissed her on the cheek. "Lass, ye've repaid him many times over with yer help," she said. "Ye dunna need tae earn yer keep. Tommy and I are very grateful for what ye've done."

Maitland smiled timidly, her gaze moving between Jordan and Thomas, who was smiling openly at her.

"Come, my lady," Thomas said. "Gather your needle and thread, and I shall escort you to the keep. It would be my pleasure."

With a genuine smile on her face, Maitland did as she was told. Gathering black thread from Jordan's sewing kit near the hearth, and a heavy bone needle, she collected Tibelda as well, and the three of them headed out of the hall and into the morning sunshine beyond.

Maitland swore that she'd never seen such a bright and beautiful day.

CHAPTER SIX

I T WAS NOON on the day after the night raid by the reivers and William was feeling that familiar exhaustion he seemed to feed off of. The exhaustion of a night of tension as a battle waged in the distance, but it was something that was as familiar to him as his own face. It was as much a part of him, as well.

The scent of battle.

The morning was dawning bright and lovely, but quite cold, and he stood on the wall next to the big iron braziers that had burned all night long, with peat, keeping the men warm. After the battle in Coldstream and the return of the men, he'd remained on the wall with his own men from Castle Questing, his seat, watching the roads and the woods in the distance for any sign of retaliation, but as the morning dawned, there was no sign of movement.

That was a good thing.

With the land beyond the walls quiet, William was seriously considering seeking out Thomas, who had returned a short time earlier. As Thomas' liege, since all of this was his property, William wanted to know about the fight in Coldstream and Thomas' assessment of the enemy. Wark Castle literally sat on the border between England and Scotland, and Thomas had seen more than his share of action since assuming command, and he'd been very good at assessing the enemy.

The man knew his way around military tactics well.

William finally decided to make his way off the wall and seek out his son, who he had seen disappear into the great hall not a half-hour earlier. As he crossed the outer bailey and approached the hall, Thomas emerged with Jordan and Lady Bowlin. William beckoned to his son, who left the women as they continued on towards the keep.

"Christ, Tommy," William hissed. "It is freezing out here. Why are you shirtless?"

Thomas pointed to the even stitches in his shoulder. "I just had my wound tended."

William peered at the injury, about three inches long. "It does not look too bad," he said. "Tell me what happened in Coldstream."

Thomas sighed heavily, his breath coming out as fog against the chill morning air. "Reivers," he said. "At first, I thought it was some of those clans you'd summoned to your conference those months ago, but I quickly realized that the clans were trying to fight off the reivers, who had attacked the village of Duns."

William nodded grimly. "The reivers again," he muttered. "How many?"

"I am not entirely certainly, but at least forty or fifty," Thomas replied. "I think it was that group that lives off to the east, between Wark and Etal, but I cannot be certain. They call themselves the Thurrock *Cú*."

"What makes you think it was them?"

"Their horses. They stole horses from Wooler last year and there were several pale horses among the group," he said. "Now, that group rides those pale horses and I am fairly certain that I saw them."

That made sense to William. "What did you do?"

Thomas shrugged. "We outnumbered them, but they are cunning, as you know," he said. "We ended up pushing them back up against the cliffs that overlook the river and driving them right over the cliffs."

William's eyebrows lifted. "*All* of them?"

"Most of them," Thomas said. "Papa, you know that it is not

enough to simply drive them away. Drive them away and they only appear somewhere else. We must eliminate them."

William nodded. "I could not agree more," he said. "Driving them over the cliff was a brilliant move. It should have killed some of them, but not all of them. The drop really isn't enough to kill them, but they could easily drown."

"I know." Thomas scratched at his head, tweaking his wound and then gingerly rotating his shoulder because it hurt. "It did not kill all of them, but it thinned their ranks."

William thought on that. "Well," he said finally, "it will cause them to regroup, anyway. Mayhap we shall have a reprieve from their raids for a time."

Thomas wasn't so sure. "I know that Northwood Castle is having an even worse time than we are," he said. "Hector came to visit last month and said the reivers have been so bold that they try to tie up Northwood so the army cannot open the gates as a group of them raid the village."

"We are fortunate they did not do that to Wark."

"Agreed."

William pondered the reivers a moment longer before spying someone coming out of the keep. Edmund de Vauden was up very early for some reason, and William zeroed in on the man. He hadn't had the opportunity to speak to him last night about the betrothal between Thomas and Adelaide, and now that he spied the man alone, he was keen to have the conversation that had been the whole point of inviting Edmund to Wark. Putting his hand on his son's good shoulder, he turned him for the keep.

"That is enough for this morning," he said. "Go inside and sleep. Your mother and I will watch your castle and your men while you do."

Thomas shook his head. "Papa, I am perfectly capable of functioning without sleep," he said. "It is you and Mother I worry over. Neither one of you is getting any younger."

William cast his son a sidelong glance. "Will you tell your mother that to her face?"

Thomas grinned. "Not me," he said. "And if you tell her I said that, I will deny it."

"She will not believe you."

"Then I shall run very fast."

William smirked, giving his son a little shove in the direction of the keep. "Go," he said, his gaze finding Edmund as the man hurried towards the warmth of the hall. "I have business with Edmund now that he is awake."

Thomas saw Edmund, too, as the man rushed through the outer bailey. "About his witch of a daughter?"

William's gaze lingered on Edmund for a moment before he began to walk away. "That is for me to know," he said. "I will see you later."

Leaving Thomas standing there, suspecting what his father was going to speak to Northumbria about, William picked up the pace and rushed to intercept Edmund before the man could get to the great hall. He almost didn't make it because Edmund moved surprisingly fast, but he managed to catch him before he could make it to the entry. Literally, he put himself between Edmund and the door.

"Good morn to you, Edmund," William said pleasantly. "What has you up so early?"

Edmund appeared tired and cold, his nose pinched red. "I could not find any servants in the keep," he said, disgusted. "It seems that I must get my own food this morning, de Wolfe."

William's attempt to be kind and polite was already being tested. "The servants were required to tend to the wounded in the hall," he said. "You know that the army rode out to defend Coldstream last night and we have wounded as a result. My apologies for having disrupted your morning."

Edmund grunted with disapproval. "Is the skirmish over?"

"It is, for now."

"Good. I am leaving today. I do not wish to be where there is fighting going on."

William's patience was thinning. "You are a border lord, Edmund," he said. "You know there can, and will, always be some manner of fighting. Twizel Castle belongs to you and it protects a very important bridge over the River Tweed. There is constantly fighting there."

Edmund looked at him in frustration. "That is true, but I am not there," he said, snappish. "I am safe at Kyloe Castle, which is a goodly distance away. I do not make it a habit of being at castles that are under siege."

William could see that the conversation was never going to be pleasant. It was probably only going to get worse, given Edmund's agitated state because he'd had to seek his own food, so he decided to bring up the subject he needed to speak with the man about, especially if Edmund was departing Wark soon. William didn't want to miss his chance.

"Then I apologize for your discomfort," he said, "but the reason I invited you to Wark was because I have a need to speak with you. Would you care to go inside out of the cold so that we may discuss it?"

Edmund eyed him, wary of William's words. "Speak to me of what?" he asked.

So the man wasn't going to make it easy for him, nor did he intend to seek a warm haven. William was starting to become irritated. "It would be better if we go inside out of the cold," he said. "Come inside and let us break our fast together."

He started to move, but Edmund didn't. He stood there, looking at William. "*What* did you want to speak of?"

Now, William's goodwill towards the man, or at least the attempt of it, was gone. If Edmund intended to be difficult, then William was fully capable of delivering the same.

"Very well," he said, folding his big arms across his chest. "I will begin. You lied to me."

Edmund blinked. "I *lied* to you? About what?"

"Your daughter," William said. "When you approached me with this betrothal, you never once mentioned how rude, unstable, and unpleasant your daughter was. You never mentioned that she cuts her arms to gain attention. You never mentioned how completely unpredictable she was, not once, Edmund. All you told me was that she is a great heiress, set to inherit the entire Northumbria fortune and, with that, you lured me in with false promises. Do you deny this?"

Edmund's face was red, his jaw working furiously. "How dare you insult my daughter," he hissed. "How dare you…"

William cut him off. "Do you *deny* any of this?" he asked, more slowly. "Do you deny she cuts her arms to gain attention? Well?"

Edmund's mouth was working, stunned by the conversation, clearly caught in a situation of his own making. But there was no way he was going to admit anything and even though William was on to him and his game, he was very good at playing the victim.

"She is a woman of great feeling," he said. "You do not understand her. She is passionate in nature."

"She has a penchant for self-destruction and dramatics," William said plainly. "And now you have saddled my son with this woman? My wife thinks you did it simply to be rid of her, but I would like to think your motive was not so self-serving. I want to know why you never told me any of this, Edmund. Why did you not tell me that your daughter was mad?"

Edmund took a step back, hissing as he did so. "You will not insult my child," he growled. "You have no right to judge her so. She has a lineage you could only dream of having, de Wolfe. She descends from the Duke of Normandy."

"And my ancestor was a premier general for the Duke of Normandy," William fired back. "Did you know that? My ancestor, Gaetan de Wolfe, was the leader of the *anges de guerre*, an elite group of knights who helped the duke conquer this country. My lineage goes back as far as yours does and is far more prestigious."

"How can you say that?"

"At least my fortune is not based on being the bastard of a prince."

Edmund was stunned. Stunned and furious. "You *dare* to say such things to me?"

William sighed sharply. "And I shall say more than even that," he said. "You lied to me when you brokered this contract. Your daughter is in no way suitable for my son and if you refuse to dissolve the betrothal, I shall take this contract to the king and leave it to his good judgement. But know this; I shall produce multiple witnesses who can attest to your daughter's behavior. I will present the picture of a completely unstable young woman, one you lied about in order to gain a betrothal with my son. When I am finished presenting my case, no man in the civilized world will want to marry her. Do you understand my meaning?"

Edmund was so angry that he was quivering. "Is that why you invited me to Wark?" he demanded. "To insult and threaten me?"

"I do not like being lied to."

"I did not lie to you."

William rolled his eye. "You are doing it now," he said. "Agree to dissolve the betrothal, Edmund. That is your only choice."

Edmund eyed him, his jaw flexing and his fists opening and closing. William could see the man's fists, wondering if he would be stupid enough to throw a punch. But Edmund backed away, clearly pondering the ultimatum he'd just been given. The man wasn't used to being challenged.

"I did not lie to you," he repeated. "I thought that with a strong hand, my daughter could be tamed. With a strong man, she could become the kind of woman he wanted her to be. Are you telling me that your son is not strong enough to handle her?"

William smiled, but it was without humor. "My son is more of a man than you could ever hope to be," he said. "But you have allowed your daughter to run amok all her life and now you expect another man to undo the damage you have done. It is too late, Edmund. Your daughter is beyond help. My son does not deserve this mess you have created, and no fortune in the world is worth the trouble you have caused."

Now, William was directly insulting Edmund, and with good reason. But Edmund only saw it one way – instead of William cowering, the man was meeting his argument face to face. He was making demands that Edmund had no intention of meeting.

His grip on the situation was slipping.

Taking a step back, Edmund forced himself to calm, knowing that he could not match William's anger. Deep down, he knew the man was right; everything he said had been right. There was no question. But Edmund would not accept responsibility.

And he could not lose this battle.

"I may be a liar, but if you go back on your word, every man in England will know that William de Wolfe cannot be trusted," he said. "You gave me your word, de Wolfe."

"I do not give my word to liars."

Edmund threatened to flare but he fought it. He had a better idea, attacking William where he knew it would do the most damage – his family.

"Then know this," he said. "If you break this betrothal, then I shall send my army out and systematically destroy each and every one of your properties. Berwick shall fall, followed by Wark and Monteviot, Wolfe's Lair and Kale Water Castle. The last to go shall be Castle Questing, and you shall watch it burn to the ground. I will command a scorched earth campaign that will destroy half of Northumberland, all of it to punish you for going back on your word. If you are prepared to fight for your life, for the rest of your life, then by all means, break the betrothal."

William had a smile on his face. "You may have a big army, Edmund, but mine is bigger," he said. "I have more allies than you do. Come for me and I shall crush you."

Edmund couldn't believe that William wasn't surrendering. A military threat hadn't worked. But he knew what would. Edmund was, if nothing else, sharp. He could think quickly on his feet and, at the moment, he had to.

He had to salvage this.

"It is a binding agreement," he said simply. "If I do not agree to dissolve it, then you cannot dissolve it on your own. I shall take it to the

Archbishop of York. What my army cannot enforce, the church will. And you cannot deny or dispute the church, de Wolfe. Not even you are that powerful."

William knew that. Unfortunately, more than all the armies in England, the church could do some serious damage to him. If they upheld the contract and William refused to allow Thomas to marry Adelaide, then it would jeopardize any marriage Thomas did have in the future, not to mention any interaction the House of de Wolfe had with the church. It was the one threat that meant something and they both knew it. But William would not surrender.

It wasn't in his nature where his children were concerned.

"I advise you to think about that," he said. "Whatever mischief you can make for me, I can make it even worse for you. Agreeably end the betrothal and I shall forget the threats you have leveled against me. Refuse to end it and there will be consequences."

Edmund was shaken and furious. He backed away from William, turning for the hall. "The marriage will happen as planned," he said. "And I am returning home today. Do not summon me again unless it is for the wedding."

With that, he turned away and rushed into the great hall, leaving William standing out in the early dawn. William was as frustrated and furious as Edmund was, only he was better at controlling it. He could see by the man's cagey response that Edmund was fully aware of his daughter's behavior and that everything Jordan had said about it was true – Edmund had knowingly tricked William into a betrothal.

And now Thomas was stuck.

It was all William's doing.

Maybe he should have let Thomas escape those months ago.

With a heavy heart, William turned for the keep, wondering what he was going to tell his wife and his son. They were bound to a contract that they'd been unfairly tricked into and, at the moment, there was nothing William could do about it.

But this wasn't the end of it.

Not even close.

CHAPTER SEVEN

"I T WAS A great pleasure to meet you both," Maitland said. "I am truly honored to have known de Wolfe hospitality."

She was speaking to William and Jordan in the inner bailey of Wark as the escort to take her and Tibelda on to Edenside waited patiently. It was just past the nooning hour on a day that had turned remarkably mild from such a cold morning, and as Maitland thanked William and Jordan, Caria ran around at their feet, playing with the two puppies she had confiscated from the hall the night before.

"'Twas an honor to have met ye, Lady Bowlin," Jordan said, taking Maitland's hand and holding it sweetly. "Edenside is in very good hands. I shall visit very soon."

Maitland smiled. "I hope you will, my lady," she said. "I hope there will be great progress when you come."

Jordan squeezed her hand. "With ye in charge, there will be," she said assuredly. "I've sent along some provisions with ye, some flour and a side of pork and a few other things. That should at least tide ye over until I send ye some goats and chickens. Ye'll need them tae feed the wee bairns."

Maitland nodded. "That would be very generous, my lady," she said. "I must admit that after our conversation last night, I am a bit wary of what I will find there."

As Jordan nodded somewhat sympathetically, William spoke. "If you find it is in terrible condition when you arrive, then simply tell Thomas," he said. "He will quickly ensure you have what you need from the first to make it a safe and nurturing environment for the children, but my wife is correct – we shall visit you soon and bring some livestock with us."

Maitland was very pleased to hear it. "Thank you, my lord, truly," she said sincerely. "You are most generous."

As William politely nodded his head, there was a commotion over by the gate that led from the inner to the outer bailey and they turned to see Edmund and Adelaide emerging. Edmund was followed by several of his well-dressed retainers, all of them carrying trunks or baggage of some kind.

The Northumbria escort was ready to depart, hovering near the gatehouse in a cluster, while Maitland's escort was nearer to the stables on the east side. The two parties were a good distance apart, both of them preparing to depart. Over near the hall, William and Jordan and even Maitland were watching Edmund and Adelaide as they headed to the Northumbria escort.

"Is he takin' his daughter along?" Jordan muttered to his husband. "Please tell me he's takin' her away from here."

William could only shake his head. He hadn't told his wife about his conversation with Edmund earlier, mostly because there hadn't been a moment of privacy between them yet. That information wasn't something he wanted to tell her in front of witnesses.

"He's not taking her," he said rather grimly, turning his attention back to Maitland before his wife could question him. "It should take a couple of hours at most to reach Edenside, my lady. It is very close to Wark. I will wish you a pleasant journey and then I shall excuse myself. I had the watch all night and now I find that my fatigue is catching up with me. And I believe I shall force my wife to come with me considering she was up all night as well."

Maitland nodded. "Of course, my lord."

She watched as Jordan tried to corral Caria, who had slept all night and had no need to go with her parents to nap. She and the puppies were having a marvelous time, but the moment Jordan grasped her and tried to pull her along, she began to wail. That, predictably, brought Thomas out from the stables.

"Mother," he said as he headed in her direction. "What are you doing to that child?"

Jordan cast her son an impatient glance. "I'm stickin' pins in her," she scowled. "What does it look like I'm doin'? I am goin' inside and the lass is goin' with me."

Thomas grinned, watching his mother try to coax Caria to go with her, while behind him, men were emerging from the stables leading horses packed with the supplies Jordan had sent along. Desmond was with them, securing the provisions, and soon it would be time to depart. Thomas watched his men gather before turning to his father.

"We should be back by nightfall," he said. "You are not planning on leaving before I return, are you?"

William shook his head. He hadn't told Thomas about his conversation with Edmund, either, and knew he needed to before he returned home. It was a depressing conversation he needed to have with both his wife and son, and something he was dreading.

"Nay," he said. "We will be here when you return."

"Good," Thomas nodded. Then, he looked to Caria, crying in his mother's grasp. "Caria, my love, come and bid me farewell."

Caria yanked herself away from Jordan, running to the safety of Thomas' arms. "Where are you going?" she wept. "May I come?"

Thomas picked her up, hugging her gently. "You may not come," he said. "I am going to take Lady Bowlin to her destination, but I shall not be gone long. While I am gone, you must be a very good girl and go with Matha."

Caria was quite unhappy. "But I want to play with the puppies!"

Thomas looked down at the little dogs, sitting on the dirt and looking up at Caria with their tails thumping. "And you shall," he said.

"Have you fed them anything today?"

That distracted Caria and she looked to the dogs as she wiped at her teary eyes. "They had some bread."

"You must feed them more than bread," he told her. "Take the puppies back into the hall where they can suckle on their mother and then go with Matha to rest. If you do these things and are a very good girl, I shall bring you something when I return."

The promise of a present magically dried all tears. "What shall you bring me?" she asked excitedly.

He kissed her cheek and set her to the ground. "I am not sure yet," he said. "But you must be very good or there will be nothing. Do you understand?"

Caria nodded solemnly, already rushing over to the puppies to return them to the hall. With Caria calm, and Jordan trailing after the child, Thomas turned his attention to more important things, including Northumbria's escort. Lifting a hand, he shielded his eyes from the sun as he spied them over by the gatehouse in their fine clothing and fine horses, with standards that had gilded ribbons streaming from them.

"Northumbria is departing," he said to his father. "So soon? He only just arrived."

William cleared his throat softly. "Let him go," he said. When Thomas looked at him curiously, he simply held up a hand. "Ask no more. We will speak on it when you return."

Thomas didn't press his father, although he was very curious. Northumbria's trip to Wark had been very brief, considering the effort it took to travel from Kyloe to Wark. As he stood there for a moment and watched the Northumbria escort assemble, he saw clearly when Adelaide broke off from her father and headed across the bailey in his direction.

Dressed in a fine gown, elaborate, with her gold jewelry reflecting the sunlight, any other man might have thought she was a pretty sight, but not Thomas. All he could manage to feel when he looked at her was disgust and impatience. He didn't want to talk to her because there wasn't anything she had to say that he wanted to hear. Quickly, he turned away.

"It is time for us to depart," he said, politely taking hold of Maitland's elbow. "Come along, my lady."

Maitland lifted a hand to Jordan and William, waving farewell, as Thomas turned her for the escort. They hadn't taken five steps when Adelaide called Thomas' name. He didn't respond until she called him a third time, when he finally came to a reluctant halt and turned towards the woman. She called his name again, for a fourth time, to make sure he had heard her, lifting her hand as if to catch his attention. He simply stood there, impatiently.

"What is it, my lady?" he asked with thin patience. "We are just preparing to depart."

Adelaide was looking at Maitland as she spoke. "I know," she said. "But I wanted to know why you were going. The lady arrived without an escort, I am told, so I am not sure why she needs one to reach her destination."

Immediately, Thomas could feel his anger rise. He wasn't going to let Adelaide make any decisions for him and he particularly didn't like her questioning decisions he'd already made. This was his castle, and ever would be, and her role in it would be as small as he could possibly manage.

"Although this is none of your concern, I will be polite and respond," he said. "We are escorting Lady Bowlin and her traveling companion because we were attacked by reivers last night and it is not safe for the lady and her companion to ride alone through dangerous territory," he said. "Is that all?"

Adelaide's gaze lingered on Maitland. "I wanted to bid the lady a good journey."

Maitland was surprised to hear that but she sensed something sinister behind the goodwill gesture. "Thank you, my lady," she said. "I hope you will come visit Edenside someday."

Adelaide cocked her head. "Why?"

It was a stupid question as far as Maitland was concerned, but it was also a question with no real answer. She'd only said it to be polite.

"Because great ladies are patronesses of such places," she said, scrambling for the first answer she could come up with. "Since Sir Thomas has agreed to be a patron, I am sure you would like to see where his money is put to use."

Adelaide looked at Thomas in shock. "You are giving *money* to Edenside?"

Thomas was rather pleased in a sadistic sort of way to see that she was upset. "It is my money," he said. "And I need not answer to you. If there is nothing else, then I must go."

Adelaide wasn't stupid. Petty, vindictive, and immature, aye. But she wasn't stupid. She could see what was going on, how Thomas seemed to be particularly fond of Lady Bowlin, and it fed her anger and jealously like nothing else. The man wouldn't give her the time of day, but he certainly paid the widow enough attention. Her father had told him that William de Wolfe had tried to break the betrothal and now Adelaide suspected why –

The Beguine.

"I would speak with you before you go," she said, looking at him pointedly. "*Alone.*"

Thomas didn't say a word. He simply took Maitland by the elbow again and walked off, leaving Adelaide standing there with a shocked expression on her face. He wasn't going to give her the courtesy she had asked for. But as he walked away, Maitland came to a halt. When he looked at her curiously, she tilted her head in Adelaide's direction.

"Please speak to her," she said quietly. "It is not polite to show her such disrespect in front of others. She is to be Lady de Wolfe, after all. That title alone affords courtesy."

Thomas stared at her. Then, he exhaled slowly, showing his great displeasure, but he knew even as he did it that he would comply with her request. He couldn't look into that face and hear those calm, reasonable words and refuse her. In that brief moment, he realized that he could never refuse Maitland, not ever. Not with any little request she could ever make of him. Frustrated, he rolled his eyes at her but dutifully let go of her elbow. Then, he retraced his steps to Adelaide.

"Well?" he demanded quietly. "What do you want?"

Adelaide was already humiliated and well on her way to a tantrum. "I want you to stay at Wark," she said. "You do not need to escort Lady Bowlin to Edenside because you have an entire army of soldiers who can just as easily complete the task."

Thomas cocked his head, almost curiously. But there was nothing curious about the words that came out of his mouth.

"My lady, I want you to listen to me and listen well," he said, sounding oddly patient. "Are you listening?"

Adelaide didn't like the fact that he hadn't readily agreed. "I am."

"Good," he said. "In the first place, you will never make any decision for me, especially when it comes to the safety, health, and welfare of the inhabitants and guests of Wark Castle. My decisions are beyond question. Do you understand me?"

She began to twitch with anger. "I was not questioning your…"

"*Do* you understand me?"

He had cut her off, speaking loudly, slowly, and deliberately. Adelaide clearly wanted to argue with him; that was all over her face. But she must have sensed that any contradiction wouldn't be well met, so she didn't.

"I understand you," she said.

"Excellent," Thomas said drolly. "Now, in the second place, I do not care what you want. Not in the least. I have spent the past six months trying to be polite and understanding. There was a time I was possibly even kind. But those days are gone. You will never again make requests or demands of me because you mean less to me than the horses in the barn or the cows in the field. I do not care what you think and I do not care what you feel. Now, go inside and get out of my sight, for I do not wish to see your pitiful face when I return. Have my words penetrated that thick skull you seem to have, Adelaide?"

Adelaide was recoiling from him, a look of utter devastation on her face. Her mouth popped open in outrage but quickly shut, and he could see the tears coming. Without another word, he turned away from her and headed back in Maitland's direction, hoping beyond hope that his words were cruel enough that Adelaide would go home with her father and tell the man how terrible Thomas had been. Perhaps that would be enough to break this farce of a betrothal.

Under normal circumstances, he would have never spoken so harshly to a woman, but these weren't normal circumstances and Adelaide was not a normal woman. He was being pushed to his limit and he was tired of it all – tired of the constant tension, tired of a woman who had brought him nothing but frustration.

But thoughts of Adelaide were tempered by the sight of Maitland as she stood where he'd left her. She looked at him with some curiosity, smiling timidly as he came near, and he reached out to take her elbow again as they continued on towards the waiting horses.

"Is... is everything well?" she asked hesitantly. "Is Lady Adelaide troubled?"

He had to bite his tongue with what he wanted to say; *I do not care if she is troubled or not.* Instead, he simply shook his head.

"There is no trouble," he said. Then, he pointed to the horses that were waiting. "I hope you do not mind. I selected a better palfrey than the one you rode in on. Truthfully, I am surprised that little beast made it as far as it did. It is very old and near collapse."

Distracted from Adelaide, Maitland looked to see the horse he was indicating and she gasped at the sight. It was a beautiful, round pony that was a pale golden color from head to tail. It had a fat belly and sturdy, lovely legs, and she went right up to it and began petting it, crooning to the beautiful animal.

"She is so beautiful," she said admiringly. "Are you sure you want to let me borrow her?"

Thomas came to stand next to her as she loved up the horse. "Borrow her?" he repeated. "She is yours. Think how happy the foundlings are going to be when they can ride a golden horse. Belle is very gentle; she will be perfect for the children."

Maitland looked up at him. "Beautiful," she murmured. "Her name means beautiful. It is perfect for her."

Thomas found himself looking into her mesmerizing eyes. "Aye," he said softly. "I have also selected a palfrey for your companion. What is her name? Tibelda? My mother said she was most helpful with the wounded. It is our gift to her."

Tibelda, who had so far been standing off to the side as the escort assembled, came forward when Maitland motioned to her. When Thomas indicated a pretty brown mare for her, it was all Tibelda could do to keep from weeping. She, too, reached out to pet the horse, thrilled with the fine equine. Thomas watched the ladies, seeing how touched they were, and it pleased him.

"Excellent," Thomas said. "Everyone is happy. Shall we depart?"

The soldiers were already mounting their steeds and Thomas took charge of Maitland while Desmond took charge of Tibelda. Each woman's meager satchel was tied to her saddle and the women were hoisted onto the backs of the horses.

With the women settled, Thomas and Desmond were the last to mount their war horses, big beasts that had seen much action the night before. In fact, Thomas' horse was muzzled for this ride because it tended to snap and he didn't want anyone losing an arm. Just as they prepared to move out beneath the cool, bright skies, the gates of Wark slowly cranked open and the Northumbria party began trickling through first.

Not wanting to mingle with Edmund's group, Thomas held up a hand to his men, indicating they remain in place until he gave the order to move out. Thomas watched as the armed Northumbria escort moved fairly quickly through the gates, heading out into the countryside beyond with Kyloe Castle as their destination for the night. Kyloe was about five or six hours away, depending on how fast they traveled and, from the look of them, they intended to travel fast.

That made Thomas think about what his father had said earlier; clearly, the man had spoken with Northumbria and Thomas was eager to know what had been said. Whatever it was, it was enough to drive Edmund out of Wark in a hurry. He had hoped it was a positive conversation but the expression on his father's face led him to believe that all was not well. Edmund was fleeing and William wasn't happy.

Perhaps he wasn't so eager to hear what had been said, after all.

Pushing that all aside, Thomas gave the order to move out once Northumbria was clear of the gatehouse, and Thomas, Desmond, Maitland, Tibelda, and fifty heavily-armed soldiers passed beneath the two-storied gatehouse also, taking the road that would lead them north and east, while the Northumbria party headed southeast. Thomas wasn't sorry to see them go but, the more time passed, the more he was very anxious to know what had been said between Northumbria and his father.

A conversation that would control his destiny.

With that on his mind, Thomas took his party north into Scotland.

CHAPTER EIGHT

The ruins of Castle Heton
5 miles east of Wark Castle

"I SAW TWO escorts leaving Wark," a breathless man said. "One is heading north and west, and the other is heading right for us. I hurried back to tell you."

Heton had once been a great tower, a beacon of strength against the Scots along the England-Scotland border, but a tower that had collapsed under a siege forty years ago when Clan Elliot tried to take it and the English descended on it.

Now, it was a mound of ghostly ruins.

The tower had been four stories of stone and might, and the walls surrounding the small courtyard had been tall and impenetrable. That was when William de Wolfe, the newly-appointed commander of Northwood Castle's army, had devised a clever plan. While a part of the army had made a big show of attacking the gatehouse to draw the attention of the Scots, William had set the rest of their army to digging a tunnel from the northeast corner, undermining the wall, and into the vault beneath the keep. Part of the wall had collapsed because of the tunnel, and the northeast corner of the keep had sunk as well. After that, the English had rushed in and the Scots had been all but purged.

It would seem that those in the area had been dealing with a de Wolfe, father or sons, for a very long time.

As they did last night.

They called themselves the *Thurrock Cú*, or the Thurrock Dogs, and their leader, The Bold Hobelar. Hobelar wasn't his real name, but that was what the men knew him by, men who were both Scots and English, men with no real loyalties to anyone other than themselves. There used to be a hundred of them, spread out between Heton and another ruined tower north of the River Tweed, but now their number had been decimated by half, and even more after the run-in with the knights from Wark Castle last night.

Now, they were a weary, injured few, but there were enough.

Enough to strike back.

"An escort," Hobelar repeated in a thick Scots accent, scratching his head with a bandaged right hand. "How big?"

The breathless man came near the fire, burning in the partially collapsed but enormous vault of the castle formerly owned by Hobelar's mother's family. They could have a fire in the morning like this, when it mingled with the smell of other cooking fires in the area. Men had returned during the night wet and half-drowned, at least those who had made it out of the river once the Wark army had pushed them over the cliff.

Fifty-three men had gone on the raid at sunset the previous evening, heading up to Duns with the hope of raiding enough cattle or livestock to bring south, across the River Tweed, but so far, only thirty-two had made it back to Heton, with no cattle, and Hobelar was bent on revenge.

The breathless man knew this as he settled down by the fire, warming his freezing hands. He knew his lord and he knew the man was humiliated and furious with the loss of life and the fact the Wark's commander had outsmarted him. "I've counted at least thirty armed men and a great lord traveling on a very expensive horse," he said. "There is a wagon carrying many chests that I am certain are filled with gold."

Hobelar digested that. "What about the group that headed northwest?"

The breathless man shook his head. "Not so many, but there were two big knights from what I could see," he said. "They had women with them, too. It seemed to me that they were heading to Kelso."

Hobelar sat back on the broken stone he used for a seat, noting the expectant faces looking at him. He was the son of a great Scottish laird and an English mother from the House of de Grey, and he'd spent his childhood in Scotland in the summers and Essex in the winter. As a young man, he'd found a life as a mercenary in Saxony and Ghent, and that lust for lawlessness had never left him. He was back on the borders now, home to him, and had his own group of outlaws that had been moderately successful for the past year, successful enough to drive out another gang of reivers who had controlled the area. Now, it was just Hobelar and his men, and the defeat they had suffered last night at the hands of the commander of Wark had been devastating.

He couldn't risk another.

"The party headin' towards us," he said. "How swiftly do they move?"

The breathless man accepted a piece of roasted bird from a man who had been cooking the fowl over the fire. "Not swiftly at all," he said. "We can easily catch them to the south if we leave now. They are carrying much riches, Hobelar... the wagon was full of such things. It would be small compensation for the defeat of last night, but it would be something."

It was his way of suggesting to Hobelar that they take the easy target. Morale was terrible this morning and even if it was an easy kill, they needed it. They wanted it.

In truth, Hobelar understood that.

"We lost twenty-one men last night," he muttered. "Twenty-one men drowned by the de Wolfe bastard at Wark."

"The youngest cub," someone muttered.

Hobelar looked around to see his men nodding grimly. Most of them were still wet from the dunking they had taken last night. They smelled like rot and mold, and of a river that had claimed far too many victims over the years. That cold and clinging water had nearly claimed more, but those sitting around Hobelar's fire were strong.

They were worthy of the fight.

"Aye, the youngest Wolfe cub," Hobelar repeated. Then, he pulled something out of his belt, something that one of his men had brought to him – a beautiful dagger with a wolf's head handle. Hobelar had seen that wolf head before, on the shields used by the de Wolfe armies, and he held it up to inspect it. "There are cubs at Berwick and Kale Water Castle, and as far west as Monteviot and Sibbald's Hold in Scotland. When I was a wee lad, the Wolfe himself was only just risin' tae power. Now, his sons command the castles around here. They are all the same tae me – all killers, the bleeders of Scots. I looked the youngest cub in the face last night and saw the murder in his eyes. But we are not enough tae face them; not as we are. But we canna be silenced. We may not be able tae raise a great army against de Wolfe and his cubs, but we shall cause him pain. Aye, we will."

The breathless man was not so breathless any longer. Hughes was his name, and he sucked the last of the meat off of the skinny bird bone he'd been given. He was also English, and from the north, and he knew the de Wolfe name well. Everyone in the north of England did.

"Then what will we do?" he asked Hobelar, watching the man as he fixated on the wolf's head dagger. "William de Wolfe is still alive, in command of his seat at Castle Questing. It is quite possible that it is the man himself coming from Wark with his trunks loaded with gold. Who else would command such fine horses and weapons and trunks?"

Hobelar looked at him. "What colors are the escort flyin'?"

"Red and yellow, but it could be a ruse. It could be meant to confuse."

Hobelar shook his head. "They'd be flyin' the de Wolfe black and silver proudly were it the man himself," he said, finally lowering the dagger and looking at his men. "They would not try tae deceive anyone. Still… whoever it is, he must be important. We can cause great trouble for de Wolfe by attackin' his allies."

"Then we shall attack them?"

Hobelar nodded. "We must meet him on the road and we must move swiftly," he said. "We dunna want tae let him get within range of Etal Castle; the garrison could send out help should they see us. Nay, we *must* catch them on the road before they reach Branxton. Beyond that, we will lose them. We will show de Wolfe that he canna destroy us. We will make the man hurt."

Already, the wet and exhausted reivers were moving, putting out the fire and gathering their weapons. The horses, those that had made it out of the river, were resting beneath the overgrowth of trees that infested the bailey of Heton, and the men rushed out to prepare them.

The day was advancing and they had little time to waste. Soon enough, they were charging from the bones of Heton's stone rib cage, out into the landscape beyond as they headed south to the road where the party from Wark had been seen. From the delay of the report, they estimated the party to be less than an hour out of Wark, which would put them on a particular stretch of road that passed through a heavily-wooded area. It was forested and it was hilly, providing an excellent opportunity for an ambush.

The reivers had swords and axes, but they also had crossbows, stolen from the dead. Hobelar sent those with the crossbows up ahead to begin the ambush and by the time they intercepted the party from Wark, the arrows were flying and men were falling, including a well-dressed lord at the center of the escort. When he went down, his men panicked.

After that, it was chaos, but Hobelar's men were the better for it – the wagon containing all of the expensive trunks somehow ended up back at Castle Heton, and just a couple of hours after the ambush, Hobelar and his men were celebrating a very lucrative ambush of a de Wolfe ally.

Victory was theirs.

Hobelar fell asleep in the sunshine of the afternoon wearing the expensive silk robes of Edmund de Vauden.

CHAPTER NINE

Edenside

I T WASN'T WHAT she had expected.

In truth, Maitland wasn't sure what to expect, but the dilapidated tower and outbuildings hadn't been among any of her hopes.

It was worse than she could have imagined.

Edenside had been a fortified pele tower complex once, built with the gray granite stones so prevalent to the area. There was a two-storied tower, overgrown with weeds and moss, and two long outbuildings, single-storied, with roofs of sod that were badly in need of replacement. The entire fortress looked old, worn, and crushed.

Stepping into the walled bailey, there was only a pair of dilapidated gates to keep those inside safe, gates that a child could have kicked down. In fact, as Maitland and Thomas and Desmond entered the bailey, which was covered with grass and weeds, Thomas had a couple of his men take immediate notice of the gates to see what they could do about making them more secure. If Thomas was feeling disillusioned and a little apprehensive of the place, he couldn't even imagine what Maitland was feeling.

The whole thing seemed deserted. No sounds of children, no signs of life. As Maitland and Tibelda left their fat palfreys just inside the wall, over near the gates, Tibelda went towards the yard to the east of the outbuildings to look for children while Maitland made her way towards the two-storied tower, hoping to find someone there who could tell her where her charges were.

The tower, in fact, was rather large. In its prime, it must have been a mighty sight, indeed. It looked as if it could hold thirty people simply by the sheer size of it. It could certainly hold twenty children, as there had been at one time.

But now, it appeared dark and vacant.

"Halt!"

A shout came from off to her left and she immediately stopped, turning to see a skinny, ill-dressed boy standing in the doorway of one of the long outbuildings. He was barefoot, filthy, and very cold, with blue lips and pale skin. But he had a big stick with him and he came towards her, wielding it menacingly.

"Who are ye?" he demanded. "Why have ye come?"

Maitland remained calm, feeling Thomas come up beside her. She knew he was armed, and heavily so, but she held out a hand to him, silently telling him not to draw his weapon.

"My name is Lady Bowlin," she said calmly. "I am the new guardian of Edenside. Who are you?"

The child frowned at her. "New guardian?" he repeated. "We dunna need a guardian. Go away!"

Maitland shook her head. "I will not go away," she said. "I have been sent by Kelso Abbey. I am to be in charge now and I promise it will be much different from the way it was before. Where are the other children?"

"I'll not tell ye!"

"Can you at least tell me your name? You know mine. What is yours?"

The boy hesitated a brief moment. "My name is Artus but they call me Wrath," he informed her. Then, he lifted the big stick. "Make another move and ye'll feel it!"

Beside Maitland, Thomas growled. "And you'll feel mine, you little..."

Maitland shushed him, keeping her gaze on the child. "Artus, thank you for telling me your name," she said steadily. "But I am in charge now and you will lower that stick. I am no threat and neither are these knights. They come as friends, I assure you. Now, where are the children, please? You will tell them to come out. There is no longer any reason to hide, I promise."

Artus wasn't so certain. He didn't drop the stick, but he didn't charge her, either. He seemed to be debating what she'd told him and, from what Maitland had been told of this place, she had to admit that she really didn't blame him. God only knew what that child had gone through and how he'd had to defend himself. She stood still as the child came near, walking a circle around both her and Thomas, inspecting them very closely.

"We dunna need ye," he finally said, holding the stick up for emphasis. "Queenie has taken good care of us."

"Who is Queenie?" Maitland asked.

The child suddenly darted off, disappearing into the long building before emerging a short time later with a tiny, round, and fairly old woman who was weaving all over the place. The woman couldn't seem to stand on her own and she leaned heavily against the boy as he pointed to her insistently.

"This is Queenie," he said. "She can take care of us. You go away!"

Frowning with concern, Maitland glanced at Thomas, who lifted his eyebrows dubiously. Trying to assess the situation, Maitland took a few steps towards the child and the seemingly sick old woman. Thomas followed along closely, unwilling to let her get too close to that child with the big stick if he could help it.

"Queenie?" Maitland said to the old woman. "Queenie, my name is Lady Bowlin. Are you ill?"

The old woman looked up at her, her eyes glazed over as if she was simply exhausted or terribly ill. It was difficult to tell. Her gray hair was like a bird's nest on her head and her jowls quivered as she lifted her head. When she opened her mouth, she belched so loudly that it startled the birds roosting on the sod house. As the birds scattered, both Maitland and Thomas caught a whiff of her breath.

Ale.

"Oh!" Maitland's head snapped back and she put her hand over her nose. "God's Bones, the woman is drunk!"

Artus simply lifted the stick as if to beat her for slandering the old woman. As Thomas stepped forward to snatch the child and shake the defiance right out of him, Maitland grabbed hold of Thomas and turned him around, pulling him with her as she walked several feet away.

"Thomas, we must be compassionate about this," she said, her voice low. "Scaring that child and old woman will not help. We must realize what has driven them to this point. From what your mother told me, life has been terrible for them, indeed. I do not blame them for not trusting us."

Thomas growled. "That lad needs a hand across his backside."

But Maitland shook her head, her hand on his big arm. "That will not help the situation," she said. Then, she eyed the provisions on the horses and an idea came to her. "I think I know what to do."

"Beat him until he screams?"

She rolled her eyes at him. "Nay," she said firmly. "Be serious. I meant the pork side that we brought... have your men build a fire and put it on a spit. Let's cook it. Mayhap the sight and smell of a decent meal will bring these children out. You know what they say – earn trust with a full belly."

He was looking at her, a rather amused expression on his face. "Is that what *they* say?"

She nodded seriously, struggling to keep the smile off her face. "That is exactly what they say."

"What idiot goes around speaking words like that?"

"Me."

The corners of his mouth twitched. "My apologies," he said. "I did not mean to call you an idiot."

She grinned at him, pointing to the provisions. "You may apologize by starting to cook that side of pork. Go and tell Tibelda what we are doing and she will help."

With a lingering glance at her, and a lingering grin, Thomas moved back to the horses and began to quietly issue orders to his men. Then, he made his way over to Tibelda, who was still rooted to the spot where she'd come to a halt when Artus had first appeared. He muttered something to the woman, who nodded faintly. As everyone began to move, Desmond came to stand next to his sister, surveying all that was before him.

"I do not think this is the happy reception you were expecting," he said.

Maitland turned to look at the drunk old woman and the boy standing next to her, still bearing the stick. "As I told Thomas, from what they have been through, I do not blame them for being suspicious."

Desmond nodded faintly before turning to her. "Speaking of suspicious," he said, his voice low. "Mae, you know I would never intrude in your affairs, but you must not think of Thomas as anything more than what he is."

She looked at him curiously. "What do you mean?"

Desmond sighed heavily, turning his head to see Thomas directing the men to remove the pork from the back of one of the horses. "Just that," he said quietly. "He seems quite attentive to you but, believe me, he is not someone you wish to become mixed up with."

Maitland tried to remain as neutral as possible. "I do not intend to become 'mixed up' with anyone," she said. "He has been kind to me and nothing more. Where did you get such an idea, Des?"

Desmond lifted his eyebrows. "I know Thomas de Wolfe," he said. "He has more troubles than you will ever know. He is the best knight I have ever seen, an outstanding commander, and treats his men well.

There is no finer warrior on the borders. But he has also been known to drink and gamble, and I cannot count all of the women he has taken to his bed. Now, he is betrothed to that… that meat poppet, Adelaide, so do not think to enter into any kind of clandestine relationship with him. It would only end badly for you."

By this time, Maitland was feeling ashamed and defensive. "I have no intention of entering into anything clandestine, Desmond," she said. "And I do not like you calling a woman a meat poppet, no matter how poorly behaved she is. That is a terrible thing to call any woman. Do you understand me?"

Desmond put up his hands. "I do not want to fight with you," he said. "I simply want to protect you. Do not believe Thomas has any altruistic intentions, and that he will break his betrothal with Adelaide to marry you, because it will not happen."

Hurt, and feeling confused, Maitland sighed sharply and turned away from her brother. "No one has said anything about marriage," she said. "Thomas and I have agreed to be friendly with one another and nothing more. Satisfied?"

Desmond looked at her suspiciously. "Then he brought it up? He asked you to do something unsavory?"

She shook her head. "Nay," she said. "He has been a completely gentle man in all ways. But I would be lying if I said there was no attraction between us. There is, and we have acknowledged it. But it goes no further."

"Are you certain?"

"I said so, didn't I?"

Desmond didn't press her, for he could see that he had offended her. But ever since the introduction of his sister to Thomas, Desmond could see the spark of attraction between them. There was something there, something obvious, and he had to stop it before it got started. He loved Thomas, but he knew the man too well when it came to women, well enough that he didn't want his sister to end up a concubine to a married knight. Even if the knight was married to Adelaide.

"Very well," he finally said. "I just want to make sure you are taken care of, Mae. I do not want to see you hurt."

Maitland didn't say anything. She was already hurt by his words, perhaps not because Desmond had taken the initiative to speak them, but perhaps because of the message he bore – *he has also been known to drink and gamble, and I cannot count all of the women he has taken to his bed*. That, in and of itself, had hurt her, thinking of Thomas with nameless, faceless women, showing them affection that she would never know from him.

Perhaps that was what hurt her most of all.

Moving away from Desmond, Maitland headed towards the tower as Thomas, Tibelda, and Thomas' men set up the fire pit. His soldiers were already building a big fire in the yard as some of them were still working on the gates. There was much going on to give them warmth, food, and security. But Maitland wasn't paying any attention to them. Her attention was on the big, squat tower.

And, perhaps, she was thinking of putting a little distance between her and Thomas.

Desmond's words had her needing to clear her mind a bit, and the tower was her destination. Over by the long outbuilding, Artus didn't stop her from entering the tower, but he did watch her with great suspicion. The tower, in fact, didn't even have a door, and Maitland looked around to see that it was propped up just inside the entry.

Inspecting it, she could see that the door was intact, but the hinges were warped. In fact, she didn't go any further, heading back out into the overgrown yard to find her brother and tell him about it. As Desmond went in to inspect the door to see if they could at least rehang it before they returned to Wark, Maitland headed over to the provisions that were being organized around the fire.

As she moved towards them, she could see Thomas and Tibelda as they worked with the men setting up the provisions. While Tibelda busied herself with the sacks, Maitland could see Thomas working alongside his men preparing the fire pit. She rather liked seeing that he was working with his men rather than simply standing there, ordering them about. Thomas seemed to be a man that was very much in the middle of his men, working alongside them, just as he had fought alongside them the night before. It seemed that he didn't expect them to do anything he wasn't willing to do, and that was an endearing quality.

But watching him also brought her back to what her brother told her as she watched his big body strain under the weight of a sack of dried beans that his mother had sent along. Had Desmond truly been trying to protect her by warning her off of Thomas? Desmond had always been very protective of her, even as children, but he'd also been controlling. He liked to have things done a certain way, always his way, and, perhaps, this was just another one of those times. Surely Thomas couldn't be a bad as Desmond said he was.

... could he?

She wondered.

"Where did Des go?" Thomas asked her.

Distracted from her thoughts, Maitland pointed off towards the tower. "There is no door on the tower," she said. "It is leaning on the wall just inside the entry. He went to take a look to see if it could be hung."

Thomas nodded, his attention shifting to the big side of pork. "We may have a problem with this," he said. "We can build a fire, but we didn't bring any iron rods or spit forks with us. If you want this side roasting over a fire, then we're going to have to find something that will support it."

Maitland turned to look at Artus and Queenie, still standing where they had left them, now watching everything that was going on with both interest and suspicion.

"I have a feeling they might not be so forthcoming with such things," she muttered, turning back to Thomas. "In fact, they might not even like us searching for them. If I distract them, can your men hunt round on the other side of this outbuilding? There has to be a kitchen yard around here. You might find what you're looking for."

Thomas pursed his lips, as if not thrilled by her suggestion. "That boy has a big stick," he pointed out. "I will be very unhappy if he uses it on you."

Maitland fought off a grin. "Trust me," she said. "If he uses it on me, it will be a very painful lesson for him. I am not beyond taking the stick from him and whacking him across his arse."

Thomas grinned, flashing that big dimple in his left cheek. "I believe you," he said. "Then you distract them and we shall see what we can find."

Maitland nodded and headed off, back to where Artus and Queenie were still standing. She tried to angle herself to stand over towards the tower so that when they looked at her, their backs would be to Thomas and his men as they snuck around the side of the outbuildings. As she hoped, Artus' gaze followed her until she came to a halt and, in her periphery, she could see Thomas and his men on the move.

"Artus," Maitland said. "I wonder if you will tell me how old you are."

Artus still had the stick, but it was down at his side now. "Why do ye want tae know?"

"Because I should like to be friendly with you. Won't you tell me?"

He eyed her. "I canna tell ye."

"Why not?"

"Because I dunna know."

Maitland nodded, looking at him closely. "I would say you are at least ten years of age," she said. "Have you always been here, at Edenside?"

Artus nodded reluctantly. "As long as I can remember," he said. "Ye said Kelso Abbey sent ye?"

"I did."

"Why?"

Maitland thought carefully on her answer. "Because I was told that some terrible people did terrible things to the children here," she said.

"I am an honest woman and I only want to help. So, they asked me to come and make sure the children of Edenside have the best of care."

Artus seemed to be more and more indecisive on his hostile stance. He looked at Queenie, who was so drunk that she could hardly stand, before returning his attention to Maitland.

"What do ye intend tae do?" he asked.

Maitland hoped they were making some progress. "The first thing I intend to do is make sure you have a hot meal," she said. "And then I intend to make sure you have clothing that is warm and a warm bed. Where do you sleep now?"

Thomas pointed to the outbuilding. "There."

"Why not the tower?"

"Because it doesna have a door."

Maitland nodded. "I saw," she said. "My brother is going to try and fix it."

Artus strained to look around her, where a big knight was in the doorway of the tower, looking at the hinges. "That's yer brother?"

"Aye."

"He's a *Sassenach*?"

Maitland smiled. "So am I," she said. "Mayhap that makes me different from the Scots who were cruel to you. I promise I will never be cruel to you and I hope that you will believe me someday.

Artus wasn't sure what to say to that. It was clear that he was becoming less hostile to her appearance and increasingly interested in what was going on. Out of the corner of her eye, Maitland could see Thomas and his men coming around the side of the outbuildings and they seemed to be holding a few things, though she couldn't make out what they were. Not wanting Artus to see them, she pointed towards the tower to keep his attention away from the covert operation behind him.

"I have not been inside the keep yet," she said. "Can you tell me about it? Is it inhabitable?"

Artus cocked his head. "Inhab… habit…"

"Inhabitable. It means livable. Can people live in it?"

The boy looked up at the tower while over by the gate, Thomas and his men had evidently found what they were looking for and were setting up a spit with the large pork side impaled on it.

"Only Laird Letty would sleep there," the boy said.

"Laird Letty? Who is that?"

Artus' face twisted, his expression turning both grim and painful. He shook his head as if unwilling, or unable, to answer her question.

"It was his home, with his wife," the boy said. Then, he pointed to the outbuilding. "This is *our* home. We sleep here."

Maitland looked at the dilapidated building. "We? As in you and the children?"

"Aye."

Maitland turned to look at the tower. "Laird Letty," she said. "Was he your guardian?"

Artus lowered his gaze. "He was our king. He told us he was our king."

Maitland began to suspect who Laird Letty was, especially by the expression on the lad's face. Everything Lady de Wolfe had told her came to mind, of the horrors of Edenside and the servant who was selling children, so she had a feeling that Laird Letty was that servant. She felt very sorry for Artus. Looking at his face, she could believe the terrible tales that she'd been told. The child was skinny, beaten, and woefully underdressed for the cold weather. Even in June, the weather here was cold. He didn't even have shoes.

Impulsively, she went to the lad.

"Artus," she said quietly. "I know what happened here. I was told how someone sold children and how some of the children died. I swear to you that it will never happen again. I am here now and I will take very good care of you. In fact, you will have the protection of these big *Sassenach* knights and you need not be afraid, not ever again. No one will hurt you."

Artus lifted his head, looking at her with big, if not suspicious, eyes.

Then, he began to back away, taking his stick and Queenie with him, dragging the raggedy old woman backwards as he lifted his stick, silently threatening Maitland not to follow him. She stood there, watching him sadly, as he stumbled back into the outbuilding and disappeared.

Perhaps it was just too much for the boy to absorb – a change in his life, and a very big change, following the horrors that he'd endured. Maitland truly didn't blame him for his mistrust. She wasn't sure what she could do to earn it other than what she was already doing – preparing food and repairing what they could of the place would be a start. She could only earn his trust by her actions and not her words.

Sometimes, words were simply useless.

The day began to deepen and as the children remained hidden, progress was made in several areas – the keep door was rehung, but it didn't fit particularly well and Desmond promised to send a smithy and a carpenter from Wark to set it properly. The same could be said for the gates of the complex, which had been secured for the most part but were badly in need of solid repairs. Lastly, the pork side was roasting beautifully over the open flame, sending the smell of roast meat into the air, that heavy and lovely scent.

To eat with the pork, Tibelda had managed to find a big iron pot in the scattered kitchen yard behind the outbuildings. She put the dried beans and enough water to cover them, and they soon began to bubble over the same fire that was roasting the pork. Maitland and Tibelda both went over what provisions they'd brought from Wark, carefully planning daily meals with what they had. Tibelda was excellent at managing provisions, so Maitland left her with them. While Tibelda watched over the simmering beans, Maitland went back to the tower to inspect it.

The tower had the unusual ground-floor entry and the door Desmond had rehung was heavy and fortified with iron, certainly sturdy enough to protect the ground-level entry. Immediately to her right was a stairwell, with steep spiral stairs that not only went up, but went down. She discovered that there was a vault below, which didn't have much in it by way of supplies or anything of use, but it did have a well, and the ground-level floor above it had one large room, which looked as if it had been used as a hall because there was a long table, two long benches, and a hearth that had an old bucket in it.

The spiral stairs led to a second floor above the ground level, and this floor contained two chambers with various broken beds, a broken trunk, and other items that could have been chairs or tables at one time. It was difficult to tell because everything was smashed and broken, but there were fortified chamber doors on this level. Even if the enemy made it into the tower, it would be very difficult to get past those doors. Unlike the entry door, they were intact and solid.

Finally, the stairwell led up to a roof that contained a very tiny wall walk around the tower, and there was a great iron basket, raised from the roof itself, that was for signal fires along the borders. All pele towers had them, only it appeared as if it had been many years since the signal fire of this particular iron basket had been used.

For a moment, Maitland simply stood there, looking out over the green countryside, thinking that Edenside was really no more than a ruined tower and a few outbuildings. Nothing grand, nothing honorable, where foundlings were tended and prepared for the world. This wasn't the noble venture she had expected or hoped for. In fact, the entire trip had been completely unexpected once she and Tibelda had reached Wark Castle, but there was one redeeming quality about this place –

It was hers.

Looking around, Maitland felt like a queen ruling over her people. All of this belonged to her and she was going to do the very best that she could, but that meant the children, wherever they were, were no longer going to sleep in that sod outbuilding. She wanted them in the keep where it was safe and warm, so she left the roof to go to the level below where there was broken furniture spread out in two chambers. Each chamber had a large hearth, and this was where they were all going to spend the night. She intended to clean it up, and warm it up, as best she could.

It was time to take action.

As the hours of the afternoon continued to trickle on into dusk, and the smell of meat continued to fill the air, Maitland took Tibelda with her as they moved their meager belongings into the tower. The men were still milling around outside, fixing gates and doors and inspecting the grounds, while Maitland and Tibelda turned their attention to the keep. They would now do what women did best.

Out came the lye soap and rags.

They had carried them with them from Newcastle and it was a good thing they did. The tower needed to be scrubbed, and scrubbed it was. Using the old bucket they'd found in the hearth on the ground level, they took the rags and soap and began to clean the floors of the dust, cobwebs, and bird droppings. Tibelda, a woman of very few words, was a hard worker and while she scrubbed floors, Maitland cleaned out the hearths on this level and eventually started a fire in one of them with a flint and stone she carried in her satchel and some of the broken piece of furniture that could surely not be repaired.

Soon, the old tower began to show signs of life again.

And that was how Thomas found her when he came hunting. Maitland's head stuck into the chimney of the hearth on the upper level of the tower, her hair was pulled away from her face and a sooty kerchief around her head. He just stood there a moment, watching her and realizing that when it came time to leave, he didn't want to go.

He simply didn't want to leave her.

"Do you see anything interesting up there?" he asked.

Maitland pulled her head out of the chimney, grinning when she saw the amused twinkle in his eyes. "Not really," she said. "Bird's nests, mostly. I was trying to clean it out a little before lighting a fire. I do not want to set the entire tower on fire."

Thomas looked across the landing to the second door, which was open. He could see the flickers from a flame inside as well as Tibelda as the woman vigorously scrubbed the floor.

"You managed to clean out that hearth," he said, gesturing. "It looks as if you will soon have this place cleaned and ready."

Maitland stood up, brushing off her hands. "I hope so," she said. "I do not want the children to sleep in the outbuildings tonight. Has Artus come out, by the way?"

Thomas shook his head. "Nay," he said. "He remains inside, which is where I suspect the rest of the children, if any, are hiding."

Maitland nodded, wiping at her face with the back of her hand. "Those are my thoughts, too," she said. "And what about that old woman? Queenie? Who do you suppose she is?"

He snorted. "Who can say?" he said. "But that belch she delivered was impressive."

Maitland lifted an eyebrow. "And that's another thing," he said. "Where do you suppose she got the money to buy ale? If she was a servant here, which I am assuming she must have been, then surely there is not any money left in this place. Clearly, there is nothing at all."

Thomas lifted his big shoulders. "If Edenside is supported by Kelso Abbey, then mayhap they have given them some money or provisions."

"I hope that is true," Maitland said. "But that lad looks as if he hasn't eaten in a month, yet the old woman has money enough to buy ale?"

"Mayhap she took the only money they had. But the lad seems quite protective over her."

It was all a perplexing mystery to be sure, one that Maitland could only shake her head at. "I suppose the only way to know the truth is to lure the children out of their hiding places," she said. "The pork should be ready to eat, as should the beans. Tibby?"

She called into the other chamber and the silent Tibelda set aside her scrubbing rags, wiping off her hands on her coarse skirt as she stood in the doorway. She lifted her chin at Maitland as if to answer the summons, and Maitland replied.

"It is time to see these children we have come to help," she said.

"Should you check to see if the beans are ready to eat? I am getting hungry, too."

Tibelda simply nodded her head and quickly made her way to the spiral staircase, which swallowed her up as she descended. Thomas turned to Maitland with his eyebrows lifted.

"She does not say much, does she?"

Maitland shook her head. "She has a rather severe speech impediment," she said. "A very heavy stutter at times, so she does not like to speak. But she is an excellent worker and a kind friend."

"You have known her long?"

"We were in Newcastle together for at least two years. We became friends when I saw some nuns harassing her for not saying her prayers properly. I defended her and now she is my shadow. Shall I tell you a secret?"

"Please do."

"She carries a big dirk beneath her skirts. And she is not afraid to use it."

Thomas laughed softly, his eyes glimmered at her. "Then I shall make certain to avoid angering her," he said. Then, he sobered, but the humor, the appreciation, never left his eyes. "I am quickly coming to see that you are the defender of the weak and less fortunate. That is a noble calling, my lady. And admirable."

There was that warmth again, something that Maitland had sensed from Thomas since nearly the beginning of their association. At first, she thought it was simply flirting, but now... now it was something different, something deeper. Something confusing but thrilling. It would be so easy to give in to his warmth, but Desmond's words kept ringing around in her head – *I cannot count all of the women he has taken to his bed.* Maitland had always thought she was too strong, too noble to fall victim to someone like that but in Thomas' case, she realized that she wasn't so strong when it came to him.

That made him a little frightening.

Unsure what to say to him that wouldn't begin that fluid repartee that started so easily between them, she simply nodded her head gratefully and turned for the stairwell. But Thomas shot out a big arm and blocked her path, his hand on the wall as his arm prevented her from moving forward. When she looked up at him, curiously, he smiled faintly.

"Will you answer a question for me?" he asked softly.

It was a tone that sent chills down her spine. "If I can."

Even though his arm was still up, somehow, he was moving closer to her. "I told you that if I had met you before that harpy came into my life, I would have pursued you," he said, his voice low and purring. "You said that you would have let me catch you. Is that really true?"

Maitland quickly averted her eyes, fearful of what would happen if she looked at him. "I said it," she said. "I meant it. May I pass now? There is much to do and Tibby cannot do it alone."

He dropped his arm but when she took a step to move past him, he grasped her left hand and lifted it to his lips, kissing it gently. It was enough to cause a gasp to come from Maitland's lips, feeling a chill run down her arm as her heart began to race. Breathing became a chore as she struggled to stay on an even keel.

"Please... do not do that," she whispered.

"Why not?"

"Because you said you came to Edenside with me as a friend and patron," she said. "A friend would not have taken the liberty you just took."

He didn't let go of her hand, although he knew she had a point. But he simply couldn't help himself. "I lied," he murmured, his mouth against her flesh. "God help me, I lied. Mae, I cannot help my attraction to you. I cannot help any of it."

Maitland was growing increasingly frightened, mostly because she knew if he sincerely pressed his attention, she wouldn't be able to fight him off. She wouldn't *want* to fight him off.

"Stop, Thomas," she begged softly. "*Please.*"

"Must I go through the rest of my life wondering what could have been between us?"

With her last shred of strength, she yanked her hand from his grasp, turning to him as she backed away. "It is infatuation and nothing more," she said. "You are in a miserable existence with Lady Adelaide and I am a fresh, new face. That is all it is. Would you truly treat me with such disrespect? Am I worth nothing more than a passing fancy? Please do not tempt me anymore, Thomas. I beg you. It is not fair to me."

With that, she fled down the stairs, leaving Thomas standing in the doorway, feeling ashamed and disappointed, more than he'd felt in a very long time. God, was she right? Was it really only infatuation and nothing more? He didn't think so. He'd been infatuated before and it never felt like this.

Never like this.

Maitland wasn't simply another pretty face; she was smart and creative and compassionate. She was everything a woman should be but, in that instant, he realized that she was right – he had been treating her with disrespect. If she'd let him, he would have bedded her, right now on the cold and dirty floor. God help him, he would have.

But it would not have been a mere conquest.

It would have been something more, something… *emotional.*

A sampling of what could have been.

Feeling contrite and weak, Thomas realized he couldn't do that to her. If he had a shred of respect for her, he couldn't treat her as he'd treated nearly every other woman who had ever caught his eye. She'd been absolutely right.

She deserved his respect.

Feeling disheartened as he hadn't felt in his entire life, Thomas followed Maitland's path down the stairs.

It was nearing sunset now, with streaks of orange and pink across the sky as the clouds moved through the coming dusk. The smell of the meat was very heavy in the air as he made his way over to the spit where the soldiers were starting to cut off succulent strips of pork and eating it. Maitland was there, as was Tibelda, and the women had been given small wooden cups to put their pork and beans in.

But Thomas stayed away from the fire. He couldn't face Maitland at the moment so it was best he simply avoid her. He was greatly confused by his words to her, and her subsequent reaction. As he headed over to his horse, kept away from the other animals, he caught movement out of the corner of his eye, seeing Maitland with her cup of beans and meat heading towards the outbuilding where Artus and Queenie had disappeared. As she moved away, he watched curiously.

He watched her with longing.

He simply couldn't help it.

For her part, Maitland knew Thomas was looking at her. She could feel his eyes upon her like a gentle touch, inviting and warm, like something she couldn't shake. But she didn't look at him in return because she was still trying to overcome their encounter in the tower. Part of her was wishing she hadn't walked away, so she kept her focus away from him. She couldn't let that weaker part dictate her morals or actions.

Therefore, she kept her focus on something other than Thomas' heated kiss – she focused on the children, hoping to lure them out of their hiding places, so she made her way to the doorway she had seen Artus and Queenie enter, standing just outside as she called out to the occupants.

"Artus?" she said. "I have a nice, hot meal for you and the others. I know you can smell the meat and you must surely be hungry. Please come out. This lovely food is for you."

There wasn't an immediate answer, but she could hear hissing back in the darkness of the outbuilding. In fact, there was a good deal of conversation and she thought she heard a child crying. Seizing the opportunity, she took a big bite of the pork.

"The food is delicious, Artus," she said, mouth full. "Won't you have some? There is so much of it and we cannot possibly eat all of it. Please come out and bring the children. Surely they would like to fill their bellies with this wonderful food."

There was more hissing and it was growing louder. Maitland leaned forward, trying to hear what they were saying, but she couldn't quite make out the words. She could, however, hear Artus as he whispered loudly in a somewhat pleading tone. But still, no children were forthcoming.

Thinking her plan to lure them out of their hiding places was not working, Maitland turned her back on the outbuilding, finishing off the piece of pork in her cup because, much like those children, she was quite hungry. She thought to, perhaps, return to the fire and consult Thomas and Desmond on what they should do to bring the children forth, but just as she began to walk away, she could hear something behind her.

Turning around, she saw a little girl with beautiful long, curly blonde hair standing just outside the door. She couldn't have been more than five years of age, a tiny little creature no bigger than a sparrow. Before Maitland could open her mouth and speak, the little girl rushed towards her, wiping at her teary eyes and smearing dirt across her pale cheeks.

"I'm hungry," she said. "I want a'bit."

Her Scottish accent was heavy, coupled by the fact that she was simply very little and not particularly articulate. Maitland immediately held out a hand to her.

"Then if you are hungry, you must come with me," she said. "I will make sure your belly is full. Will you come?"

The little girl nodded firmly, still wiping at her watery eyes, and reached out to take Maitland's hand. When Maitland clutched the little fingers, they were like ice. She was so little and so very cold.

"What is your name, lass?" Maitland asked.

The little girl simply looked up at her as if she didn't understand the question. Maitland was very gentle with her as she bent over to ask her again, but the words didn't come forth before she heard a voice by the outbuilding door.

"'Tis Pride, she is."

Maitland looked up to see Queenie standing there with a group of children around her. She didn't look so drunk any longer. In fact, she sounded rather sober. But Maitland wasn't really looking at her. She was looking at the children, shocked by what she saw.

It was worse than she thought.

She'd never seen such destitute children in her life, all of them in rags, all of them skinny and malnourished. They were all bunched up around Queenie and Artus, and the younger ones were weeping. Queenie pointed to the little girl in Maitland's grip.

"Her name is Dyana, but I call her Pride," she said. Then, she began to point to the children around her. "This is Lust, Gluttony, Sloth, Wrath, Greed, and Envy. Ye have Pride with ye. 'Tis the only way I can remember their names."

Maitland took a few steps towards the children, getting a better look at them. The sun was nearly down now, but the moon was bright. Bright enough to light up the yard and the landscape beyond the walls, with the smell of the river blowing on the evening breeze. The children were looking at her with a mixture of apprehension and hope – four boys, two girls, and then a third little girl in her grip. All of them dirty and ill-dressed for the cold. Truly, it was as tragic as Maitland had ever seen.

"But surely they have real names," she said. "What are their real names?"

While Queenie shrugged, Artus pointed to the two girls standing next to him. "This is Marybelle and Nora," he said. Then he moved to the boys standing nearby. "The tall one is Phin, and those two are Renard and Roland. They're brothers. Lust, Gluttony, Sloth, Greed, and Envy."

He pointed to them in the order he'd introduced them. Maitland thought it was a rather horrible thing to name these children after the seven deadly sins, but she didn't say so. It wasn't the time. Instead, she motioned them all towards the fire.

"Come along with me, children," she said. "We have food for everyone and a fire. You shall be warm and have a meal. Come along, now."

She turned around again, little Dyana still in hand, only to see that Thomas, Desmond and Tibelda had come up behind her and were watching the interaction. As soon as Maitland saw Thomas, she hissed pleadingly.

"Cloaks," she said. "Cloaks and blankets, whatever you may have with you. These children are freezing."

Thomas and Desmond nodded, turning back for the horses where cloaks had been packed for inclement weather, but Tibelda came forth, to Renard and Roland, respectively, because they were twins and not much older than Dyana was. They were tiny, dark-haired lads with bird-bones and Tibelda was surprisingly gentle with them as she took each boy by the hand and began leading them over to the fire.

The rest of the children, and Queenie, followed.

Thomas, Desmond, and the soldiers with them had managed to unpack several cloaks from their possessions and, soon, the children were wrapped up in them, sitting next to the fire and eating great pieces of roasted pork. Maitland and Tibelda, with their cups of beans and each with a wooden spoon they'd confiscated from the soldiers, moved from child to child, spooning the soft, delicious beans into their little mouths, feeding them like mother birds feeding their babies. There were a great many open mouths, starving, and they fed them carefully, making sure each child was fed.

But it was quite a process.

Artus was one of those with his mouth open for the hot beans. With pork hunks in both hands, he alternately stuffed himself on the meat and slurped down the beans. Maitland waited until she got a goodly portion of food into the lad before she started asking him more questions.

"What have you been living off of, Artus?" she asked. "Have the priests from Kelso come here to provide you with food?"

Artus' mouth was full as he spoke. "Sometimes," he said. "They come when they have somethin' tae give us. Sometimes they bring us sacks of barley and oats."

Maitland's gaze moved to Queenie, who was dozing by the fire. She didn't seem to be too interested in the food. "And you," she said. "Queenie? Why are you at Edenside?"

Hearing her name startled her out of her doze, and Queenie snorted as she became alert. "Me?" she said, wiping at her eyes. "I'm the cook."

"I see," Maitland said. "When was the last time the priests from Kelso brought food for these children?"

Queenie scratched her bristly head. "Weeks ago," she said. "The wee bairns have been livin' on oats not fit for the pigs. So ye know what I did? I took it with the barley they brought and I made ale. I give it tae the bairns tae fatten them up."

That explained how the old woman was drunk and it also explained why the children were so skinny – the old woman was making ale rather than feeding them the grains. She happened to glance at Thomas, who was standing back in the shadows with Desmond, listening to everything. When he saw that she was looking at him, he shook his head grimly, knowing they were both thinking the same thing.

These children have been neglected.

"From now on, we shall have proper food for the children," Maitland said evenly. "I know you have done your best with what you have been given, but I will worry about food for the children from now on. Tomorrow, we shall go through the stores and see everything there is, and I will plan accordingly."

Queenie looked as if she had no idea what Maitland was talking about. "Plan for what?"

Maitland lifted her shoulders. "Everything," she said frankly. "I shall make sure we have enough food stores, and I will make plans so that Edenside will be a productive place. I shall teach the children their bible verses, and I can even teach them skills. We can even make money someday, enough to help sustain us so the children can learn the value of good, hard work."

The little ones weren't paying much attention to the conversation as they continued to eat, but Queen and Artus, the eldest child out of the group, were clearly perplexed. In their minds, there wasn't anything beyond the daily struggle to survive, so Maitland's words were completely foreign to them. Queenie eventually went back to dozing and Artus went back to eating as Maitland made her way over to Thomas and Desmond.

They had been standing well back and out of the way, observing everything with critical eyes. The conversations and the actions of the women had been touching as well as orderly and nurturing. It was clear they were used to dealing with children. As Maitland approached, they looked at her with interest.

"Well?" Desmond whispered loudly. "What are you going to do, Mae? You've gotten yourself into a mess."

Maitland was quite calm about it. "Only for now," she said. "We shall sleep in the tower tonight where it is warm and, tomorrow, I will go about assessing the grounds. We will see what we have to work with, but I know even now that the provisions we brought will not be enough. Thomas, can you send us a few craftsmen along with the carpenter and smithy for the doors? I will need people to build beds and fortify the gates, and even more people to help build livestock pens for the animals. I have not seen any pens or fences, and I would be willing to wager there are not any in the kitchen yard."

Thomas, who had seen the kitchen yard, shook his head. "There is very little in the kitchen yard at all," he said. "Des and I will head back tomorrow morning, but we will leave the soldiers here. They can help you start getting things repaired around here."

Maitland nodded gratefully. "I need rope and fabric for beds and mattresses, and clothing. God only knows how badly these children need clothing. Will you see what your mother can send me? I shall be grateful for anything she can donate. She will understand."

Thomas looked out over the children huddled by the fire. "Sloth,

Greed, Gluttony, Pride, Wrath, Envy, and Lust," he muttered. "If there was ever a place sincerely in need of salvation, it would be this place. I would say you have your work ahead of you, Lady Bowlin."

Maitland knew that, but she'd never been one to back down from a challenge. Before she could reply, however, the soldiers who had been over near the gates, watching the landscape beyond, suddenly began calling out the approach of riders. No one panicked, but a couple of the soldiers near the fire pit drew their swords. Most of the children were too involved in their food to notice, but Artus did and he tensed, preparing to grab the children and run with them.

It wouldn't have been the first time he'd had to do so.

But no one moved and no one ran. When the soldiers at the gate determined there was no threat, they threw the big iron bolt on the gates and opened them, admitting a rider. As the man moved in the direction of the fire where everyone was standing, Thomas recognized him.

The soldier was from Wark.

"What is it?" Thomas demanded as he rushed to the man with Desmond on his heels. "What has you riding across the borders in the darkness?"

The man reined his horse to a halt and the frothing animal tossed its head, throwing foam. "Your father has sent me, my lord," he said. "Lord de Wolfe demands you return to Wark Castle immediately. Northumbria was killed in an ambush earlier today."

Thomas didn't react outwardly, but Desmond did – his eyes widened and he audibly gasped.

"Northumbria is *dead*?" he hissed. "What happened? Who ambushed him?"

The soldier leaned forward on his saddle, lowering his voice. "Survivors of Northumbria's party said they were attacked by reivers," he muttered. "Your father needs you back at Wark immediately, my lord. He says you must return tonight."

Truth be told, Thomas wasn't all that shocked. Surprised at Northumbria's death, of course, but not shocked that it had happened. "Are they sure it was reivers?" he said. "They do not normally ambush and kill. Their purpose is raiding and looting, not murder."

"Unless it was the men you swept over the cliff into the Tweed last night," Desmond said. "You know that group to the east has been known to murder for profit. It could have been them."

Thomas was aware of that. "The Thurrock *Cú*," he said quietly. "I thought that might be the group last night who raided Coldstream and told my father so. We know they watch Wark and other outposts of my father's, but an attack from them against travelers is rare. But mayhap they were watching when Northumbria departed Wark for home and decided he would be a good target."

"It is a distinct possibility."

"And now Edmund is dead."

It was still difficult to believe, even as he said it. In fact, Thomas was having some difficulty grasping the sudden turn that life had taken. With Edmund gone, that meant Adelaide was now the sole heiress and commander of Northumbria's vast armies and the marriage, with no date set, would now be pushed upon him.

Thomas knew that before he even spoke to his father.

Whatever his father and Northumbria had discussed during the earl's visit to Wark didn't matter now. Thomas was certain his father, even if he'd begged Northumbria to break the betrothal, would now ask Thomas to do his duty, to marry Adelaide, and inherit a vast empire that would keep the northern ties of de Wolfe strong and wide.

Everything he'd ever hoped for his life was now ended.

He turned to Desmond.

"I will return home immediately, but you remain here with Lady Bowlin for the night," he said. "Make sure she and the children are adequately protected and then return on the morrow. I am sure I will have need of you."

Desmond nodded, but Thomas couldn't even look at Maitland as he moved swiftly to his horse. He couldn't say goodbye. Looking at her, and speaking to her, would emphasize the tremendous disappointment he felt at the moment, how the death of a man could force him into a lifetime of misery.

And a lifetime without Maitland.

Did he love the woman? He'd only known her a couple of days. He'd known love, once, so he knew he wasn't in love with her – yet. But given more time with her, he was fairly certain that he could be. He had no reason to believe that, given time, he would *not* love her. From the beginning, he'd felt differently towards her than almost any woman he'd ever met other than Tacey. But Tacey was in his past. He only wished Maitland could be in his future. Attraction for her had turned to interest, and interest to disappointment.

What was it he'd said to her?

Must I go through the rest of my life wondering what could have been between us?

The message from the weary Wark soldier only a few minutes ago had answered that question.

Yes.

CHAPTER TEN

Wark Castle

"HOLD THE BANDAGE tighter," Jordan commanded. "Keep her arm up above her head."

The servants were trying very hard to carry out Lady de Wolfe's orders, but it was difficult when the woman they were trying to help was being so difficult.

At least, she was trying to be difficult without actually resisting too much. With Adelaide, it was mostly noise and weeping and some wriggling, but nothing to suggest she was really trying too hard to pull away. She was letting Jordan and the maids inspect her cut arms and wrists, and weakly struggling when they wrapped them to stop the bleeding, but not much beyond that.

She was in the midst of a performance of a lifetime.

Jordan was trying to be sympathetic. God help her, she was genuinely trying because the lass had only just received word that her father had been killed in an ambush. The man's battered body had been brought back to Wark Castle, where it was placed in the cool vault until arrangements could be made to return the remains to Kyloe Castle for burial. Adelaide had been told of her father's death and promptly collapsed, whereupon she was brought to her chamber to recover.

Her German nurse, a woman who was rarely seen and even more rarely heard, remained with her in case she awoke, but when next Jordan and William realized, the German nurse was screaming that Adelaide had cut her wrists and had smeared the blood on her fine bed curtains. Why she smeared the blood there, neither Jordan nor William could guess, but she'd done it before. They could only assume it was for dramatic effect. Now, Jordan and several female servants were bandaging up Adelaide's arms as her nurse stood on the landing outside the chamber and loudly wept. William stood just inside the doorway watching everything that was happening.

Sincerely, it was a nightmare.

"My father," Adelaide wept listlessly. "My dear and sweet father! Why did they kill him? And where is Thomas so he might comfort me? I need him!"

Although William did not blame the woman for her grief, her manner of dramatics had him on edge. Perhaps he was used to women who were more mannerly and in control of their emotions, which Adelaide was not. She wailed and writhed weakly on the bed as Jordan and the maids tightened up her bandages. When she finally seemed tightly wrapped, Jordan dared to leave her post by the woman's side and went to her husband. Sighing heavily, she pulled William into a corner of the chamber, away from the German nurse on the landing and away from Adelaide's bed.

She didn't want to be overheard.

"She's not cut herself deeply enough tae do any real damage," Jordan muttered to her husband. "'Tis just enough to be bloody."

William was trying not to react with complete and utter disgust. "I am truly sorry for Edmund's death," he whispered. "But what she has done…"

"What she has done is try tae play upon our sympathies," Jordan said quickly. "Make no mistake, English; as sorry as I am for the death of her father, she is usin' it as an excuse tae gain attention from us, and particularly, from Tommy. Can ye hear her callin' for him?"

William nodded. "I do, indeed," he murmured. "I have sent for him. I expect him shortly, as it is not a long ride from Edenside, but we have a crisis on our hands now. With Northumbria dead, Adelaide is now the head of a very powerful army. That unstable girl controls an empire."

"What are ye sayin'?"

It was William's turn to sigh heavily as he brought forth words he didn't want to speak. But he'd had time to think on the situation and the words, unfortunately, were necessary.

"Tommy is betrothed to her," he said simply. "Northumbria would not break the contract, Jordan. I have not had the opportunity to tell you of our conversation, but I asked him to break the betrothal and he refused. That is why he fled this morning, because of our rather contentious conversation. The betrothal *is* intact."

Jordan looked at her husband, long and hard. Somehow, she sensed he didn't seem so angry about the fact that Northumbria had refused to break the betrothal. Knowing her husband as she did, God help her, she knew what he was thinking.

"Ye're goin' tae make Tommy marry her, are ye not?"

"He would be the biggest land holder in the north."

Jordan tried to become angry but she didn't want to explode in front of Adelaide. She bared her teeth and balled her fists, struggling not to lash out at her beloved husband. Still, she couldn't help the passion in her actions or in her voice.

"But the man would have tae marry *that!*"

She was pointing to Adelaide now, so very infuriated. But in the same breath, she understood her husband's position perfectly. Even if they could somehow break the betrothal, the chance of Adelaide marrying someone who would assume that great power and create a great upheaval in the north was always a grim possibility. The king had favorites that would salivate to have such wealth in England.

It would create a crisis of power, which was what her husband was trying to avoid.

"Let us be realistic," William said, sounding as if he were trying to rationalize the situation. "We have been very fortunate that all of our children have found love matches. If Thomas does not... most men do not find love matches. It is the truth. Marriage is made for alliances, not love."

Jordan didn't believe him for an instant. "*Ye* married for love."

"But you were also a chieftain's daughter. We have been through this. What happened with us was very fortunate."

"But Tommy willna be so fortunate."

William just looked at her. He didn't have to speak because Jordan already knew his answer. She was thinking of her son and his happiness. William was thinking of the future of his entire family as well as Thomas', as the next Earl of Northumbria. It was an incredibly powerful position, one that would make Thomas a major player in the north, even more than his brothers were.

As Scott and Troy had once said, on the day that they were all trying to talk Thomas into the betrothal with Adelaide, the older de Wolfe brothers had all made good for themselves with properties and wealth. But even all of those properties, and all of that wealth, couldn't compare to what Thomas would have when he married Adelaide de Vauden.

The Earldom of Northumbria.

"He will thank me for this one day," William finally said. "Mayhap he will not find happiness with his marriage; mayhap it will only be tolerable for him. It is an unfortunate thing, but he will make a fine earl and he is badly needed, Jordan. I will not live forever, and when I go, I want to make sure my sons, and my family, are protected and the family legacy shall live on."

Jordan could feel great disappointment on behalf of her son, disappointment that he would sacrifice his happiness for wealth and position.

"Ye werena so determined for him tae marry Adelaide before the death of the earl," she said in a low voice. "Ye told Tommy as much. Ye told *me* as much, English. Ye even spoke tae Northumbria tae see if the betrothal could be broken. Why the change of heart now? What has changed?"

William's gaze traveled to Adelaide, who lay upon her blood-smeared bed with maids all around her. "Up until this morning, Northumbria was still in control of his earldom," he said quietly. "A man with a reasonable mind was in command. Tommy inheriting the earldom was still years away, far enough away that, mayhap, a suitable replacement could be found should the betrothal be broken."

"But now there is no more time for that."

William shook his head. "Nay," he said, his gaze returning to his wife. "We *have* no more time. That madwoman over there is in control, but more than that, she is alone. When Edward discovers that Northumbria is without an earl, she becomes the most valuable commodity in England. God only knows who we will have on our doorstep if Edward has his way, and it is my intention to control the situation."

"With yer own flesh and blood."

William's jaw ticked, torn on a decision he knew he had to make. "That has been my intention from the beginning," he said quietly. "It was a moment of weakness for me to think otherwise, Jordan. I was thinking with my heart and not my head when I suggested breaking the betrothal. I was angry because I felt deceived by Edmund. But I've had time to think, to understand what is best for us all – Tommy *must* marry the girl. He must do it now before Edward catches wind of Northumbria's death."

Jordan sighed faintly. "Ye sent a man for him, did ye not? He'll be here in a few hours. Ye can tell him tae his face that ye've changed yer mind. I wouldna be surprised if he doesna agree with ye."

"He will do what he is told."

Jordan looked at her husband. In truth, he was an old man. He'd been involved in the politics of England for over sixty years and he'd been making difficult decisions for nearly as long. He hadn't achieved that longevity by being weak or fickle, and she knew that he'd been trying to gain something quite valuable for Thomas with the marriage to Northumbria's heiress. That had been his goal from the beginning. It would have been a perfect situation if the heiress hadn't been a madwoman.

Jordan wondered if her own feelings were causing her to neglect her son's political and financial future. Did she want her son to find love and happiness over financial gain that would make him a very important man in England?

It was the worst decision she and William had ever had to make.

Confused, and saddened, Jordan turned away from William, making her way over to the bed where Adelaide lay, a bandaged arm over her eyes as she dozed. Seeing that there was nothing more she could do at the moment, Jordan whispered instructions to the servants, to watch over the woman and to send for her if needed, before motioning to William to follow her from the chamber. Together, they quit the chamber as the weeping German nurse slipped in.

In silence, they moved to the chamber across the landing, only to see that Caria and her nurse were missing. Thinking they were probably in the yard somewhere, as it was a mild day outside, Jordan and William took advantage of the vacancy of the chamber to catch up on some much-needed rest. It was what they had been trying to do when panicked servants had told them about Northumbria's tattered escort.

In fact, William was almost afraid to close his eyes, afraid that something else would happen. Wark had been chaos since nearly the moment they arrived, so he forced himself to lay down next to his wife on the very large, comfortable bed that belonged to Thomas. This was his chamber, after all, loaned to his parents, William no sooner shut his eye than Jordan was gently shaking him awake.

"English," she whispered. "Get up. Tommy has returned."

Opening his eye, William could see that it was now dark outside. That suggested a significant amount of time had passed, but it hardly felt like any time at all.

Rubbing a hand over his face, he sat up wearily, giving a yawn. He could see that the chamber door was open and a soldier stood there, one Jordan quickly sent away and shut the panel. William shook his head.

"I did not even hear anyone knock on the door," he said. "How long have I been asleep?"

Jordan was running her hands over her pinned hair, smoothing back the strands. "Several hours," she said. "It is supper time. Tommy just rode intae the bailey, so let us go down tae greet him."

William stood up, more tired now than he was when he'd lain down. "Nay," he said quietly. "I will go. You go in to Adelaide and sit with her. I will deal with Thomas."

Jordan turned to look at him. "I should go with ye," she said. "Tommy wouldna dare fight back if I'm there."

William simply shook his head, running his fingers through his mostly-gray hair. He still had a head full of hair, but it had been very dark once, thick and wavy. Oddly enough, he didn't have a vast amount of wrinkles for a man his age, so it was really the hair color that gave him away more than anything, and it had probably gotten far more white during Thomas' betrothal.

The situation was aging him rapidly.

"I will go alone," he reiterated, going to the door. He put his hand on the latch, pausing, and there was some lethargy in his movements. His expression turned wistful. "It is times such as this where I miss Kieran. We look at the situation as Thomas' parents, but Kieran had the ability to look at it from another angle. It was always the right angle and he was always able to advise me. God, I miss him so much."

Kieran Hage had been William's best friend and second-in-command until five years ago when the man had passed away. Kieran had been the most enormously powerful man on the border, a knight of incredible skill and a vast amount of wisdom. Kieran and William, and a third knight, Paris de Norville, had squired together at Northwood Castle and had literally spent their entire lives together. Their children had all intermarried, and the three men themselves had married cousins from the same family – Jordan, Jemma Scott Hage, and

Caladora Scott de Norville. They were all first cousins and the marriages irrevocably made the knights family.

The three knights had been closer than brothers, bonded by blood and marriage in the end. While Paris still commanded at Northwood Castle, Kieran had gone to Castle Questing with William when the man assumed his new earldom nearly five decades earlier, and William had come to depend greatly on Kieran. *His brother.* There were times when he still wept for the loss of Kieran, whom he'd held in his arms as the man died. It had been one of the most difficult moments of William's life and something he still hadn't recovered from.

He never would.

Jordan knew that. Every time William brought up Kieran's name, she knew he was feeling particularly emotional and vulnerable. Though she loved her husband deeply and they shared a bond that few couples did, she knew that the bond William had shared with Kieran had also been powerful and deep. When William lost Kieran, he'd lost a piece of his soul. Quietly, she made her way over to him, putting her gentle hands on him in a show of support and sympathy.

"I know," she whispered, hugging him. "He left a hole with us that will never be filled. Mayhap, ye should consult with Paris about this. Ye know he'll tell ye the truth."

William wriggled his eyebrows. "I *have* spoken to Paris about this," he said. "You know that Paris sees the logical side of things. He believes that Tommy should marry Adelaide. To have Tommy as Northumbria would bring great stability to the region."

"And he knows that Adelaide is an unstable lass?"

William nodded, pursing his lips irritably as he opened the door. "He knows," he said. "His solution was to tell Tommy to keep her drunk all the time so she would be easier to manage."

Jordan opened her mouth in outrage, but that sounded very much like something Paris, the perpetually arrogant and flippant man, would say. In fact, she realized that she had to fight off a grin.

"That is *not* funny," she said. "And not helpful."

William stepped through the door. "Helpful enough that I may end up suggesting it to Thomas myself."

As he walked away, he could hear his wife calling after him. "Dunna ye dare!"

He knew she was smiling.

"Tommy!"

Thomas had no sooner dismounted his horse than he heard Caria's cry. Turning around, he saw her running into the stable yard, heading right for him. Opening his arms to her, he scooped her up.

"What are you doing out at night?" he asked, even though the whole of Wark was brightly lit with torches against the cold spring night and there were people all around. "You should be in your chamber, eating sup."

Caria's arms were wrapped around his neck. "I was waiting for you," she said, and Thomas caught a glimpse of her nurse over by the yard entrance. "I knew you were coming back, so I was waiting. Did you go into Scotland?"

Grabbing his saddlebags with one hand, he carried them in one arm and Caria with the other as he headed out of the stable yard.

"I did," he said. "I went to Edenside. Do you remember hearing us speaking on it last night at sup? It is a foundling home. Do you know what that is?"

Caria thought on that. "Is it sinful folk?"

He shook his head. "Not really," he said. "It is for children who do not have mothers or fathers. I met them today."

Caria's face lit up. "Can I meet them, too?"

He shrugged. "I do not see why not," he said. "But we must ask Matha and Poppy."

They were in the outer bailey now, heading towards the great hall. Light streamed from the lancet windows and the ventilation holes at the roofline, with smoke billowing from the chimney and out into the night. But Caria wasn't looking at the hall or anything else; she was still fixed on Thomas and the idea of the foundlings.

"Why do these children have no mother or father?" she asked. "What happened to them?"

Thomas glanced at the child; technically, she was a foundling, too, with both parents dead, only she didn't know that. Caria had no idea who she really was and probably never would if his father had anything to say about it.

"They must have died," he said. "I did not ask them what happened to their parents, but I am sure they must have died. Now they live at Edenside and Lady Bowlin is going to take care of them."

Caria remembered Lady Bowlin and how she'd described how a penny could feed the poor. "Lady Bowlin is nice," she said.

"Indeed, she is."

They were drawing near the hall now and Caria seemed surprised to see just how close they were, as if only noticing it for the first time. Her arms around his neck tightened.

"Tommy," she said slowly. "I… I must ask you something."

"What is it?"

"I want to live here with you."

He came to a halt. "We have been through this before, Caria," he said. "You must return to Castle Questing with Matha and Poppy. Think how heartbroken they would be if you did not live with them."

Caria frowned, looking very much like Tacey in her expression. "But I want to stay here with you," she said earnestly. "You have no one to take care of you and I could do that."

He smiled. "And you would do a remarkable job," he said. "But it would hurt Matha and Poppy terribly if you came to live here. Would you be so cruel to them?"

She was beginning to tear up. "Can I stay for just a little while?"

Thomas kissed her cheek. "Mayhap you can stay a little while," he said. "The next time I go to Edenside, mayhap you and Matha can come with me so you can meet the children. Would you like that?"

Caria nodded, wiping at her eyes. "I would," she said, pushing the issue. "But I do not want to go back to Castle Questing. Will you ask Matha if I can stay with you?"

From the corner of his eye, Thomas caught sight of William as his father emerged from the inner bailey, heading towards the great hall. Knowing he and his father had much to discuss, he kissed Caria on the cheek and set her on her feet.

"We will discuss this later," he said. "I must speak with Poppy now. If you want to wait for me, I shall eat supper with you."

Caria nodded, still wiping her eyes, as her nurse snuck up behind her and took her by the hand to lead her away. Thomas watched her go, heading back to the keep and back to the big bedchamber, even waving at her when she turned her sad face to him. She managed to pass William on her way to the keep, who put his hand on her dark head as he passed by.

"Why is Caria weeping?" William asked as he drew close. "What is it now?"

Thomas smiled weakly. "She is a weepy one."

"She is."

"She wants to live with me at Wark."

William snorted. "She speaks of that constantly," he said. "Your mother and I have denied her, but she is headstrong. She will not stop asking."

Thomas thought on Caria's strong-willed personality. "Her mother was not that way at all," he said. "Remember? Tacey was so timid and shy. And she was so tiny – I think Caria is going to be her mother's size. Even now, she looks smaller than her age."

William nodded, thinking of the tiny little girl who had been so remarkably strong. "She may be small, but she is mighty," he said. "I have no doubt that little Caria will grow up to do great things."

Thomas could hear Caria in the distance as her nurse tried to take her into the keep, squealing unhappily about something. He grinned.

"She would make an excellent Princess of Wales," he said. "Or even a queen if you marry her off to some Saxon king. Think of the Welsh bloodlines that would take flight through the nobility of the German kingdoms. She would become the mother of nations."

"Possibly," William said. "But I am not certain it is safe to ever divulge her bloodlines, especially with Edward the way he is at the moment. If he knew we had a Welsh princess in our midst, he could bring the whole of England down around me and accuse me of being a traitor. He would tear up the north to get to me and to Caria. Which is why you and I must have a serious discussion about Northumbria's death."

Thomas immediately sobered. He knew what his father was going to say. He'd resigned himself to it during the ride that had brought him home from Edenside. He knew this discussion was coming and he was prepared, as difficult as it was for him to accept.

"I know, Papa," he said quietly. "I must marry Adelaide."

William wasn't surprised at Thomas' response. The man wasn't a fool. He knew what William did and, for once, they were thinking alike when it came to this betrothal. But still, there was something inside of him, buried deep, that made him feel so damned guilty about it.

"Aye," he replied honestly. "Tommy, please know that this gives me no pleasure. All of my children have found happiness in their marriages and I had sincerely hoped that for you. But it seems as if it is not to be. Right now, the Northumbria earldom is without a strong commander at its head, and the moment Edward hears of Edmund's death, my guess is that he will have a dozen Scots and French nobleman lined up to assume the earldom. We cannot allow that to happen, lad. That would throw the north into turmoil."

Thomas groaned faintly, folding his big arms across his chest in a gesture that looked a good deal like his father. "It was only this morning that you were apologizing for the situation," he said. "I received the impression that you spoke to Northumbria about it."

William nodded. "I did," he said. "I tried to force him into breaking the betrothal, but he would not do it. I was hoping that, with time, I could present him with suitable candidates to take your place, and that was my intention. But with his death today, we no longer have that luxury of time. It *must* be you, Tommy."

They were standing on the steps leading to the great hall and, suddenly, Thomas felt inordinately weary. His father's words were as he'd expected but, still, the reality of them was almost too much to bear. He sank down onto the top step as his father followed suit. Together, they simply sat there, letting the news of what must happen sink in.

"What about Troy's son, Andreas?" Thomas asked. "He is much closer in age to Adelaide and he is a de Wolfe."

"Andreas is a remarkable knight, but he has much to learn. To give him a powerful earldom would be a mistake at this point. Northumbria needs an experienced man."

"What about Brodie de Reyne?" Thomas was thinking of all of the single knights he knew. "The man has served Troy for many years and lost his wife several years ago. He is a son of Baron Hartlepool of Throston Castle. The House of de Reyne is a major house in the north."

William was nodding before Thomas even finished. "And they are great allies," he said. "I knew Brodie's grandfather, Creed de Reyne, as a young man and he was an excellent knight and a wise commander."

"Then Brodie is a candidate?"

William shrugged. "If you can convince Adelaide to see him, and to agree to him, and if Brodie agrees, then the marriage would have my blessing. But I must ask you a question."

"What is it?"

"Would you really see the most powerful earldom in Northumberland in Brodie's hands? Or would you rather control such power?"

Thomas thought on his older brother's knight, a man who had been with Troy for at least twenty years. Brodie de Reyne was close to Thomas' age, in fact. They were friends, of course, and Brodie had been a talented and skilled knight, much as his father and grandfather had been, but his father had him thinking about giving over Northumbria to Brodie.

In fact, Thomas saw a major issue with that scenario – Brodie would probably end up hating him for saddling him with a madwoman like Adelaide, and that didn't sit well with Thomas. As much as he didn't want to be married to the woman, he wouldn't wish her on his worst enemy.

Or a dear friend.

"I suppose I could not do that to Brodie or to Andreas," he muttered after a moment. "If either one of them married her, he would end up hating me. But, damnation, Papa… I wish there was an easy answer to this situation. Of all the times for this to happen."

William looked at him. "What do you mean?"

It occurred to Thomas that he really didn't want to explain that comment, but it wasn't as if he could take it back or his father could unhear it. Struggling not to feel foolish, he waded into unfamiliar territory.

"I mean…" He stopped, paused, and then started again. "I mean that if this whole betrothal with Adelaide hadn't happened, I might have chosen another lady for my wife."

"Who?"

"Desmond's sister, Lady Bowlin."

William's brow furrowed. "The Beguine?"

Thomas nodded. But when he saw the expression of disbelief on his father's face, he felt very much like explaining just so his father would know he wasn't foolish. "She is unlike any woman I have ever met, Papa. She's brilliant, so very brilliant, and she's kind and compassionate. She would make a Lady de Wolfe that I could be so proud of, and the truth is that I never thought I would say those words about anyone. Up until two days ago, Tacey was the only wife I had ever wanted. But now… damn the unfortunate timing, but Lady Bowlin has made me change my mind. If I was not betrothed to Adelaide, I would marry Lady Bowlin tomorrow."

William looked at his son with some astonishment before puffing out his cheeks and turning away. It was a good deal to absorb.

"Truly, Thomas?" he finally said. "In the past eight years, you have lived a wild life from England to The Levant and back again and, all the while, Desmond de Ryes was holding the key to your happiness?"

Thomas smiled weakly. "I am as surprised as you are," he said. "I knew Des had a sister but nothing more than that. Many men have sisters, including me, so there was no reason to think Desmond's sister was any different from the rest. But she is, Papa... she *is*."

"And you... *like* her?"

"A great deal."

William pondered that irony for a moment, looking up and seeing the glittering stars spread across the heavens.

"I was lamenting to your mother tonight about the absence of Kieran to counsel me in this time of great decision," he said. "Someone told me once that the stars in the heavens are really the souls of every great warrior who has ever lived. Achilles, Alexander the Great, Charlemagne... all of them are up there, looking down upon us, and I know for a fact that your Uncle Kieran is up there, looking down upon us as well. Someday, I will join him, and you will look up at the stars with your own son and tell him of your father. I wonder what you will tell him, Tommy. That he was the greatest knight you ever knew? Or that he forced you to marry a woman you did not love for strategic gain?"

Thomas was looking at his father seriously. "I will tell him that my father was the greatest *man* I have ever known," he said. "I know I was born well after your prime as a knight, and I never knew you with two good eyes, but you are the greatest man I have ever known, Papa, and I am very proud to be your son. I know... I know there are times when I have disappointed you. From the time when I was *Dhiib aleasifa*, and then I returned and served the Duke of Dorset until I grew bored of that. It took me some time to find my way home, but I *did* find my way because I knew you would be here, waiting for me. Do you know *why* I eventually came home?"

William cocked his head slightly. "Because you missed your family?"

Thomas took a deep breath and shook his head. "I did, but that was not the real reason," he said, feeling a lump in his throat. "It was because I was with Kevin Hage when he was told that his father had passed away. The look on Kevin's face, Papa... I could see such raw pain. Kevin knew he had disappointed his father and he never had the chance to tell him how sorry he was. Even now, I know he is happy with his new wife and children, but that pain of not telling his father how sorry he was is something that will never leave him. I never, ever want that to happen to us, Papa, so for everything I have done that hurt you, please know how sorry I am. I can be stubborn and foolish, but when I was trying to run from this betrothal and you told me how disappointed you were in me... you were right. I was a horrible disappointment and I am sorry."

William had tears streaming down his face as he listened to his youngest son lay himself wide open. It was so unlike him and such a difficult thing to do. Reaching out, he put his big hand on his son's stubbled face.

"Fathers say things that they do not mean sometimes," he said hoarsely. "I told you that you had disappointed me because I was frustrated with you, but I should not have been so cruel. You are so much like me, Tommy – proud, stubborn, determined to do things your own way. That is why I understand you so well. But you have never truly disappointed me. Every decision you made in your life, every path you took, has made you the man you are today and I could not be prouder of you. Never forget that."

Thomas was teary eyed at this point, wiping at his eyes so he wouldn't openly weep. "I needed to hear that," he said. "I needed to hear that I have made you proud in some way."

"In *all* ways."

"I hope to continue that," Thomas said. "And if you want me to marry Adelaide, then I shall do it. But I will be honest... I wish that it was Mae I was betrothed to. I never thought I would be happy again, but with her... I know I could have been."

William put his hand on Thomas' shoulder, a show of support and sympathy. "I am sorry, Tommy, I truly am," he said. "I do want you to be happy, but sometimes we must make decisions that do not include personal happiness, only the greater good."

Thomas sighed heavily. "And you believe this is for the greater good?"

"Unfortunately, I do."

Thomas didn't question him any further. He knew his father was making the best, and perhaps the only, real decision he could make no matter what it personally cost Thomas. It wasn't that he didn't care, because he did... but sometimes a sacrifice was needed for the greater good of all.

And that sacrifice would be Thomas.

"Very well," Thomas said. "If you think it is best, then I shall comply. Where is Adelaide now?"

William wiped the tears from his face. "In the keep," he said. "She cut her arms again when she heard of her father's death. Your mother is with her."

Thomas resisted the urge to roll his eyes at more of Adelaide's dramatics which, in this case, were understandable. She had seemed inordinately attached to her father. Now, the subject turned from deeply emotional things to the immediate future facing them.

"I see," he said. "And what of Edmund? Where is he?"

"In the vault. We must transport him back to Kyloe Castle for burial."

"I was told that the reivers ambushed him and killed him."

William nodded. "That is true, at least from what the witnesses have told us," he said. "I think you and I have some strategic planning to do. We know the reivers have a hiding place somewhere near Etal and I think it is time we cleaned them out for good, especially after the death of Northumbria."

Thomas couldn't agree more. "Indeed," he said. "Let me go see to

Mother and Adelaide, and I shall meet you in the hall later to discuss this very thing."

With that, he stood up, pulling his father to his feet. For a moment, they simply looked at each other, smiling, until William grasped him behind the neck and kissed him on his dimpled cheek. So much had been said this night, so many words of worth, that it had been an important moment for them both. The youngest, foolish son of The Wolfe had grown up and was becoming a wise and thoughtful man of his own.

But William couldn't help thinking, as they walked to the keep, that all of that wisdom and growth would be wasted on a woman like Adelaide de Vauden.

It was a terribly disappointing thought.

"MY LORD!" ADELAIDE cried out weakly. "You have come!"

Thomas had just entered her lavish bower, immediately noticing his mother sitting next to the bed. As Jordan stood up and patted her boy on the cheek, Adelaide extended a bandaged arm to him.

"I am so happy you have returned," she said. "I kept the weather clear so your journey home would be unhindered by terrible weather. The night is still clear, is it not?"

Thomas' resolve to do his father's bidding was already in danger of wavering as he listened to her spout nonsense. "It is a clear night," he said. "May I express my deep regret at your father's death. We are all very sorry for you, my lady."

Adelaide's face twisted into a grimace. "He was murdered," she hissed. "Murdered by thieving scum."

"I know," Thomas said evenly. "I intend to do something about it."

Her face lit up. "You do?" she gasped. "I am deeply touched that you would do such a thing for me. You have my deepest gratitude."

Thomas was uncomfortable with her thinking that he was doing this just for her. "My father and I were just discussing it," he said, clarifying that William was in on it, too. "We shall come up with a plan to punish those responsible for your father's death, I assure you."

Adelaide suddenly sat up in bed, waving about her mummy-wrapped arms. "And I should like to help," she said. "I shall turn the weather terrible and stormy, and flush them out of their holes with torrents of water. You can catch them more easily that way."

Thomas honestly had no idea what to say. He turned to his father as if to beseech the man for help, but there was no help to give. He'd come into the chamber resigned to do his duty and marry the woman, but as the seconds ticked away, he was losing ground. He didn't want to disappoint his father; he truly wanted to do his duty. But that duty included marrying a psychopath.

"Adelaide," Jordan spoke up. Having been sitting near the bed, she clearly heard the woman's madness and could no longer keep silent. "Whoever told ye that ye could control the weather, lass?"

Adelaide looked at Jordan as if only just noticing her. "Well… *everyone*," she said. "My mother told me that I had the gift."

"What gift?"

"As a *tempestarii*."

"A storm witch?"

Adelaide smiled. "My mother passed the gift to me," she said. "She was *tempestarii*, also. She could control the weather by spitting into the wind. I can control the weather with my blood."

Jordan's eyebrows lifted slowly. "Yer blood?"

Adelaide nodded. "I know you think it is foolish, but it is true. These cuts on my arms are not for my benefit, but for the benefit of the weather. Something in my blood controls the weather – like tonight, for example. I ensured the weather was clear so that Thomas could return to me unhindered."

Jordan didn't tolerate foolishness, not with her children or husband or anyone else around her. She knew that Thomas was more than likely hanging on by a thread to his vow to do his duty, to marry Adelaide, but that wouldn't last if the woman kept going on about being a storm witch.

"Adelaide," she began. "I want ye tae listen tae me, lass. Can ye do that? Stop lookin' at Thomas and look at me. I am speakin' tae ye."

Adelaide complied, but it was difficult. "I hear you, Lady de Wolfe."

"Good," Jordan said. "Now, I am goin' tae tell ye somethin' truthful, somethin' that no one else, includin' yer mother, has evidently told ye. Only God can control the weather, lass. Yer blood has nothing tae do with it. When ye cut yer arms, ye're only hurtin' yerself and upsettin' Thomas. Do ye understand that?"

Adelaide expression morphed into one of confusion. She looked between Jordan and Thomas. "But why should it upset him? He is a warrior. He has seen blood before."

Jordan struggled not to become annoyed. "Because it is unfittin' for a young lady tae cut herself up and smear her blood on the curtains."

"But that is how my blood controls the weather," Adelaide insisted. "And I shall pass the gift along to my children. My daughters will be *tempestarii,* also. It is passed from one generation to the next."

Jordan sighed heavily. "Lass, have ye spoken tae the priests about yer gift? Have they told ye anythin'?"

Adelaide seemed to falter. "My mother said the priests would not believe us," she said. "I've not been to church since I was a very young child. In fact, I do not remember the last time I prayed."

"Ye dunna pray tae God, lass?"

"My mother did not believe in God. She only took me to church because my father insisted."

Jordan turned to look at William, then. So much of Northumbria's deception was becoming clear now – a mad wife and, clearly, a mad daughter she had passed her insanity to. As Jordan struggled to think of what to say next, Adelaide turned to Thomas.

"You needn't worry, Thomas," she said. "I know you told me that I mean less to you than the horses in the barn or the cows in the field, but I have decided to forgive you for saying such things to me. I will prove to you what a worthy wife I shall be when I provide you with bright and powerful children. My mother left me an amulet that will ensure we conceive only the strongest children."

Thomas' eyebrows flickered as Adelaide, a virgin, spoke freely of conceiving children, in front of his parents no less. More than that, she mentioned those very harsh and hateful words he had spoken to her earlier and he wasn't entirely sure he wanted his parents to hear how nasty he'd been to his future wife.

"Mayhap this is not the best time to discuss this," he said, laboring against the inherent annoyance the woman provoked in him. "Rest for tonight and we shall discuss it on the morrow."

But Adelaide would not be silenced. She had Thomas' attention, and he was being polite to her, which was rare. She intended to take advantage of it. She climbed off of the bed, pushing the servants aside as she moved for her dressing table, which was piled with all manner of possessions that a very wealthy young lady should have. She began shuffling things around, looking for something in particular.

"But I want to assure you that I mean what I say," she said. "The amulet was passed down in my mother's family, from Celtic goddesses, she said. My mother is directly descended from the goddess Cuda, the goddess of fertility, and this amulet has come from her."

Thomas was watching her with a mixture of concern and distaste before looking to his mother, who appeared rather worried. Just as he thought to say something to Adelaide, to end this conversation before it got out of hand, the woman apparently found what she was looking for and abruptly raised a small object.

"This is it," she declared, holding up something Thomas couldn't quite see. "It is the fertility amulet that will ensure our children are gifted and strong. It has been used to conceive hundreds of children in my mother's family. The woman puts the amulet into her womb and it magnifies the man's seed, and…"

"Enough!" Thomas roared. "You dare to speak of such things in front of my parents? Put that vile thing away and shut your mouth.

How dare you offend my parents with talk of fertility and wombs and… God have mercy, woman, have you no shame at all?"

Adelaide's eyes widened and she quickly put the amulet back into its box. "I only wanted to prove to you that I will make a worthy wife, Thomas. You needn't bellow at me."

Thomas was afraid to say anything more. Truth be told, all of the resolve he'd mustered to go through with this marriage had vanished, and that same disgust and frustration he'd always felt with Adelaide had returned, stronger than ever. Beyond rage, he turned on his heel and stormed from the chamber, leaving his parents behind. When William tried to follow, Jordan called out to him.

"Nay, English," she said. "Let him go. Tommy must reconcile all of this in his own way, so let him go. But ye… ye go and find Caria. Stay with the lass. I am going to have a discussion with Lady Adelaide now and I dunna want ye here."

William gladly departed. When his wife used that tone, it only meant one thing – that she, too, had been pushed past her limit. In truth, William pitied Adelaide. He knew what was about to happen. There were times, with all his might, that his wife was even stronger than he was. This was one of those times.

Swiftly, he closed the chamber door behind him and did as he'd been told.

He would seek out a young lass who wasn't speaking of fertility amulets and men's seed. Caria, for him, would be much better conversation this night, and wherever Thomas had gone, he hoped the man was finding better conversation, as well.

God help the man.

CHAPTER ELEVEN

A Week Later

"I THOUGHT I'D find you here."

In the dim mustiness of the stables, Thomas glanced up from the hoof of his war horse to see Desmond approaching. At midday on a bright day, he was busy with his animal, busy staying out of Adelaide's reach. His gaze lingered on Desmond for a moment before returning to what he thought was the beginning of a split in his horse's hoof.

"And so you have found me," he said. "What do you want?"

Desmond leaned up against the stable wall, watching Thomas pick at the hoof. "Your father is looking for you," he said. "And if I did not know better, I would swear you were hiding in here."

Thomas dropped the hoof. "Of course I am hiding in here," he said. "You know I am hiding. What does my father want?"

"I did not ask him," Desmond said. "Probably something about Adelaide. She's in the hall, you know, pushing the servants around. She is taking over the chatelaine duties and no one can stop her."

Thomas didn't say anything. He simply dropped the hoof, picked up his horse's comb, and began brushing the animal. "You left this morning to go to Edenside," he said, changing the subject because he didn't want to waste any energy talking about Adelaide. "How is the situation over there?"

Desmond planted his bottom on a stool against the wall. "I've been going there all week, you know."

"I know."

"The place is looking much better," he said. "The gates have been fortified, animal pens built, the yard cleaned up, and your parents have delivered a flock of chickens and a herd of about ten goats. The children are getting regular meals now, thanks to the eggs and milk."

"And Queenie the Cook isn't making ale from the grains?"

Desmond grinned. "My sister caught her doing it a few days ago and dumped everything into the grass," he said. "Unfortunately, it was potent and the goats ate the grass, resulting in a herd of drunken goats. It was the most humorous thing I have ever seen, but Mae didn't think so. The Billy goat kept head-butting everything that moved, including her. She tied him up until the drink wore off."

The thought of Maitland struggling with a drunken Billy goat brought a smile to Thomas' lips. In fact, he chuckled. "I would have liked to have seen that."

Desmond waved him off. "You will not have the chance," he said. "Mae discharged Queenie, so no more ale. Now Tibelda is doing all of the cooking and the children are also learning how to do for themselves. Mae has them learning all kinds of things now."

As Desmond rattled off all of the skills his sister was teaching the foundlings, which was mostly milking the goats and learning to make cheese at this point, Thomas' thoughts drifted to Maitland herself. Not the children, not the drunken cook... *Maitland.*

He couldn't help it.

He'd spent the past week trying desperately not to think of her and feeling jealous of Desmond every time the man left for Edenside, which had been daily. He'd wanted to go with him, but his parents were still at Wark and he was genuinely trying to please them by doing his duty. Going off to see the woman who had his attention, the woman he very much wanted to be with, would not have pleased them.

But, God, he just couldn't shake her.

And it was only getting worse.

"And the tower?" he asked, pretending to pick at his horse's mane. "Is it repaired?"

Desmond nodded. "You would not recognize it," he said. "Mae and Tibelda scrubbed it from top to bottom, and the carpenters reinforced the entry door and built beds for the children. Mae has the girls in one chamber and the boys in another, downstairs. Mae and Tibelda sleep upstairs with the girls, but the children all have their own beds. And the fabric your mother sent a few days ago has already been put to use – now all of the children have warm clothing from that big roll of fabric your mother sent, the one of blue wool."

Thomas snorted. "She told me about it," he said. "That very fabric has been at Castle Questing for a very long time. My father will not wear the color, nor will any of my sisters or any of the grandchildren wear it because it is stiff and smelly, if it is the same stuff I am thinking of. It has been in her solar for as long as I can recall."

Desmond grinned. "You are not going to believe this, but Mae soaked that fabric in vinegar and now not only does it not smell, but it is soft," he said. "The children all have comfortable new tunics to wear. You should see how much better they look. Truly, Mae has worked wonders with those little waifs. Even Artus, who still insists on being called Wrath, is coming around. He is not nearly so hostile."

It was increasingly difficult for Thomas to focus on what he was doing. He could just picture those children, happy with their new tunics that Mae had made for them. It sounded as if she had been very busy. He wondered if she had thought about him, just a little.

God, he hoped so.

"And the coinage I sent with you a few days ago?" he asked. "What has she done with it?"

Desmond sat back against the stable wall. "I went with her into Kelso on Market Day," he said. "We purchased all manner of food stuffs – flour, grain, dried carrots, beans and peas, mostly stuff that was dried and will keep for months on end. But she also bought some fresh food, like quince and lemon. You know you cannot get them too readily this far north. Mae is very good at negotiating with the farmers and she purchased quite a bit for what you sent her. It should keep the children fed for months to come."

Thomas slapped the horse affectionately on the neck, appearing casual about the conversation when the truth was that it was consuming everything about him right now. He could hardly think straight for thoughts of Maitland.

"And your sister?" he asked the question he'd been dying to ask. "How does she seem these days?"

Desmond nodded. "Well," he said. "She is doing what she was born to do. She did tell me to thank you for the money you sent her."

Thomas was moving around to the front of his horse. "There is more where that came from."

"She asks about you every time I see her. She wants to know how you are doing with Adelaide."

Thomas glanced at him. "What do you tell her?"

"That you are miserable but you are doing your duty."

Thomas' gaze lingered on him for a moment before he growled and dropped his hand from his horse. He could no longer pretend that he was casual about this conversation. With a grunt, he ended up slumping back against the wall of the stable.

"My duty," he muttered. "I hate this duty. More than anything I have ever hated in my life."

Desmond's good humor faded. "I know," he said. "No one blames you."

Thomas looked at him, then. "I told Mae once that I was going to punch you in the face for not introducing us sooner," he said. "You cannot know the times I have wanted to follow through with that threat."

Desmond's eyebrows lifted. "Me? Why is this my fault?"

Thomas tossed the comb in his hand aside. "Because I would have married your sister, you dolt," he said. "Have you not figured this out yet, Des? Your sister… if there was no Adelaide, I would have married her the day I met her. I think she is the best thing I have ever known."

Desmond watched him for a moment. "She is," he said, his voice suddenly low and none too friendly. "She has been through a good deal, Thomas. You know this. I hope you have sense enough to stay away from her because I will not allow her to fall victim to your unhappiness."

Thomas' eyes narrowed. "What is that supposed to mean?"

Desmond stood up, suddenly quite serious. The subject was his sister and he was, and always had been, very protective of her. Now that Thomas had confessed his feelings for Maitland, which Desmond had suspected all along, it was time for him to make the situation plain.

"I mean exactly what you heard," he said. "My sister is a good woman who has been treated abominably by both my father and her husband, and now she has a chance at doing something good with her life. I'll not let you ruin it by running to her for comfort because you're unhappy with your wife. Is that clear? I know you have feelings for her; I could see it the day you two met. And I further know that she has feelings for you, too, but it ends there. I will never let you do anything clandestine with her. I will not let you hurt her."

Thomas scowled. "*Hurt* her?" he repeated, aghast. "Where did you get an idea like that? I would never hurt her and your threats are unnecessary."

Desmond stood his ground. "You and I have known each other for several years," he said. "I have seen how you are with women. I have seen you flatter them, shower them with affection, bed them, and leave them devastated. I've *seen* you do it, Thomas, so do not deny it, and I happen to know that you have at least one bastard in Berwick. The one you send money to every month. Does your father know about that?"

Thomas' gaze turned cold and deadly. "Why do you ask? Are you going to tell him if I do not stay away from your sister?"

Desmond shook his head. "It is not my place to tell him," he said.

"Nor have I told my sister. I am simply saying that I have seen how you are with women in the past and I do not want my sister to become another Thomas de Wolfe casualty. You cannot become angry with me for wanting to protect my sister."

Thomas' gaze lingered on him. Nothing he had said was untrue; that was the problem. Thomas knew it was all true. But with Mae...

Things were different.

"I cannot help what I feel," he finally said. "But I swore to my parents that I would do my duty by marrying Adelaide. She is my duty and duty only. But Mae... she is my life that could have been. If you do not think that tears me apart, you would be wrong. And I would never hurt something as priceless and respectable as Mae. You have my word on that."

With that, he quit the stable, heading out into the cool, breezy day, thinking that somehow, someway, his heart had become a pile of ashes in all of this. Desmond's fears were all valid. He genuinely could not become angry with the man for trying to protect his sister. But that heart that had become so damaged with Tacey's death had now collapsed into cinder in the wake of his loss of Maitland. Loss in an emotional sense. The woman was alive and healthy, and would ever be as long as he had any say in it, and he had no intention of making her his concubine as much as he would have liked to. He simply couldn't do that to a woman that magnificent. For once, he'd grown a conscience and he hated himself for it.

But it was the right thing to do.

Thomas needed a distraction, badly, so he headed towards the keep with the intention of finding Caria. Perhaps he'd take her down to the river or, perhaps, he'd even let her ride the pony he'd purchased for her recently. He hadn't had the opportunity yet to show it to her and he knew she'd be thrilled. It gave him something to think of other than Maitland. Just as he turned for the keep, however, he heard someone call his name.

"Thomas!"

He knew that voice and it turned his stomach. He almost ignored it but thought better of it. Coming to a halt, he simply stood there, looking off towards the keep.

He knew what was coming.

"I have not seen you all morning, Thomas," Adelaide said. "I thought you might like to see what I have done in the hall."

Thomas wouldn't look at her. "I do not need to see it," he said. "It does not matter to me what you do."

He started to walk away but she followed him. "I have arranged it for our wedding," she said. "I want to return to Kyloe Castle, but I have decided we shall be married here before we return. I vowed not to return to Kyloe unless I was married, so we must marry first. It has been six months since our betrothal, Thomas. With my father gone... this is what he would have wanted. There is no reason to delay."

Thomas came to a halt and looked at her. "Return to Kyloe?" he said. "We have never discussed that. I have no intention of leaving Wark at this time."

Adelaide was puzzled. "But as the Earl of Northumbria, Kyloe is your seat," she said. "Wark is merely an outpost for your father. It is not worthy of the Earl of Northumbria. Ask your father; even he will tell you that. As the earl, your place is at Kyloe."

Much as he hated to admit it, Adelaide was correct her in her assessment of their marriage and what his responsibilities were. Kyloe Castle was an enormous bastion that housed an army of nearly two thousand. It was the earl's seat, and when Thomas married Adelaide, he would become the earl. That went with marrying the heiress.

But, God... he didn't want to go.

His heart sank.

"Let me speak to my father about this," he said after a moment. "If I am to go to Kyloe, then my father will need to find a replacement for me here at Wark."

"Then you will agree to a wedding by the end of the week?"

He looked at her sharply. "I will agree to a wedding when my father finds a replacement for me," he said. "We are all trying to come to terms with your father's passing, Adelaide. You are not the only one it affects."

"But we must return to Kyloe soon. I must bury my father in the chapel with his ancestors."

There was the little matter of the body in the vault, which would not stay incorrupt for an over amount of time. Thomas felt a good deal of pressure knowing that his time as a single man was limited. Now, there was a timeframe on it that he could not refute.

"And we shall return him." Thomas put up a hand to stop her from whining. "As I said, let me speak with my father about this and we will make definitive plans. I simply cannot run off and leave him without a commander at Wark."

It was clear that Adelaide didn't like that answer. "I will not wait weeks," she said, pointing towards the gatehouse where the vault was. "I *cannot* wait weeks to bury my father. It is not proper."

He was nodding even as she finished her sentence. "I realize that," he said as he turned for the keep again. "I will seek my father's counsel in the matter."

Thomas headed off towards the keep, moving swiftly away from her to keep her from arguing with him. He passed through to the inner bailey and was nearly to the stairs that led up to the keep when he heard something behind him and turned to see that Adelaide was following him. He stopped.

"Where are you going?" he asked.

She looked at him expectantly. "I am going with you so that we may speak with your father."

He shook his head. "I will speak to him alone. Go back to the hall and I shall find you there later."

Adelaide sighed sharply. "Why can I not come? We will be discussing *my* wedding and *my* father."

The familiar annoyance with the woman was starting to flood his veins. "Adelaide, let me be plain," he said with thin patience. "You cannot always have what you want. In this family, the men make the decisions and the women do what they are told. I told you to go back into the hall, and you shall. Do whatever it is women do in preparation for a wedding and let me talk to my father alone."

He took the steps, but Adelaide remained at the base of them, watching him. "I will not be cast aside," she called after him. "My father permitted me to help with his decisions and I shall do the same for you. I am no one to be trifled with, Thomas, and I will not allow you to continue to show me such disrespect."

Thomas didn't even answer her. He wouldn't argue with a fool but, with every step he took, he was feeling sicker and sicker to his stomach. He was going to have to deal with that woman for the rest of his life and he was certain it was because God was punishing him for all of the sins he'd committed, for the men he'd killed and the women he'd widowed and the bastards he'd produced. Everything *Dhiib aleasifa* had ever done, everything Thomas de Wolfe would ever do.

It was the only explanation.

God wasn't going to let him be happy.

Once inside the cool, dark keep, he shut the door behind him as if to block out Adelaide. She hadn't come up the stairs behind him, but that didn't mean she wasn't going to. He knew his father was up in the master's chamber, so he set his sights on that, but as he headed for the stairwell, he passed the chamber that Desmond used.

The one that Maitland had stayed in during her brief visit.

The door was closed but it brought him to a halt. He'd passed the door many times since Maitland had departed Wark but, every time, the sight of the door brought back memories of a woman who had captured his attention. Their week of separation had done nothing to cure those feelings. If anything, they'd only grown stronger.

He paused by the door, putting his hand on the jamb and running his fingers over it as he thought on the lovely woman with the reddish-brown eyes. Life was such a cruel thing sometimes. But as he sadly turned away from the door, thoughts lingering on Maitland, he caught movement out of the corner of his eye and the dagger he always kept on his belt was abruptly unsheathed. He lifted it just in time to see Adelaide's German nurse nearly on top of him. Startled, he jumped back, away from her, as she gasped.

"*Verzeihen!*" the woman cried. "Forgive me, *mein herr*. I did not mean to startle you!"

Realizing he wasn't about to be gored by a petite old woman, he sheathed his dagger. "No harm done," he said.

He tried to push past her and go up the stairs, but she stopped him. "*Mein Herr*," she said quickly. "I must speak to you. Please."

Thomas wasn't in the speaking mood but he paused, out of courtesy. "What could you possibly have to say to me?"

The woman appeared nervous, *very* nervous. Her fingers, her jowls, everything about her was trembling. "There is not much time," she said in her heavy accent. "I must tell you about Lady Adelaide."

"What about her?"

The woman was beginning to look distressed on top of being nervous. "Where *is* Lady Adelaide?"

Thomas lifted his big shoulders. "Outside," he said. "I left her at the bottom of the stairs. I assume she is going back to the hall. Why do you ask?"

The woman put her hand to her mouth. "*Gott hilf mir*," she whispered. Then, she looked up at Thomas, utter terror in her eyes. "God help me, she is not who she seems. Be very careful, *mein herr*. She can kill you."

Normally, Thomas would have disregarded such rantings, but something in the woman's eyes made him take notice. "What are you talking about?"

The woman glanced anxiously at the keep entry before continuing. "I must tell you what I know," she said. "While the *herr* was alive, I could not, but now that he is dead, I fear only Adelaide, and I trust that you will not tell her what I say."

"What do you have to say?"

The woman leaned towards him, lowering her voice. "That she has planned for you," she whispered. "Adelaide has been betrothed to two men in the past and she killed both of them."

Thomas looked at the old woman as if she'd gone daft. "*What?*"

But the woman nodded steadily. "It is true," she said. "At first, she was fond of them, but then she grew bored. She pushed one down the stairs, and the other one, she poisoned. Her father took the bodies away and buried them in the storage vault. He told the families that the young men had run away. But she killed the second man after she had seen you in Carlisle. She told me about it. You were there with other lords at a great gathering, and she had also attended with her father. Do you not remember seeing her?"

Thomas was struggling to remember what the woman was referring to. "Carlisle?" he repeated. "That was over a year ago. It was a gathering of warlords of the north and I do not recall seeing any women there."

The old woman nodded. "She was there," she said. "The *herr* and Lady Adelaide attended and she saw you and she wanted you. She killed her betrothed and told her father that she wanted to marry you."

Thomas stared at the woman, torn between shock and disbelief. "She is a *murderess*?" he hissed. "I cannot believe that. She is not that clever!"

The old nurse nodded, wringing her hands. "She is more clever than you know," she said. "She paid men to find out what they could about you and one of them told her that you were called StormWolfe. That is why she speaks of *tempestarii* – if you are the StormWolfe, then she wants to be the storm witch. She thought you would love her better that way."

Thomas was truly taken aback by what he was hearing. "Then she really does not believe herself to be a *tempestarii*?"

The old woman shook her head sharply. "*Nein*," she said. "It is for your benefit."

Thomas' mouth popped open in astonishment. "Then all of that has been an act? The cutting of her arms and the belief that her blood controls the weather?"

The woman nodded fervently. "It is not true," she said. "She does not believe it. She does this to gain your attention and your sympathy, and nothing more. But the cuts on her arms... she has been doing that since she was a child. She would do it to gain her father's attention and get her way. The earl would always give in to her but I believe the man was afraid of her."

The astonishment that had swept Thomas was turning into something else, something dark and terrible. "My God," he muttered. "She must be mad."

"She is," the woman insisted. "Please believe me, *mein herr*... she *is* mad. She is mad and she is wicked. You must protect yourself. All of the shouting and the insults you have dealt her, I wanted to tell you to be careful, but I could not. Lady Adelaide is deadly."

With that, the woman dashed off as if terrified, rushing from the keep, perhaps going to find her charge and pretend as if she had not just divulged the woman's sordid secrets. But Thomas simply stood there, struggling to absorb what he'd been told. Adelaide was evidently not the foolish woman they'd all believed her to be. All this time, it was an act for his benefit. He'd always known her to be mad – that was clear. But beneath that giddy, foolish, mad façade lay the heart of a killer.

Or so her old nurse wanted him to think.

He had to talk to his father.

"THAT WOULD EXPLAIN a great deal, actually," William said calmly. "It would explain why Northumbria pursued you so much. I did not initiate this betrothal, Tommy. Northumbria came to me and specifically asked for you."

Standing in his big, cluttered bower where his parents and Caria were staying, Thomas' eyebrows lifted to his father's revelation.

"And you never questioned that?" he said. "It never seemed strange to you?"

William shook his head. "Surely you jest," he said. "The Earl of Northumbria comes to me and wants to make my son his heir? I did not question that, but as we now know, I should have. Evidently in more ways than one."

Jordan, who had been listening carefully to the conversation, came to stand next to her son. "What will we do, English?" she asked William fearfully. "We canna allow Tommy tae marry a murderess!"

William could hear the fear in his wife's voice. In truth, he wasn't entirely immune to that fear, either. His son had just delivered a shocking revelation to him about Adelaide de Vauden and he was still reeling. But even in his shock, so much of this betrothal made sense to him.

Now, things were falling into place.

"We cannot prove anything," he said frankly. "What you heard were the spoutings of an old woman. She could very well be lying and, certainly, if we ask Adelaide, she will deny it. Unless we have witnesses to her madness, I am not sure there is anything we can do. And the fact remains that she is still the heiress to Northumbria's earldom. That has not changed."

Jordan was beside herself with worry. "Then ye must send men tae Kyloe tae discover the truth behind Adelaide," she said. "Discover what they know, English. Ye must!"

William knew that. "I will go myself," he said. "This mess is of my doing, so I must discover the truth personally. Meanwhile, I will send you and Caria back to Castle Questing. If Adelaide really is a murderess, then I do not want either of you here at Wark. And Tommy..."

"Aye?" Thomas said.

"Get out of here for a few days. Leave Desmond in command and get out of here. If she really has murdered the two men she was betrothed to before you, then I do not want you around her, either."

Thomas almost refused, but the words of resistance died on his lips.

Suddenly, he saw an opportunity he never thought he'd have again – *get out of here for a few days*. He knew exactly where he was going to go.

There was no question.

Edenside.

"What about you, Papa?" Thomas said. "Northumbria was ambushed trying to return to Kyloe and I will not see you become another victim. We know those reivers are somewhere to the east. If they have struck before, they'll strike again."

William held up a hand to ease his son. "I will return to Castle Questing with your mother and Caria first and collect a sizable army, one that will protect against a handful of reivers," he said. "My army and I will travel to Kyloe and I will get to the bottom of these rumors about Lady Adelaide."

"And if they are true?"

William sighed heavily. "You are not going to like this."

Thomas frowned. "Why not?"

William was thoughtful as well as grim. "If there are witnesses to her madness, then by law, she can be arrested," he said. "But if she is arrested before your marriage, Northumbria will revert to the crown and we will once again be apprehensive of who Edward will grant the earldom to. But if you marry her first…"

Thomas got his meaning right away. "Then I retain the earldom while she rots in the vault."

"Exactly."

Jordan's hands flew to her mouth. "Nay," she breathed. "Tommy has to marry that… that *killer*?"

William looked at his wife. "I realize that this sounds hard and calculating, but it is the reality of things," he said. "Tommy marries her, I arrest her on the king's authority as a murderess, and Tommy remains the Earl of Northumbria, never to see Adelaide again. We may even be able to have the marriage annulled while he retains the title. If Edward is in a generous mood, and the church is convinced that Adelaide is possessed with the devil or worships the devil, as she has professed not to believe in God, then that may be possible."

It was complicated. So very complicated. But strangely, Thomas wasn't opposed to it. He saw what his father was trying to do. If he could get the marriage annulled, that meant Thomas would be free to remarry.

And he knew just who he would choose.

Maitland would make a magnificent countess.

"Then we must do as we must, Papa," Thomas said quietly. "I am with you."

William reached out, putting a big hand on Thomas' shoulder. "Good," he said. "Meanwhile, we all depart at dawn. Mayhap you will come back to Castle Questing with us, Tommy?"

Thomas shrugged casually. "I was thinking of going to Northwood Castle," he said. "I will go visit Uncle Paris for a few days. And then I may go to Edenside to see how my money has been spent. Des told me that Lady Bowlin has been doing remarkable things with the place."

The part about Northwood Castle was a bit of a lie, to throw his father off of his train of thought, but he included the part about Edenside just so he wouldn't be lying completely. Still, William was on to him. Knowing how Thomas felt about Lady Bowlin, he didn't think that was a particularly good idea for the man to go to Edenside, not in the middle of this crisis, but he didn't say so. Thomas was a grown man and he was capable of making his own decisions. The main thing now was that they clear out of Wark. Adelaide would be left alone, wondering where everyone had gone, but that couldn't be helped.

No one wanted to be bottled up with a killer.

That night, William, Jordan, Thomas, and Caria slept behind a bolted door in the master's chamber. While William and Jordan slept on the bed, Thomas slept in a big chair with Caria snuggled against him. No matter how much Jordan coaxed, the little girl wouldn't come and sleep between her parents. She wanted to sleep in the chair with "her" Thomas.

It had been a tense night and no one but Caria seemed to get much sleep. But just before dawn, they moved out in silence, loading Jordan and Caria up in the fortified carriage while Thomas informed Desmond that he would be escorting his parents home. It was a lie, of course, but he did it for two reasons – he didn't want the man tipped off about Adelaide's ghastly character because he wanted him to behave normally with the woman, and he didn't want the man tipped off to the fact that Thomas' true destination was Edenside. Given their conversation the day before, he didn't think Desmond would take that too well.

Therefore, as the sun began to rise in the east, the great gates of Wark Castle opened and the de Wolfe party headed out into the cold, gray dawn.

CHAPTER TWELVE

Edenside

"TIE UP THE goat, Artus!" Maitland called to the boy. "Do not let it push you around!"

Artus was trying desperately not to fall victim to an aggressive nanny goat. He'd milked the goat every day for the past four days and thought he was doing a rather good job, but the goat must have thought otherwise. Maitland had shown him three times how to properly milk the goat, but he simply didn't have the hang of it yet, whilst the girls, Marybelle and Nora, were doing a much better job of it. They had soft girl hands, or so Artus had been told, and the nanny goats liked them much better.

"She doesna like me," Artus declared as the goat swung her head at him, clipping him on the arm. "Do I have tae milk it?"

Maitland had been standing a few feet away, watching the scene unfold with Artus and his enemies, the goats. They really didn't like him much and Maitland had been trying to figure out why but, ultimately, she decided that Artus simply didn't have a way with the animals like the others had. Therefore, she waved him off.

"Nay," she said. "You'll have to work in the kitchen with Tibelda, making the cheese. The others will do the milking. Go on, now, to the kitchen with you. Tibelda will be requiring your help."

Defeated by the horned beasts, Artus walked past her, dejectedly, heading for the kitchen yard where Tibelda was boiling goat's milk over a flaming hearth, making the cheese with the help of Renard, Roland, and little Dyana. The younger children remained in the kitchen with Tibelda while the older ones handled the herd, but now Artus was relegated to the kitchen and he wasn't particularly thrilled about it.

While Marybelle and Nora continued to milk the nanny goats, at least the ones who were cooperating, Maitland turned away from the animal pen and headed for the kitchen to collect another bucket. They had eight nanny goats, three of which were pregnant, two with baby goats that produced the most milk so far, and one Billy goat who remained in another pen and away from the others. He was very mean, this goat, so mean that Maitland had given him the name of Addy.

It was short for Adelaide.

The children didn't know that, of course, and Tibelda really didn't, either. That was a joke known only to Maitland, and every time the goat misbehaved, she scolded "Addy". It was wrong and she knew it, but she really didn't care. Naming the nasty goat after Thomas' betrothed was perhaps her own personal rebellion against a situation that was well out of her control, and had been from the moment she'd met Thomas.

It was a situation that had been over before it ever really got started.

It was midafternoon on a day that had been surprisingly mild. It was late spring, which could be stormy and cool, but this day had been calm and clear, with puffy white clouds scattering in the breeze. As Maitland crossed over to the kitchen for the bucket, she found herself looking up, thinking it was a beautiful day and reflecting on the past week at Edenside. In spite of the situation with Thomas, things were going better than she could have imagined.

There were a few things to be happy for.

The small herd of goats was being used to teach the children how to milk and make cheese, which had been part of her master plan. The animals had been a gift from the Earl of Warenton and his wife, brought from Castle Questing, which really wasn't very far away, by stable servants and a few soldiers who herded them into the newly-built animal pen at Edenside. True to her word, Lady de Wolfe had sent for the goats and the animals had arrived along with a flock of chickens.

The beginning of Edenside's self-sufficiency had arrived.

With the chickens housed and the goats penned, Maitland had turned her considerable skills to the seven skinny, cold, and dirty children she was in charge of. The morning after her arrival to Edenside, she and Tibelda had boiled water and filled up a big trough that had been used to water the animals of past occupants. Using the precious soap they'd brought with them, they'd washed the girls first and then the boys, washing their clothes as well and then drying everyone, and everything, before a great fire.

But the rags they wore were only temporary. The goats and chickens had arrived a short time later along with a pile of blue woolen fabric, courtesy of Lady de Wolfe. Maitland had been thrilled. Finally, something warm for the children to wear. The next day, Desmond had visited with money from Thomas, and he had escorted Maitland into Kelso where it was Market Day, and Maitland had purchased a great many things with Thomas' money – foodstuffs, including vinegar and wine so she could start making her own vinegar, among other things.

It had been a productive trip.

Maitland and Desmond had returned to Edenside laden with goods, and the children and her brother had enjoyed a good supper that night of baked eggs and bread while Maitland soaked Lady de Wolfe's woolen material in some of the vinegar she had purchased. It softened the material enough so that she and Tibelda were able to make seven tunics the following day, with long sleeves and high necks, going all the way to the children's ankles to keep them nice and warm.

With bellies full and bodies clean and warm, the next order of business was to begin the children's education. Lessons had started almost immediately and, even now, the children were doing very well with their lessons. They were learning cheese-making skills and in the evening after a day of chores, Maitland would read to them from the bible, writing letters in the dirt of the kitchen yard so they could learn them. There would be more lessons tonight on letters, and words, and as Maitland picked up the bucket she'd come for, she could hear Artus yelling.

A visitor had arrived.

Thinking it was Desmond, Maitland rushed to the animal pen and handed the bucket off to Phin, who was helping Marybelle and Nora milk the goats. As Maitland rounded the outbuilding from the kitchen yard, she fully expected to see Desmond coming through the gate.

But that was not who she saw.

It was Thomas.

Startled at his unexpected appearance, Maitland watched the man dismount his muscled war horse and look around at the small ward, which looked much different from when he last saw it. As he secured the horse and turned to walk towards the stable yard, he caught sight of Maitland standing there and he immediately lifted a hand to her in greeting.

She waved back.

In truth, Maitland wasn't sure how she felt to see him again. The week of separation from the man had done nothing to purge him from her mind. As she watched him walk towards her, a hint of a smile on his face, it was all she could do to keep her breathing steady.

The man had the ability to make her heart leap in all directions.

It wasn't that she didn't want to see him. Of course, she did. But Desmond had told her about Northumbria's death and the imminent wedding between Thomas and Lady Adelaide, and even though she'd always known that the marriage would happen at some point, some-how, the news had crushed her. All of Thomas' sweet words, of his vow that he would have married Maitland had he not been betrothed to Adelaide, had gone to her head.

And her heart.

She tried not to feel too badly about it.

"Good day to you, my lord," she said as Thomas drew close. "We are honored by your visit."

Thomas' grin broadened, the dimple in his left cheek deep. "Good day, Lady Bowlin," he said. "I have heard that you are doing marvelous things here and I came to see for myself."

Maitland smiled weakly. "I am trying," she said. "Did my brother relay my thanks for the money you sent us?"

Thomas nodded. "He did," he said. "And you are welcome. I have brought you more because I am sure you have more needs."

Maitland nodded. "Always, but we have come along splendidly this week. Would you like to see?"

Thomas nodded. "Very much so."

Maitland flashed him a smile, her gaze lingering on him as she beckoned him to follow her. "Come with me."

Thomas did, gladly. Already, it was a pleasant conversation and just seeing the woman did something to him. It was as if his heart had wings, and even now as he followed her, he felt as if he were walking on air. The escort for his parents to Castle Questing had taken less than an hour, as the fortress was only a few miles south of Wark, so on the entire ride to Edenside, which had also taken a short amount of time, he contemplated what he would say to Maitland when he saw her.

But the words didn't come so easily.

Tongue-tied.

He'd actually been rather speechless when he beheld her for the first time in a week. Whatever he felt for her, or whatever he thought he felt for her, hit him full-bore and all he could do was smile. And now, they were having a conversation of superficial words when what he really wanted to do was tell her everything he'd considered over the past week, of his inability to push her from his mind.

But he simply couldn't do it.

He promised himself he would never disrespect the woman and were he to speak what was in his heart, he couldn't guarantee that he would keep that promise.

"I must say, it does look quite different here," he said, looking around the neat kitchen yard with its animal pen and chicken house. "Did my carpenters do all of this?"

Maitland was looking at what had his focus. "Aye," she said, lifting a hand to shield her eyes from the sun. "They built the chicken house first to protect the fowl. Then, they built the pens for the goats."

Thomas could see two small girls and one small boy as they milked the nanny goats. They were working very hard at it as the baby goats moved around them nervously, trying to get to a teat that hadn't been milked. He grinned.

"The children look as if they know what they are doing already," he said. "Did you teach them to milk the goats?"

Maitland nodded. "I did," she said proudly. "But they learned quickly. Come over here. Let me show you what we are doing with the milk."

He turned away from the goats and followed her over to the repaired kitchen area, looking around with some surprise.

"This does not look as it did when last I saw it," he said. "The hearth was broken and the bread oven had no door. And there was certainly no roof."

He was pointing to the cover that had been repaired. The kitchen was an open one, with a hearth and chimney built into the enclosure wall, a bread oven that looked like a beehive, and a covering overhead to keep out the elements. It was really nothing more than an open stall, but now it was neat and organized and clean, and smelled divinely of baking bread.

"Your carpenters fixed the shelter," Maitland said, looking up at the covering. "They also fixed the bread oven and unclogged the hearth. Truly, the men you sent have worked miracles. This is not the same place you left."

Thomas lifted his eyebrows in agreement. "That is for certain," he said. Then, he noticed Artus, the two small twin boys, and the tiny little girl all standing at the kitchen table where they were working on what looked like curds. He pointed. "What are they doing?"

Maitland was quite proud of her production line. "Making goat cheese," she said. "I told your mother I was going to teach the children how, and it is really very simple. See the hearth? Tibelda is bringing goat's milk to a boil, and when it is nice and hot, she brings it over to the table where Renard and Roland put lemon juice into it. This makes it curdle."

Thomas was leaning over the small boys, watching what they were doing. "Des mentioned you had purchased lemons with the money I gave you," he said. "This far north, they are a precious commodity. Is this what they were for?"

Maitland nodded. "There is something in the juice that starts the cheese-making process with the hot milk," she said. "I can use vinegar, too, but something about the lemons makes it taste better. Once the juice is stirred in, we wait until it curdles and then we spoon it into linen that has been placed over a bowl. We fold the linen up and let it sit overnight so the cheese becomes a little firmer."

Thomas nodded his approval. "Fascinating," he said. "Then what?"

Maitland pointed to Dyana, the little girl, as she stirred and stirred a soft, white mixture. "Then Tibelda or I put salt and herbs in the cheese, which Dyana is mixing in. We did cheese yesterday that had wild garlic and dill in it. The cheese today has wild rosemary; it grows all along the southern side of the tower wall."

"And then what will you do with the cheese?"

Maitland looked at him as if surprised by the question. "Sell it in Kelso on Market Day," she said. "I believe we can make good money selling the cheese to travelers or to inns. In fact, I was going to go into Kelso and talk to the innkeepers to see if they would be willing to buy our cheese. It is quite delicious."

He cocked an eyebrow. "*I* will talk to the innkeepers in Kelso and tell them they must buy your cheese," he said. "They would not dare deny me. In fact, I shall go to a few other small villages around here and sell your cheese to the innkeepers. Can you meet the demand?"

Maitland nodded. "I think so," she said. "If I need more goats, I can always ask my great patroness, Lady de Wolfe."

Thomas grinned, gazing into her lovely face and feeling a pull towards her that he'd never felt in his life. A week of separation had done nothing to quell what was growing. Distance could not kill something that was starting to have a life of its own. In fact, his feelings must have been written all over his face because Maitland suddenly looked away, breaking whatever spell was hovering between them, but Thomas' gaze was still on her.

He couldn't look away.

Maitland kept her eyes averted, focused on the bread that Tibelda had just taken out of the oven. She ripped a piece of bread from a hot loaf and smeared it with some of the soft cheese that little Dyana had just stirred up with salt and rosemary.

"Here," she said. "You must try the cheese so you know how delicious it is. We make it during the day and move it to the vault of the tower at night to keep it chilled, but try some of our freshly-made cheese from today."

Thomas sensed a nervousness in her movements, as if she were abruptly nervous around him. He could only surmise that she'd seen his longing for her in his eyes and it had startled her. She'd told him once that she would never do anything improper with a betrothed man, and he realized with both respect and disappointment that she was a woman of her word.

Disappointed because he had hoped that she would fall.

It would make it easier for him to, also.

But she had remained strong. Thomas watched her as she extended the bread to him and he took it, making sure to brush her fingers as he did so. With his eyes on her, he took a bite of the warm bread and creamy cheese, realizing as soon as he began to chew that it was utterly delicious.

"It is the best cheese I have ever tasted," he said, mouth full. "I shall demand that every innkeeper from Kelso to Berwick buy your cheese.

In fact, I shall take some with me when I leave so that they may taste the product."

Maitland looked at him hopefully. "It would be wonderful if we could sell it locally," she said. "It does not keep very well, so it must be eaten within just a few days. I do not think we could sell it any further than just a few hours' ride from Edenside."

"You shall make a fortune, my lady. Well done."

With that, he put the rest of the bread into his mouth and chewed it up, telling the children around the table how wonderful their cheese was. The twins seemed rather shy around him, but little Dyana beamed, and all Thomas could see was happy children, so completely unlike the little waifs he saw the first night at Edenside.

In truth, Maitland had already worked miracles.

He ended up eating two more pieces of bread with the soft cheese because it really was delicious and he was rather hungry. Satisfied with his snack, at least for the moment, they headed out of the kitchen and back into the yard so that Maitland could show him the repaired tower.

However, they had picked up a tail in Artus, who followed them across the yard. Thomas wished the lad wasn't trailing them, hoping to have a few moments alone with Maitland. He knew he shouldn't but, at this point, he didn't much care. As the seconds ticked away, the more he felt as if he had to tell her what was on his mind and in his heart, even if the words would never translate into action. He wasn't a man to keep things to himself, for he believed in being forthright and honest. Perhaps it was foolish of him, but then again, he'd been known to be foolish from time to time.

Especially when it came to women.

"The last time you were here and you left so swiftly, my brother told me it was because of the Earl of Northumbria's death," Maitland said, breaking into his train of thought. "May I offer my sympathies. It is terrible what happened to the man."

Thomas glanced at her as they walked. "He told you about the reivers?"

"He did."

Thomas grunted. "Northumbria's death was a surprise," he said. "The reivers do not usually attack travelers, so that was an unusual happenstance."

Maitland shrugged. "Mayhap not so unusual considering you had just confronted them in Coldstream the night before," she said. "If I was a fighting man, I might think it was revenge."

He looked at her, smiling. "Are you always so smart?"

She laughed softly, embarrassed. "Not really," she said. "It just seemed logical."

"Your instincts are good."

Maitland blushed furiously at the compliment. She wasn't usually the blushing type, but Thomas had that effect on her.

"Thank you, my lord," she said. "I try to be a reasonable and gracious woman at all times. In fact, I must again thank you for all you have done for Edenside. Without your help and your craftsmen, we could not have repaired as much as we have. We owe you much."

Thomas kept glancing at her as they walked towards the tower. "I am happy to be of assistance," he said. "In fact, if there is anything more that you think you need, all you need do is ask. I shall make sure you receive it."

Maitland paused, looking around the yard. "For now, I believe we are content," she said. "I am going to see the abbot of Kelso next week to discuss the charity and the fact that we can accept more children if there is a need."

Thomas frowned. "The abbot has not been by to see you yet?"

She shook her head. "Not yet," she said. "We have had people traveling to mass pass us by and I know they have seen all of the work that was going on here, so I can only assume that information has made it to the abbot. He must know that I have arrived."

Thomas scratched his neck as he looked off in the direction of Kelso. "It is quite possible that he does not want to show his face considering it was his sister who nearly destroyed the charity," he said.

"Mayhap I shall go into town with you when you go. It may help to have a de Wolfe present when you meet the man."

She looked at him curiously. "Why?"

His eyes glimmered at her. "He will know that there will not be another failure, and if *he* fails you, then he will have to answer for it – to me."

Maitland's expression softened. "You are too kind to me," she said. "I am not sure what I ever did to deserve such devotion."

"I wish I could give you more." The words slipped out before Thomas could stop them and, abruptly, he hung his head, hissing at his lack of control. "I am sorry, Mae. I did not mean… God's Bones, I *did* mean it. I meant every word. I am not a liar and I cannot lie to you and tell you that I did not mean what I said. Forgive me."

He was rambling a bit, something that was rather endearing. Maitland smiled at the big, nervous knight. "For what?" she said. "For saying the words? Or for meaning them?"

"Both. But I will not take it back."

She nodded faintly, a gesture of understanding. "I did not ask you to," she said quietly. "My brother tells me that you and Adelaide will be married very soon now that her father is dead."

Thomas rolled his eyes. "Did you say that just to rub it in my face?" he asked, annoyed and off-balance. "I know what has to happen, but believe me, there is no joy in it. There never has been and there never will be. I just… I just do not want you to hate me for it."

"Why would I hate you for it?"

He was starting to say too much, heading down that slippery slope that would have him spilling out all manner of feelings and he would be unable to stop. Shaking his head, he turned for the tower.

"Come along," he said. "Show me the tower now. Des says that the carpenters have repaired everything."

Maitland scurried after him, but not because she wanted to show him the keep. She ran up behind him and grasped his hand, pulling him to a halt. But then, she began pulling him over towards an enormous yew tree that was growing big and wild near the wall, which was terrible for the defenses. Anyone could easily climb onto the wall and then hang on the branches to descend into the yard.

But Thomas wasn't looking at the bad positioning of the tree. He was looking at Maitland, feeling her soft hand around his callused one as she pulled him over to the wall where there were some big rocks, as the landscape itself was quite rocky and most of the yard was rocky as well. It was quiet here, away from everything, and she pushed Thomas down onto one of the rocks and faced him.

"Now," she said. "You and I must have a serious discussion, Thomas. I am a forthright woman and I do not like the games that men and women play, so if you think to play a game with me and feed me tantalizing words as you just did, know that I will not stand for it."

Thomas looked up at her, feeling as if he were about to be scolded and knowing he deserved it. "Aye, my lady."

Maitland was firm. "I told you that I am nothing more than a passing fancy and I further told you not to tempt me because it is not fair. Do you recall that conversation?"

He nodded, dejected. "Aye, my lady."

"Then why do you continue to make comments like the one you just made?"

"Because I cannot help myself, my lady."

She sighed sharply. "You are only making this harder for us both, and if taking your money means I must continue to take your leading comments, then I will refuse your money. I am quite serious, Thomas. I shall find another patron who will not say such things to me."

Thomas hung his head. She was such a fine, upstanding woman and he was scum. There was nothing about him that was worthy of her. Heavily, he exhaled.

"May I say something, my lady?"

"I wish you would."

His head came up, his gaze fixed on her. "You are not a passing fancy," he said. "A week ago, I met the most remarkable woman I have ever met and I cannot forget her no matter how I try. Do you know *why* I stayed away for an entire week? Because I was trying to put you from my mind. I am about to enter into a marriage that will be loveless and contentious. That will be the rest of my life, Mae, but that has nothing to do with my feelings for you. A bitter bride is not causing me to seek comfort elsewhere. If there was no Adelaide, I would still feel this way about you. I will feel this way about you until I die."

Maitland was so very touched by his words. She knew his betrothal to Adelaide was loveless. She knew it was arranged. When she closed her eyes at night, she could see Thomas' handsome face and powerful body, and it was almost more than she could bear. He was attracted to her, and she to him, and if they were to let it run wild, there was no telling where it would go. But she also knew that she couldn't – nay, *wouldn't* – carry on with a married man.

Even if that man was Thomas.

But the truth was that she had spent her married life in a loveless marriage of her own. She had always craved for a man to care for her; since she had been a child, with a father who disdained her, she'd always yearned for a man's affection and attention. There was a very large part of her that wanted to give in to whatever relationship Thomas wanted to conduct, yet the rational part of her – the part that knew such a thing would only come to a terrible end – refused to let her give in to the woman who needed love so much. It was a terrible tempest inside of her, mirroring the one inside of Thomas, only she was better at concealing it.

With a resigned sigh, she went to sit on the rock next to him.

"You have been honest with me, so I suppose I should be honest with you," she said after a moment. "I told you once that if you had pursued me, I would have let you catch me. That is still true. But I would not do it simply to fulfil your whim. But if you were sincere in your pursuit…"

He cut her off. "I would have been. I swear to you that I would have been."

She looked at him. "Then the proudest moment in my life would have been to bear the title Lady de Wolfe."

Thomas looked at her. They were just a few inches apart, but close enough that he could feel the heat coming off of her body. He'd never felt such emotion, such horrific sorrow paralleled by wild joy. It began to occur to him that what he'd felt for Tacey hadn't come close to what he was starting to feel for Maitland, at least not in the beginning. What he'd felt for Tacey had grown gradually, a sweet affection like the warmth of a mild summer's day. What he felt for Maitland was starting to feel like he was walking on the surface of the sun.

It could easily consume him.

Thomas couldn't describe it better than that. And in that moment, he knew what he felt for her and what he would always feel for her. He realized that whatever attraction and infatuation he had for her had run away from him until it was something he could no longer control.

He knew.

"I cannot give you my name," he said hoarsely. "But I can give you something else."

"What?"

"My heart."

Maitland's eyes widened and she gasped, leaning away from him, but she didn't get up off the rock. She continued to sit there, looking at him with wide eyes.

"Do not tell me that," she breathed.

"Why not?"

"Because… because it is simply not fair."

"To whom? Me or you?"

"Both of us," she said, the shock in her expression replaced by pain. "Don't you know that I would take your heart and never give it back, Thomas? Don't you know that I would keep it forever?"

Thomas could see, in that statement, that she was feeling as much angst and pain as he was. He had to tear his gaze away from her or risk reaching out for her.

"So what do you we do?" he asked. "And do not tell me to go away, because I will not. And do not tell me to forget about you, because I cannot. Even if I never touch you, Mae, I want to come here to visit you, to hear you laugh and see you smile. Don't you know what joy I feel when I see how happy you are now? How happy a little money and a few goats have made you? Please do not take that away from me. Do not take away the only true happiness I may ever know."

"I won't," she murmured. "I could not take that away from myself. I do not know what we are to do, Thomas. Mayhap simply speaking about what we feel will suffice for now. Mayhap it will be a test of willpower, to see if our pretty words are stronger than what is in our hearts. Have you punched Des in the face yet for not having introduced us sooner?"

Thomas broke down into soft laughter at the unexpected humor. "I have not," he said. "But he and I have had a discussion about you. He told me to stay away from you."

"Will you listen to him?"

He looked at her, shaking his head slowly. When he spoke, it was simply to mouth the word.

"Nay."

No sound came out, but Maitland didn't have to hear the word to know what he'd said. It was like a dagger through her heart but, in the same breath, it was everything she wanted to hear. She could feel the beauty of his feelings, no longer truly concerned that they were simply a whim. She could feel the truth of his words in the purest sense, and she believed him implicitly. It was at that moment she realized that she was denying herself something that every woman wants – the adoration and attention of a man. She'd never had it for herself and, damnation, she wanted it.

The strong stance she was taking against him was starting to crumble.

It was already gone.

Lowering her gaze, she stood up and held out her hand to him.

"You wanted to see the tower?" she said. "Let me show you."

She was changing the subject, which was probably wise. Thomas couldn't say much about it other than to simply follow her. In truth, he was feeling depressed and lost, having finally found a woman he could feel something for and unable to act upon it. He had no idea how he was going to navigate the situation and not have his guts ripped out every time he saw her. He wondered if, in the years to come, he'd simply become accustomed to the pain.

It was a sorrowful thought.

The tower loomed before them and Thomas could immediately see the fortified door, which took his mind off his troubles for the moment. The carpenters he'd sent from Wark had done a remarkable job on it and as Maitland opened the door, he ran his hands over the panel, inspecting it.

There were two big iron bolts on the interior of it, plus a lock, all of it nicely securing the door. He shut it, throwing the bolts to see how strong they were. He was bent down, inspecting the iron bolts, but as he came up, a body suddenly pressed against him. Hands were on his face and before he realized what was happening, Maitland was slanting her soft lips over his.

Off-balance, Thomas slammed back into the wall next to the bolted tower door, his arms going around Maitland of their own volition. One moment, he was startled and in the next, she was in his tight embrace. He was surely squeezing the breath from her. Maitland's arms were around his neck, her mouth on his, and when Thomas realized what was happening, instinct took over.

He could hardly believe it.

His heart was pounding in his ears as he suckled her lips, forcing her mouth open with his tongue and tasting her sweetness. Maitland didn't resist him, not in the least, and whatever fire was burning in his belly was burning just as hotly in hers. She was soft and pliable in his arms, and he kissed her furiously, so hard that he drove his teeth into his soft lip, drawing blood, which Maitland licked off hungrily. When she pulled back to look at him, he saw his own blood on her lips and it drove him wild.

He was on her again in a flash, picking her up in his arms, her feet dangling a foot or more off the ground. He was suckling her lips, her cheek, her neck, moving against the wall until they stumbled into the chamber on the lower level that had once been used as a hall. The hearth was dark but daylight streamed in through the small lancet windows, giving some light to see by. But all Thomas knew was that he'd never been so hungry for a woman in his life. Light or dark, he didn't need to see her.

He only needed to feel her.

In truth, he could hardly believe he found himself in this situation. Up until a few seconds ago, Thomas was positive he would have to go the rest of his life never having touched Maitland, and he was still shocked that she had thrown herself at him. But he didn't question it. He was bloody well thankful. Somehow, they ended up backed into the repaired feasting table and he slammed his thigh into it, which caused him to pause in his sensual assault. He pulled back for a moment, finding himself looking into her wide, beautiful eyes.

"Why, Mae?" he breathed, licking his swollen lips. "You told me not to tempt you."

Maitland's lips and cheeks were red from his bristly beard, her chest heaving with the force of her passion. "I know," she whispered. "All you've done is talk. All I've done is resist. I… I have never had a man speak so to me, not ever. I do not know what came over me, Thomas. Suddenly, I had to touch you. I cannot explain it more than that."

Thomas had his big hands on her head, swallowing it up as he leaned in and kissed her gently. "You are *not* a passing fancy."

Maitland sucked in a ragged breath. "Swear it to me."

"I swear. God, I swear."

"I… I have never had anyone love me before, Thomas."

"If you give me the opportunity, I will."

She put her hand over his mouth before he could kiss her again and when he looked at her, he could see tears glistening. "But I cannot carry on with a married man."

He cocked a dark eyebrow. "I am not married yet."

He had a point – an indisputable point. He *wasn't* married at that moment, technical as it might be. Realizing that, Maitland could no longer control the passion that was burning holes in her. Leaning forward, she captured Thomas' lower lip between her teeth, biting him gently, and Thomas groaned.

Madness consumed him. His mouth claimed hers once again and Maitland gave herself over to him, willingly and completely. His big, warm body settled her back on the tabletop and he wedged himself between her legs, but she hardly cared. She knew what was coming and she welcomed it. She was eager to know the man, in every sense of the word.

Thomas didn't keep her waiting. As his lips feasted on hers, he reached down and pulled up the edge of her long garment, pulling it up and sliding it past her hips. Yanking it over her head, he pulled her shift off with it, and both landed in a pile on the table behind her.

Then, he took a good look at her body, slender and white, with full breasts and narrow hips. She was magnificent. He was in full protection, which was a problem, so he pulled off his gloves as Maitland moved to his belt, unfastening it. The gloves and belt hit the floor, followed by his de Wolfe tunic.

Bending forward, he held out his arms and Maitland took hold of his mail coat, pulling it off as he shimmied out of it. That, too, ended up on the floor, followed by his padded tunic. Naked from the waist up, his lips claimed hers once more as he unfastened his breeches. They slithered to his knees as he put his hand on her buttocks and pulled her hips to the edge of the table.

Thomas devoured Maitland's lips as a big hand closed gently over a breast, feeling the silken skin against his palm. Maitland groaned when he began tugging at her nipple, toying with the hard, little pellet, and when his mouth left hers and began nursing against that nipple, her head tipped backwards as she gasped in ecstasy. Every suckle sent bolts of excitement shooting through her body and between her legs, a flame ignited that she'd only felt once before, back in the days when Henry had drawn arousal out of her. Instinctively, her pelvis rocked forward, seeking his manhood, silently begging for him to fill her.

Thomas could feel her squirming and he knew exactly what she wanted. As he worked her breasts hungrily, his fingers sought out the curls between her legs and he pushed his fingers into her. She was already wet and swollen, her body preparing for his entry, and he thrust his fingers into her tight, wet passage, moving in and out of her, mimicking the thrusting that would soon be taking place. Maitland groaned and opened her legs wider to him, demanding his entry, and Thomas could wait no longer.

Carefully, he positioned his engorged phallus at her threshold, thrusting into her slick body. He was so big that Maitland gasped with the shock of his intrusion but thrust her hips forward to capture all of him. Thomas had managed to arouse a side of her she never knew she had, one that was willing to overlook the complexities of the situation and surrender to the myriad of emotions she was feeling for the man. None of that seemed to matter any longer. She needed to be touched, to be loved.

She needed to belong to him, forever.

Carefully, Thomas began to thrust, his arms going around her as he gathered her up tightly against him, her chest to his, the feel of her soft breasts against his skin, feeding his lust. Against him, Maitland groaned and gasped at the pleasurable sensations, her legs wrapping tightly around his hips, begging him to plunge deeper.

Thomas had never experienced anything so sweet in his entire life. His body pounded into hers and she accepted all of him, moving with him as her pelvis met him, move for move. It was magical, his manhood burying itself in her wet folds as her body tried to coax forth his seed. Maitland's hands moved from his shoulders to his buttocks, holding his body against hers as if to force him ever deeper.

Thomas surrendered without a fight.

His hot seed released and Maitland felt him shudder. But he kept moving within her, his hand moving to the junction between her legs and stroking her until she, too, experienced her own powerful release. Gasping as waves of pleasure rolled over her, Maitland had never known anything like it in her life.

It was all she ever hoped it could be.

As the ripples of satisfaction died down, Thomas remained buried in her, kissing her gently, showing her without words of the feelings that were growing for her. Come what may, she would always have his heart and there was nothing in the world, and no earldom powerful enough, to change that.

But he knew, even as he held her, that the difficulties of their situation had just exploded in all directions. The Beguine had now become a mistress... God, how he hated thinking of her in that context. She deserved so much more, more than he could give her at the moment. But that didn't stop him from being selfish about it.

He was in deep.

CHAPTER THIRTEEN

H E WAS OVER near the stables, helping Artus with the Billy goat by turning the animal out in the yard to graze, only the goat wasn't so fond of Artus and began chasing him around. Thomas just stood there and laughed.

The goats had a serious dislike for Artus.

Maitland could hear Thomas, that deep and booming laughter. He sounded so... *happy*. Two hours after their unexpected and sizzling encounter in the tower, she could still feel his body against hers and when she smelled her hands, she could smell his musk all over her.

It was enough to make her lightheaded.

Truly, she still had no idea what had come over her in that moment with Thomas. She'd been so strong and resolute to resist him, to deny him and whatever relationship he wanted to carry on with her, and then suddenly she was throwing herself at him like a harlot. It was like she couldn't control herself.

She simply wasn't sure how to feel about it. Regret? Guilt?

Or... *joy?*

Supper was on the horizon and she busied herself in the kitchen with Tibelda and the three littlest foundlings as they began to pack the soft cheese away for the night. The children, supervised by Tibelda, had the cheese curds tied up in squares of linen, enough to hold the curds together but porous enough to let the liquid drain out. They were tied to branches, at least six or ten packages hanging from a branch, for easy transporting down to the vault.

With the goats milked for the night, Maitland waved the older children over to the kitchen, where two of them would take a branch of goat cheese bundles and carry it off to the tower with the vault down beneath. Even Thomas got into the act as he and Artus took a branch between them, carrying everything down to the vault with Tibelda to direct them.

That left Maitland in the kitchen alone, focused on preparing supper. She'd been trying to figure out what to say to Thomas for two long hours, wondering if there was anything she could say at all that hadn't already been said. Truth be told, she felt embarrassed by her behavior but she wasn't sorry about it. She supposed that time would tell if she was just a whim with him or not, if he'd finally gotten what he wanted from her and would now move on, but something told her that wasn't the case. No man could look into her eyes so sincerely and speak such words of depth and beauty if they were meaningless.

At least, she hoped so.

With the children packing away the cheese for the night, Maitland's thoughts lingered on Thomas as she prepared the sup. With the eggs gathered from the chickens, she made another egg dish with the eggs, a little goat's milk and salt, and dill blended in. Two days ago, they'd slaughtered one of the chickens and after they'd picked the bones clean, she boiled the bones with carrots and onions and salt, making a delicious broth into which she put cabbage, more onion, and a little wild thyme. It made a wonderful pottage to eat with the baked eggs and the bread Tibelda had made, and by the time everyone came out of the vault, they could smell the delicious meal cooking.

But before they could eat, the animals had to be secured for the night, so the children raced to make sure everything was tied up and the gates of the pens were locked. It was all part of the responsibility Maitland was determined to teach them – responsibility for themselves and for their surroundings. She felt it important to give the children a sense of being responsible. Meanwhile, Maitland and Tibelda carried the meal into the tower, into the very room where Maitland and Thomas had made love.

In fact, when Maitland entered the chamber, it made her pause, her cheeks growing warm as she remembered that old, worn table with the fondest of memories. It was difficult to keep the smile off her face. She set everything down and passed out the wooden bowls that Thomas' carpenters had made for them, as the children, followed by Thomas, entered the chamber and clustered around the table.

Maitland began to dish out the food as Tibelda started a fire in the hearth, and Thomas sat down at the end of the table. The last time he was in that exact spot, he'd been doing naughty things to Maitland, and as she made sure all of the children had a bowl full of pottage and baked egg dish, Thomas sat there and ran his hands over the edge of the table as if remembering. He looked at her, she looked at him, and it was enough to cause Maitland's heart to skip a beat.

She could see it in his eyes.

Pure, unadulterated warmth and attraction. *Adoration.*

Things were different now.

Feeling breathless, giddy, Maitland struggled to return to what she was doing, spooning out bowls of pottage and passing them around the table. Once the children were slurping up pottage and eggs, she dared to look at him again, only to see that he was still looking at her with a smile on his face.

She smiled in return.

Filling the last wooden bowl with a heaping amount of the egg dish and a great hunk of bread, she went to the end of the table and put it in front of Thomas. His eyes never left her, not even when she put the bowl in front of him. He continued to smile at her and she continued to smile at him, so much so that she nearly forgot what she was going to say to him.

"I gave the children the pottage first," she said. "They will be busy eating soup, so you can eat your fill of the eggs and leave the rest for them."

Thomas' smile grew. "Thank you, Lady Bowlin," he said as he took the spoon she was handing to him. "But I could have just as easily eaten pottage as well."

She shook her head. "You are a grown man and you need more food than the children do," she said. "They are quite happy with their pottage and bread."

"And you?" Thomas said softly. "Will you not eat with me?"

Maitland nodded, perhaps a little shyly, and went to claim her own bowl of pottage and her piece of bread. As the children sat at one end of the table and stuffed their faces, laughing and chatting because, for the first time in ages, their living situation allowed them to be joyful, Maitland sat down with Thomas at the other end and began to eat her pottage in silence.

Thomas eyed her as he ate. All they'd done is smile at one another, but there was still a measure of uncertainty in the air. The dynamics between them had changed now, but he found it interesting that he didn't want to run from her. He couldn't count the number of women he'd bedded and then run away, so this was quite a new experience for him.

He didn't want to leave her at all.

"Now that you have all of this cheese, what next?" he asked after a moment. "When is Market Day?"

Maitland swallowed the bite in her mouth. "It is tomorrow, actually," she said. "I have already spoken with the market patron, the commander of Roxburgh Castle. He has agreed to let me sell the cheese on behalf of Edenside."

Thomas knew Roxburgh Castle, an English-held castle on the Scots side of the border. "Roxburgh Castle is garrison by Northwood Castle," he said. "I know the commander very well. I grew up with him, in fact."

"Oh?" she said, interested. "He told me his name was de Bocage, I believe."

Thomas nodded. "Tobias de Bocage," he said. "His father serves at Northwood Castle with my Uncle Paris and host of other cousins."

"He is very tall," Maitland said, spooning more pottage into her mouth. "I have never seen such a tall man."

Thomas grinned. "You should see his father," he said. "As tall as a tree. His father, Michael, served with my father many years ago when my father was the captain of Northwood's armies. In fact, my father was the commander of ten or eleven of the best knights who ever fought in the north, and Michael was one of those knights."

"But why did your father leave Northwood?"

"Because he received an earldom from King Henry and the gift of Castle Questing," he said. "Of course, I was not born at the time, but my mother tells the tale. My father and Uncle Paris, and another uncle named Kieran Hage were the best of friends. When my father went to Questing, it was a very difficult decision for Paris to remain at Northwood while Kieran went with my father. It is a difficult thing to separate best friends like that."

Maitland was listening with interest. "And your Uncle Kieran is still at Questing, with your father?"

Thomas shook his head. "He died about five years ago," he said. "The physic said it was a bad heart. He'd been suffering for years, but he was so attached to my father, and my father to him, that he simply held on as long as he could. My father still has not gotten over his death and, at his age, I doubt he ever will. For warriors, sometimes it is easier, and there is more of a sense of closure and finality, when men die in battle. That is a glorious death. But when a man lives as long as Kieran did and dies a slow and painful death, that is very difficult for fighting men to stomach. It seems to go against the natural order of things."

Maitland had stopped chewing, listening to the sorrow in Thomas' voice. "He must have been a great man."

"He was," Thomas agreed. "One of the greatest men I have ever known. He raised great sons as well. In fact, I went to The Levant several years ago with one of his sons, a man who is now the Duke of

Dorset. It is a long story how he obtained that title, but suffice it to say that I know his father would have been extremely proud of him for it."

Maitland was quite swept up in the conversation. "I did not know you went to The Levant."

"I did."

"What was it like?"

He wriggled his eyebrows. "Hot," he said. "Hot, dry, and dirty. And the fighting... brutal. Very, very brutal, but it was something that helped me grow as a warrior. It is not an experience that I would trade for anything, barbaric as it was."

Maitland thought on a hot land that was dry. "That seems so strange to hear you speak on a land that is hot and dry," she said. "Is it like that all year?"

"Very nearly."

"No water at all?"

"It depends where you were. Sometimes there was water. Sometimes there was not." He watched her face as she pondered such a place with awe. "The Mamluk warriors had a name for me."

"What was it?"

"Dhiib aleasifa."

He said it just the way the Mamluks did, such a foreign and beautiful tongue, but before Maitland could comment, someone nearby shouted in her ear.

"What does that mean?"

It was Artus, who had snuck over to their side of the table, unnoticed by either of them because they'd been so swept up in each other. As Maitland jumped at the sound of the child's voice and rubbed the ear he'd yelled in, Thomas laughed softly.

"It means StormWolfe," he said. "I create my own storms when I fight."

Artus had been listening to most of the conversation, captivated by the English warrior. "Is it true?" he asked. "Are ye a witch, then?"

Thomas shook his head. "It is only a figure of speech," he said. "It simply means I bring strength and chaos with me when I fight."

Artus was chewing on a big piece of bread, open-mouthed. "Can I see ye fight?"

Thomas shrugged. "There are no battles around here, lad."

"I think I know of one," Maitland said thoughtfully. "Tomorrow's market also coincides with a fair and there will be games of skill for knights. I saw some in town already when I was there. I thought it would be fun to take the children so they could enjoy the festivities and, mayhap, you could come along and let the children see you fight in the contests."

Being a great competitor, Thomas was immediately interested. "What kind of games?"

Maitland lifted her shoulders. "I am not certain, but there were several knights in town already," she said. "I also saw a posted bill that spoke of a large purse for the winner."

Thomas scratched his head. "A large purse, you say?" he said. "I suppose I could win it for the charity. It would be enough money to keep you supplied for a very long time."

Maitland grinned. "Then you will come with us and compete?"

Thomas looked between Maitland and Artus, who seemed very excited about the whole thing. The thought of competing for a prize was thrilling enough, but the thought of competing so that Maitland could see him... that was more appealing to him. It made him very proud to think of her cheering him on. But he was hesitant.

"I do not know," he said. "I do not have any of my joust equipment with me. All I have is my sword and usual equipment, but nothing specialized that they use at contests."

"Like what?" Artus demanded.

Thomas tried to explain. "It really depends on the contest," he said. "Mass competitions will not allow me to use my broadsword, but I haven't any clubs or blunt weapons with me. And if there is a joust, I will not be able to complete because I do not have any of my poles with me."

Artus would not be dissuaded. "Do ye have yer shield?"

"Always."

The boy threw up his hands. "'Tis all ye need. I can find ye a club in the yard."

Thomas was genuinely hesitant because he knew these fairs and tournaments were followed by men who did that kind of thing for a living. They were well-equipped for the games and he simply wasn't. But he realized, as he looked at Maitland and Artus, that he didn't want to disappoint them.

Besides… it had been a very long time since he'd attended any manner of tournament. They didn't get many of them in the wilds of the borders where he was, so he was thinking that, perhaps, he didn't want to miss this one.

It might be fun.

"Very well," he reluctantly agreed. "I will go, but I cannot promise I will be able to compete. Yet I will not go at all if you do not finish your supper. Lady Bowlin went through all the trouble to make it for you, so you will finish it."

Artus grinned broadly, displaying his yellow teeth, as he ran back to the children eating around the table and announced that Thomas would be competing at the fair in Kelso and make them all rich. That brought a round of cheers from the children, who leapt up in their blue tunics and began jumping around with glee.

Thomas and Maitland laughed as Tibelda tried to force them back to the table to finish, but it was a difficult fight. The little waifs, who had so little to be excited about in their lives, were overwrought with joy. Tibelda finally gave up and went to sit with Maitland and Thomas as the children danced around, ate their bread, and spoke of what they would do with the money Thomas won for them. When it finally came time for bed, only a bellow from Thomas sent them scattering to their chambers like skittish rabbits, but it wasn't out of fear.

It was out of excitement for what the next day would bring them.

When the children were finally in bed and the dishes were taken back to the kitchens by Tibelda, to be washed and used the next day, Thomas went out to take care of his horse, penning it with some grain and water, and returning to the tower with his saddlebags.

Truth be told, spending the night in the same building as Maitland after what had happened earlier in the day made him a little anxious. They hadn't spoken about it because they were both trying to process it, but their casual conversation at supper had been encouraging. Maitland showed no signs of being awkward towards him. Even so, Thomas knew, at some point, they would speak on what had happened. For him, it had been a powerful experience, perhaps one of the most powerful experiences he'd ever had because he'd shared it with someone he was very quickly coming to care a great deal about.

But because he was coming to care for her, he was coming to think that he probably shouldn't bed her again, at least not until they talked things out. He didn't want her to think he was only interested in having relations with her. There was far more to it than that. For the first time since Tacey, Thomas was thinking about someone else and trying to be conscientious of her feelings. Not that he'd bedded Tacey; he never had. His feelings for her had been far more emotional and far less physical because of their circumstances at the time. There was something in him that had connected with that lonely young woman. But with Maitland, the physical pull was overwhelming and he didn't want her to think that he was trying to disrespect her, or take advantage of her, in any way.

That was a new thought process for him.

Therefore, he spread his traveling cloak out on the warm stones in front of the hearth in the feasting chamber and using his saddlebags as a pillow, he lay back, listening to Maitland move around on the floor above, scolding children who were too excited to sleep. Somehow, he drew comfort simply from hearing her voice. He never knew such a thing was possible.

When Tibelda finally came back to the tower and bolted the entry door, Thomas remained awake as the woman went up the stairs and the voices above him grew quiet. At some point, he drifted off to sleep, warmed by the fire, perhaps even a bit exhausted from the events of the day. For certainly, it had been eventful.

Perhaps even life changing.

When Maitland tiptoed downstairs less than an hour later, she found him snoring softly before the fire. She'd only come to bid him a good sleep, but she ended up watching him sleep for a few minutes. Leaving him with a gentle kiss to his forehead, she went upstairs and fell asleep, dreaming of dark-haired knights with big dimples.

CHAPTER FOURTEEN

Kelso, Scotland
The Borders

IT WAS A far bigger fair than Thomas had been led to believe.

The day was brilliant, a bright blue sky above and the sun was giving off some warmth that was positively glorious. The village of Kelso was full of people at the early hour of the morning, farmers and merchants and potential customers, all of them moving through the occasionally muddy streets of Kelso on Market Day.

Kelso had a charter to hold a market and they did, every Sunday, one that was especially busy when the pious emerged from mass, as they were now. Matins was over and people were spilling out into the vast market area to purchase their goods. But more than the customers and merchants at this hour, there was also a deluge of knights and armed men filling the town as well.

It was almost three miles exactly from Edenside to the market street, which ran next to Kelso's vast abbey. On the east side of the town, on an island between two branches of the River Tweed, stood Roxburgh Castle, and Thomas could see the mighty fortress as they arrived at the market. It was a magnificent bastion, rising up over the land with its gray towers and powerful gatehouse. With the morning sun glistening off of it, it almost looked white, like something straight from the halls of heaven.

It was difficult to keep his mind on what he was doing as he spied the castle, knowing his close friends were there, but he'd committed to helping Maitland set up the stall to sell their cheese. It was rather demeaning work for a man of his reputation and stature to be helping with menial tasks, but anything to keep him close to Maitland, he would do without question.

Where she was concerned, he had little pride.

The ride to Kelso that morning had been quiet between them, with no meaningful words but meaningful glances the entire way. They still hadn't spoken about what had happened the day before, but the more Thomas spent time with her that morning, helping her set up her stall and speaking of things that were related to those tasks, the more he could sense that she wasn't troubled by what had happened. Considering she had initiated it, he wasn't entirely sure she wouldn't feel terribly ashamed and guilty about it, but as the morning deepened, and the more time they spent together, the more he could see that she wasn't bothered by it.

If anything, there was a light in her eyes that he'd never seen before.

It put a zest in his step, giving him that feeling of walking on air again. He'd never known such foolish joy, and when the stall opened for business, he started grabbing people off the street and dragging them over to the stall, forcing them to taste the cheese and then forcing them to buy it, even if they hadn't come to the marketplace for cheese.

After the fifth customer he'd commandeered bought four round blobs of the delicious goat cheese, he began to walk up and down the avenue, grabbing anyone who looked like they had the money to buy the cheese. Terrified people were pulled over to a stall that contained two women and seven small children, all of them delighted to sell the goat cheese that was truly delicious. Even if the cheese had been awful, the force-fed customers would have bought it anyway, simply to spare them the wrath of the big, muscular knight who seemed to be their champion.

Thomas' strong-arm tactics worked. By mid-morning, nearly all of the cheese had been sold. It sold for two pence for a half-pint of the cheese, and they'd brought almost fifty half-pint blobs with them. Now, they only had seven left and the children were wildly excited about the money they'd made. Maitland took the opportunity to teach them a little about counting, and money, and she counted out the coins in front of them, and they had a little over seven shillings total, which was an astronomical amount of money to them.

Already, their Market Day had been a success.

Thomas watched as Maitland taught the children about money, giving each one of them a pence to keep. To see their faces when she gave them the money, one would have thought that the crown jewels had just been handed over to them. Maitland told them to save it, but Artus wanted to know if he could buy himself some shoes because the only ones he had were worn and had holes in the sole.

In truth, Thomas thought it was a little sad that the child should want to buy himself shoes – not a toy, or sweets, but shoes. That was the extent of his lavish thinking. That gave Thomas an idea and he told Maitland he would return shortly. Heading out of the stall, he went in search of a tanner, but he hadn't taken ten steps when he caught sight of a group of knights heading in from the east. Ever observant, he peered at the group, coming in from the far side of the town, before coming to realize that he knew them.

He recognized the colors.

The first thing he saw was the de Longley crest, three hugely clawed falcons imposed over a sword, framed in a three-point shield. The colors of scarlet and black announced that the knights of Northwood Castle were making an appearance. Thomas knew those colors, and that crest, as well as he knew his father's own standards. They were colors that dominated Northumberland because everyone in the north knew of Northwood Castle and the House of de Longley, the Earls of Teviot.

Thomas' nearest and dearest had arrived.

So, he stood in the middle of the road, facing them as they approached, his big arms folded across his chest and a smirk on his face. He could see them drawing closer and closer, paying more attention to what was going on around them than what was in front of them. Then, someone caught sight of him because he heard his name shouted. The entire group looked in his direction and he could see expressions of glee spread over the familiar faces.

"Thomas!"

It was Hector de Norville, a man who also happened to be married to Thomas' sister, Evelyn. A big man with a crown of red hair that had now mostly gone to gray, he lifted a gloved hand to Thomas, who lifted his in return. Behind Hector were his two sons, Atreus and Hermes, strong young knights who saw their Uncle Thomas and made a dash for him on their new Belgian war horses that were difficult to control. Fledgling knights and excitable horses almost always made a bad combination.

In fact, Thomas had to get out of the way when Hermes came too close because his cream-colored horse didn't seem to want to stop. The horse roared past him, all mane and tail and thundering hooves. Irritated, Thomas slapped the horse on the rump, which caused the horse to start and ended up nearly dumping Hermes. Thomas threw up his hands as he turned to Hector.

"You let them bring beasts like that into town?" he asked. "They are going to kill everyone."

Hector snored. "Or they shall teach my sons a very valuable lesson," he said, watching his sons dismount the horses so they wouldn't be thrown. "Those are a gift from their grandfather. I told my father not to give them those horses, but he insisted when he saw them at a dealer in Berwick. He says every young knight must have a wild horse to tame."

Thomas snorted. "That sounds like Uncle Paris," he said, looking at the group of knights behind Hector. "He did not come with you?"

Hector shook his head. "My father is lazy in his old age," he said. "He did not want to come."

"Where is Teviot?"

He was referring to the Earl of Teviot, the lord and master of Northwood Castle who, long ago, had also been a knight under the command of William de Wolfe before his father passed away and left him the title. He had made a very fine earl for over forty years, as he'd been young when he'd inherited the title, and Adam de Longley had earned himself the name of "Teviot the Good" because of his benevolence over the years. His manner, his fairness, had been a tribute to the fine training of William de Wolfe those many years ago.

"De Longley has not been well," Hector said, his mood dampening a bit. "He has something in his chest that the doctors cannot seem to cure, a cough that has become worse over time. His lady wife thought it best for him not to exert himself with a trip to Kelso."

Thomas knew that Adam had not been in the best of health as of late. It was troubling to hear. "I will make a point of visiting Northwood one of these days to see him," he said. "His sons did not come, either?"

Hector shook his head. "One is in France and the other is in London," he said. "Why are *you* here? Did you come for the tournament?"

Thomas opened his mouth to tell him, but something made him hesitate. Telling Hector that he'd escorted two women and seven children into town didn't sound very masculine, in retrospect, but he couldn't very well lie.

"I am the patron of the Edenside foundling home," he said, trying to make it sound prestigious, like he hadn't just herded a bunch of women and children into town. "The woman in charge has brought the children into town to sell their cheese. She is trying to make the home self-sufficient and I support her efforts."

That sounded masculine enough, or at least benevolent enough, and Hector nodded his head as if impressed. "Tommy the Benefactor," he said with a grin. "You are taking after your parents. I swear, they support half the charities in Northumberland."

"Aye, they do. A worthy thing, don't you think?"

"I do," Hector agreed. "So you are telling me you are not here to compete in the tournament? I am disappointed. I wanted you on our team."

Thomas glanced at the men behind Hector, recognizing all of them. A smile spread across his lips. "No wonder you want me," he said. "Look at that motley crew you have brought with you. You should be ashamed of yourself."

Hector laughed softly, turning to the men behind him. "Even if my father didn't come, old Deinwald did," he said, catching the man's attention and waving him forward. "Have you nothing to say to Tommy, Deinwald?"

Sir Deinwald Ellsrod was perhaps the surliest, bitterest, and meanest man on the border. A knight who had served with William and Paris and Kieran in his prime, he had been a wild man on the field of battle, looking like a barbarian with his blond ponytail and big muscles, and he rarely had a kind word to say to anyone. But the truth was that a fairer, more just man had never existed, and he had surprisingly mellowed in his old age. But not too much; he spied Thomas and simply lifted an eyebrow.

"I have much to say to that de Wolfe whelp," he said. "Where should I start?"

Thomas grinned as he moved back in the group, going to Deinwald and putting a hand on the old man's leg.

"Tell me how much you love me," he said. "Tell me how much you miss me."

"Never. I loathe the sight of you."

Thomas pointed at him. "I can see a tear in your eye right now," he said, grinning as he turned to the men next to him. Deinwald's grandsons, Garr and Hugh Ellsrod. "God help you with a grandfather like that. It is a miracle you did not turn out exactly like him."

Hugh was two years older than his twenty-year-old brother. "I would be proud to be as nasty and bitter as he is," Hugh said, "but it seems I have inherited my grandmother's fine disposition. I am a rose to my grandfather's thorn."

Thomas nodded. "Your Grandmother Aloria is a remarkable woman," he agreed, looking to the dark-haired younger brother. "Greetings, Garr."

"Do not talk to him!" Hector suddenly yelled. "He has asked to court my daughter, Lisbet, so I am in the process of being very cruel to him. You will not speak to him, Thomas. I mean it."

Thomas started laughing. "Lisbet is a lovely young woman of sixteen years," he said, pointing to Garr. "You would deny her this magnificent specimen of a potential husband?"

Hector waved a stern hand at him. "Bah," he scoffed. "Ignore him, I say."

Thomas looked at Garr and shrugged, who shrugged in return. There didn't seem to be any real animosity, merely a father who did not want to lose his youngest child yet. In fact, Garr was trying not to grin. Thomas headed back in Hector's direction.

"If you want me on your team for the tournament, I would be willing," he said. "But I have no equipment with me. I would have to borrow yours."

Hector nodded firmly. "I will be happy to let you," he said. "One de Wolfe is worth ten men of another team. Will you come with us now? We are heading to Roxburgh to see Tobias. He will be on our team, as well."

Thomas thought on his friend, Tobias, the big and powerful knight with a long reach, which would work to his advantage in a competition. "Collect Tobias and I will meet you back here," he said. "Where is the competition field?"

Hector pointed back the way they had come. "If you came in on this road, you passed it," he said. "It is in the open area to the north, outside of town. Meet us over there around midday. That is when the teams will be selected and the rules established."

Thomas nodded. "I will be there."

Hector's gaze lingered on him a moment. "Tommy," he said. "Is your intended with you?"

Thomas' features stiffened. "She is not," he said. "Why do you ask?"

Hector shrugged. "My father has mentioned the situation you are going through," he said, lowering his voice. "I am sorry, Tommy. It does not sound ideal."

Thomas didn't want to think of Adelaide, not today, but he was polite to Hector's statement. "It is not," he said. "I will tell you more about it later, but not out here in the middle of the street. Get going to Roxburgh and I will see you at the field in a short while."

Hector simply nodded, giving the man a brief smile as he moved out and taking his men with him. Thomas stood aside as everyone passed him, grinning when Deinwald cast him a typically nasty scowl.

It was good to see that again.

As the party from Northwood moved past him, heading for Roxburgh Castle, Thomas headed back to the stall to inform the eager children that he would, indeed, be competing in the tournament this day. As he moved down the road, the crowd thinned out and, suddenly, children in blue tunics were running at him.

"No more cheese! No more cheese!"

They were grabbing at his hands, pulling at him, and he looked down into happy little faces. Marybelle, a little blonde, and her sister, Nora, who was older with bushy red hair, each had a hand, while Artus and the twins, Renard and Roland, were pulling on his tunic. Behind him, he could feel more little hands tugging at him.

"We have no more cheese!" Artus said excitedly. "We sold it all!"

Now, Thomas understood the excitement. "I see," he said. "Congratulations. You have done well today."

That was all they wanted to hear. The children let him go, excited with their pence, and it reminded Thomas that he'd been intending to find a tanner before the knights from Northwood distracted him. He intended to have seven pairs of shoes made. But that would have to wait as Maitland approached him, her lovely face glowing with delight.

"We made over eight shillings today," she said. "Truly, I did not expect to sell everything. I was hoping to sell just a few."

Thomas grinned at her as the children danced around them. "It is an excellent product and people will like it a great deal," he said. "You must make sure you are here every Market Day so they can find you and buy more. But I still intend to go to all of the taverns in town and get a commitment from them to buy your cheese, so you had better plan on making a great deal."

Maitland nodded excitedly. "We will," she said, watching the happy children around her. "Can you believe it, Thomas? A week ago, these were sad and starving children, and now look at them."

Thomas watched her face as she looked at the children. "You have shown them what kindness and compassion can do," he said quietly. "*You* did this, Mae. You showed a measure of compassion to children who had known none, and now see the result. You should be very proud."

Maitland looked at him, warmth and gratitude in her expression. "But I could not have done it without you," she said. "Your generosity and your mother's generosity have made this possible."

He had the sudden urge to kiss her. He wanted to pull her into his arms and kiss her until she gasped. In fact, he almost forgot himself and started to reach out for her, but he caught himself in time, putting his hands behind his back in the hope that it would help his self-control.

But, God's Bones, it was difficult.

"Anything for you," he murmured, for her ears only.

Maitland smiled at him, a glorious smile that made his heart flutter. He could tell that she wanted to say more to him but refrained for propriety's sake, perhaps. Or perhaps it was because she wasn't sure what to say in this strange, new world the day after she had thrown herself at Thomas.

It was obvious that things were different between them now.

Averting her gaze, she turned to help Tibelda, who was packing up the bowls and buckets they'd brought, putting them into a hand cart that had been found on the grounds of Edenside and repaired.

As Maitland and Tibelda loaded up, all Thomas did was stand there and stare at Maitland. He'd once questioned himself as to whether or not he'd loved her, knowing that, given time, he would. But as he watched her work, he realized that he didn't need any more time to realize that he did, indeed, love her. There was so much there to love, from her kindness to her intelligence to her beauty. He'd fallen hard and fast for her, but he didn't care. It brought him joy he couldn't begin to describe. Maitland had been so worried that she was a passing fancy and, as he'd told her yesterday, she wasn't. In fact, she would never be rid of him. He was hers for life.

All would have been perfect except for one thing…

Adelaide.

Thomas had told his father he would marry the woman and he would not break that promise. Too much was at stake and, in spite of everything, he still agreed with everything he and his father had discussed. Only now, he was coming to cling to the hope that his father would get evidence on the murders Adelaide had committed so the woman could be locked up and the marriage annulled. He knew it was a nearly impossible hope; God help him, he knew it. But he wouldn't give up hope that, somehow, it would all work out in the end. He would marry Maitland and spend the rest of his life proud and happy with the woman he married.

He would pray for a miracle.

But until that day came, he would enjoy each and every moment with her because he knew that from this point on, their time together would be few and far between. Today was a gift from God as far as he was concerned.

He wasn't going to waste it.

"I saw some friends of mine in town," he said after a few moments. "Did you see the big group of knights ride in a few minutes ago?"

Maitland looked up from securing a wooden bowl in the hand cart. "I think so," she said. "But there have been a great many groups of men moving about. The group with the red and black banner? The men you were talking to?"

He nodded. "They are from Northwood Castle," he said. "The knight in command is my brother-in-law, married to my sister, Evelyn. He has my nephews with him, among others. He has asked if I would compete with them in the coming games and I have agreed, so it seems as if you and the children will have some great spectacles to view today. These are very skilled knights, so it should be quite a show."

Maitland's face lit up. "How exciting," she said. "I know the children will be thrilled. Do you think we will have time to take our cart back to Edenside before the festivities begin? If we go to the field to watch you, we have nowhere to put it for safe keeping."

Thomas shook his head. "Not to worry," he said. "I shall take it over to the livery across the road and pay the man a pence to watch over it for you."

And he did, taking it across to the livery at the end of the market street, wedging it back into a stall and paying the livery keep to watch over it. By the time he returned to Maitland, the children had been told that Thomas was to officially compete in the upcoming games and they were thrilled beyond measure. Marybelle and Nora grabbed on to his hands again, as it seemed to be their favorite thing to do with him. Thomas, Maitland, Tibelda, and all of the children headed from the market street and into the avenue of the merchants.

With the fair in full bloom, the avenue was lined with entertainers that had come in from out of town. The first thing they saw was a man who wore painted masks to frighten and thrill the children, and little Dyana and Roland burst into tears at the sight. Maitland picked up the little girl to comfort her while Thomas forced Marybelle and Nora to let his hands go so he could collect Roland. He convinced the little boy that there was nothing to be frightened of, or at least tried to, and as they came upon some dancing dogs, the boy's tears seemed to miraculously vanish.

Eager, excited children crowded around a man who had five trained dogs. The dogs could dance on command, spun circles, climb up on a stool and beg, and a host of other tricks that had the children laughing and clapping. At least, it had six out of the seven clapping and laughing. Dyana, the youngest, was tired and yawning and weepy, and Maitland held the little girl on her hip as she rubbed her eyes and wept. Not even the dancing dogs could lighten her mood.

But then a man walked by with candied slices of apples and pears on a stick, and Dyana suddenly wasn't quite so tired. Thomas noticed her interested but she stopped short of asking for anything; she simply looked at the treats with big eyes. Thomas saw what had her attention and he purchased seven of the sticks, each with three apple and three pear slices that had been coated in honey and cinnamon.

The children took the candied fruit sticks as if someone had handed them a hunk of gold. A treat like this was so very precious and rare. At first, they looked at it mostly, unsure what to do, until Thomas told them to eat it. The only child among them who had ever had sweets was Artus, who gobbled down the confection. When the other children saw how much he liked the treat, they followed suit and soon they were all sticky with the honey from the fruit, eating it eagerly. The little dogs, distracted from their performance by the children eating, broke rank to lick hands until their master yelled at them. Dejected, the dogs went back to performing.

Watching the children eat their treats had Thomas rather hungry and he looked around, spying smoke from the chimneys of the bakers. They seemed to be located behind the street of the merchants, so he convinced Maitland that they should find some food before the festivities began, and she grasped the children, moving them away from the dogs as Thomas headed across the avenue. Thomas could hear Roland and Renard weeping now, as they evidently wanted to take some of the dogs with them. Having much experience in weeping children as a result of Caria, Thomas backtracked his steps and took the little boys with him, one in each hand, as he herded everyone towards the street of the bakers.

The street of the bakers turned out to be more of a central court-yard of bakers, with three of them churning out bread and other food for hungry visitors. Thomas went from baker to baker, buying bread and butter, and anything else they happened to have. The first baker had stuffed eggs, which were hard-boiled eggs filled with the cooked yolk mashed with herbs and cheese, while the second baker had fruit bread and pies filled with meat, apples, and carrots.

While Tibelda and Maitland settled the children down beneath a small tree that was behind one of the baker's ovens, spreading out the feast before them, Thomas went to the third baker to find a pie of honey and apples, all baked up with clove. Bringing two big pies back to the children, he set them down on the ground before them and watched the children stuff themselves. In fact, they ate so much that he had to return for more eggs and meat pies for himself, Maitland, and Tibelda.

"Truly, Thomas, you have done so much already," Maitland said as he handed her a meat pie of her own. "Tibby and I could have shared with the children."

Thomas had a mouthful of eggs. "You do not need to share with them," he said. "You deserve your own food. You have worked hard enough for it."

She looked down at her pie as if unsure. "You have been far too kind," she said quietly. "I do not think I have ever known anyone so generous."

He stopped chewing and looked at her. "It is for you, you know," he said softly. "Everything I do is for you. Do you not realize that yet?"

She looked at him, smiling weakly. "I do not even know what to say."

"Tell me you know why I am doing all of this."

"I know."

He resumed chewing, swallowing the bite in his mouth. "Good," he said. "Now – *eat*."

It was a subtle command. With a grin on her face, Maitland tucked into the meat pie, using her fingers, and it was utterly delicious. Hungry, she plowed through most of it, giving over a small corner to Artus, who was still hungry. But it didn't matter; her belly was full, as was her heart.

Truly, she didn't think it could be any fuller.

Tucked back behind the warm stone ovens of the baker's circle, the children were beginning to grow sleepy. Having been up well before sunrise, and now with full bellies after an eventful morning, they were now lying down in the grassy patches or resting on each other. Dyana was already sleeping on Tibelda, while Renard and Roland had lain down on each other, sleeping like puppies in a pile. Phin, the silent young lad who was the same age as Nora, sat with the sisters as Marybelle lay her head on her sister's lap and fell asleep. That left Artus standing off by himself, but when he saw Thomas and Maitland in quiet conversation, he wandered over to them.

"I dunna want tae sleep," he said flatly. "Can I go out and look at the fair?"

Thomas looked at the boy, amused. "You do not wish to rest? It has been a busy day already."

Artus shook his head, frowning. "I'm not a bairn," he said. "I want tae see the fair!"

He was quite enthusiastic about the festivities, disdainful that Thomas should think he needed to sleep. Therefore, Thomas took pity on him.

"You would get swallowed up out there if you went out alone," he said. "I will go with you. In fact, Lady Bowlin should come with us, too. She may see something that she needs for the home."

Maitland wasn't sure what that could be but she didn't give him any argument; she simply nodded. Artus was thrilled to be able to go out along the avenue and see all of the sights, with Thomas and Maitland bringing up the rear. Leaving Tibelda with the children, the three of them headed out onto the main road again, now onto the street of the merchants where there were all manner of tradesmen and importers.

Artus raced up ahead, immediately mesmerized by a smithy who was pounding at something on his anvil. Sparks flew and the child stood there, entranced, as Thomas and Maitland walked through the crowd, catching up with the boy. Thomas' gaze lingered on the lad.

"I've not had the opportunity to ask you how Artus has been this past week," he said. "He was quite defiant on the night we arrived at Edenside but seems to have settled down well enough."

Maitland's gaze was on Artus. "All things considered, he has settled in admirably well."

"Has he stopped calling himself Wrath?"

She grinned. "Aye," she said. "He has. I was afraid we would have trouble with him when I forced Queenie out, and initially he was upset, but that quickly passed when he realized I would not be stealing the food from the children. It seems that Queenie had stolen nearly everything and the children were subsisting on very little, but they had no one else to care for them."

"Did Artus tell you that?"

She nodded. "Aye," she said. "He spoke a little of what happened with the abbot's sister and the servant. It would seem that Artus hid all of the children that were left from a servant he called Laird Letty, a man who took children away who would never return."

Thomas shook his head sadly. "And he does not know what became of the children?"

"Nay. But he knew enough to hide those he could."

"Where did he hide them that the servant could not find them?"

They were nearing Artus at this point and Maitland came to a halt, turning to speak to Thomas so Artus wouldn't hear her.

"He told me that he took them down by the river," she said softly. "He took them out of Edenside completely and it was Queenie, who was the cook, who smuggled them food and blankets. The old girl may have stolen food out of their mouths, but it sounds as if she helped them through the crisis, at least a little. Some of the coinage you gave me went to Queenie when I sent her away to reward her for helping the children. I do not want her at Edenside, but I am appreciative of what she did for them. I cannot even imagine the horrors these children have endured, Thomas. That is why it makes me so happy to see them laughing and eating and making cheese to sell. They need someone they can trust, and they need a sense of normalcy, a sense of security."

Thomas was nodding as she spoke. "And you have given that to them," he said, glancing over at Artus, who was asking the smithy a question. "And that lad is a hero, whether or not he knows it. He seems smart and resourceful."

"He is," Maitland said, looking over at the boy. "He is very bright."

"But he does not know who his family is?"

"Not at all. He has been at the foundling home since he can remember."

Thomas cocked his head thoughtfully. "How old would you say he is?"

Maitland shrugged. "Ten years of age," she said. "At least, that is what I told him. He does not really know."

"He is old enough to foster at Wark," Thomas said. "The lad can become a page and mayhap even a soldier someday. It would be good training for him beyond making cheese. It would give him a profession."

Maitland looked at him in surprise. "You would take a child with no family and no background to foster?" she said. "That is astonishing, Thomas. What would your family say? A position in a de Wolfe household is a coveted thing."

It was his turn to shrug. "I can do as I wish," he said. "Smart lads are always welcome. Believe me, I have seen lads from the finest families who are as stupid as a fence post. An intelligent boy is a valuable commodity."

Maitland thought that was a rather magnanimous view. "I do not know many men that would say that," she said. "In fact, I do not know any, except mayhap Lord de Vesci. He was a generous man, too, much as you are. But what will your wife…"

She suddenly came to a halt, realizing she had brought up the one subject they'd been dancing around since he appeared yesterday. She hadn't meant to bring it up; it simply came out. When she glanced at him, embarrassed and smiling apologetically, Thomas took a step towards her and lowered his voice.

"Finish what you were going to say."

She shook her head. "I should not have said it," she muttered. "It just slipped out. Forgive me."

He sighed in understanding. "There is nothing to forgive," he said. "You want to know about Adelaide."

She wouldn't look at him, lifting her shoulders weakly. He continued.

"I am glad you brought her up," he said. "We've not spoken about anything that we should have, so let us get it all out in the open. First, let us speak on what happened yesterday. I will be honest when I tell you that it was, mayhap, one of the most important experiences of my life and I want you to know that come what may, I shall always belong to you. I told you that Adelaide may have my name, but you will always have my heart, Mae. I know that it is not proper, but I cannot help what I feel. You know the situation with Adelaide... it is only an arrangement, and an unhappy one at that. I wish things were different. I wish that with all my heart."

Maitland was looking at him now, her expression somewhat guarded. "I do not know what came over me yesterday," she said. "One moment I was looking at you and in the next..."

"Are you ashamed?"

"Of my behavior? Aye. But not of what I feel for you."

He smiled faintly. "Tell me what you feel for me, Mae. Please."

She grimaced and averted her gaze. "I have tried not to feel anything, but I cannot help it. There is nothing about you that I do not adore."

"Nor I about you."

She looked at him, then. "You asked me once if you were to go through the rest of your life wondering what could have been between us," she said. "I have held you off and told you it was not fair to me to press your affections, but the truth is that I have affection of my own towards you. Mayhap when the affection is as strong as it is between two people, that affection will find a way."

"And that is the case with us?"

"I believe it is."

He stared at her a moment, a glimmer in his eyes that wavered between delight and sorrow, before suddenly reaching out to grasp her hand.

"Come with me," he said.

After telling Artus to remain at the smithy stall, Thomas hauled Maitland down the avenue, pulling her through groups of people, clearly in search of something. Maitland went along with him, knowing she couldn't very well pull away, but also quite curious as to what he was searching for. He was a man on a mission, towing her through the crowd under the midday sun until he found what he was looking for.

Maitland found herself being pulled into a rather large merchant stall. In fact, the stall was at least four times the size of a normal stall – there was a stall section in the middle, and on both ends, and then it stretched back away from the street, and the entire place was loaded with more merchandise than Maitland had ever seen. Thomas marched right up to a man who appeared to work there, as he wore expensive clothing and an elaborate cloth around his head.

"Is this your establishment?" Thomas asked.

The man turned to look at him, a very big knight with expensive clothing, expensive protection, and a very expensive sword. He perked right up.

"Aye, my lord," he said. "What do you have need for?"

Thomas pulled Maitland forward. "Her," he said. "Do you have garments you can sell her? Things she can wear today?"

As Maitland gasped and shook her head, the man nodded. "I do," he said. "Let me bring my wife. She sells pre-made garments to some of the finest ladies in the north. I am sure she has something to suit your... your..."

"Wife," Thomas said without hesitation, digging into the purse on his belt. "Give her at least three or four things she can wear. They must be durable and well-made, and pretty, but not too elaborate. She serves the church in a capacity and it would not do for her to wear something gaudy. Is that clear?"

As the man looked rather confused, Thomas put a gold coin in his palm, a truly princely sum. The man's eyes widened and he quickly nodded his head.

"Aye, my lord," he said, suddenly darting away, calling for his wife. "Leave your lady in my hands, my lord. She will be properly clad!"

As he rushed off, yelling for his wife, Maitland turned to Thomas. "You know I cannot wear what has not been given to me by the church," she said. "I cannot…"

"*I* am donating the clothing to you," he said. "Mae, you are a beautiful woman. You deserve to wear something other than these sacks and rags that you have on. I am not trying to hurt your feelings, but a durable dress that is somewhat better fitting would be much better than what you have on, don't you think?"

Maitland was both horrified and interested. She'd had nice clothing, once, but it had been too elaborate for her charity work with the church. Beguines didn't wear silks and damask, so when Henry had died, she'd given her finery away in lieu of more appropriate clothing. But, God help her, she missed wearing something soft and figure-fitting. Perhaps it was vain of her, but she missed it nonetheless.

"Well," she said reluctantly. "I suppose it would be all right if the garments were not too elaborate."

Thomas held up his hands as if to ease her. "You may pick anything you wish," he said. "You will choose what you shall wear, but please let me do this for you. You deserve everything I can provide for you, Mae."

Maitland looked at him, realizing that her eyes were stinging with tears. *I can give you everything but my name, he'd said once.* Perhaps he'd really meant it. Perhaps he was actually a man of his word in a world that saw little of that. Now, he was trying to take care of her – *her.*

Not the charity, not the children, but her.

It had been so long since anyone had taken care of her and, at that moment, Maitland realized how much she had missed it. It was wrong to be so weak; oh, so very wrong. She was allowing him to buy her things and to call her his wife when she wasn't. She swore that she would never carry on with a married man, but as Thomas pointed out, he wasn't married – yet.

Yet.

Perhaps she was simply living in a fool's paradise.

But Maitland didn't say anything more as the merchant and his wife rushed towards her, both of them very eager to help the lady, and Thomas stood off to the side and grinned as the pair fussed over Maitland and discussed what would be best for her. She seemed uneasy, and uncertain, and she kept looking at Thomas as if to seek reassurance that this was the right thing to do. He nodded at her, encouragingly, and then she simply seemed resigned. As the wife dragged Maitland back into the rear of the stall, Thomas' attention found the jewelry cases that the man had against the wall.

The cases were literally that – locked boxes that contained precious items. Thomas knew this because he'd seen enough merchants in his travels to and from The Levant to know how they transported their fine gems and gold. Curious, he called the merchant over to unlock them, and the man did, presenting Thomas with a multitude of beautiful gold and silver jewelry.

"I have many things from the lands of The Levant and beyond," the merchant told him, knowing he had a customer with a lot of money on his hands. "See these golden earrings? They are from Greece, my lord. Can you see the shape? They are bees. They would look beautiful on the lady."

Thomas wasn't interested in earrings although had to admit that they were lovely. He looked at the fine necklaces, bracelets, and rings, an entire variety of them – purple stones, blue stones, Mother of Pearl, and more. The merchant had quite a selection. But then he came to something that caught his attention; it was a small, gold ring with a gemstone in the middle of it, in a gold setting, and he lifted it up to look at it. Turning it about in the light, he realized that it was the exact color of Maitland's eyes – that light brown color that had a hint of red in it. An astonishing color he'd never seen before, now in a gemstone on a ring. He handed it to the merchant.

"What kind of stone is that?" he asked.

The merchant held it up. "It is called *krustallos*," he said, inspecting the stone. "It is a stone that comes in many colors – yellow, brown, sometimes even blue or pink. The ancient Greeks believed it was a very powerful amulet. It is meant for protection."

Thomas rather liked that idea. "I will take it," he said. "Now, can you have shoes made for the lady?"

The man nodded eagerly. "I can, my lord," he said. "I work with a fine tanner because sometimes my customers want boots or slippers. What do you need?"

Thomas could see the man's eyes lighting up with the thought of coins, mayhap even multiple coins, hoping for a great sale. He fought off a smile.

"Shoes for the lady, so make sure you mark the size of her feet," he said. "Something durable, I should think. Not slippers, but boots."

"Aye, my lord."

"And seven small pairs of shoes."

The merchant lifted his eyebrows. "*Seven* small pairs, my lord?"

"For children."

The merchant looked surprised. "You... you and your wife have seven small children?"

It was taking a lot of effort not to grin. "Seven," he said. "Four boys and three girls. I shall mark out the size of their feet, approximately, and you shall have them made for me. Deliver them to Edenside Foundling Home as soon as you can and I shall pay you handsomely. Do you know where Edenside is?"

The merchant nodded, only now he wasn't looking too terribly surprised. Concerned was more like it. "Edenside," he breathed. "You… you are there with your children?"

Thomas nodded. "They all belong to me now and I intend to take good care of them," he said. "Have you heard of the House of de Wolfe?"

The man nodded quickly. "I have, my lord."

"Good," Thomas said. "My father is William de Wolfe and I am the commander of his outpost at Wark Castle. You will make sure the lady is properly clothed, ensure she has a pair of new boots, and deliver seven new pairs of leather shoes to me at Edenside and I will make sure my father and mother purchase goods from your establishment. Fail at anything I have asked for and I will ensure my parents, and everyone else I know, has nothing to do with you. Is that clear?"

The man was overwhelmed with what he'd just been told, but he nodded firmly. "It is, my lord," he said. "Leave me with the sizes of the little feet and I shall ensure they are delivered to you before the next week is out."

Pleased that he had the merchant properly awed and frightened, Thomas was about to turn to look at any number of other wares in the stall when Maitland suddenly appeared from the rear of the establishment with the man's wife trailing after her. She was out of the woolen long tunic she wore, the one that concealed her beautiful figure, and she was wearing a simple brown surcoat over a soft white shift with long sleeves. The garment had ties on the side, along her torso, and it was a little long, but it flattered her figure beautifully. She looked like an entirely new woman in it and Thomas could feel his heart flutter at the sight of her.

She was stunning.

"You look utterly beautiful, Mae," he said, unable to take his eyes from her. "Is it comfortable?"

Maitland looked a little embarrassed by all of the fuss, but she nodded to his question. "So very warm and soft," she said, sticking out her arm. "Feel the shift? It is of a very fine broadcloth."

He touched it, feeling how soft but sturdy it was. "Do you like it?"

Hesitantly, she nodded. "I do, Thomas, but…"

He cut her off, turning to the merchant. "We will take this one," he said, returning his focus to Maitland. "Is this the only one available?"

Maitland shook her head, looking down at herself. "Nay," she said. "There is another one, light blue in color, that is of nearly the same style."

"Then we shall take that one, too. Anything else?"

"Thomas, *stop*," Maitland put her hand on his arm insistently. "It is too much. All of this; it is too much."

Thomas ignored her as he turned back to the merchant. "We shall take both of these garments and she shall wear this one out of the shop," he said. "When I return next week, have more ready-made garments for her to look at."

The merchant and his wife scattered, going to collect the other blue surcoat as well as the ring that Thomas has purchased. As the wife rushed forward from the rear of the stall, she was carrying the pale blue surcoat with her, but she also had a small purse in her possession. It was mustard-colored silk, with a drawstring, and as she approached Maitland and held it up, they could see that there was a swarm of bees embroidered on it.

"To go with your new surcoat, my lady," the woman said proudly. Then, she opened up the purse and pulled forth two big tortoise shell hair combs. "May I?"

She meant to put them in Maitland's hair and not knowing what else to do, and afraid to refuse for fear of insulting Thomas, Maitland simply nodded her head and the woman pulled off the kerchief she kept around her head, revealing her lovely, dark hair. Maitland locked eyes with Thomas, clearly overwhelmed by everything that was happening to her, but he simply smiled as the merchant's wife quickly drew the combs through Maitland's hair to brush it out swiftly before braiding it and wrapping the braid at the base of her skull. Then, using those two big combs, she shoved them into Maitland's hair to secure the braid.

Thomas stood there and looked at her, shaking his head in awe.

"Beautiful," he breathed. "Absolutely beautiful."

Maitland was flattered, giddy, and ill at east all at the same time. She ended up smiling bashfully at him and he snorted at her reaction, turning to the merchant and telling the man he'd have to return with the sizing for the children's shoes after the tournament. He didn't want to be late and they'd already taken up enough time to shop.

Taking the blue surcoat and Maitland's old clothing under one arm, he held out his elbow to Maitland, who timidly took it. Thanking the merchant and his wife, Thomas quit the stall with Maitland on his arm.

Truly, he felt puffed up like a peacock with Maitland on his arm. This lovely, exquisite creature meant something to him, feelings he honestly never believed he would ever experience. Glancing up into the sky, he could see that the day was starting to lean towards the afternoon and, soon enough, the contests would be starting. Before they got to the blacksmith's stall to collect Artus, he came to a halt and turned to Maitland.

"Here," he said, pulling out a small pouch that had been wrapped up with the blue surcoat. "I bought this for you."

Maitland just shook her head. "*More*, Thomas?" she said, as she hesitantly took the pouch. "How much does one person need? Truly, you have done too much already."

He watched her open the pouch. "I have not done enough," he said. "You had better get used to it."

She started to frown, to say something to him, but she dumped the pouch into her palm and out came the ring. Mouth open, she simply stared at it.

"What... what *is* this?" she finally asked.

With a smile playing on his lips, he plucked it out of her palm and held it up to the light. "The stone is the color of your eyes," he said. "See it? The merchant says it is called *krustallos* and it is meant for protection. I want you to have it."

He was handing it back to her. Maitland looked at him for a moment before taking it, looking at the beautiful stone set in the dark, hammered gold.

"It is the most beautiful ring I have ever seen," she said, somewhat emotional about it. "But, Thomas, a ring? You should not give such things to me. It is not..."

She trailed off and he finished for her. "Proper?" he said, certain that was what she meant. Taking the ring from her, he lifted her right hand and put the ring on the third finger. It fit perfectly and he lifted it to his lips to kiss it. "Mae, we must stop thinking about what is proper and start thinking about what is right for us. Not to say I will flaunt you all over the north, because that would shame you. I would not do that to you. But we may be discreet with what we do, and what we feel for one another, because I told you that I belong to you forever. I meant it. And if I want to give you a ring that will cause you to think of me every time you look at it, then I shall do so. Please, Mae. It would make me happy."

Looking at the ring, Maitland was swamped with a myriad of emotions. Since yesterday, everything seemed like a dream to her, feelings and sensations that were something she'd always hoped to experience but never believed she would. When Henry died and she committed herself to religious service, deep down, she believed her life was over. She thought she would be taking care of orphans for the rest of her life. Not that it wasn't a noble calling, but she truly believed there would be no other chance for her. No love, no man of her own, no home and no children. But then came Thomas and all of that seemed to change, though the situation was far from simple. It was as complicated as it could be.

Was it right?

Was it wrong?

She was starting not to care. All she knew was that she was surrendering to the man in ways she could not have imagined.

Everything.

As Thomas led her back down the avenue, Maitland couldn't imagine a finer thing than going through life with Thomas de Wolfe at her side. Truth be told, she would probably take him however she could get him. Even if he was married to another.

God help her… even if he *was* married to Adelaide.

She simply didn't care any longer.

CHAPTER FIFTEEN

Wark Castle

"WHERE *IS* EVERYONE, Hilde?"

The German nurse was picking up a few haphazardly thrown articles of clothing from the floor of Adelaide's bower at Wark Castle. The lavish chamber, with the old blood smears on the bed curtains, and the stink of the apple bark wrapped around horse dung that Adelaide burned constantly. An apothecary from the village of Kyloe had told her that the smell would ward off evil spirits and ensure that only the good would remain, so Adelaide had taken that to mean it would keep Thomas in good spirits, good enough to like her and want to marry her. But, so far, it hadn't worked. The more it didn't work, the more she burned it.

All it did was stink up the entire keep and drive Thomas away.

"Sir Thomas escorted his parents home, my lady," the nurse said steadily. "He told you this."

Irritated, Adelaide turned to scowl at the woman. Spread out over her bed, she was restless and bored, and had been since Thomas had left the day before.

"I know that, you insipid sow," she snapped. "But why is he gone so long? And why did he not invite *me* to go?"

Hilde, the nurse from a small village in Saxony that had been sacked by the Northmen, didn't want to have this conversation with her again, mostly because the last time they'd had it, Adelaide had resorted to throwing a cup at her head, which had hit her. She still had the welt. But that wasn't unusual with Adelaide, who treated her servants abominably. Even those who had raised her since birth. The manners and propriety Hilde had tried to instill in the young girl, Edmund de Vauden and his spoiled tactics had bled right out of her.

"He did not invite you to go because of the reivers that killed your father," Hilde said as she put the clothing away in the wardrobe. "Sir Thomas had enough to worry over with escorting his parents safely home. There was no need for you to be exposed to such danger."

That actually made some sense to Adelaide, who sat up on her bed. "Do you really think so?"

"I do."

She thought on that a moment. "But he is so nasty to me at times," she said, muttering. "Nasty and cruel. Don't you think so? And he seems to have no respect for my claims of being a *tempestarii*. Do you think I should try something more to convince him that we are meant for each other? It has been six months and trying to convince him that I control the weather has not worked."

Hilde didn't answer right away, mostly because she knew Adelaide didn't want to hear what she had to say. Adelaide wanted people to confirm her own wants and opinions, not give her their own.

"I think that if you are kind to him, he will be kind in return," Hilde said steadily. "Mayhap, you should stop trying to convince him you are a storm witch. Clearly, he does not care. Mayhap, you should simply be kind and obedient."

As she knew, Adelaide didn't like that answer. She frowned. "Is that why has he not returned?" she said. "Because I am not kind and obedient?"

"You saw how he responded to Lady Bowlin, who was kind to everyone."

That was definitely not something Adelaide wanted to hear or be reminded of. "A Beguine," she scoffed. "A mindless chit whose only desire in life is to tend foundlings. What a bore. Is that why Thomas has not returned to Wark? Because I am not like Lady Bowlin and he does not wish to return to me?"

Hilde was careful in her reply. She was still in the wardrobe, looking at the very expensive pieces of clothing, some of which needed mending, and trying hard not to enrage her young charge with the conversation.

But it was a difficult task.

"He probably remained at Castle Questing to see his family for a day or two," she said. "You must not worry, my lady. He will return soon enough."

Adelaide sat on her bed, pondering the situation. Truth be told, she'd been worrying about all of this since the de Wolfes had departed yesterday. It had been an abrupt departure and a cold one. Lord and Lady de Wolfe didn't even bid her a farewell. Standing up, Adelaide went over to the lancet windows that overlooked the river beyond the walls.

"They left rather quickly," she said thoughtfully. "Don't you think they left rather quickly? I wonder why. I thought Lord and Lady de Wolfe were planning on remaining until the wedding. And my father… he is still in the vault. Why would Thomas go off and leave my father in the vault and not take him home, as I wished?"

Hilde pulled out a shift that needed mending in the hem. "I am sure he will return soon and do just that," she said. "You told him that you wish to return home, didn't you? He will take you home."

"And he will stay," Adelaide said firmly. "Kyloe Castle will be his and he shall remain there with me. Wark is nothing compared to Kyloe. The House of de Wolfe is nothing compared to Northumbria. Won't Thomas make a magnificent earl?"

"He will, my lady."

Now, Adelaide was smiling as she looked from the window, the warm rays from the sun touching her cheek as she dreamed of her future as the Countess of Northumbria.

"He will make the *best* earl," she said. "The most handsome in the north. I will be the envy of everyone with Thomas de Wolfe as my husband. He was destined to be the earl, Hilde. I had to *ensure* he became the earl. Everything my father and I have worked so hard for is so close that I can almost taste it. When Thomas returns, we shall be married immediately. Has the priest from Kelso arrived yet? I sent word to him yesterday, you know."

"No one has arrived, my lady," Hilde said.

Adelaide sighed sharply. "Not yet," she muttered, turning away from the window. Her gaze was on the chamber now, looking it over. "This place holds nothing but misery for me. Why, in this very room, Lady de Wolfe told me to stop being so silly and selfish the day my father was killed. Can you believe that? She had the audacity to scold me. A Scots! As if she can tell me anything. She is nothing but a Scots rat."

Hilde wasn't paying much attention to her but pretending that she was. Too much inattention and Adelaide would throw things. She might even strike her, as she had before. Hilde lived in fear of Adelaide and had ever since she'd been a young girl and stabbed her in the arm with a knife when Hilde said something to displease her. That was the first instance of Adelaide's violent nature, something that had only gotten worse with time.

The woman had no boundaries and therefore knew no fear when it came to expressing her anger or getting what she wanted. That included ridding herself of fine young men because she no longer wished to be betrothed to them. Like rubbish, she simply disposed of them.

That was Adelaide's deep, dark secret.

"Lady de Wolfe is a powerful woman," Hilde reminded her. "You would do well not to speak ill of her in her husband's outpost."

Adelaide looked at her. "I am not speaking ill of her," she said. "I am simply stating a fact – she is an inferior Scots who happened to marry well. But she cannot tell me how to behave in my own home. This is my domain and my husband will be a more powerful earl than William de Wolfe."

Still fumbling with the garment that needed to be mended, Hilde went on the hunt for the sewing kit to repair the torn shift.

"Have you not stopped to think that your husband is half-Scots?" she said. "That means your children shall have Scots blood in them. You should be careful how you speak of the Scots, my lady. You are about to be related to them."

Adelaide looked at her as if taken aback... but taken aback by what? The truth? The fact that Hilde had the impudence to say such things that were obvious to anyone else but Adelaide? The old woman was in the wardrobe looking for the sewing kit and Adelaide marched over to her and slammed the wardrobe door against her head, clipping the old woman's ear. As Hilde gasped and fell back, Adelaide kicked her. Hilde ended up on her arse.

"Keep your stupid words to yourself," Adelaide hissed, standing over her menacingly. "I will hear no more from you about Scots or Lady de Wolfe, do you hear me? Thomas will marry me and we shall live at Kyloe. I will become his world and it is a world with no Scots and no old women telling me what to think. Do you understand me?"

Hand over her bruised ear, Hilde nodded quickly but she didn't reply. She was afraid to. However, Adelaide's words struck fear into her heart – *no old women telling me what to think*. To Hilde, that meant Adelaide meant to get rid of her. She'd known the woman long enough to know that the meaning was clear. Adelaide de Vauden was many things, but she was not one to make idle threats and, in that statement, she'd revealed her future intentions. She could call it a slip of the tongue, or deny it altogether, but Hilde knew better. She had seen many examples of the woman's follow-through over the years.

She knew that Adelaide meant to kill her.

It was a shocking realization, but given who spoke the words, perhaps not so shocking. Hilde was quite sure that she was not being paranoid. Fear in her heart kept her quiet, but Adelaide was evidently looking for an answer because she kicked her again, her pointy toe against Hilde's tender thigh.

"Well?" Adelaide demanded. "Do you understand me?"

Hilde kept her gaze averted. "I do, my lady."

Adelaide's gaze lingered on her for a moment before turning away. As quickly as the storm had arisen, it had passed. That was usual with Adelaide. It was a trait, just as she had the trait to seem rather mad but harmless to the world. But that wasn't Adelaide at all; she was anything but harmless and those who fell victim to her only discovered that too late.

Evil didn't even begin to encompass what she was capable of.

Which was why Hilde had warned Thomas. While Edmund de Vauden was alive, there was nothing Hilde could do because Edmund was complicit in his daughter's behavior. She created the chaos and he cleaned up the mess. She had killed two unsuspecting young knights from good families, and Edmund buried the bodies in secret and made excuses to the families. So long as Edmund had been alive to clean up his daughter's wickedness, Hilde had feared for her life should she speak out. Adelaide would kill her and Edmund would make her disappear. But with Edmund gone, there was no one to fill that void. What Adelaide did would be laid open for the world to see.

And Thomas had to know.

"I want you to see what is taking the priest from Kelso so long," Adelaide broke into Hilde's panic-driven thoughts. "Go find de Ryes and find out what is taking so long. Mayhap he will know."

Quickly, Hilde got up off the floor and straightened her wimple. "Aye, my lady."

She nearly ran from the chamber, leaving her sewing kit scattered on the floor. She waited until she was at the keep entry before allowing the tears to come, tears of pain and fear, tears she kept bottled up so Adelaide wouldn't see them. Adelaide fed off of fear and the torment of others, so Hilde was very careful not to show anything other than obedience around her. But now that she knew what Adelaide's intentions were, or at least suspected what they were, she wasn't going to allow herself to fall victim to a madwoman. She had to plan her escape or die.

And she wasn't ready to die yet.

CHAPTER SIXTEEN

Kelso

"**I**S HIM?"

"'Tis."

The Bold Hobelar could hardly believe his luck. The youngest de Wolfe cub, the commander of Wark Castle, was in Kelso on this day evidently without his army, which was shocking. Hobelar could hardly believe it until his men confirmed it.

"'Tis shockin', I say," Hobelar said. "I thought I recognized the man when we came intae town from the north, when he was in the crowd with those children. Do ye suppose the children are his own?"

The man who had confirmed the identity of Thomas de Wolfe was the same man who was always scouting for Hobelar, always breathless and quick of movement. He lifted his slender shoulders.

"He's with a woman," he said. "I saw him kiss her. It could be his wife."

Hobelar's bushy eyebrows lifted. "The man has come tae town with his wife and children, and no army?" he said in disbelief. "It is possible this is tae be too easy for us."

"What do you intend to do?"

Hobelar turned towards the tournament field where the mass competition was currently taking place. He could hear the crowds cheering in the distance. He was huddled with a small group of his men in the cold shadows of Kelso's big abbey while the rest of the group was wandering the crowd at the fair, stealing what they could.

Even the reivers had heard of the great fair today and they'd made a point of coming to steal, pickpocket, and otherwise wreak havoc on an unsuspecting crowd. But what he hadn't counted on was seeing the man he'd sworn revenge against after the disaster in Coldstream. He'd managed to ambush one party from Wark, resulting in several deaths, but now to find the youngest de Wolfe cub within his sights, with no protection of soldiers, in fact, was almost too good to be true.

"I'm not certain," he said. "Where is he now?"

The breathless man threw a finger in the direction of the tournament field. "He's joined with other knights," he said. "He's fighting in the mass competition."

That brought Hobelar pause. "Other knights," he muttered. "Friends?"

"They fly the standard of Northwood Castle."

That brought recognition to Hobelar. It also brought pause. "Northwood and de Wolfe are brothers tae the bone," he said. "We thought the man was alone with his wife and bairns, but he's not. He'll stick with Northwood's men."

"Then what do you want to do about it?"

It was the second time the same question had been asked and Hobelar wasn't entirely certain now, but the news that de Wolfe was with the Northwood knights had him thinking. He would go after one knight alone, even a de Wolfe, but he wasn't about to go after several heavily-armed Northwood knights, too. Still, he was an opportunist and knew he had to take his chances, for another one might not come. Revenge, if not taken when presented, often slipped away into oblivion.

His heart was pounding with the possibilities.

"Clearly, the man has come tae enjoy the fair and the competition," Hobelar said. "He's not come prepared tae do battle. But I'll not let him slip away. We've found him in a moment of weakness and I'll not let this go."

"Then what do we do?" the breathless man demanded.

Hobelar had to look decisive to his men; he knew that. Any sign of weakness and the faint of heart lost faith.

"We go tae the field," he said firmly. "We watch tae see if de Wolfe and the Northwood knights part ways. I am willin' tae take on one lone knight, but I'm not willin' tae take on several, and especially not men from Northwood Castle. There's an opportunity in this, lads, but we must be smart about it."

The men glanced at each other, some of them even nervously. They'd taken a massive beating in Coldstream several days before and they hadn't come to Kelso with the intention of going into battle, but Hobelar was seeing this as a chance to seek vengeance on de Wolfe. No one had expected to see the man here. Now, a trip to the fair for some easy targets was becoming something else and the breathless man, always the man of reason, summoned his courage to speak on it.

"If the man is with his friends from Northwood, then it would be foolish to challenge them all," he said. "If you want to be smart about it, then we wait for de Wolfe to leave Kelso and we follow him. Mayhap he'll leave with just the woman and the children and, if that is the case, we can catch him on the road. If we try to take him now, with his friends around, we could all end up dead."

Hobelar was eager but he wasn't stupid. "Then we follow the man," he said decisively. "We go tae the field and we watch him every moment. When he leaves Kelso, we leave. We follow him wherever he goes and look for the chance tae strike. I'll not let the deaths of my men go unanswered. God has given me this chance tae seek vengeance and de Wolfe is goin' tae pay with his blood, do ye hear?"

The breathless man nodded reluctantly. "But if you kill him, you bring the whole of de Wolfe down around us," he pointed out. "Kill one and they'll all come. They'll tear apart the north looking for us and we cannot survive such a thing."

Hobelar lifted his eyebrows. "I dinna say I was tae kill him," he said. "But his wife and children are with him. Damage the family and ye damage the man."

Some of the outlaws didn't care about the age or sex of those they robbed or murdered, but others did. Attacking a man was one thing, but attacking his young children was another. Hobelar's intentions were brutal but not unexpected given the man and his reputation.

It was simply his way.

As Hobelar pulled his woolen cloak over his head and dashed out towards the tournament field, followed by most of his men, the breathless man lingered by the abbey for a moment, wondering if Hobelar's sense of vengeance was going to kill them all. Ambushing a party of men from Wark was one thing, but ambushing a man and his family?

The breathless man suspected this was not going to end well, for any of them.

CHAPTER SEVENTEEN

Northwood Castle

"I HAVE COME looking for my son but I am told he is not here."

In the lavish keep of Northwood Castle, and specifically in a hall on the entry level of the keep, William was facing a big man who put his arms around him and hugged him tightly. He'd known the man the better part of his life and several of his children had married several of the man's children, but when Paris de Norville put his arms around William and hugged him, William simply stood there and didn't respond.

He was far too angry to do so.

Paris felt the man stiffen up in his arms and he squeezed him tighter for it. The more William resisted, the more Paris squeezed until he ended up squeezing so hard that William grunted.

"Release me, you idiot," William snapped softly. "I am in no mood for your foolery."

There wasn't a day, a time, or a place that Paris couldn't give in to foolery of any kind. He cupped William's stern face, looking him in the eye.

"Nay, Tommy is not here, but why take that out on me?" Paris said, his blue eyes twinkling as he dropped his hands. "Is he supposed to be here?"

William sighed heavily, a weary sound. He began to pull off his heavy leather gloves, aiming his body for the nearest bench. He was so weary he had to sit down or fall down. The gloves ended up on the tabletop as he plopped down at the feasting table that stretched nearly the length of the chamber.

"I am too old for this, Paris," he muttered. "Far too old."

Paris came around to sit at the end of the table, next to him. "You *do* look much older than I remember," Paris said, just to get the dig in considering they were both the same age. "What is the matter with you, William? Why are you here looking for Tommy?"

William rubbed his good eye before looking at the man. He was still quite handsome at his age, a man who had been blond and fair in his youth, but that blond hair had turned to gray a long time ago and Paris refused to admit it. He still insisted he had blond hair even though everyone could see he clearly did not. Such was the proud, arrogant man that William had known all of these years, but Paris was also his dearest friend in the world. Beneath that vain exterior beat the heart of gold, with the wisdom to match when Paris was feeling particularly cooperative.

At the moment, William desperately needed that cooperation.

"I have trouble," he muttered. "Bring me food and drink. You and I have much to discuss."

Paris was usually glib, sometimes inappropriately so, but he could see by the expression on William's face that something serious had happened, indeed. He sent a servant for refreshments before returning his attention to William. His manner wasn't so glib as he faced him.

"Tell me what has happened," he said quietly. "Why do you look so exhausted?"

William groaned in response, leaning forward to wipe his hands over his face. "Northumbria is dead."

Paris' eyes widened. That wasn't something he had been expecting to hear. "Northumbria?" he repeated. "De Vauden is dead?"

"Aye."

"What in the hell happened?"

William looked at him. "He had departed Wark and was returning to Kyloe Castle when he was set upon by reivers," he said. "Edmund was killed in the attack and his body was returned to Wark. Even now, it is in the vault, awaiting return to Kyloe. You know that Tommy is betrothed to the Northumbria heiress."

"I know."

"Paris, she is a murderess."

Paris' face twisted in shock. "She's *what?*"

William nodded unhappily. "De Vauden has saddled Tommy with a daughter who has murdered the two men she was betrothed to before her betrothal to Tommy," he said. "This is all my fault. When Northumbria came to me and wanted to negotiate a marriage between his daughter and my youngest son, I was quite thrilled for Tommy. He will inherit the Northumbria earldom, and you and I both know it is the largest earldom in the north. Of course I took the offer. Why wouldn't I?"

Paris was hanging on his every word. "*But?*"

"But I never insisted on meeting the daughter before I agreed," he said, sounding despondent. "But I should have. God, I should have. The woman is a nightmare, Paris. She tells Tommy that she is a *tempestarii* who can control the weather. She cuts her arms and smears her blood on the walls, on her bed, and tells him that it is her blood that controls the weather. She does it every time she wants attention from him and the more she cuts, the more distant he becomes. She is mean and demanding, and certainly not sane. But that is not the worst part."

Paris was beginning to feel the horror that William was; it was bleeding out of the man, in every direction. "But a *murderess*, William? Truly?"

William nodded. "Adelaide's own nurse told Tommy that Adelaide killed the two men she was previously betrothed to," he said. "You want to know why I am so exhausted? Because I have just come from Kyloe

Castle where I informed the majordomo that Edmund de Vauden is dead and Adelaide is now in control of Northumbria. I spoke to the man privately and when I confronted him about the truth behind the men Adelaide had been betrothed to before Tommy, the man looked as if he'd seen a ghost. He became pasty and pale, and refused to give me a straight answer. I would have thought that mayhap the old nurse was lying until the very end of the conversation when the majordomo begged me not to repeat what I had heard to Adelaide if I valued Tommy's life."

Paris was staring at him with his mouth hanging open. "My God," he hissed. "The majordomo was terrified!"

"That is my opinion, as well."

"He is terrified of Adelaide!"

"I could see it in his eyes."

Now, Paris was worked up about the situation and Thomas' fate. "What will you do?" he demanded. "You cannot let Tommy marry this... this *killer*."

William eyed him. "Listen to me, Paris," he said quietly. "As much as I do not relish the idea of Tommy marrying that woman, we must look at the bigger picture here. If Tommy does not marry her, Edward will surely marry her off to any number of his Savoyard favorites and we will have a French bastard in command of the largest army in the north. If that happens, it throws all of us into jeopardy – our security, our families – everything."

Paris was looking at him in both understanding and horror, an odd combination. "God," he breathed. "So you *do* intend to let Tommy marry her."

"And then I intend to arrest her for murder," William hissed, pounding his fist on the table. "Patrick is the Constable of the North, Paris. Edward himself gave Atty that title and I will arrest Adelaide on their wedding night and throw her in the vault at Berwick. It is an unbreachable jail and with Patrick as her jailor, she will rot there. Consider it justice for those poor men she murdered."

Paris didn't like the plans, but he understood them. "Then Tommy is the Earl of Northumbria, unopposed and safe from the murderess."

"Exactly."

Parish grunted. "God's Bones, William," he muttered. "You were correct when you said you had trouble. And Tommy? How does he feel about all of this?"

A servant approached the table at that point, placing wine, cheese, and fruit in front of William. Neither man spoke until the servant left the hall completely, and when he was gone, William spoke quietly.

"He agrees with me," he said. "When Tommy marries Adelaide, he becomes the Earl of Northumbria. I believe I may even be able to have the marriage annulled based on Adelaide's behavior. I am sure the majordomo isn't the only one who knows what crimes that woman has committed. I am sure there are many others who will attest to her evil. The church will not allow Tommy to remain married to a woman of such wickedness."

Paris was struggling to digest everything he'd been told. He watched William drain nearly half of his cup of wine before cutting up the tart, white cheese and feasting on it.

"You are taking quite a chance with your son's life, William," he said quietly. "But I understand why you are doing it."

William glanced at him, mouth full. "And you disagree?"

Paris shook his head. "It is not that," he said. "I do agree with you completely. If Edward plants a French nobleman as Northumbria, then our lives will be hell."

William swallowed the bite in his mouth. "I do not like that Tommy is in the middle of this but, as I said, it was of my own doing," he said. "I never met the girl before agreeing to anything and Jordan believes Edmund simply wanted to be rid of his daughter. When he first brought her to Wark, he dumped her off and fled home like a coward. That should have been the first indication that all was not well."

As William ate, Paris poured himself a measure of the sweet, red wine and took a healthy swallow. "And what does your wife think of your plan to go through with the marriage?" he asked.

William lifted his big shoulders. "She is not happy about it, but she understands," he said. "There is no pleasing alternative to this, Paris. Either Tommy marries the witch or one of Edward's favorites does. I have not lived all of these years, building an empire, only to see it threatened by a Frenchman."

Paris shook his head. "That is a very real possibility if Edward discovers the Northumbria heiress is unwed."

"My thoughts exactly."

The weight of the situation was settling on two old knights who had seen much in their lifetime. Power and politics and battle had always been their stock and trade, so this latest issue was nothing new. It was simply uglier than most, and the pair had the ability to overlook the emotion in the situation and focus on what needed to be done. William began cutting up an apple, his thoughts lingering on his missing son.

"Thomas told me he was coming to Northwood to visit," he said. "That is why I came here after leaving Kyloe. When I came through the gatehouse, I was greeted by Deinwald's son, Edric. He said that everyone has gone into Kelso for a fair and tournament."

Paris nodded. "They have," he said. "I remained here, of course, and Edric chose to remain behind. Deinwald went with his grandsons."

William snorted. "Grandsons," he muttered. "And I even have great-grandchildren. Scott is a grandfather with Will's children through his wife, Lily de Lohr, and his second son, Thomas, has also married and is expecting a child."

Paris grinned. "Your father, a close and dear friend of Christopher de Lohr those years ago, would have been delighted to see the two families joined," he said. "Will has a son, doesn't he?"

"Two."

Paris nodded his approval. "They shall be the greatest knights England has ever seen with de Wolfe and de Lohr blood."

William fell silent a moment, his thoughts turning from Thomas to the vast legacy he had. "Children, grandchildren, and great-grandchildren," he muttered. "It is enough to make a man believe that he shall live forever."

Paris wriggled his eyebrows in agreement. "And you shall," he said. "So shall I. Do you know how I know this? Look at Kieran's children. Alec and Kevin and Nathaniel are just like him, and Kevin now is the Duke of Dorset. His own son is named Kieran, which means Kieran Hage, in time, will become the next Duke of Dorset. Kieran the Old is in every inch of that boy, so I'm told. That is not simply immortality, William – it is legend."

William smiled faintly, thinking on the grandchildren he shared with Kieran. "Edward and Axel already have Kieran's size, but they have too much of Jemma in them," he said. "Only the youngest, Christoph, has Kieran's manners. Eddie and Axel are aggressive and fearless."

Paris cocked an eyebrow. "They have too much of the banshee in them."

"You had better stop calling her that. She's not beyond taking a fist to you."

Paris grinned. He and Jemma Hage, Kieran's wife, had shared a love/hate relationship from the moment they met, decades ago when she was a tiny, fiery Scotswoman and he was an arrogant young knight. Truth be told, he still missed harassing her on a regular basis, but in the times they were together these days, the old spark of aggravation was there. It made reunions rather fun until she took a stick to him.

"She would die of a broken heart if I stopped pestering her," Paris said. "She looks forward to it as much as I do."

William couldn't help but grin, but that gesture soon faded as he thought of Jemma, alone now that Kieran was gone. The woman still lived at Castle Questing since her husband's death, making herself useful, but the light had gone out of her.

"She has changed since Kieran's passing," he said quietly. "She is not the same. Something in her died right along with him."

All jesting aside, Paris knew that. He'd seen it in her, too. "I know," he said. "She loved him, William. We all did."

William nodded faintly, thinking on Kieran. "I miss him greatly," he whispered. "I held him in my arms as he breathed his last and I will say this; it was a privilege. It was a privilege to be with him as he took his last breath. I was speaking to him of the battle near Whiteadder Water when someone cut the garter of the mail of his left leg. Do you remember that? The mail slid down and took his breeches with it, and suddenly, Kieran is fighting with his bare arse exposed. I laughed so hard I nearly got myself killed because I was not paying attention to my opponent."

Paris was grinning. "I remember," he said. "It was even more humorous because once the fighting stopped, he refused to pull up his breeches. He left his backside hanging out and made it back to the encampment that way. Then he went to the Scots prisoners and made them all look at his bare buttocks to punish them for what their kinsmen did."

William was starting to laugh, as he always did when they discussed the battle at Whiteadder Water. Anyone who had been there those years ago, fighting in the skirmish against the Scots, remembered that battle with humor because it was the beginning of the infamous Helm of Shame. William began to howl and Paris right along with him.

"And so came the Helm of Shame," William said, wiping the tears from his eye. "Do you remember what Kieran did that moment when it all began?"

Paris was giggling like a fool. "I do," he said. "But I know that Michael put him up to it. Those two were merciless in their pranks."

It felt so good to laugh. William had spent so much of the past several days being depressed and troubled that to laugh over Kieran's antics after Whiteadder was cathartic.

"As Kieran was walking around, holding up his breeches in the front so his manhood was at least covered, he comes across Corin de Fortlage, a younger knight who pulled out of the battle early," William said, starting to cry again because he was laughing so hard. "He was so angry that Corin pulled back early that he pushed the man to the ground and sat on his head with his bare buttocks. He called it the Helm of Shame and told Corin if he ever left the field of battle early again, he would punish him with the Helm of Shame again. Corin was always the last man to leave the field of battle after that."

They burst into a new fit of giggles, reliving memories that were so precious to them. The Helm of Shame was legendary amongst the de Wolfe armies and it was something that Kieran had done more than once. If a young knight displeased him, they were threatened with the Helm of Shame. Humor, brotherhood, and battle had a special meaning to old knights. They'd known so much death and pain that to relive the better moments somehow took the sting of horror away.

"Corin was the last man from the field until the last battle he ever fought," Paris said, wiping his eyes of tears as he sobered. "It was difficult to lose Corin when we did. He was just starting to become an excellent knight."

William, too, sobered, remembering the young, blond knight who fought so fiercely but could be lazy at times. "How long has it been now?" he asked. "At least thirty years since we lost him?"

Paris nodded. "Almost exactly thirty years now," he said, sobering dramatically. He sighed heavily, looking to his oldest and dearest friend. "Are we really so old, William? Look at all of the men who have gone before us – Corin, Ranulf, Kieran and more. Ranulf was the first, as I recall, but he was old even back when he was training us as young knights. His death from old age was not surprising. But still… I do miss the man. He was gruff and hard as only Ranulf could be."

William smiled as he thought on the knight who had been well into his fifth decade when William and Paris and Kieran were in their prime. It was a moment of reflection on men who had passed on before them, keeping their memories alive by speaking their names. Wistfully, he smiled.

"I think the point I was making is that the Helm of Shame battle was the last thing Kieran ever heard in this life," he said, thinking on that moment of loss and still feeling as if it had happened only yesterday. "I hope that when my time comes, I will hear you in one ear and my wife in the other. She can speak of her love for me and you can speak of our days of glory."

But Paris shook his head. "You do not want to hear my voice in your ear," he said. "You only want to hear Jordan, for the two of you have shared a love that most men only dream of. It is only right that she should be the last thing you ever hear."

William forced a smile. "I hope so," he said quietly. "But I want you to know something, Paris. You and I have been friends for almost seventy years. Aye, it has been that long, and there is no man on earth, save Kieran, that I would rather go through this life with. You have been a thorn in my side, and a pain in my neck at times, but a more loyal and true friend has never existed. If I never again have the chance to tell you that, then I am telling you now. Much as it was a privilege to be with Kieran as he drew his last, know that it has been my greatest privilege to call you my friend, and we will continue to be friends in the next life. The bond we have between us does not end with death."

Paris reached out, grasping William's hand that was on the tabletop. They held on to one another for a moment, tightly, reaffirming ties that had always been there and would forever be intact. It was a rare moment of emotion between them.

"Nay, it does not end," Paris said, uncharacteristically emotional. "It will never end with us. Other than my wife, you are the one person in this world who understands me and I am a difficult man to understand. I know that."

William smiled faintly. "Caladora was a saint."

Paris' blue eyes took on a distant and sorrowful reflection. "It is strange, William," he said. "I lost Caladora last year, but to me, it does not seem as if she is gone. It is as if she is only in another chamber, or out with the chickens, or in the kitchens. I feel as if all I have to do is turn a corner and there she'll be. She is a ghost that is with me always, but it brings me comfort. I do not know if that makes sense, but that is how I feel."

William squeezed his hand. "It makes sense," he said softly. "I believe she is with you. She was always so worried about you, so attentive, and I do not think she has left you. I do not think she can. I think that when you die, she will be standing right next to your bedside to take your hand and lead you into eternity."

Paris forced a smile. "It is a good thought," he said. "Do you know something, William? In our entire life together, she never once scolded me or admonished me. Never once, in all of the foolish things I said or did. How is it that I deserved such a gentle creature?"

William shook his head. "You were fortunate, I suppose."

"Verily."

The conversation faded as each man was lost to his own thoughts, about the days and loves of the years that had passed them by. A pair of servants entered the cold, cavernous hall at that point, carrying peat and kindling, and they moved to the great hearth to start the fire for the evening. William and Paris simply sat there in silence, thinking and reflecting. Finally, William stirred.

"We seem to have gotten off of the original subject," he said, scratching his head. "I came here looking for Tommy and being that he is not here, I have a suspicion on where he might be."

Paris looked at him, curiously. "Where do you think he is?"

William was back to the expression that suggested his entire existence was in turmoil. "You know Desmond de Ryes."

"I do. He serves Tommy at Wark."

"The man has a sister, a Beguine, who has taken over the foundling home at Edenside."

"The one with the recent scandal? With the servant who was selling the children?"

"The same." William paused. "Tommy has feelings for the woman. He might have gone there to see her."

Paris' eyebrows lifted in disbelief. "Surely you jest."

"I wish I was."

There was more disbelief on Paris' part. "Great Bleeding Christ, William," he hissed. "Tommy has enough trouble without... without bedding a widow pledged to the church. What in God's name is he thinking?"

William held up a hand to ease Paris' outrage. "You've not met this woman," he said. "She is beautiful, young, and intelligent. Jordan thinks very highly of her, and if the situation were any different, she would make a perfect wife for Tommy and he would have my blessing. But the situation is *not* different and I'll not let him complicate things, at least until we can settle the immediate situation with Adelaide. After that... after that, we'll deal with whatever Tommy might be feeling for Lady Bowlin."

Paris could only shake his head. "This is all madness," he said. "If you think your son is at Edenside with this Lady Bowlin, then go and retrieve him. He does not need this complication."

"I know."

"In fact, I will go with you. I need to get out of this place, anyway, and clear my head."

"Why do you say that?"

Paris shrugged. "Adam is not well," he said. "Even now, he sleeps a great deal. Death lingers at Northwood, William. First it came for Caladora, now it comes for Adam. They say that death always comes in threes, so it makes me wonder who is next. I did not want to go to the fair today because I simply did not want to leave the castle with all that is happening here. But going with you to beat some sense into Tommy... that, I *will* do."

William chuckled as Paris stood up, calling to the servants to have his horse prepared. "We can go at first light," William said. "The sun will be setting soon and we can just as easily take care of this on the morrow."

"Pah," Paris said. "There is more than enough daylight left. It will take us a couple of hours at most. We can stay the night and return on the morrow with your son in chains."

William was still grinning, now shaking his head. "Do not be too harsh with him," he said. "Tommy has a great weight on his shoulders, greater than you or I ever had at his age. He genuinely feels something for Lady Bowlin, so we must tread carefully."

"And I will," Paris said. "But Tommy needs to realize that you are under a great strain as well, and he must not make it worse."

"He knows."

"*Does* he?"

It was a pointed question and William nodded, although he truthfully wasn't sure. Thomas tended to be selfish at times, but William knew his son understood the gravity of the situation he was in. Whether or not he thought of others before his own wants was in question, especially when it came to a woman.

It was a mystery.

As Paris went to change into his protection at the armory, William sat back down at the table and finished off the wine and food. When the last drop of wine went down his throat and the last grape was swallowed, he pulled his gloves back on and headed out to the inner bailey of Northwood, a vast area, where his war horse was waiting in the shade.

In the outer bailey beyond, three hundred of his soldiers waited, men he had taken with him to Kyloe Castle when he'd left his wife off at Castle Questing. Considering what happened to Northumbria, William wasn't going to travel lightly these days. He wasn't going to take that chance, as he'd proven when he'd taken so many men to Kyloe.

Off to the east, William could see that they were expanding the already enormous keep by adding on a large section. Stonemasons were working beneath the bright sun; William had seen them when he'd ridden in. He paused a moment, watching the building going on as he tightened up his gloves.

"They're building a chapel."

William turned to see Edric Ellsrod standing next to him. The man was the spitting image of his father in his youth; shorter, muscular, and with long blond hair and an edgy look about him. He was hell with a sword.

"Is that what it is?" William asked. "I was wondering. But why a chapel? Northwood already has one."

Edric cast him a long glance. "A *private* chapel," he said. "Lady Teviot does not like to worship with the rank and file, and you know how pious she is. She wants a family chapel."

William nodded with understanding. "Ah," he said. "But it is two-storied. What is on the top floor?"

"Lady Teviot has brought in her own priest. That is where he will live."

William looked around at what used to be a larger area than what it currently was. "If she keeps building, there will no longer be an inner ward," he said. Then, he returned his focus to Edric. "Where is your mother? I've not seen her since my arrival."

Edric pointed to the second floor of the keep. "She is keeping company with Lord and Lady Teviot," he said. "I am sure Paris told you that the earl is not doing well."

"He told me."

"It has hit my mother fairly hard. She says that Lord Adam was always kind to her."

William thought on the Earl of Teviot when he'd first met him. A tall, sinewy young man with a crown of pale red hair, William had liked him a great deal. He'd knighted him, in fact. Adam had been young, but he'd been a hard worker and an excellent knight. Kieran never had to bestow the Helm of Shame on Adam's head, which was something of a tribute to his diligence and character.

"Teviot's father and I were very close," he said after a moment. "My father died when I was young and Adam's father was something of a surrogate to me. Mayhap I shall go and visit Adam before I leave."

Edric nodded. "That would do the man a world of good."

As Edric headed off, returning to the gatehouse and his duties, William glanced up at the great keep of Northwood, bracing himself for the visit to a dying man. Paris' horse was brought around at that point, and Paris emerged from the keep at nearly the same time, so William thought he might have to delay his visit for now. He had pressing matters to attend to and he knew that Adam would understand.

Resigned, he began to move towards his horse just as Paris mounted his steed. Paris' horse was young and excitable, having been purchased in Belgium when Paris bought the horses for Hermes and Atreus, and William watched Paris wrestle with the big, white horse.

"Mayhap you need a horse that is not so excitable!" he shouted across the ward. "Send that horse back and get one that is more suitable to an old man."

Paris struggled with the beast. "Bah! He is only spirited."

"You should not have to fight your horse so much simply to ride him."

But Paris ignored him. He'd spent his life riding horses and there wasn't one that had bested him yet. William shook his head at his arrogant friend and went to mount his own horse, but as he got near his animal, Paris' horse suddenly bucked and sent Paris flying. The horse, now riderless, charged around the inner ward, crashing into William's horse just as the man went to climb into the saddle.

Startled, William's panicked horse bucked and bashed into William, sending him sailing off-balance into the newly-built wall next to him, and William, completely unprepared, hit the wall full-on with his unprotected head.

He collapsed in a heap.

Men were running from all directions, trying to contain the horses. As Paris lurched to his feet, rubbing the elbow he'd hit when he'd slammed into the ground, he saw William crumpled in the dirt over by the wall. Men were rushing towards William, so Paris began to run, too, pushing away men who were asking him if he'd hurt himself. The closer Paris drew to William, the more he could see that the man was unconscious. Men rolled him over onto his back and as Paris came up to his side, he suddenly saw the big, bloodied spot on the wall where

William had hit his head.

It was all Paris could do to keep from screaming out loud at the sight.

CHAPTER EIGHTEEN

Edenside

"ARE YOU SURE I cannot tend your wound?"

Maitland seemed very concerned, but Thomas valiantly brushed her off. "This is a mere scratch, my lady," he assured her. "I've had far worse, believe me."

That part was true. He'd had far worse wounds in the past, including a goring a few years ago in Dorset that nearly took his life. But the current wound that Maitland was speaking of was a gash to his head, received in the mass competition when a Carlisle knight clipped him with a club, trying to bring him down. Thomas, however, had remained on his feet. The same couldn't be said for the Carlisle knight, who went down when Thomas cocked his fist and plowed it into the man's face.

But it had all been great fun.

They were on the road home from Kelso now under fair skies as the calm afternoon waned. The days were getting longer, so sunset was still a few hours off yet. There was plenty of time for the party from Northwood to reach home once they dropped their precious cargo off at Edenside.

Since the children and Maitland and Tibelda had walked from Edenside, being that it was very close to Kelso, some of the Northwood knights were off their horses, allowing the children to ride as they led the steeds along the road. Roland and Renard were on Garr Ellsrod's horse, having a grand time and pretending they were knights, as Deinwald himself walked along with Phin and showed a surprising amount of patience with the lad as they discussed some of the duties that knights had. Phin, the slender and usually-silent boy, was getting quite an education.

Artus was walking alongside Thomas, who was explaining to him about the differences between the horses around them – some were rounceys, comfortable riding horses but not war horses, while the others, including Thomas' steed, were actually war horses. Hector and Thomas' horses were destriers, true war horses in every sense of the word, kept muzzled so they wouldn't bite anyone.

Marybelle, Nora, and little Dyana were in the hand cart with all of the bowls and buckets they'd used to transport the goat cheese, pulled along by Maitland and Tibelda. Thomas had offered to pull the hand cart himself, but the women had refused, so he walked alongside, leading his horse and explaining to Artus about the different types of steeds until Maitland began pointing out the gash on his head. As Edenside came into view in the distance, he continued to brush off her concern, much to her distress.

"You really should have it bandaged," she said to him. "At least put a cold compress on it to bring the swelling down."

Thomas put his hand on his forehead, feeling the lump. "It will go down on its own by tomorrow," he said. "But if it will make you feel any better, I will put a cold cloth on it when I return to Wark. It does not even need any stitches."

"Are you certain?"

"I am."

"If Tommy is to suffer a wound, Lady Bowlin, then let it be to his head," Hector said, on the other side of Thomas. "It is the part of his body where a wound can do the least damage."

Maitland grinned while Thomas scowled. "It was truly thrilling to watch all of you compete today, my lord," Maitland said to Hector. "I had forgotten how exciting a mass competition can be. It has been years since I have seen one. I am sorry you did not win the purse, but it was a good fight."

Hector, having only met Maitland at the beginning of the contests, hadn't had any real opportunity to speak with her. But throughout the mass competition, he saw that Thomas' attention kept going back to the lovely woman in the brown broadcloth. The woman, Thomas had informed him, was the Guardian of Edenside, known as Lady Bowlin, and Hector immediately thought that Thomas' support of the foundling home had an ulterior motive now that he saw the woman in charge. He'd never known Thomas to be overly supportive of charities and seeing the stunning Lady Bowlin told Hector why Thomas was suddenly so interested in Edenside.

Quite a lot made sense after that.

"We did not win the purse because Carlisle cheated," Hector said flatly. "I know for a fact that several of his men were knocked down, but they resumed fighting, anyway. That is a flagrant foul."

Thomas lifted his eyebrows. "Only if they are caught, and they were not."

Hector pursed his lips irritably. "Bastards," he muttered. Realizing he had used harsh language in front of a lady, he hastened to change the subject. "Are you from Northumberland, my lady?"

Maitland nodded, not oblivious to Hector's quest to divert the conversation away from his bad language. "A small town called Lesbury," she said. "It is near Alnwick. That is where my family home was."

Hector knew Alnwick well; most knights in the north did. "And now you intend to remain at Edenside?"

Her eyes twinkled. "I am rather enjoying it," she said. "We are making cheese to sell and making a little money. To be self-sufficient is our goal so we will not take up so much of Sir Thomas' time and money."

Thomas looked at her, feigning hurt. "I rather enjoy being a great benefactor," he said. "The next time I come, I shall bring my little sister with me, the one you met at Wark. Caria could learn a thing or two from these children on how to be productive and grateful."

On his other side, Hector snorted. "She will never learn such things if you continue spoiling her, Tommy," he said. "I have told you that before. But you may be right – it may do her good to spend some time with the foundlings and understand what it is to work for your survival. It would be a good experience for her."

Thomas thought on that. He was aware that Hector knew of Caria's true parentage. Hector had gone on that fateful trip to Wales, escorting Penelope de Wolfe to her new husband, so he was well aware of who Caria really was. But like the rest of the family, he kept the secret and went along with the story that Caria was simply William and Jordan's youngest child even though Jordan had been well past her childbearing years when Caria had been born. No one questioned where the child had come from and the family kept up a united front about it.

"It's not a bad idea," Thomas replied to Hector's suggestion, noting that the gray stone walls of Edenside were looming closer. "It might also not be a bad idea to post a few soldiers here at Edenside. With all of the trouble we've been having with the reivers, and the fact that there are now things of value there, I think I will send a few soldiers over to help with the security of the place. Would you accept them, Lady Bowlin?"

He had been rather formal with her in front of witnesses, for obvious reasons, and Maitland went along with it. But she did so miss hearing him call her "Mae". Coming from his lips, it was like a gentle caress to her ears.

"I should ask the abbot at Kelso to provide us with some soldiers, but considering what happened when he put his sister in charge, I do believe I will accept de Wolfe assistance instead," she said. "I thank you for your offer, my lord. We can house them in one of the outbuildings, the one that has a hearth."

Since Thomas was being so generous, Hector spoke up, too. "Is there anything else you need for the foundlings?" he asked. "Anything that Northwood can provide?"

Maitland thought a moment. "Your offer is kind, my lord," she said. "I suppose we can always use more goats to milk. More goats means more cheese and, according to Sir Thomas, we are going to have the whole of Northumberland demanding our product."

Hector grinned as Thomas nodded his head firmly. "It *is* delicious," he said. "Lady Bowlin is ensuring that Edenside is self-sufficient for years to come. More than that, I promised her I would go to the local taverns and demand they buy her cheese."

Hector cocked an eyebrow. "Certainly, they will not deny an armed knight."

"My point, precisely."

They had finally arrived at the gates of Edenside. Garr removed the twins from the back of his horse and Deinwald took Phin by the hand, leading him over to the gate as Tibelda opened it. Thomas and Hector lent a hand at ushering the children inside, going so far as to enter the compound just to make sure all was well and no one was lying in wait for seven children and two women. In the wilds of the north, one had to be careful of marauders. With everything secure, Hector bid a polite farewell while Thomas lingered by the gate.

The men from Northwood were waiting for him, unfortunately, and Thomas knew he couldn't linger. It was time for him to return to Wark and wait for word from his father about the information from Kyloe. He'd stayed away as long as he dared, considering Wark was his command, so he knew he needed to go.

At Edenside's repaired gate, he faced Maitland a proper distance away.

"I will return in a few days to see how things are coming along," he said, rather neutrally because Hector was still in earshot. "If Hector is sending goats, is there anything else you need?"

Maitland hated to see him go. She really did. They'd spent such a wonderful two days together that she was becoming rather attached to having him around. It was difficult to see him off.

"I do not believe so at this time," she said, "but if you could see your way to donating more fowl to our home, it would be appreciated. We can use the meat and the eggs for the children."

Thomas nodded. Then, he lifted his voice and turned to Hector. "Did you hear that?" he said. "Along with the goats, send chickens and geese for meat and eggs."

Hector lifted a hand and waved, acknowledging the request, and Thomas returned his attention to Maitland. "You shall have your goats and chicken and geese delivered, my lady," he said. "And when I return in a couple of days, it will be with ten men. Meanwhile, you can prepare the outbuilding you spoke of so they have a place to sleep. You will also need to feed them."

"I can do that, my lord."

He smiled at her. "Good," he said. Then, he lowered his voice so that only she could hear him. "It will seem like an eternity until I see you again, love. Wear the blue dress for me the next time I come."

Maitland's cheeks flushed a soft pink. "I will," she murmured. Then, she lifted her right hand slightly, rubbing on the ring. "I shall think of you often."

"Swear it."

"I do."

He winked at her. "Good," he muttered. "I shall return."

With that, he turned for his horse, vaulting up onto the animal's back as the party from Northwood began to move out. Hermes and Atreus, astride their wild stallions, began to tear off down the road at a gallop, causing the others to follow suit. Soon enough, the entire group was thundering off down the road and Maitland watched them for a moment, shielding her eyes from the sun, watching Thomas tear down the road until he was out of her sight.

With a smile on her lips, she came back into the yard, closing the gate and throwing the big bolt on it to seal it up.

What a day it had been.

Maitland was feeling rather dazed and dreamy as she wandered back into the kitchen yard where the children were washing and drying the bowls and buckets used for the cheese. Out of habit, Maitland jumped in to help, but her mind wasn't on it. It was on the day, on the moments she spent with Thomas, and on his return in a couple of days. Odd how a man she'd tried to stay away from, or at least keep at a metaphorical arm's length, had broken down her barriers in more ways than one.

She couldn't wait to see him again.

Maitland returned to work with renewed vigor, making sure the children took the clean buckets to milk the goats again before they were sheltered for the night. Since she wanted to increase the milk production, milking the goats twice a day would stimulate more milk. Marybelle and Nora took their buckets and headed into the pen to milk, followed by the twins and Dyana, who wanted to play with the baby goats. Artus and Phin remained outside of the pen to watch, and Maitland remained in the kitchen, cleaning out the bowls with Tibelda. She kept an eye on the children as they milked and played, thinking that her little charity was coming along better than she could have ever hoped for.

Thanks to one rather handsome and powerful knight.

But what Maitland didn't know was that Edenside was being watched from the trees to the north, just over the road. That handsome and powerful knight had attracted the wrong kind of attention, and the eyes that had followed Thomas de Wolfe and the Northwood knights from Kelso had also decided not to follow the knights any further. Women and children made a much better target, for none of Hobelar's reivers wanted to tangle with seasoned knights.

That had been a group decision.

When they figured out that de Wolfe was either a sponsor or somehow responsible for the women and children of the old pele tower, even if the woman he seemed to be attentive towards wasn't his wife, they decided that the tower with the women and children inside was to become part of their revenge against the stalwart commander of Wark Castle.

Damage the family and you damage the man.

That was exactly what Hobelar intended to do.

Whoever these people were to him, Thomas de Wolfe would get the message loud and clear.

ARTUS HEARD THE noise first.

Awoken from a dead sleep, he could hear the goats making a great deal of noise and, suddenly, Maitland was rushing past his open chamber door, heading for the bolted tower entry.

"M'lady!" Artus leapt out of bed and rushed to the chamber door in time to see her throwing the entry bolt. "What's amiss!"

Maitland was in a panic. "Something is in with the goats," she said, yanking open the door. "Artus, grab a fire poker or anything you can get your hands on. Hurry! Bring it!"

Artus scrambled over to the hearth, now burning low with fire due to the lateness of the hour, and grabbed a heavy iron poker. He rushed from the chamber just as Phin and the twins were waking up.

"Stay here!" Artus hissed at them.

Fearfully, the boys remained in their beds as Artus rushed out with Lady Bowlin, a big iron poker in his grip. He handed it over to Lady Bowlin, however, as the two of them rushed out into the yard, by the big tree that hung over the wall.

That was their terrible mistake.

It was dark, with the moon to the west of the tower creating eerie shadows along the yard. Rushing into the yard, Maitland and Artus failed to see men in the tree branches over their heads, men who had climbed onto the wall and then into the tree. As the pair ran out, the men dropped down, catching the boy first, who screamed angrily. They grabbed Maitland a split-second later and, panicked, she began swinging the iron poker around, pounding it on anyone who came too close.

It was so dark that Maitland couldn't really see who she was hitting but she knew she made contact based on the painful grunts she was hearing. At the moment, all she could think of was retreating into tower and bolting the door, but there were bodies behind her, preventing her from fleeing. Terrified, she began to scream.

"Artus!" she cried. "Get inside and bolt the door!"

Artus, however, was in his own battle, which really wasn't so much of a battle as it was an outright capture – of him. He wasn't very large, and he couldn't fight off a group of men, but he did the only thing he could do – he used his teeth and legs. He was biting anything that came near, kicking with all of his might, but it wasn't enough. He was overwhelmed. As Maitland watched in horror, two shadowy figures dashed into the tower.

Unnatural strength seized her, strength she summoned to save the children. With a roar, she leveled off the poker, swinging it at her head-level and hoping to catch her attackers in the head as well. She began screaming for Tibelda to bolt doors, but then she heard crying as the attackers began emerging from the tower with children in their arms. Renard, Roland, and Phin were carried past her. She could hear them screaming as they whizzed by and she remembered that the chamber door to the boy's dormitory had been open.

The boys had been left vulnerable.

Then, there was screaming from the second level of the keep as the attackers reached the girl's dormitory. She could hear things slamming and the girls screaming, and she knew it was because Tibelda was putting up a fight. The woman always carried a dagger in her skirts and, clearly, she was using it because she heard men yelling as well. She could only pray that Tibelda had bolted the door to the girl's dormitory.

The fighting in the tower seemed to go on forever.

As Maitland beat down her attackers, someone yanked the poker from her grip. An old blanket was abruptly thrown over her head and as she fought and struggled, men were wrapping rope around her, tying her up in the blanket. The sounds of a battle in the tower became eerily still and, shortly thereafter, she could hear Marybelle and Nora crying as they were carried from the keep. Maitland ended up slung over someone's shoulder, but she was still kicking and fighting as much as she could until they managed to get a rope around her ankles to still her legs.

Disoriented and suffocating in the stifling woolen blanket, she was forced to stop her struggles for fear she really would suffocate. Whoever had her was rushing off with her and she was bounced around painfully, the sounds of the panicked goats growing further and further away. She could hear the crying of the children and she called out to them, hoping to calm them. They were caught up now, prisoners, and there was nothing more she could do. She'd fought the battle and she'd lost, at least until the next battle, and once she assessed the situation, she would certainly give their abductors another fight. Maitland never had been one to lie down and surrender. But for the moment, the fight was over as she and the children were spirited off into the night.

What Maitland didn't see was the last act of the abductors before they left the tower completely, and that was the careful placement of a wolf's head dagger right at the entry to the tower, so it was sure not to be missed. The reivers were sending a message, very loudly, and they wanted to ensure Thomas de Wolfe received it.

They wanted Thomas to know who was in charge.

BACK AT EDENSIDE, the newly-repaired entry gate had managed to slam shut when the abductors fled, the hinges broken on the western gate, wedging the panel closed and immovable. The goats in the kitchen yard were untouched, as were the chickens, although the door to their coop had been knocked open, giving them the opportunity to escape so they could find food.

The goats, having been harassed by men in an attempt to draw out those in the tower, were now moving through a breach in the pen, wandering out into the kitchen yard and into the kitchen itself where several sacks of grain, stored in a stone storage cabinet, drew their interest. Having been disturbed from their sleep, they were now wandering around, finding things to eat, whether or not they were meant to be eaten.

Being goats, they would strip everything.

Now, Edenside was a community of goats and chickens, having the run of the place and lots of delicious things to eat, but up in the tower, on the roof, a tiny figure emerged from her hiding place and began to fearfully make her way down the stairs.

When the screaming had started, little Dyana had run. She was young, but not so young that she did not know a bad sound when she heard one. Back in the days of Laird Letty, she'd been a toddler and whenever there was screaming or raised voices, Artus had taught her to run and hide.

This time, it had saved her from abduction.

She'd run straight up to the roof and hid in a little crevice between the roof and the wall. But now that she'd come down the stairs, she could see that the tower was empty. No sounds, no people. Dyana made her way down to the level where the girls slept and she wandered into the dormitory, finger in her mouth, as she looked at the empty and somewhat disheveled chamber. Marybelle and Nora had tried to hold on to their beds as they were grabbed, so the beds were in disarray and scattered on the floor. As Dyana stood there, looking at the chaotic mess, she heard a groan.

She followed the sounds.

Tucked over behind her own little bed lay Tibelda.

The woman had a dagger in her chest, her own dagger in fact, turned on her by one of the reivers when she'd tried to defend the girls. Blood soaked the woman's woolen clothing and pooled on the floor beside her as Dyana knelt down beside Tibelda and put a timid little hand on the woman's head. Tibelda's eyes fluttered open.

"B-babe?" she said with her heavy stammer. "Is it the b-babe?"

Dyana leaned over so Tibelda could see her little face. When the woman blinked, cleared her vision, and recognized her, she smiled weakly.

"'Tis the w-wee b-babe," she said, reaching up a weak hand to stroke the terrified child's cheek. "Are ye w-well, lass?"

Dyana nodded, finger still in her mouth and tears in her eyes. "Where'd they go?"

Tibelda was fading fast. "Is everyone g-gone now?"

Again, the child nodded her head. "They ran away."

Tibelda thought as quickly as her muddled mind would allow. "And t-they didna take ye?"

Dyana was chewing furiously on her finger. "I hid."

Now, things were coming a little clearer to Tibelda, but she knew her time was limited. Frankly, she was shocked to see the child. But in that little one, she saw hope. She couldn't go for help, which meant only the child could.

A tiny little girl against the world.

But she didn't want the child to go to Kelso Abbey or into that big town; she'd only become lost, or worse. Kelso Abbey, and the abbot, only had bad connotations for Edenside and Tibelda didn't trust them to help those at Edenside. They never had before. Therefore, that meant the child had to find help elsewhere. She tried to smile, cupping the child's face in her hand.

"I-it was good that ye should hide," she said. "B-But now ye must find help. Do ye understand? Y-ye must find Sir Thomas and tell him w-what has happened."

Dyana's eyes widened with confusion. "Where is he?"

Tibelda could see how frightened the child was. She could feel her strength fading and breathing was becoming more and more difficult. She felt as if she were drowning, but she summoned the last of her strength to calmly give instructions to a terrified child.

Too many lives depended on it.

"G-go into my chamber," she told the little girl as calmly and steadily as she could. "T-there is a cloak on a peg. T-take it with ye and go out to the road. D-do ye remember the way the knights went when they left us?"

The child shook her head, perhaps not completely understanding the question, and Tibelda held up a finger. "I-if I give ye a pence, w-which hand do ye take it with?"

The little girl was puzzled for a moment, but took the finger out of her mouth and held out her right hand. "Here!"

Tibelda smiled faintly. "G-Good lass," she said. "N-now, get the cloak and go out to the road. A-and follow the direction of yer pence hand and stay to the river. W-When ye come to a bridge, cross it, and there will be Wark Castle. T-That is where Sir Thomas is. D-do ye understand?"

Dyana nodded solemnly. "Will he come?"

Tibelda closed her eyes; her vision was starting to go. "H-he will, lass," she said quietly. "H-Hurry, now. T-The cloak will protect ye from the night, b-but ye must hurry. T-tell Sir Thomas that the bad men t-took everyone away and he must help. P-please, lass. Y-ye must go."

Dyana nodded, but the finger went back in her mouth. She sat there and chewed on it until Tibelda closed her eyes and stopped breathing.

Then, everything grew terribly still.

No breathing, no speaking, no goat bleating down in the kitchen yard. Simply utter and complete stillness. Frightened of the stillness, Dyana didn't really understand that Tibelda had died. She shook her, twice, but Tibelda didn't move, so the child thought perhaps she was only sleeping in spite of the blood on the woman and on the floor. Death really didn't register with the young girl. However, knowing she'd been asked to help, Dyana stood up and left Tibelda's body, going to the adjacent chamber in search of the cloak she'd been told to find.

In spite of her young age, Dyana was obedient and smart. She could see the cloak, hanging up on the peg, and she pulled on it a few times until it came tumbling down over her head. Wrapping it around her body and having to double it up because it was far too big for her, she headed out of the tower and onto the front steps where she kicked the wolf's head dagger that had been placed there by the reivers. It scattered out into the dirt and, curious, Dyana went after it, picking it up and seeing that it was a big knife. It had the head of a dog on the end and the dog had gem-stone eyes. She could see them glittering in the weak light.

Because it was pretty, and because she knew that big people often used knives for protection, Dyana thought to take it with her on her journey to find Sir Thomas. She'd even seen Artus with a big knife, back in the days of Laird Letty, and she knew something sharp like this was meant to protect. It made her feel less frightened simply to carry it and the good Lord knew how badly she needed the courage.

Desperately.

Making her way to the front gates, Dyana could see that one of them was broken. She couldn't open it. Still, at the angle it sat, there was a small hole at the base of it, near the wall, so she got down on her knees and crawled through it. The cloak came off because the hole was so small, so she reached in her little hand and pulled it through. Now, she had her cloak again, protection against the night, and her dog-knife in her hand.

She was ready.

Sitting in front of the broken gates, Dyana held up her "pence hand". It was on her right and she turned to look down the road on that side. She had no way of knowing it faced east, or that Wark was only a few miles in that direction. All she knew was that Tibelda had told her to follow the road until she came to a bridge, and over the bridge was Wark Castle. Looking up in the sky, it was covered by a smattering of glittering stars and the moon was sitting low to the west. There wasn't much light to travel by, but that didn't matter. She'd been told to find Sir Thomas and find him she would.

Heading off in the direction of her "pence hand", the first step of her journey – and saving her friends – began.

CHAPTER NINETEEN

Wark Castle

I T WAS JUST before dawn.

Thomas was already awake, already going about his usual rounds. In spite of his reasons for fleeing Wark, it felt good to be back again. This was *his* command, *his* home. He stood on the battlements just as the sun began to break over the eastern horizon, thinking that the land looked green and lovely. The ribbon of the River Tweed reflected the golden morning light and a slight mist arose in the fields. It had a rather surreal look, one that Thomas had seen a thousand times, but on this morning, things were different.

More beautiful.

It all had to do with Maitland. He was looking at things differently now, seeing beauty in the world around him. Off to his left, he caught a glimpse of Desmond and his dreamy mood faded somewhat. Reality returned. Desmond was coming down from the part of the wall that was built on a slope, as the keep of Wark was on a fairly high motte and the wall ran up and over that motte. There were many stairs on that part of the wall, making it a bit of a hike for a man to do his duty, and Desmond lifted his hand in greeting to Thomas as he approached.

Thomas lifted his hand in return, thinking of what he'd done to

Desmond's sister two days ago. Desmond had told him to stay away from Maitland, not wanting his sister to be another of Thomas' conquests, so Thomas would make certain to stay off of the subject of Maitland for now. At least, stay off of it on a personal level. He didn't want an angry brother trying to throw him over the wall of his own castle. And until he could think of a sincere, calm way to speak on his feelings for her, he would simply refrain. Desmond had to be in the right mood for it, and so did he.

But it was a conversation that had to come sooner rather than later.

"That gash on your head does not look as bad as it did when you rode in yesterday," Desmond observed. "Does your head ache this morning?"

Thomas shook his head. "Not in the least," he said. "I told you the knights from Carlisle cheated. How do you think they were able to knock me in the head like this? And they seriously went after Garr and Hugh Ellsrod. Those two are battered and bruised."

Desmond snorted. "They went after those two because they are young and arrogant," he said. "I've seen them taunt others before. Did they do that this time?"

Thomas gave him a half-grin. "It *was* fairly humorous."

"Then their beat down is no surprise."

Thomas continued to grin, thinking about Hugh and Garr and how they insulted and slandered nearly every opposing knight in the mass competition as they attempted to prove their superior worth.

"I suppose it is no wonder that Carlisle went after all of us with a vengeance," he said. "But it was great fun. Oh, and I saw Lady Bowlin in Kelso, by the way."

Thomas thought he was rather smooth in the way he brought the subject up. He wanted Desmond to know he'd seen the woman and Desmond looked at him with surprise.

"Mae?" he said. "What was she doing there?"

Thomas folded his big arms, leaning back against the parapet. "She is teaching the foundlings to be productive and self-sufficient," he said.

"My mother gave her all of those goats and Mae has taught the children how to milk them and make cheese. It is very delicious cheese, in fact, and I told her that I would scour the taverns around Edenside and make sure all the tavernkeepers purchased her cheese. She sold her entire stock at the fair in Kelso."

Desmond grinned. "That sounds like her," he said. "She is very industrious. In Newcastle, she had the children making soap. Did she tell you that?"

Thomas nodded. "She mentioned something about it to my mother on the night she met my parents," he said. "My mother is greatly impressed with your sister, by the way. She will provide her with whatever she needs for the charity, and now Northwood is donating chickens and geese. Before long, your sister is going to have more donations than she knows what to do with."

Desmond shook his head. "Not her," he said. "She will know exactly what to do with them. You have never seen a woman of such organization."

Thomas stopped short of praising Maitland, too, because he didn't want it to look suspicious. He'd gush about her, unable to contain himself, and Desmond would catch on to the situation, so he simply nodded his head and returned his attention to the sunrise.

"I told her I'd have my mother send her more goats," he said. "I wonder if she could use a milk cow, too? The next time you go there, you should ask her."

He was turning it on to Desmond, thinking himself very clever for not suggesting *he* go and ask her. But Desmond scratched his head and yawned.

"Mayhap," he said. "But for now, I think I shall go to bed. I was up guarding the night while you were sleeping safely away, you little prince."

Thomas chuckled. "Off with you, then," he said. "But before you go, we will need to discuss returning Edmund de Vauden home. He's still in the vault, is he not?"

Desmond sobered. "Still," he said. "It is cold enough in there that the body isn't decaying, but the man must go home, Tommy. I know you do not want to go to Kyloe with Adelaide but, in this case, she is right – the man has to go home and you must go with her."

Thomas nodded, his mood dampening as it so often did when Adelaide was the subject. "I know," he said. He hesitated a moment before looking at the man. "Des, there is something you need to know. When I left here the day before yesterday, I told you that it was to escort my parents home."

Desmond nodded. "And you did," he said. "I saw you. And then you ended up in Kelso for some reason."

Thomas lowered his voice. "I did not want to tell you before I left, but for your own sake, you should know the truth," he said. "The day that I left, Adelaide's nurse found me. She had quite a bit to say. Have you seen that woman around, by the way?"

Desmond nodded. "I saw her yesterday," he said. "Why? What did she say?"

Thomas exhaled, an unhappy sound. "She told me that Adelaide's *tempestarii* act is just that – an act. Adelaide heard that I was called StormWolfe and she has put on this storm witch act thinking it would somehow endear her to me."

Desmond was listening seriously. "I knew it," he muttered. "It was too bizarre to be believed, and far too coincidental. She lied, did she? Utterly typical of the woman."

Thomas held up a hand. "There is more," he said. "The nurse also said that Adelaide has been betrothed twice before, and both young men were murdered – by Adelaide. The last one was murdered because Adelaide saw me in Carlisle last year at the great gathering of northern warlords and she told her father that she wanted to marry me. Whoever the man was that she was betrothed to at the time met an untimely death, clearing the way for a betrothal to me."

Desmond's eyes were wide with shock. "A killer?" he hissed. "That freakish madwoman is a killer?"

Thomas ran his hand through his dark hair wearily. "That is what my father is intent on finding out," he said. "That is why we left so suddenly. My mother did not want to be here, and she did not want Caria here, and my father intended to ride to Kyloe Castle and speak to anyone he could about it. He wants eyewitnesses, or at least testimony to that effect, because he wants to arrest Adelaide. But he wants me to marry her first so I can assume the earldom."

Desmond was truly shocked by what he was hearing. "God's Bones, Tommy," he breathed. "He still wants you to marry her? Even with what he knows?"

Thomas nodded. "If I do not marry her and my father arrests her, then the Northumbria earldom reverts to the crown," he said. "That means Edward can give it to one of his favorites, and my father does not want to see that happen. It would throw the entire north into turmoil. So, he wants me to marry the woman so I can assume the earldom before he arrests her. That way, we are all protected from whatever fool Edward would grant the earldom to. Although it makes sense to me, I must say that I am not happy about it, as I have not been happy about this betrothal from the beginning. However, if my father can get enough evidence to arrest Adelaide, then she will rot in the vault. I will never have to see her again."

Desmond could see the logic of it all, but it was still a horrific situation. "And if your father cannot get enough evidence against her?"

Thomas lifted his big shoulders. "I would normally never say this where it pertains to a woman, but if she tries to kill me, I have a right to defend myself. And I will."

"Then you will be accused of killing your wife. Do you have any idea how that will look for you?"

Thomas looked at him. "Do I have a choice?"

Desmond shook his head, leaning against the wall next to Thomas as he struggled to process what he'd been told. "Nay," he said. "Unfortunately, you do not. Adelaide has been asking for you constantly since you left with your parents. She is determined to marry you before you return her father's body to Kyloe."

"I know."

Desmond looked at his friend. Thomas looked weary and defeated already. He didn't like to see that where Thomas was concerned.

"I am sorry, Tommy," he said sincerely. "If there is anything I can do, simply say the word."

Thomas pushed himself off of the parapet, wandering over to the portion of the wall that overlooked the inner and outer baileys. "I will," he said. "But for now, we act normally, as if we do not know what Adelaide is capable of. Until my father returns from Kyloe Castle, that is all we can do."

"Agreed."

The expression on Thomas' face suddenly seemed to change as he looked over the inner and outer wards, causing Desmond to see what had his attention. Immediately, he could see Adelaide emerging from the keep and descending the stairs down to the inner bailey. The murderess herself had made an appearance and the mood instantly seemed to change. It went from one of tense but quiet understanding to one of foreboding. *A killer was in their midst.*

Desmond sighed heavily.

"There she is," he muttered. "Best of luck, Tommy."

Thomas braced himself. He refused to see Adelaide when he returned yesterday, pleading exhaustion, but Adelaide was smart – she knew he'd be seeing to his duties early this morning and she was going to intercept him. Knowing he couldn't put off the inevitable, he simply headed for the tower with the stairs that led down into the bailey.

"Tell the men on the wall to keep an eye out for my father," he said. "I want to know when he is sighted."

Desmond nodded. "I will stay on the wall myself," he said. "Not to worry."

Thomas paused. "I thought you were exhausted after being up all night?"

Desmond shook his head. "Not after what you just told me," he said. "I am eager for your father's return, too."

Thomas simply lifted his eyebrows in agreement and took the stairs, down the darkened tower and emerging into the cold, damp bailey. As soon as he hit the ground, he could see Adelaide coming through the far gate from the inner to the outer bailey. She was dressed in yellow, bright against the dawn's shadows. He headed right towards her because, clearly, she was heading for him.

He couldn't avoid her any longer.

"My lord," she called out, her voice echoing against the stone walls because she'd very nearly shouted. "Welcome back. I came to see you yesterday when you returned but I was told you were not to be disturbed."

They came to a halt in nearly the center of the outer bailey, but it was an uneasy halt. For every two steps Adelaide would take in his direction, he'd take a step away from her. There was about six feet between them and he refused to let her close the gap.

"It was a strenuous ride," he said simply.

Adelaide was expecting more of an explanation. She looked at him, lifting her eyebrows with the beginning of that annoyed expression she so often had on her face. "And I trust your parents made it home safely?"

She said it rather sarcastically. Thomas simply nodded. "They did."

"They did not even bid me farewell."

He could have given her a nasty reply, but he refrained. "My... mother was not feeling well," he said. "She simply wanted to get into the carriage and depart as quickly as she could."

It was obvious that Adelaide didn't believe him. She was becoming more annoyed by the second. "I see," she said. "Now that your parents are back at Castle Questing, I must speak to you about the return of my father's body to Kyloe Castle. It has been over a week, Thomas. I really must insist that we marry immediately and return his body to Kyloe for burial."

"Define immediately."

"Today."

He shook his head. "Nay," he said. "We will wait until my mother is feeling better and can return for the mass. As for your father's body, it is my understanding that it is in a decent state since it is so cold in the vault. If we marry by the end of the week and return him then, that should be sufficient."

His answer infuriated her. "Unacceptable," she said, crossing her arms angrily. "It will be today."

Thomas cocked an eyebrow at her. "I told you that you cannot have everything you want, when you want it," he said, losing his patience. "I further told you that I will make the decisions when it pertains to us or any other matter of my house and hold. You do not have a say in these things."

Adelaide's face was starting to flush. "I have a say," she hissed. "If you want this earldom, and I know you do, then you will do as I say."

He smiled thinly at her. "I do not care about the earldom, nor do I care about you. I am only in this contract because our fathers brokered it. Please – if you want out, just say the word and I will be happy to release you from this burden. I beg you to release us both."

That wasn't the answer Adelaide was looking for. She was hoping to force him into obedience with her threat. Just as she was gearing up for a retort, the sentries on the walls sounded and Thomas was distracted. He turned for the gatehouse, trying to hear what the sentries were saying, as Adelaide snarled behind him.

"I am *not* finished," she said, struggling to regain his attention. "Look at me, Thomas. I am not finished with you yet."

He ignored her. The sentries seemed somewhat excited and Thomas began heading for the gatehouse. As he moved towards it, the ropes on the portcullis went taut and the massive iron grate began to lift. Overhead, Desmond shouted down to him.

"De Wolfe colors!" he shouted down.

Thinking it might be his father, Thomas quickly made his way to the gatehouse, leaving Adelaide where he left her in a furious mess. But

Thomas was very eager to speak with his father so he stood at the mouth of the gatehouse as the portcullis lifted, seeing the rider come down the road that led right into the gatehouse.

Immediately, he saw that it was not his father, but he did recognize Markus de Wolfe's horse. It was a very big, black horse to support an enormous knight, and he stood aside as Markus charged through the gatehouse and reined his sweaty, weary horse to a halt. He ripped his helm off as Thomas approached him.

"Tommy, it's grandfather," he said breathlessly. "There has been an accident."

Thomas felt a wave of shock wash over him. "What accident?" he demanded. "Where is he?"

Markus wiped the sweat out of his eyes as he threw his leg over the saddle and plopped to the ground. "Northwood," he said. "There was an accident with the horses and grandfather was badly injured. You must go to Northwood immediately. Grandmother is already heading there with Uncle Blayth and several other men. Riders were sent for Troy, Scott, and my father this morning."

Thomas knew he had gone pale. His hand went to his heart as if to hold it into his chest, for his father was his heart and soul and then some. He simply couldn't believe what he was hearing.

"Oh, God," Thomas breathed, grabbing hold of Markus. "What happened to him? God, Markus, tell me he is not dying."

Markus was a mature young knight but, emotionally, he still had some growing to do. He was still only nineteen years old. When he saw the fear in Thomas' eyes, his composure took a hit.

"His horse threw him head-first into a stone wall," he said. "He was not wearing his helm. Garr Ellsrod arrived at Castle Questing some-where around midnight to tell us what had happened. Will has gone after Uncle Scott and Atreus has gone for Uncle Troy, and Alec rode for my father at Berwick. I was told to summon you. I do not know how badly grandfather is injured, Uncle Tommy, but I know you must come. You must come *now*."

Thomas put his hands over his face, trying to hold back the gut reaction of tears and horror. "Oh, God," he breathed. "Oh God, not my papa. Please, God, not my papa."

By this time, Desmond had come off the wall and had heard most of what Markus had said. He began shouting for Thomas' horse to be brought as well as his own. Men began running with a purpose as the stable servants flew into a frenzy. Everything and everyone was moving and as Thomas turned around to head to the armory, Adelaide was suddenly behind him.

"Why was your father at Northwood Castle?" she asked without a shred of emotion. "You said that you escorted him to Castle Questing."

Thomas didn't reply; he didn't trust himself to. He pushed past her but she reached out, grabbing his arm and trying to physically prevent him from walking away from her. He reacted strongly, so strongly that when he jerked his arm from her grip, she tripped backwards and ended up on her arse. But Thomas kept walking. In fact, he started running. He ran to the armory with Desmond behind him and, between the two of them, they managed to get themselves dressed rather quickly. A few soldiers had piled in after them, grabbing shields and other items, making sure the knights were equipped.

It didn't take long for both Thomas and Desmond to be fully dressed, and they spilled out of the armory with soldiers following behind, carrying the items they had grabbed so they could secure them to Thomas' saddle. Thomas wasn't any less panicked than he had been moments before, but he managed to speak somewhat coherently.

"Des, put the gatehouse sergeant in command while we are away," he said. "Lock up Wark and make sure the men know that they are to remain here and remain vigilant while we are gone. I do not want that portcullis raised for anyone."

"Aye, Thomas."

"Make sure they know that."

"Aye."

Desmond was slightly behind Thomas as they walked, eyeing the man with worry. On top of everything else Thomas had to worry over, now his father had been injured. Knowing how attached Thomas was to his father, he could only imagine the man's concern. They were just heading back into the outer bailey where the horses were being brought around and Desmond began shouting at some of the soldiers to mount a small escort when they caught sight of Adelaide again.

Now, she was over by the steps leading into the great hall with her nurse standing behind her. It was clear that Adelaide was terribly upset, brushing at her yellow skirt that had become dirty when she fell back. She was talking to the nurse, waving her hands around when she wasn't batting at her skirt, but the sight of Thomas emerging from the armory had her rushing towards him again. She put herself right in front of him.

"Wait!" she shouted. "You are not leaving Wark until we settle a few things, Thomas. The priest will be here this evening and you and I shall be married. And I want an honor guard assembled for my father so we may…"

Thomas walked right past her without acknowledging her and she whirled around as he moved past, her fists clenching as the man soundly ignored her. She was beyond fury at that point as her betrothed refused to listen to her in any fashion, consumed with going to his father based on what he'd been told.

But Adelaide would not be ignored and she would not be brushed off. Grabbing a small dirk that she kept in the purse hanging from her waist, she lifted it and began to scream.

"This is all your fault, Thomas de Wolfe!" she screamed as she dragged the blade across her forearm and immediately drew blood. "You have caused my suffering and your father's injury is God's punishment! I hope he dies so that you may feel my own pain at my father's death, do you hear me? *This is your punishment!*"

She was shrieking like a madwoman, slicing the blade across her other forearm as the blood began to flow. In truth, the only reason Thomas stopped and turned around was because of only one thing she said – *I hope he dies.* Thomas lost all self-control at that moment, spinning in Adelaide's direction and charging. He was fully intent on killing her. But Desmond was there, putting himself between Thomas and Adelaide because he knew, for certain, that Thomas was going to murder the woman for what she'd said about William. There was no doubt in his mind.

Markus, seeing his uncle being restrained, jumped in to help, all the while confused and disgusted by the woman who was cutting up her arms in the middle of the bailey. He had no idea who she was, but based on family gossip, he suspected he was seeing Adelaide de Vauden. It was a horrific, chaotic scene.

"Nay, Thomas," Desmond hissed, struggling against Thomas' strength. The man was like a raging bull. "Ignore her, do you hear? She is attempting to get a reaction out of you. Do not give it to her!"

But Thomas couldn't seem to hear him. All he could see was Adelaide, standing there with her arms bleeding, gazing at him with nearly as much hatred in her expression as he felt for her in his heart. At that moment, lines were crossed – it was no longer Thomas and his clear disdain for Adelaide, but now Thomas and his abject hatred for the woman. Even though both Desmond and Markus were restraining him, he still managed to get an arm free, pointing at Adelaide as she stood there and loudly wept.

"Bleed out into the dirt and die, you bitch, for if you do not, when I return, I will kill you myself for what you have said," he growled. "I am at an end with you."

Desmond managed to get a hand on Thomas' head, turning him away so he wasn't looking at Adelaide. With Markus' help, they began to steer him back towards the horses that were being loaded with shields and weapons. Thomas was so shaken, so angry, that he could barely walk.

"Des," he said hoarsely, "have that woman thrown in the vault with her father's body. She can sit there and rot alongside him until I decide to release her."

Desmond looked at him, somewhat shocked by the brutal command but not completely surprised. "Thomas..."

"*Do it.*"

It was an order, not meant to be disobeyed. Desmond sighed faintly. "It will be done," he said. "Anything else?"

"Aye," Thomas said as he reached his horse. "Lock her in and keep her there until I return. If anyone lets her out, or if anyone opens the cell door before I return, I will personally kill the man. Is that clear?"

Desmond knew he meant every word. "It is clear, Thomas."

As Thomas mounted his war horse, Desmond relayed quick but succinct orders to the gate sergeant, including the arrest of Lady Adelaide. As Thomas turned his steed for the gatehouse, the next sounds he heard were those of Adelaide's screams as she was set upon by a dozen Wark soldiers. Crying his name, she was dragged off to the vault.

Her screams of terror were like music to Thomas' ears and perhaps the only thing that settled the murderous rage in his heart. Thundering out of the gatehouse with Desmond, Markus, and about two dozen Wark soldiers behind him, he turned for the road north, the one that would lead him to Northwood Castle.

With every step his horse took, Thomas could feel his fury cooling. It was a forced cooling, because if he didn't force himself to calm down, he would go on a murder rampage. With a few deep breaths and distance between him and Adelaide, it became easier. He wasn't so blinded by his rage any longer but, now, fear took hold. Fear for his father, fear for what had happened. Markus knew nothing more than what he'd already told him, so there was a greater fear of the unknown. If Garr Ellsrod had ridden in the dead of night for Castle Questing, that told Thomas that the injury his father suffered must be very bad, indeed.

But he couldn't panic, not yet.

He was hoping it wasn't as bad as it sounded. He could get to Northwood and William could be up and moving with nothing more than a bump on his head, or he could get there and find his father dead. At this point, any scenario was possible, and Thomas found himself praying that it wasn't all that bad. His father was immortal, wasn't he? A man who was elderly, but incredibly healthy and active. Truly, William was ageless, and a foolish accident wasn't going to steal away England's greatest knight.

The Wolfe of the Border...

Nay, an accident wasn't going to take him away.

Thomas refused to believe it.

Up ahead was the bridge that Wark guarded, the one that crossed the River Tweed. But instead of going over the bridge, Thomas intended to take the road that veered to the right and ran along the river. That road would take them straight to Northwood Castle, which was easily less than an hour's ride. They would be there quickly. In fact, Thomas was so focused on the road turning east that he failed to see a tiny figure crossing the bridge, running as fast as the little legs would move.

In fact, Desmond saw it first and he threw up a hand, catching Thomas' attention as he reined his excited horse to a halt.

"Thomas!" he shouted. "Look!"

Thomas did. He wouldn't have thought anything of a lone child except for the fact that she was dragging a dark, heavy cloak and he happened to recognize the fabric on the child's tunic.

The blue fabric his mother had donated to Edenside.

Shocked, Thomas pulled his horse to a halt, directing it back towards the bridge as the soldiers accompanying him nearly crashed into each other at his swift change in direction. Thomas found himself thundering over to the bridge where the child dropped the cloak and tried to climb onto the railing, terrified of the big horses. When Thomas saw that, he reined his horse to a halt and vaulted off the saddle, landing on the ground with his feet running. He ran straight up to the child, seeing that it was the tiny little girl, Dyana.

He fell to his knees in front of her.

"Dyana?" he said, great concern in his voice. "What are you doing here, sweetheart? Did you wander away?"

The little girl realized that it was Thomas, the man she had been looking for. She was so cold that her lips were blue and, somewhere, she'd either lost her shoes or never had them on because her feet were filthy, bloody, and cold. She let go of the railing on the bridge and came towards Thomas.

"Tibelda is sleepin'," she said, sounding frightened. "She told me tae tell ye that bad men came and took them away."

Thomas was trying to make sense out of it. "Bad men?" he repeated. "Who was taken away?"

The little girl was pale with exhaustion and fear from her night on the road, but she knew that Thomas was safety, as was Desmond, whom she also recognized. She went straight to Thomas and put her little arms around his neck.

"Everybody," she said. "The men came and they were screamin'. They took everyone away."

Thomas was seized with dread. "Everyone at Edenside was taken away?" he clarified, realizing that he was starting to tremble. "Men came and took them away."

The little girl nodded as she tried to climb on Thomas. As he put his arms around her and picked her up, something fell out of her hand and onto the dirt of the bridge. Thomas found himself looking at the wolf's head dagger he'd lost at Coldstream when battling the reivers, something he thought was forever lost.

Until now.

Horror such as he'd never known swept him. Bending over, he picked up the dagger.

"Oh, God," he breathed, looking at it in shock. He held it up to the child. "Sweetheart, where did you get this? Did... did someone give this to you?"

Dyana was finally safe, so her manner had eased considerably. She petted the top of the wolf's head as if it were a living animal. "Pretty," she said, pointing at the bejeweled eyes. "See? Pretty."

Thomas was trying very hard to keep his composure in the face of a weary, frightened child, but Desmond wasn't so calm. He put his hands on the little girl, trying to force her to look at him.

"Where did you get the dagger, lass?" he demanded. "And where is Lady Bowlin? Where is my sister?"

The little girl looked at him with her big, blue eyes. "The bad men took her," she said. "Tibelda is sleepin'."

Desmond and Thomas looked at each other over the top of Dyana's blonde little head. The child wasn't making much sense, but what she was saying was wholeheartedly alarming.

"I must go to Edenside," Desmond muttered, his voice trembling. "I must see for myself what has happened."

Thomas was struggling desperately not to panic alongside Desmond. He was overwhelmingly worried for his father, and now his fear for Maitland was exploding. What in the hell had happened at Edenside after he'd left? He'd only just left there and he'd inspected the entire place for threats. There hadn't been any sign of hazard.

Not one...

Was this his fault? Had he missed something?

Clearly, something had occurred. He could only imagine that there was some level of truth to what the little girl was saying because Maitland would have never let the child out of her sight if she could help it. Thomas felt as if he were being pulled in all different directions and trying so very hard to keep his wits about him.

It was a nightmare.

Taking a deep breath, he forced himself to evaluate his priorities – his father was crucial, but so was whatever happened at Edenside. He had a frightened little girl that told him something very bad had happened. He wanted so badly to go with Desmond to Edenside but, in the same breath, he knew he had to go to his father first. The man was badly injured, perhaps even dying, and Thomas would never forgive himself for not being there when his father needed him. It was a horrible choice to have to make, but he made the only one he could – he had to go to Northwood.

He prayed that Maitland would understand, wherever she was and whatever had happened.

I'm so sorry, Mae.

It was a choice that broke his heart.

"Go," he barked at Desmond. "Take some men with you and go. Find out what has happened and then send someone to Northwood to inform me of your findings. I will take the child with me."

Desmond was already running for his horse, shouting at the soldiers and taking at least six with him. Thomas handed Dyana up to Markus, who took the child until Thomas could mount his horse. Then, he handed the little girl back to Thomas, who then tore off down the road, heading for Northwood, as Desmond took off in the opposite direction for Edenside.

Even though Thomas wasn't heading for Edenside, his focus was with Desmond, wondering what in the hell had happened at Edenside that a tiny little girl had wandered miles away trying to find help. The more he thought about it, the more his heart sank because he knew, over and over again, that Maitland would have never let Dyana wander away from Edenside had she been able to help it. Unless the child simply slipped out and wandered off when everyone was sleeping… *but no.* He stopped himself from thinking that because he knew it wasn't true.

Something very bad had happened.

Something very bad, indeed.

CHAPTER TWENTY

MAITLAND HAD NO idea where she was.

  She hadn't slept all night, tossed around and battered with the old blanket over her head, dulling her senses, until the group finally stopped moving. Then, someone pulled her off of the horse she'd been slung over and dumped her onto the ground.

The blanket came off her head.

It was just before dawn and the land was covered in dew, a mist rising from the fields all around her. She'd been brought to the ruins of a castle or some other type of structure. It was difficult to tell, but the entire thing was crumbling around them, set amongst a gentle landscape of green fields and tall trees.

But there was nothing bucolic or gentle about the ruins. It smelled like human habitation, that acrid stench that assaulted her nostrils. Men had been living in these old stones, exposed to the sky and the elements except for one small area that had once been part of the vault, for it had a barrel ceiling and was buried under rocks and grass and fallen trees. The interior of the ruins was stripped for the most part, as men cleared the ground for them to live and sleep and eat, and burn their cooking fires when they could.

It was a den of animals.

Fortunately, Maitland had been dumped with the children, who now huddled with her. She had her arms around most of them, as many as she could, and Artus sat on the other side of them, pressing his body against Phin and Nora for some heat and protection. They were notably missing Dyana, the littlest, but Maitland was afraid to ask about her, afraid that if she asked and the abductors didn't realize there was a child they had missed, that they'd go back to Edenside and look for her.

She didn't want to tip them off.

So, she sat there with the six children and kept her mouth shut. The children were terrified, exhausted, and hungry, and Maitland tried to comfort them as best she could. Considering she had no idea what was going on, it was rather difficult to do so. She had no idea what to tell them. As she sat there rocking the twins, trying to soothe them, a shadow fell over the group. Looking up, she could see the figure of a man as he blocked out some of the morning sun.

"Greetin's, my lady," he said in a Scottish accent, although it wasn't particularly heavy. "I apologize for yer rough treatment, but it was necessary."

He sounded gallant, which enraged Maitland. "Necessary for what?" she asked. "Necessary to frighten us half to death? You know that you raided a foundling home, don't you? We have no money to give you and no one to pay a ransom. It was a wasted effort on your part."

The man crouched down a few feet away, a poorly dressed wretch with dark-circled eyes and a mop of shaggy gray hair. "It was not, I assure ye," he said. "They call me The Bold Hobelar, my lady. May I have yer name?"

Maitland was angry and weary, and very frightened for the children. "I am the guardian of these children," she said warily. "What do you want with us?"

Hobelar didn't seem offended by her reply. "Ye're valuable tae us," he said. "Ye're very valuable tae the de Wolfe pup."

"Who is the de Wolfe pup?"

"The commander of Wark Castle."

Maitland stared at him a moment before averting her gaze. "I do not know what you mean."

Hobelar's pleasant manner changed in an instant. He picked up a nearby stick and whacked it against the ground in a startling motion, causing Maitland and the children to jump with fear and surprise.

The message was clear.

"Dunna lie tae me," Hobelar growled. "We followed ye from Kelso. We saw every move de Wolfe made and we saw his attention tae ye. Are ye goin' tae tell me again that ye dunna know him?"

The whistling stick in Hobelar's hand had Maitland's attention. She didn't want any of the children to be hit by it so she thought better of her resistance.

"I know him," she said. "He is a patron of Edenside's foundling home."

Hobelar's pleasant manner returned frighteningly fast. "Is he, now?" he said, though it was more of a statement than a question. "Then ye do mean somethin' tae him."

Maitland wasn't sure where the conversation was going, but she knew it couldn't be good. "He is very generous and so are his parents," she said. "Please... the children are cold and hungry. We can do nothing for you. Won't you please let us return home?"

"Not now," Hobelar said. "Ye're goin' tae tell me what ye know of Thomas de Wolfe."

"I told you that he is our patron. He lives at Wark Castle. Beyond that, I do not know much."

Hobelar eyed her for a moment. Then, he reached out, quick as a flash, and grabbed Artus by his skinny arm. As the boy yelled and Maitland screamed, Hobelar picked up the stick he'd so recently smacked on the ground and lifted it to Artus as if to strike him. The children were screaming and crying as Maitland bolted to her feet, holding out her hands.

"Nay!" she cried. "Please do not strike him, I beg you!"

As Artus squirmed in his grip, Hobelar brought the stick to a halt just shy of Artus' face. "Then ye'll tell me what I wish tae know, woman," he said. "If ye dunna tell me, I'll take it out on these bairns."

Maitland nodded quickly, reaching out to pull Artus from the man's grasp and tuck the child behind her. She stood there, the only barrier between the children and a man who would abuse them. Her heart was pounding with fear.

"I swear that I will be honest with you, but leave the children alone," she said, her voice trembling. "They have been through enough. They are parentless, for God's sake. Would you really abuse children who have no one to love them?"

Hobelar lifted his shoulders. "I had no one tae love me and I'm no worse for the wear," he said as his men chuckled behind him. Then, he crooked a finger at Maitland. "Come here, woman. We are goin' tae have a talk."

Maitland was becoming more frightened by the moment. "What about?"

"De Wolfe," Hobelar said. "I want the man. He killed many of my men and I want him."

Behind Hobelar, Maitland could see a host of unhappy faces. Scruffy, dirty, smelly men who lived like beasts in the wilderness. *Outlaws*, she thought. *They must be outlaws.* The men didn't look like Scots to her, or even English, and she was quickly trying to assess just, exactly, who they were. The only thing she could come up with was outlaws.

"Did he kill your men in battle?" she asked.

Hobelar shrugged. "Ye could say so."

"And you were fighting against him?"

"Aye."

"Then I am sure you killed many of his men, too."

Hobelar eyed her. "It is not so easy," he said. "What de Wolfe did was murder. He murdered my men and I *will* have my revenge on him."

Maitland could hear the thirst for vengeance in his tone. Even if he hadn't spoken the word, she would have still known. Now, she knew why she and the children were here and it frightened her to death. The man wanted revenge and those kinds of men were the most irrational to deal with, fed by the anguish of others. Her heart began to beat faster as bile rose in her throat.

"And you are going to murder the children and me in revenge? Is that why we are here?"

Hobelar shook his head. "Not yet," he said. "But dunna give me any ideas, woman. First, we'll do it easily."

"What do you mean?"

Hobelar's eyes narrowed. "I want ye tae draw the man out of Wark," he said. "I'll let ye walk tae the castle and draw him out, and if ye dunna do yer duty, I'll kill the bairns. I swear I will."

Maitland's jaw dropped in shock as she looked at Hobelar and the dirty, filthy scum behind him. "But they are *children!*"

"I'll litter the road with little bodies if ye dunna bring the de Wolfe pup tae me."

She gasped in horror. "You would kill innocent children for no reason at all?"

"I have a reason!" Hobelar shouted over her. He thrust a finger at her. "I have a reason and ye'll not stop me. Now, go sit with the bairns. Do what I say, woman, or it will go badly for ye."

Maitland did as she was told. Rushing to the children, she sat down and quickly pulled Roland and Renard into her arms, holding them tightly as she pulled the others towards her as well. She wished they hadn't heard Hobelar's threat, because they were all trembling and weeping, but there was nothing she could do but comfort them. She couldn't make them un-hear what they'd already heard. She wished with all her heart that *she* could un-hear it.

They were in quite a bind.

Quickly, she began to relive the last conversation she'd had with Thomas. He'd told her he would return to Edenside in a couple of days with men to guard the place. That meant she had to survive at least two days before he figured out something was amiss. And Dyana? What had happened to her? And Tibelda? Hopefully the pair was together and safe. That was all Maitland could pray for because she had enormous trouble on her hands at the moment.

Sacrifice six children or sacrifice Thomas.

God help her, that's what it might come down to.

The disbelief, the horror of it, was unfathomable.

CHAPTER TWENTY-ONE

Northwood Castle

I T WAS A vigil.

A sickening, horrible, heartbreaking vigil that Thomas could barely stomach. He could hardly believe any of this was real.

The news wasn't good. His father, while trying to mount his horse, had been thrown into a wall, head-first, smashing his temple and his good eye. Knocking himself unconscious, Paris and several knights had brought William into a chamber where Paris had personally tended to him, as he'd done so many times in the past. Paris was one of the best warrior-physics in all of England, as he'd proven many times, but this instance was particularly difficult for him.

He'd caused it all.

It was something he'd confessed to Jordan when he arrived, in tears because of it, but Jordan had been stoic and calm. It had helped Paris' manner immensely, but the guilt he felt was overwhelming. He'd stayed right by William's side, applying every technique he'd ever learned to address the head injury. His attention to the massive lump on William's head was constant.

Thomas, because he was closer to Castle Questing, was the first brother to arrive behind Blayth, who had brought their mother. Patrick arrived a few hours later, followed by Troy. Scott was the last to arrive and he came just before sunset, a man who was also an excellent healer in his own right. He tried to be professional about it, discussing his father's state with Paris, but the emotion of the situation was just too overwhelming. Thomas saw Scott wipe his eyes after a particularly intense discussion with Paris.

That gesture, small as it was, didn't give Thomas much hope.

Evening fell and William abruptly began to stir, muttering something to Jordan about getting a baby out of bed. She told him to go back to sleep and he did. Rising from her chair next to the bed with her favored shawl wrapped around her slender shoulders, Jordan called softly to the servants for some food and drink before going about lighting the tapers in the chamber so that they would have some light during their long and terrible wait.

As Paris left the room in search of more moss for a compress, Jordan brought a lit taper over to the table where her sons were gathered. As she passed Thomas, who was seated in a chair with a tiny little girl in his arms, dead asleep, she came to a pause. Handing the taper to Troy, who set it down on the table, Jordan smiled weakly at Thomas.

"Some people find stray dogs, but it appears ye may have found a stray child," she said. "I saw ye come in with her, Tommy. Who is she?"

Thomas shifted, looking down at Dyana as she slept heavily. "She is from Edenside."

"But why do ye have her?"

Thomas grunted; he didn't want to bring his troubles into his father's sick room, but his mother had asked a question. He had to tell her something. "Because as we were heading to Northwood, we found this little lass walking along the bridge," he said. "She told us bad men had come to take everyone at Edenside away. Desmond has gone to see what has happened, but I've not heard from him yet. He said he would send word as soon as he could."

Jordan's smile faded and a look of concern crossed her face. In fact, all of the brothers in the chamber heard Thomas, all of them now listening.

"Someone has raided Edenside?" Jordan asked. "What of Lady Bowlin?"

Thomas put his big hand over the child's ear as she lay against his chest so she wouldn't awaken with the conversation. "I do not know," he said, his stomach twisting in knots even as he said it. "As I said, I sent Desmond and several soldiers to see what has happened to them. I'm simply waiting for word."

Jordan frowned, distressed. "Sweet Jesus, Joseph, and Mary," she breathed. "Who would raid a foundlin' home?"

Before she could get worked up, Thomas held up his hand. "I think I know," he muttered. "God help me, I'm fairly certain I know."

"Who, Tommy?" Patrick had moved away from his position against the wall and was now standing next to their mother. "Who did this?"

Thomas looked up at his enormous brother, who happened to be the Constable of the North. The north of England may have been fairly lawless at times, but Patrick maintained good control of it. From his seat at Berwick Castle, he was the heavy hand of justice in the area. Thomas looked his brother in the eye.

"The same reivers who have been giving us trouble for the past year, Atty," he said. "The ones that call themselves the Thurrock *Cú*. They were in Coldstream almost two weeks ago, raiding the village, and my men herded them off of a cliff overlooking the river. I do not know how many of them made it out of that river alive, but those who did are evidently bent on revenge."

Patrick's eyebrows furrowed. "But how do you know?"

Thomas glanced around the room. "Because it was in that same battle that I lost the dirk Papa gave me when I was first knighted," he said. "We all have the same dirk, the one with the wolf's head on it. I thought I would never see it again but this little girl showed up holding it. She said the bad men left it."

Scott and Troy were listening, too, along with Blayth. "But how would they know about Edenside?" Scott wanted to know. "If they are looking to seek revenge against you, what is your connection to Edenside?"

Thomas looked at his eldest brother. "I am a patron," he said. "So are Mother and Father. We have been giving Edenside supplies and livestock so they can sustain themselves. I also believe these same reivers are the ones who ambushed Edmund de Vauden last week as he left Wark and killed him. Clearly, they are watching Wark and they are watching me. I can only surmise that they saw me go to Edenside at some point and that was why they raided it – to punish me."

The brothers reacted to the shocking news of Northumbria's death. "Northumbria is *dead*?" Patrick said, aghast. "Why was I not informed of this?"

Thomas held up a hand to ease the big man. "So much has happened in the past week, Atty, truly," he said. "Papa and I have had as much as we can handle. We did not intentionally withhold the information, I assure you. There simply has not been time to send word."

It calmed Patrick down a little, but not much. As he shook his head, frustrated that he had to find out about a fairly crucial death in his jurisdiction this way, Jordan was looking at her son with great fear.

"Do ye think it's true, Tommy?" she asked. "Do ye truly think the reivers are truly tryin' tae punish ye?"

He shrugged. "I can think of no other explanation."

"Those poor children," she said sadly. "They survived the scandal of the abbot's sister only tae fall victim to reivers. God help those sweet bairns."

With that, she sighed heavily and walked away, wandering back to her husband's bedside. Jordan was a woman of deep feeling, in all things, and the raid of Edenside upset her greatly. But she couldn't let herself get too swept up in it, not with her husband so badly injured. He needed to be her focus, so as she sat next to him and put a gentle hand on his battered head, Thomas looked up at his brothers.

"I expected word from Edenside by now," he said quietly. "I realize this seems like a trivial thing compared to Papa's injury, but it is important to me."

"We can see that," Scott replied. "But why? What is Edenside to you that it means so much?"

Thomas lowered his gaze uncomfortably. "I have grown attached to it," he said. "I am not sure I can explain my feelings on the matter, but let me try. I have spent my life rather... directionless. I was born the youngest of six powerful brothers and I spent my life watching all of you and wanting to be just like you – Scott's command presence, Troy's aggressiveness, Atty's air of power, Blayth's resilience, and Edward's smooth manner. Each of you had something I lacked. I think it is fair to say that I have been the wild colt of the group."

He watched grins spread across the faces of Patrick, Troy, Scott, and even Blayth, who was listening intently.

"You were the incorrigible baby," Scott said, rolling his eyes. "Troy and Atty and I were young men when you were born. It was as if Mother and Father had two groups of children – me, Troy, Atty, Blayth and Katheryn, and Evelyn were one group, and then when we were older, suddenly, there were three more little de Wolfe whelps to tend – you and Edward and Penny. I can still see Katheryn and Evelyn chasing you and Edward around when you were just a few years old because Mother had just given birth to Penelope and it nearly killed her. I remember that very well."

"I remember the screaming," Troy said, shaking his head. "God's Bones, the screaming at all hours. With Edward, not too much, but Tommy and Penny – you are both very lucky we did not smother you while you slept."

Thomas grinned. "It was my intention to make your lives as miserable as possible, you know," he said, watching them laugh. "That was always my goal."

"It seems that you succeeded," Blayth said in his slow, deliberate speech. "Although I do not remember you in your youth, I have heard stories. Someone told me once that when you were about five years of age, I made you angry so you spit on me. I grabbed you and took you to the stable, where I tied you to a post and left you. The screaming brought Mother and she evidently tried to beat me."

The three older brothers were nodding and laughing. "It is true," Patrick said to Blayth. "I remember that. We tried to tell Mother that all four of us tied Tommy up but, somehow, it did not work. She knew it was you and she took a switch to you."

Blayth was laughing at the mere suggestion even though it wasn't something he could recall. He'd been robbed of most of his memory due to his head injury years ago, and it was times like this when he truly wished he did remember things. An obnoxious brother and a protective mother would have been a fun recollection.

"An angry mother is a fearsome thing," he said. But he sobered, looking to his youngest brother. "Nothing we seemed to do did any damage to Tommy. In spite of being a spoiled, screaming child, he seems to have matured reasonably enough."

"You all matured reasonably enough."

It was a low, mumbling voice that came from the bed. All five of them looked over to the bed, startled, where their father was starting to stir. He was mumbling other things they couldn't quite hear, but it clear that he was somewhat lucid. Jordan, sitting next to the bed, stood up and leaned over her husband.

"Are ye awake, English?" she asked softly. "Can ye hear me well enough?"

"I hear you."

Her head snapped over to her sons. "Atty, fetch Paris. Tell him that his patient has awakened."

Patrick headed out of the chamber, quickly, while the remaining sons stood up and headed over to the bed to see their father. William's only good eye, his right one, was bruised and cut, but it was open. They could see that he was looking at them.

"Welcome back, Papa," Scott said. "I thought I told you never to ride wild horses at your age."

William blinked. "Is… is that what happened?"

It was clear in that question that he was understandably muddled. Scott came along the other side of William's bed, taking a candle from the bedside and holding it up to see the reaction of his father's pupil. "That is what happened," he said. "What do you remember?"

William didn't say anything for a moment. He simply lay there, his eye opening and closing slowly. His left eye, the one he'd lost long ago, was without its customary eye patch, having been removed by Paris after the accident because the strap went over the part of the head that William had hit.

William had lost the eye to a Welsh archer those years ago, and a thick purple scar ran crossways across his eye, starting near his nose and ending right over the brow bone. The eye was closed, a little sunken, but nothing catastrophic. His sons, who had never known their father without his eye patch, got a good look at his face without it. It made him look very different, the reality of what a warrior looked like with William's years of experience.

No man emerged from that many years of battle unscathed.

"I remember riding to Northwood," William muttered after a moment, closing his eye. "I had to speak with Paris about… something. It was Tommy. I had to speak with him about Tommy." He fell silent for a few seconds when suddenly, his eye flew open and he turned his head, struggling to look around. "Tommy? Where is Tommy?"

"I am here, Papa," Thomas was standing at the end of the bed, holding Dyana against him. He came forward, passing the sleeping baby off to his mother as he came to stand beside his father. "Here I am. Do not be troubled."

William struggled to clear his vision, seeing his youngest son standing right alongside him. He lifted a hand to him, which Thomas took. He gripped his father's hand tightly.

"I remember that I went to Kyloe Castle," William said. "I went to tell them about Northumbria."

"I know," Thomas nodded soothingly. "Do not become upset, Papa.

We can discuss this later, when you are feeling better."

William simply held on to him tighter. "We will discuss it now," he said. "It is all true, Tommy – Adelaide is a murderess. The major-domo... he became frightened when I asked him about her. He would not discuss it but, as I was leaving, he told me not to speak with her about it if I valued your life. The man warned me off."

Thomas stared at him for a moment before emitting a hissing sigh. "Then it is true," he said. "God's bones... she *did* kill them."

William squeezed his hand in agreement but, in truth, it had taken nearly all of his strength to speak. His head was throbbing and his entire body hurt – face, neck, arms – everything. He couldn't recall why but, at the moment, he didn't much care. He remembered *why* he'd come to Northwood, at least – looking for his son to tell him what he'd discovered at Kyloe.

That was all that mattered.

"Be... careful, Thomas," he said, the grip on Thomas' hand weakening. "Be careful with her."

With that, his eye closed and he drifted off, in pain and exhausted. Thomas kissed his father's hand before setting it back on his chest. When he glanced up at his brothers, he found himself looking at a host of curious and very concerned faces.

"What is he speaking of?" Scott demanded quietly. "What in the hell is happening with the House of de Vauden?"

At that point, Paris rushed back into the room with Patrick on his heels. He went straight to William's bedside as Thomas held up a hand to silence his brothers, drawing them away from his father's bed. Troy grabbed hold of Patrick, as he was oblivious to what William had just said, and the five of them gathered near the door of the chamber, away from their father.

It was a tense little huddle.

"I've not seen any of you lately, at least not enough to tell you what is transpiring with Northumbria and my betrothal, but the truth is this," Thomas said. "As you heard, Edmund de Vauden was murdered last week in an ambush, the day after I routed a large group of reivers who were raiding Coldstream. That is where I lost my wolf's head dagger, the one that showed up today with the child I was holding. With Northumbria dead, his daughter – and my betrothed – is now in command of a massive army. You know the hell I have been going through with Adelaide so I will not repeat it. But three days ago, Adelaide's nurse confessed to me that Adelaide is evidently far more dangerous than we suspected. The nurse told me that Adelaide has murdered two men she was previously betrothed to and that her father was complicit with these deaths. That is why father has been to Kyloe Castle – to get to the truth of it. What he discovered is what you just heard him tell me."

All four brothers were looking at Thomas with varied degrees of shock and disbelief. "My God," Patrick finally breathed. "Tommy, I may have heard of this. Two years ago, a minor noble family that lives near Berwick, with the name of Horncliffe, came to ask for my help to locate their missing son. He'd been betrothed to Adelaide de Vauden and, according to Adelaide's father, Alexander Horncliffe simply disappeared one day. The family did not blame de Vauden, or suggest he was to blame, so I did not think to mention it because it did not seem relevant."

Thomas was listening intently. "Did you ever find the missing man?"

Patrick shook his head. "Horncliffe is still missing to this day."

That bit of information greatly concerned everyone. "You are the Constable of the North, Atty," Scott said rather passionately. "You would know if there are any other disappearances associated with Northumbria and Adelaide de Vauden."

Patrick shook his head. "I am not for certain," he said. "At least, no one else has come forward with a missing son who was once betrothed to Adelaide de Vauden other than the Horncliffe family, but I did hear of another young man from a local noble family who had been pledged to the great heiress down towards Alnwick. At least, I thought it was

Alnwick. Mayhap it was Kyloe. In any case, his name was Cabot de Berck and I seem to remember hearing my wife speak of him. I do not know what became of him, however."

"Then you must find out," Troy said, interrupting Scott when the man tried to say the same thing. "For Tommy's sake, you must find out if de Berck was the second…"

Thomas cut him off, shushing them because they were raising their voices. "I appreciate the concern; you know I do," he said. "But Papa and I have already discussed the situation and we have already made plans – Northumbria would make a fine prize for Edward to award to one of his favorites now that Edmund is dead, and Papa cannot allow that to happen, so Papa and I both agree that I should go forward with my marriage to Adelaide to secure the earldom for the House of de Wolfe. Papa's entire trip to Kyloe was with the intent of obtaining witnesses against Adelaide."

"Yet he only found a majordomo who was terrified to speak on the subject," Troy said. He shook his head. "God's Bones, Tommy. You tried to run from this betrothal once and we stopped you. If you run now, no one will stop you at all – in fact, we will *help* you."

Thomas smiled weakly. "I am not running. Mayhap I should, but I cannot, not with the safety of Northumberland at stake." His attention turned to Patrick. "Atty, mayhap you can find witnesses and arrest Adelaide for the murders of Horncliffe and the unknown second betrothal. With her in the vault, I may be able to have the marriage annulled and the earldom would remain mine."

It was an outlandish scheme at best. The brothers were now looking at each other, dubiously. Quite a bit had gone on with their youngest brother and the Northumbria betrothal, far more than they could have guessed. It was quite a quagmire now.

"I can try to find witnesses to this situation, Tommy, but you are taking a terrible chance," Patrick said. "What if I cannot find witnesses willing to give testimony against Adelaide? You will be married to a murderess."

Thomas lifted his big shoulders. "If she really is a murderess, then sooner or later, I suspect she will go after me," he said. "There is no love lost between us. In fact, we have had some terrible discussions and I have been more than cruel to her. At some point, she may snap and make an attempt on my life. If she does, I will be ready for her."

It was a confident statement that bordered on arrogance. "All for an earldom, Tommy?" Scott wanted to know. "You will go into this marriage knowing that you may have to fight for your very life?"

Thomas pointed to their father, lying on the bed. "Papa was willing to do everything he could to secure Northumbria for me," he said. "I cannot, and *will* not, disappoint him. If I must be vigilant for the rest of my life against a madwoman, so be it, but Papa feels that this is enough of an important situation to take the risk."

It sounded final. As the brothers looked at each other, trying to find some kind of argument that would make Thomas realize marriage to a murderess wasn't the only solution, a servant entered the chamber and made his way to Thomas.

"My lord?" the woman said timidly. "A man has come for you. He says it is about Edenside."

Thomas hardly remembered moving. One moment, he was standing in his father's chamber with his brothers and in the next, he was racing down Northwood's rather treacherous stairs. The keep of Northwood had a large, two-storied foyer, something that could be seen from a balcony on the second floor, and he raced past the balcony and down the last flight of stairs only to see Desmond and Hector standing in the entry. Markus was there, too, all of them standing in a nervous huddle.

Desmond nearly broke down when he saw Thomas approaching.

"It's true," he said, sounding edgy and emotional. "Tibelda is dead and everyone is gone. When we took Tibelda to the priests at Kelso to be buried, we searched the town and the surrounding area, but there is no sign of them anywhere. We even went to the garrison at Roxburgh Castle and had them help us, but we found nothing."

Thomas' breath caught in his throat at the mention of Tibelda's death and no sign of Maitland. Although he'd been hoping for better news, the truth was that he hadn't expected it.

Still... the reality was a blow.

"Nothing at all?" he asked, incredulous and frightened. "No one saw anything?"

Desmond was pale and exhausted. "Nay," he said. "We asked people in Kelso if they had seen anything. We even went to the abbey and asked, but no one knew a thing. Roxburgh even sent his men all over the countryside, but there was no trace."

"And Edenside?" Thomas demanded. "Is it destroyed?"

Desmond shook his head. "Surprisingly, it is not," he said. "The front gates are broken, which may be how the intruders entered, and the interior of the keep was in disarray, but nothing was burned or broken. The goats are still there, as are the chickens and all of the supplies Mae had. But everyone is simply gone."

"My God," Thomas breathed. "But the littlest one somehow managed to escape."

Desmond nodded. "God only knows how she managed it, but thank God she did," he said. "I left all of the soldiers I took with me at Edenside to watch over the place while I came to tell you what we'd found. Everyone... *gone*."

Thomas digested that. After the initial shock, he'd cooled dramatically, realizing he couldn't help Maitland if he was in a panic. He was a de Wolfe and a de Wolfe was always calm in a crisis. In fact, the family motto was *courage in times of trouble*. All of the de Wolfe brothers held to that motto, including Thomas. If there was any hope of finding Maitland and the children, he had to think clearly.

Perhaps now, more than any other time in his life, the youngest de Wolfe brother had to show his courage.

It was time.

"I know who has taken her," he said with surprising calm. "I have known from the start, but I suppose I was hoping against hope that I was wrong. That dagger that the little girl brought us, the one with the wolf's head? You saw the dagger, Des. You know that it is mine, but I did not think to tell you that I lost it in Coldstream on the night we drove the reivers into the River Tweed."

Desmond was listening intently. "Then how –"

"Because the reivers took Mae," Thomas said, cutting him off. "Those bastards who call themselves the Thurrock *Cú*. They are seeking vengeance against me for driving their number into the river that night. Somehow, they found my dagger and considering that very wolf's head is on the de Wolfe standards, they knew it was mine. I firmly believe they are the ones who killed Northumbria when they saw him leaving Wark, and I further believe they have been watching my movements. It is the only thing that makes sense."

Desmond's brow furrowed. "But why should they go after Mae?" he asked. "Why would they even go near her?"

Thomas looked at the man. He'd refrained from telling him anything about his feelings for Maitland, but now he had no choice. He had to confess everything in what would perhaps be a confession not well received, but it couldn't be helped.

Desmond had to know.

"Because I was at Edenside yesterday," Thomas said quietly. "Des, I know you told me to stay away from Mae, but the truth is that I have feelings for her. In fact, I love her, and if that upsets you, I am sorry, but I cannot help myself. I was with her in Kelso when she sold her cheese and I escorted her back to Edenside when the day was through, but I swear to you that I left Mae and the children safe and sound."

Desmond had gone pale as he listened to Thomas' confession with rising disbelief. "And the reivers were watching you," he hissed. "They have been watching you since Coldstream and when they saw you with my sister, they went after her."

Thomas sighed with regret. "I believe that is true."

Desmond went from pale to flushed all in a split second. "You bastard," he growled. "I told you to stay away from her. I told you! This is all *your* fault!"

Before Thomas could respond, Scott stepped in. He faced Desmond with a rigid expression. "Thomas is your liege," he said in a low tone. "You will not show him such open disrespect, de Ryes, no matter what the subject."

Thomas put his hand on Scott's arm. "I am not troubled, Scott," he said, trying to push the man aside so he wouldn't get into a physical confrontation with Desmond. "He has every right to be upset. He did tell me to stay away from her but I could not. She is a wonderful woman, Des, and I love her. I am sorry if I deceived you, but I did not think you would believe that my feelings are sincere for her."

Desmond was looking at Thomas even though Scott hadn't moved out of the way. He was tilting his head sideways to look around Scott's big body. "I told you I did not want her to become another de Wolfe conquest," he said angrily. "You are to marry Adelaide and then what becomes of my sister? Does she become your whore?"

Thomas shook his head. "Nay," he insisted. "I would never treat her so poorly. A whore is a name for a woman who means nothing to a man, and Mae means a great deal to me. I can give her everything but marriage, Des. I can give her my heart and my soul and my love and my money. I will treat her like a queen for the rest of her life. Does that still make her my whore?"

"Yes!" Desmond nearly screamed. "It does! Paint the picture any way you wish, but you are making my sister your concubine, Thomas. She does not deserve that!"

The situation was getting out of hand, veering away from the crisis at hand and on to Thomas' feelings for Desmond's sister. Scott, Troy, Patrick, and Blayth were listening to it all very closely. They were quite surprised to hear the declaration from Thomas. Given what had happened with Tacey those years ago, and how their little brother had lived a loose life of women and wine since then, they weren't prepared to hear him declare his love for another woman.

Even so, they were seeing all of the signs that Thomas was being sincere. Knowing the man as they did, he didn't take things like this lightly. He never said something he didn't mean. It was a most confusing situation, but one that would have to wait for clarification. Patrick finally put himself between the two men, a massive flesh and blood barrier to stop them from focusing on one another.

"You two can argue about this later," he said, "but right now, there is a woman and children that need help. It seems to me that you can put aside whatever differences you may have and focus on that for now."

"Agreed," Scott said, turning to Thomas. "What do you want to do about this? If the Thurrock *Cú* are after you, then they took the woman and those children for a reason."

Thomas was glad for Patrick and Scott's intervention because he was starting to become quite emotional in his argument with Desmond. He loved Maitland and nothing her brother said was going to change that. Raking his fingers through his dark hair, he struggled to focus on Scott's valid question.

"Clearly, they want my attention and now they have it," he said. "I am sure they killed Northumbria for the same purpose, but something tells me that they have not killed Mae and the children, at least not yet. If their intention had been to kill them, then they would have done that at Edenside. Desmond would have found the bodies. Instead, they have taken them away, which leads me to believe they have another purpose in mind."

Patrick nodded. "I think so, too," he said. "I have been dealing with the Thurrock *Cú*, Tommy, as Northwood has also, but Troy and Scott haven't, which brings me to the conclusion that they are somewhere east of Wark and west of Berwick. They are in this area."

Thomas nodded. "My suspicions as well," he said. "There are three ruined pele towers between Wark and Berwick that would be perfect for the reivers to hide in. I've had my men check those sites periodically, but they never found anyone. There are more pele towers further south, of course, but I do not think the reivers would be hiding out so far south when most of their activity has been between Wark and Berwick.

So far, they have managed to evade us."

Troy, who had remained silent throughout the conversation, mostly because he was a man of few words and more action, held up a finger to catch everyone's attention.

"Think on it, lads," he said. "Thurrock is not a name from the north; it is a town in Essex. I know because I've been there before. The House of de Grey had lands in Thurrock, in Essex, and de Grey used to be a major landholder in the north. They still hold Chillingham Castle further to the south."

Everyone was looking at Troy by now. "What is your point?" Scott asked.

Troy lifted a dark eyebrow, looking very much like his father in that gesture. In fact, out of all of the brothers, he was the one who favored William the most.

"My point is that the de Grey family also used to own Castle Heton, which is in ruins now," he said. "It is a ruinous mound that is east of Wark and south of Coldstream by a few miles, out in the wilds of Northumberland. It is not very far from here. You have speculated that the Thurrock *Cú* is mayhap in one of the ruinous pele towers around here, but what about a ruinous castle? And their name may very well give you a clue as to where, exactly, they are."

Thomas and Patrick looked at each other in surprise. "He's right," Patrick said. "My God, he's absolutely right. We were fools not to have seen that before."

Troy waved them off. "I do not deal with them regularly, so it is easy for an outsider to see something you may not," he said. "I may be completely wrong, but if you want to locate these men, then that is as good a starting point as any. You should go to Castle Heton."

Thomas was thinking that his brother made a good deal of sense. "We must start somewhere," he said. "I will go to Castle Heton first, but being that they hold Mae and the children hostage, I cannot go charging in with an army to rescue them. If they see us coming, it could go very badly for Mae and the children."

"What are you suggesting, Tommy?" Scott asked.

Thomas looked at the men standing around him, men he'd grown up idolizing. He so wanted to be great like they were, but he had no heroics behind him, no history other than his time in The Levant that suggested he was made of greater things. He hoped he wasn't being foolish by speaking his mind.

"It is not a job for an army, at least not at first," he said. "I will ride out alone to Castle Heton and see if they are there. If they are, I shall get them out myself. I will not attract any attention that way and it will be safer for Mae and the children."

Immediately, the brothers began shaking their heads. "Nay," Scott said. "You cannot do this alone. I agree that going in with an army at the outset could be detrimental, but you cannot rescue a woman and several children by yourself. You are a de Wolfe, Tommy, and by virtue of that bloodline, you are a great and powerful knight, but you are not invincible. You must be realistic."

"He is trying to do what is right." Blayth, who had largely remained silent throughout the conversation because his head injury prevented him from speaking quickly, finally opened his mouth. He stepped forward, moving to Thomas' side and putting a hand on the man's shoulder as he spoke. "You are trying to do what is good and noble, and you are trying to do it without asking for help from your older brothers. But this is a task for the family, Tommy. We are with you, whatever you wish to do. Will you let us help you?"

Thomas looked at his older brother, a man who, before his head injury, had been gentle and wise. He was still gentle and wise; the man he'd known as James for most of his life was still there, deep down. He had been the family peacemaker before and he still was.

"It is not that I do not wish to ask you for help," he said after a moment. He pointed a finger to the ceiling, indicating the floors above. "But there is so much to worry about with Papa. He and Mother need you here, with them. I will take Desmond and we will sneak into the reivers' stronghold and get them out."

"And if you don't?" Scott asked. He held up a hand to indicate patience while he continued. "Tommy, I understand you want to rescue the woman, and you should. Papa would want you to act on your instincts as a knight by saving women and children. But he would never forgive any of us for letting you go if something happened to you, so we are going to help you. Right now, Papa has Uncle Paris and Mother to tend him, so we can do no more. He has awoken, and his reactions seem to be good, so I am not as worried about him as I was before. Right now, I am worried about *you*. You want to save this woman and the foundlings single-handedly and I simply do not think it is a good idea. The reivers are seeking revenge against you and God help you if they were to capture you while you were trying to save others. Do you understand my concern?"

Thomas sighed heavily. "I do," he said. Then, he looked at his brothers, at each one of them. It was difficult to put his thoughts into words. "I have always been the screaming little brother. Troy has even said so. This is something I must do to save the woman I love and, for once, I want to be a responsible brother. I want to take my place beside the rest of you by doing the responsible and courageous thing. I have spent my entire life being the purposeless and reckless de Wolfe brother and I no longer want to be that man. I do not need you to hold my hand through this. I can do it myself."

Scott smiled faintly. "We will not be holding your hand," he said. "But we will be fighting anyone who tries to cut it off."

In spite of himself, Thomas grinned. He couldn't argue with logic like that, and the truth was that he did need their expertise. He wanted it.

"Then I am in command?" he asked.

"Completely."

Thomas looked at Desmond, who was gazing at him somewhat guardedly. "Des?" he said. "Mayhap we have differences when it comes to Mae, but can you at least put them aside until we get her to safety?"

Desmond looked at the host of de Wolfe brothers looking at him expectantly before finally nodding his head. "Aye," he said, sounding resigned. "I'd rather be at your right hand than in your path, Thomas. What do you have in mind?"

Thomas told him.

CHAPTER TWENTY-TWO

THE NEXT MORNING, a tempest unleashed from the heavens.

It was just before dawn on the day following the discovery of Edenside's abduction, and a storm lashed the lands the likes of which no one could remember in recent memory. Winds howled, rain splashed, and through it all, an army moved into the area west of Castle Heton.

Wark, Questing, and Northwood had gathered to destroy the Thurrock *Cú* once and for all. A message had been sent to Berwick overnight, and Patrick's mighty Berwick army was moving in from the east. Scouts were out all over the landscape, staying to the forests, staying off the main roads, not wanting to be sighted if, in fact, the reivers had their own scouts out. But in this weather, unless a man was going to war, there was no reason to send out scouts.

And for the House of de Wolfe and its allies, this was war.

Thomas' plan, as conceived of and discussed all night long, was simple – some of Northwood's best spies had been sent out in the darkness to Castle Heton to determine if there was human habitation there. Garr and Hugh Ellsrod had gone with them, young knights who were hungry for glory and dangerous work, and they had returned to announce that, in fact, they'd caught the smell of cooking fires near the old place. Upon closer inspection, they saw sentries in the trees around

Heton, leading them to believe that there were men inside. It seemed that Troy had been correct – the Thurrock *Cú* had a link to the ruinous Castle Heton.

After that, the plan was laid out.

Thomas and his brothers, plus Desmond and Patrick's son, Markus, would sneak into Castle Heton and locate Maitland and the children, if they were there. If they were, they would spirit them away, hopefully without being seen, leaving the clean-up to the massive armies that were being assembled. Northwood and Wark were coming from the north and west, Berwick from the east, and Questing would march south, swing around, and then come northward so that any escaping reivers would be sandwiched between four enormous armies.

But there was a catch, of course. There was no guarantee that Maitland and the children were in the ruins of Castle Heton, and only a thorough inspection would determine that. So as the storm broke just before dawn, Northwood's army moved out to rendezvous with Wark and Questing.

Coordination was the key or none of the carefully-laid plans were going to work.

There was also another issue – anyone going into Castle Heton couldn't wear armor or protection because it was heavy and noisy, and they would have to move swiftly. That meant that Thomas, Scott, Troy, Patrick, Blayth, Desmond, and Markus were all going into battle without protection. They wouldn't even carry broadswords because the big weapons would weigh them down.

They would be open and vulnerable.

As they prepared to depart Northwood with the army with the great storm overhead, they were wearing little more than breeches, tunics, and an oiled cloak to keep the rain off of them. They didn't even have helms on.

And that was how Paris saw them.

In truth, the man had been wrapped up with William, who was doing surprisingly well in spite of the injury he'd sustained, but Paris had caught a glimpse of a mustering army in Northwood's outer bailey and it was enough to prompt him to leave William's side. Descending into the outer bailey, he saw troops armed for battle, with half of the knights without protection and the other half with it.

Northwood had always had its fair share of several high-caliber knights, and this generation was no different. Edric, his brother Rhys, Edric's sons Garr and Hugh, and Rhys' son, Landry, were all suited for battle. So were Hector, Atreus, and Hermes. All of them armed to the teeth. Then, there were Thomas, Scott, Troy, Patrick, Blayth, Desmond, and Markus who were not armed in any way, yet they were gathered with the knights.

Paris had come off the steps of the keep, fully preparing to run into the midst of the gathering warriors and demand to know what was happening, but he was intercepted by Deinwald and Michael de Bocage.

Michael, a mountain of a man with bright blue eyes, had been Paris' second-in-command at Northwood for several decades. His eldest son, Tobias, commanded Roxburgh Castle. Paris had a long history with both Michael and Deinwald, but he wasn't happy with the entire Northwood army being mustered and him not knowing a thing about it.

Deinwald and Michael were able to ease Paris' irritation by explaining that the army was preparing to destroy a nest of reivers, which was the truth for the most part. No one sought to tell Paris more because anything they told him would get back to William, and the man didn't need to worry about anything other than his own health at the moment.

Therefore, Paris stood and watched, along with two of his oldest friends, as the Northwood army left the great gates in a driving rainstorm and headed out into the landscape beyond. In truth, it was a rather lonely moment for the old knights. None of the younger warriors riding to battle could have known what a sad moment that had been for the three old knights who had been left behind.

Once, it had been the three of them, and several others, riding to battle back in the glory days of William de Wolfe. Now, the army and the battle were ruled by a new generation, for their time had passed. William's time had passed, as much as anyone hated to admit it.

It was a difficult truth to accept.

It was with that thought that the three of them returned to the keep and went to sit with William as the man lay in bed with a massive bruise on his head. Perhaps in that simple gesture, of sitting with an injured comrade, they were able to find some comfort in their days of glory that had once been.

Old knights never die, went the old saying. *They simply fade into legend.*

Certainly, these men were legendary.

But Thomas wasn't thinking of his father or of the old knights who had ridden to battle before him as he headed from the gatehouse. He was focused on what needed to be done, of his coming duty, and as he looked to his left, he could see a line of his brothers riding side by side. The only one not present was Edward, and he was sorely missed. All of them, united in a line, united in brotherhood and solidarity even though this wasn't their fight.

Nighthawk...

ShadowWolfe...

DarkWolfe...

The Dragon Wolfe...

Nay, it wasn't their fight. It was Thomas' – but any fight he had became theirs, and Thomas considered himself extremely fortunate to have such brothers.

He very much wanted to be worthy of that bond.

StormWolfe...

As the youngest, directionless de Wolfe brother, he'd had a lot to live up to. He'd done what he'd done, he'd lived his life the way he wanted to live it, and he blamed his lack of interest in women on losing that tiny Welshwoman those years ago. As he pondered those thoughts, he realized he'd blamed his actions on everyone, and everything, other than himself. Now, he had an opportunity to change that, a moment in his life that would define him forever. He was going to do something great and noble with his life by saving children and saving the woman he loved.

Only to be forced to marry someone else.

It was a sobering thought, but it didn't deter his determination. Thomas wasn't exactly sure how he was going to get through his marriage mass to Adelaide, but he would have to force himself. It wasn't as if he had a choice.

He'd come this far.

Overhead, the thunder rolled and the lightning flashed as the army moved to within a mile of Castle Heton. In truth, it was a little over six miles from Northwood Castle, so the army managed to reach the outskirts fairly quickly, just as the morning began to lighten. The storm was still raging, but they had more light to see by as a vast and soggy England lay out before them. That was when Hector and his sons, as well as the Ellsrod knights, put a halt to the army and had them hunker down.

Now, it was time for the de Wolfe men to shine.

"I will wait for your signal," Hector said to Thomas, helping the man strap a crossbow onto his back. "I'll wait for your red arrows to fly into the air. When they do, we'll charge."

The rain was soaking the men who had just taken off their oiled cloaks, now strapping daggers to their bodies. Those were the only weapons they dared to carry. Thomas took his wolf's head dagger, the one he'd lost and recovered, and shoved it into a sheath strapped to his thigh. Fastened to the crossbow were two arrows, each one with a bright red flag tied to it.

"If you do not see the arrows within the hour, send Hermes and Atreus to see what is happening," Thomas said. "Tell those two to keep their heads down. I know how excited they can get. I do not want them giving the armies away."

Hector looked over at his excitable sons. They were very nearly pawing the ground, eager to get on with the battle. "They have de

Norville and de Wolfe blood in them," he said. "They are perfect warriors, Tommy. They shall perform flawlessly."

Thomas grinned over at his nephews, who were very disappointed not to be in the advance party to rescue the children and their guardian.

"Spoken like their father," Thomas said. "But if those two fail, tell them that I will revive the Helm of Shame. Do they know what that is?"

Hector started to laugh. "Of course they do," he said. "We all do. I will make sure they know that you have threatened them with his heinous thing."

"See that you do."

Thomas and Hector grinned at each other for a moment before Hector turned back to his army, making sure the men were hunkered down, while Thomas turned to his brothers and nephew. All of them were ready to go, soaking wet, with water running down over their faces and into their eyes as the storm raged. Thomas joined them, looking at everyone, making sure they were prepared. They were on a slight rise, facing southwest, looking through a dip between two hills. Through it, there was a flat plain beyond, with knee-high grass, a line of trees, and then the landscape dipped down into another flat plain.

"Let us not delay," he said, pointing southwest. "See that line of trees in the distance? That is the River Till and Castle Heton is beyond that. We leave the horses at those trees and go the rest of the way on foot. When we arrive, it will be our priority to scout out the location of the reivers before we start looking for Mae and the children. We must know where our enemy is stationed before we move."

The brothers nodded in agreement. "Once we find Mae and the children?" Desmond asked. "Then what?"

Thomas looked at him. He wanted so badly to be the one to save Maitland, but he knew Desmond wanted to get to his sister as well. Truthfully, it didn't matter how she was saved, only that she was.

"Then we slip in, unnoticed, and get to them," he said. "Grab the first child you come to, or if it happens to be Mae, grab her first. I do not care who grabs whom, only that they are all removed. Once you have a warm body, stay out of sight and go straight to your horse. Head back to the waiting Northwood army as fast as you can."

It was a sound plan. Everyone started to mount their horses but Troy hung back. He went to Thomas, putting his hand on the man's shoulder.

"You are fearless, Tommy," he muttered. "Let us prove it."

Thomas looked at the man, a smile on his lips. It brought him a moment of reflection. "I wish…" he started, then stopped. His smile turned somewhat sad. "I wish Papa was with us. I told him once that I know there were times when I have disappointed him, and I had hoped that, someday, he might see me in action and be proud of me for it. I wanted him to see the *Dhiib aleasifa* as he was always meant to be."

Troy put his hand on the man's wet head in an affectionate gesture. "The StormWolfe," he murmured. Then, he looked up to the sky. "The elements are with you, Brother. A storm has arisen in your honor and it is time to release that cunning warrior inside of you. As for Papa, mayhap you do not quite understand this because you do not have children yet, but there is nothing you have to prove to him. He was proud of you the moment you were born. We've *all* been proud of you since the moment you were born. There is nothing you need to prove to any of us."

With that, he kissed his brother's wet forehead and headed off to his own horse.

Feeling fortified and determined, Thomas leapt onto his war horse, his gaze focused on the trees in the distance. Beyond that, he could only pray that Maitland and the children were waiting. He couldn't stomach the alternative. They hadn't come this far only to fail. For Maitland, and for the children, he had to succeed.

The StormWolfe was unleashed.

IT WAS A horrible, miserable day.

The ruins of the great castle had a large barrel vault where the majority of the reivers were taking shelter on this morning, leaving Maitland and the children out in the rain. They were beneath a cluster of birch trees, and the heavy canopy provided a measure of shelter, but not enough. There was still water dripping down on them and as Maitland protected the twins, Artus tried to protect Marybelle, and Phin tried to protect Nora.

All of them were huddled together, cold and hungry and exhausted. Hobelar hadn't spoken to Maitland since yesterday, which had been a blessing, but the trade-off was that they'd basically been neglected. They'd been given one old horse blanket to warm them, but there was no fire, and the only food the reivers had given them was the scraps of a boar they'd killed.

The animal had fed thirty or more men but when it came to the hostages, they received a bone with some meat scraps on it, which Maitland fed to the starving children as a mother bird would feed her hatchlings. There were six open mouths and Maitland picked every sliver of meat from the bone, everyone receiving a piece in turn, until there was nothing left. Then, she gave the bone over to Artus, who broke it open so they could eat the marrow.

And that was all they'd had.

Now, with morning dawning, the children were hungry again and Roland was starting to sniffle. Maitland was terrified that she was going to have sick children on her hands, but she was so thankful that Hobelar had left them alone that she didn't want to catch the man's attention by asking for food or shelter.

In fact, Hobelar had them corralled over by the eastern end of the ruins, by a wall that had long had holes knocked in it, and just beyond the holes and the trees that were providing them with some shelter was a wide-open field to freedom. Maitland had seen it last night and this morning, her gaze lingered on it. But she knew they'd never make it through without being seen; at least, not *all* of them would make it.

But perhaps one would.

At this time of the morning, the men in the half-ruined barrel vault were starting to awaken. In this heavy rain, they were starting fires inside the vault because Maitland could see and smell the smoke that was billowing out of the vault opening. She could hear men coughing inside. Leaning over the twins, who were both dozing on her lap, she tapped Artus on the head. When the boy looked up, she put her finger to her lips.

"There is a hole in the wall behind me," she hissed. "Can you see it?"

Artus looked over her shoulder before nodding his head. "Aye."

"Can you get to it and escape?"

Artus' eyes lit up. He looked around, seeing men stirring at this early hour, but they weren't being watched. Yesterday, they'd had two men watching them all day and into the night, but this morning, there didn't seem to be anyone around. He returned his attention to Maitland and nodded eagerly.

"Aye," he said, pushing Marybelle off his lap and crawling towards Maitland. "I'll get through."

Maitland grasped his arm before he could get away. "Run to the nearest village," she whispered. "I do not know where we are, but find the nearest village and tell them to take you to Sir Thomas at Wark Castle. He will come and help us."

Artus nodded. "Aye!"

"Stay low and stay out of sight!"

Artus passed another long glance behind him, making sure one last time that there was no one watching them, before crawling through the foliage, between the birch trees, and finally slithering out of the hole in the wall. Once he was through, he took off at a dead run, straight east through the knee-high wet grass.

Maitland didn't dare turn around to watch him. She pulled Marybelle and the twins close, wondering how she was going to explain Artus' absence to Hobelar when he came around. And she knew, without a doubt, that he would come around at some point. She was fearful of that moment, fearful she wouldn't be able to lie her way out of the situation and Hobelar would take it out on the children. The only way to prevent that would be to remove the children entirely.

Perhaps they should all escape, too.

Looking around, Maitland was on the hunt for anyone who might be looking their way, but the reivers seemed sleepy and dazed as they started their morning fires. She tugged on Phin.

"Phin," she said. "You must help the children to escape. Can you do this?"

Phin couldn't have been more than seven or eight years of age, a skinny child who rarely said a word. He nodded fearfully, perhaps understanding danger more than most. All of these children had suffered such terrible hardships at Edenside, with Laird Letty in charge, so they understood self-preservation.

"But ye?" he asked anxiously. "Will ye come?"

Maitland wasn't sure that she should. She really only wanted the children safe and if Hobelar or another reiver saw that everyone was gone, the search would be on. Maitland thought, perhaps foolishly so, that if she at least remained behind, perhaps they wouldn't go after the children. They would still have a hostage, a prize to use against Thomas.

It was a chance she was willing to take.

"Nay," she whispered, grasping the child and turning him for the hole in the wall. "Take the children with you and scatter. Some of you run one way and some of you run another. Split up. Find a village or people who can help you and tell them to take you to Sir Thomas at Wark Castle. Can you do this? Can all of you do this?"

By this time, Marybelle and Nora were listening and they were starting to cry, frightened of what they were being asked to do. Maitland stroked their faces, touched their little heads, trying to convince them that this was the right thing to do. She handed Roland over to Nora and Renard over to Marybelle, insisting they each take charge of a little one. Phin was already moving for the damaged wall.

"Come on," he hissed at them. "Get down and crawl. Crawl with me!"

Maitland watched as the five of them slithered through the foliage, between the trees, and finally to the hole in the wall. She held her breath as Marybelle and Nora had to lift the twins through to Phin on the other side. When she finally saw the girls slip through, the relief she felt was overwhelming. At least now, they'd have a chance.

Please, God, keep them safe!

Now, Maitland had her own plans to make, plans to keep the reivers fooled for as long as she could to give the children enough time to get far away. Keeping her eye on the men moving about in the early morning hour, she began to rip up some of the foliage on the ground, making little piles of it. When she had several little piles, she threw the horse blanket over them, patting it down to make it look like huddled children were sleeping beneath it.

But Maitland remained nervous; oh, so nervous. She knew that at some point, Hobelar and his men would return and she could only hold them off so long with a story of sleeping children. But for now, the children were running off, and no one had noticed as of yet, so the more the seconds ticked away, the more Maitland had hope that the children would make it to safety. As the rain pounded and the lightning flashed, she sat and she waited.

Her wait wasn't a long one, unfortunately. As she sat there, her hand on one of the bumps under the blanket to make it look as if she were comforting a child, Hobelar appeared out of nowhere. One moment, there was no one nearby, and in the next, that wild-eyed outlaw was standing just a few feet away.

The expression on his face turned Maitland's blood to ice.

"DID YOU SEE that?"

The question had come from Thomas. He and the others had just crossed a river with thigh-high water and were huddling in a row of rain-soaked trees within sight of the old ruins of Castle Heton when they suddenly caught sight of a child bolting through the wet fields. He took it for an animal at first until he saw skinny arms flailing. It took Thomas a moment to realize that the child was Artus.

"My God!" Desmond gasped. "That is one of Mae's children!"

Thomas nodded, his heart pounding at the sight. The excitement and the fear that Maitland and the children had been found were overwhelming. As he'd hoped and prayed, Castle Heton was the right place. They found what they were looking for. He'd thank God for the good fortune when he had the time but, at the moment, he had serious things to accomplish.

God would understand.

"Go, Des," he said, waving a sharp hand at the man. "Go and get him. Hurry!"

Desmond vaulted over the branch that was in his way, charging out into the field and heading straight for the panicked child. As Thomas and his brothers and nephew watched, Desmond intercepted the child and grabbed him around the waist, racing back with him clutched against his torso. But it was then that they saw more children falling out of a hole in the old castle walls – five children to be exact. The children started running in different directions, some towards them, some away from them. Thomas pointed to the scattering horde.

"Go," he commanded. "Get the children. Get them back to North-wood!"

Scott, Troy, Patrick, Blayth, and Markus charged from the shelter of the trees, each man going after a particular child. Thomas left the shield of the trees as well, rushing across the field, trying to stay low as he approached the crumbled wall that signified the ruins of Castle Heton. He ran past Troy as the man was heading back to the trees with a little girl in his arms, and then Patrick doing the same with a tiny little boy clutched against him. All across the field, his brothers and nephew were collecting children and taking them to safety. That left Maitland and Thomas was going to rescue the woman or die trying.

He'd already made that decision.

He went straight to the hole in the wall.

Thomas hunkered down for a moment, listening for cries or shouts from those inside the ruins, but there was relative silence. Certainly nothing that could be construed as an alarm, so it stood to reason that perhaps they didn't even know their hostages has escaped.

Carefully, Thomas peered through the hole, seeing trees and foliage on the other side, but he also saw movement. Straining to make it clear, he could just see Maitland being yanked to her feet by a big, dirty man. That was all it took for Thomas to remove his crossbow and fire off a red-tagged arrow, up into the air and back in the direction from where he'd come. It was a low shot, and a long one, hoping it could be seen against the storm and rain. He was alerting the army to charge, praying they saw the signal because he didn't intend to send off another.

That second arrow was reserved for the bastard who had just put his hands on Maitland.

It was about to get ugly.

HOBELAR HAD HER by the wrist, digging his dirty fingers into her flesh.

"I hope ye've had enough sleep, woman," he said. "Ye are goin' tae complete a task for me today."

Maitland let him pull her away from the blanket. The less he saw of what it was covering, the better. "I did not sleep at all, if you must know," she said unhappily. "What do you want of me?"

Hobelar wouldn't let go of her wrist. "It is time we discuss my plan," he said as the rain pounded down on them. "Ye're off tae Wark today."

Maitland tried to yank her arm free. "Let me go," she snapped. "You are hurting me."

Hobelar tightened his grip and twisted her arm so that she gasped. "Shut yer lips, woman," he hissed. "If ye dunna want the children harmed, then ye'll shut yer mouth and do as ye're told. Are ye listen-in'?"

Maitland stopped struggling against him because he was genuinely hurting her. "I am listening," she said with contempt. "What do you want from me?"

Hobelar plastered on a feigned smile. "Good lass," he said. "Do ye know where Wark is?"

Maitland lifted her shoulders. "I do not even know where *we* are."

Hobelar indicated the direction behind him. "Wark is that way," he said. "If ye take the road tae the south, it will take ye straight tae Wark."

"And what do you want me to do when I get there?"

Hobelar eyed her for a moment before wiping the water from his face. "Tell de Wolfe he must come with ye," he said. "Tell him I want tae speak tae him, and if he willna come, tell him I'll kill the children and dump them at his gatehouse."

Maitland felt fear shoot through her even though she knew that the longer she stood there and talked to Hobelar, the less chance the man had to get his hands on the children as they fled into the storm.

Run, children, run!

"I will tell him," she said steadily. "But he will bring his army when he comes."

Hobelar frowned. "Tell him the bairns will die if he does," he said. "Ye dunna seem tae understand, woman. Explain tae de Wolfe that he must come alone. Anythin' else and I'll kill the children right in front of ye."

Maitland shook her head at the man, that slow and wagging gesture suggesting utter disgust.

"Who has been so cruel to you your entire life that you believe hurting children is acceptable?" she asked. "Did your mother beat you senseless? Did your father whip you until you screamed? What makes you think that behaving this way is the right and civilized thing to do? Those children have never done anything to you. They cannot hurt you in any way. They have never had anyone love them and I am trying very hard to raise them to be productive people. I am teaching them skills and a trade. Why would you take all of that away from them just for your foolish notions of revenge?"

Hobelar suddenly grabbed Maitland around the neck and she gasped, her hands going to his as he held her around the throat. "Ye have no idea what I've done, woman," he growled. "If ye knew the men I've killed and the women I've cut tae pieces, ye wouldna speak tae me so. For now, I'll forgive ye, but do it again, and I'll kill ye."

Maitland could feel the blood pulsing in her face. "Kill me and you'll have no one to accomplish your terrible scheme."

He squeezed tighter and Maitland knew if she didn't fight back, he might very well kill her, so she brought a foot up, kicking him right between the legs. Hobelar loosened his grip as he doubled over, but he didn't let go of her completely. As she tried to whirl away from him, he grabbed hold of her hair and yanked hard. Maitland fell to her knees as Hobelar stood over her, mad enough to kill.

"That'll cost ye, woman," he said. "I hope ye enjoy pain."

Before he could collect the dagger in the sheath on his belt, a high-pitched whistling sound filled the air and something solid hit Hobelar squarely in the chest. He staggered back and fell onto his buttocks as Maitland ripped her hair from his grasp. Terrified and startled, she turned in time to see an arrow protruding out of Hobelar's chest.

An arrow with a bright red flag attached to it.

Shocked, she turned in the direction the arrow had come from in time to see Thomas emerging from the cluster of birch trees. He had a wicked-looking crossbow in his hands and as the skies lit up with lightning, he rushed to Maitland and pulled her off of the ground.

"Thomas!" Maitland gasped in utter shock. "You're here!"

He was already running away, pulling her with him, as the reivers over in the barrel vault realized something was terribly wrong. Men were spilling out into the storm, shouting the alarm.

"Hurry," Thomas said as he pulled her into the birch trees. "No time to talk. *Run!*"

Maitland didn't need to be told twice. She was already running, leaping through the foliage and launching herself through the hole in the wall where the children had gone. Thomas was right behind her and they began running, as fast as they could, across the wet field that stretched to the east.

Thomas had Maitland by the hand, but she was running faster than he was. Terror fueled her stride and by the time they reached the river, she plunged into it, sloshing across it as Thomas kept pace with her. His horse was tethered to a tree on the other side and he grabbed Maitland, practically tossing her up into the saddle as he mounted in front of her.

"Thomas, the children!" Maitland cried as he reined his horse around. "We must find the children!"

Her hand was on his shoulder and he grasped it, kissing it quickly. "I already have, sweetheart," he assured her. "The children are safe, I promise."

Maitland didn't say anything more. She was stunned and over-whelmed with Thomas' slick rescue, hardly believing he'd been there to save her at just the right time. It seemed like a miracle. As he spurred his horse away from Castle Heton, coming towards them over a rise was a massive army. Maitland caught sight of the mounted army, hundreds and hundreds of them, and as Thomas charged through their lines, they continued on towards Castle Heton.

But that wasn't all.

To the north, she could see another army moving towards Castle Heton and then, to the south along the road Hobelar had wanted her to take to Wark, she could see yet another line of men. It seemed like an entire army was surrounding them from all side, all of them converging on Castle Heton.

It was a rescue the likes of which no one had ever seen before.

After that, Maitland pressed her face into Thomas' back and held on, weeping softly now that she was safe. They were tears of thanks, of joy, and of fear that hadn't quite left her yet. *The children are safe, I promise*, he'd said. She wasn't even sure she believed him until they reached an enormous castle and charged through the gates, and there she saw several big, wet men standing with her children near the entry to an inner ward.

Desmond was among those wet and weary men, and as Thomas pulled his horse to a halt, Desmond was there to pull his sister from the beast and embrace her tightly. When Maitland caught a glimpse of Lady de Wolfe emerging from the keep with little Dyana in tow, the tears Maitland had so recently stilled returned with a vengeance, and she sank to her knees, opening her arms to the seven children she'd come so close to losing. Hugging them all, alive and well, was one of the sweetest things she could have imagined.

God had been looking out for those children, for once.

Finally, they were safe.

CHAPTER TWENTY-THREE

THERE WAS A soft knock on the chamber door and Maitland, half-covered in soap and water, went to open it.

Thomas stood out on the landing, smiling weakly at her, and she waved him inside.

"Come in, Sir Thomas," she said, indicating seven children and two big copper tubs filled with hot, soapy water. "We were just cleaning up all of the Castle Heton filth. Care to lend a hand?"

Thomas' smile broadened and he shook his head as he caught sight of Artus and Phin in one tub, dunking their heads underneath to see who could hold their breath longer. Artus popped up, wiped water out of his eyes, and spied Thomas.

"Watch me, Sir Thomas!" he cried. "Watch me!"

His head went back under quickly and water sloshed over the sides. Thomas pointed to the boy. "He is not going to stay under too long, is he?"

Maitland laughed softly, wiping her hands off on a linen towel. "Nay," she said. "He becomes frightened after only a few seconds. It will not last long."

The two of them grinned at each other as the door opened again and in swept Jordan and Caria, carrying piles of garments between them into the warm and slightly damp chamber.

"Tommy!" Caria cried, dumping off the garments on the only bed in the room, a rather big bed, and then rushing to Thomas, who picked her up and squeezed her. "How long are you going to stay? I want you to stay a very long time. Will you?"

Thomas gave her a hug and she gripped his neck enthusiastically. "I cannot stay too long, but you know I will return as soon as I can," he said, spanking her affectionately on the buttocks before setting her to her feet. "Look at all of these children you have to play with. What fun you shall have."

He said it to distract her and it worked. Caria saw Marybelle, Nora, and Dyana in one of the big copper tubs and she ran to it, trying to take her clothes off as she went.

"Matha!" she said. "I want to take a bath!"

Jordan was over by the bed, separating clothing out by size, and saw Caria as the little girl tried to pull her dress over her head. Dropping what she was doing, she rushed to her.

"God's Bones, lass," she said, helping Caria yank her clothing off. "Let me help ye before ye tear yer head off."

Caria was far too excited to get into the bath with the other girls, and when Jordan stripped her down and put her in, she squealed with delight and immediately started splashing. Both Thomas and Maitland watched with a grin.

"It seems that everyone is having fun for bath time," he said to Maitland, his smile fading as he looked at her. "Do you have a moment to spare me?"

Maitland could see he meant a private conversation, away from little ears. She mouthed *"always"* before replying aloud.

"Of course," she said. "Lady de Wolfe? May I leave you with the children for a moment?"

Jordan waved her on and she followed Thomas into the corridor outside. She shut the door softly behind them, shutting out the sounds of frolicking children and splashing water.

"Your mother has been so kind," she said quietly. "I hate to impose on her, especially with your father's injury."

Thomas lifted his eyebrows. "She told you about that?"

"She did. How is he faring?"

"Much better. He was able to sit up in bed a little just now as I told him of our grand adventure."

"That is good news."

He grunted, wearily rubbing his eyes. "I have not spoken to you since we returned with the children," he said, looking at her. "I have so many questions about what happened, but that will have to come later. At the moment, all that matters to me is that you are safe and the children are safe."

Maitland gazed up at him, seeing that he was a man with much on his mind. She wanted so badly to wrap her arms around him. "There is time to speak of everything later," she said. "Do not be troubled. We need not speak of it now."

Thomas shook his head. "I must," he said. "But before I do, may… may I hold you?"

Maitland fell against him, her arms around his neck as he wrapped his big arms around her and held her tightly. Feeling his strength, his great and solid body, undid Maitland and tears sprang to her eyes.

"I was so frightened I would never see you again," she whispered. "I was so frightened for the children, but I am selfish in that I was mostly frightened for me without you. Does that sound terribly selfish?"

His face was buried in the side of her neck. "Nay," he whispered. "For I was fearful of the same. You cannot know the horror I felt when I came across Dyana and she told us that you had been taken away. Utter and complete horror."

"Desmond told me everything. It is a miracle she found you."

"It is, but I am sorry about Tibelda. I know she was your friend."

That only made Maitland hold him tighter. "She was," she murmured. "I shall miss her terribly, but the children are safe. That is all she would have wanted."

Thomas held her a moment longer before loosening his grip so he could kiss her. It was a sweet, tender kiss, one of great power and longing. The kiss grew increasingly amorous until he backed off, knowing this was not the place. But he licked her lips and kissed her again before setting her to her feet.

"I have just come from my father," he said quietly, holding her hand and lifting it to his lips as he spoke. "So much has happened since we last spoke that I do not even know where to start. I suppose the first thing I must do is ask you a question."

"What question?"

"You once said you would take my heart and never give it back. Is that still true?"

She nodded, her eyes warm with sincerity. "More than ever."

He lifted her hand and kissed it again, a painfully sweet gesture. So much had happened in the short time they'd been apart – his father's trip to Kyloe and subsequent injury, his continued determination that Thomas should marry Adelaide. That hadn't changed. Maitland didn't know about Adelaide's murder streak or anything else about the woman beyond what Thomas had told her. She knew that Edmund de Vauden was dead, but certainly none of the politics behind Thomas' rush to marry Adelaide now.

There simply wasn't any reason to tell her.

But the situation was breaking his heart.

"That is good to hear," he whispered. "Because I have given you my heart for always. I thought I was in love before, once. I have spoken of Tacey and of my feelings for her, but with you… I realize that mayhap I wasn't truly, deeply, and madly in love. Tacey gave me a taste of what I was capable of feeling, but you have brought out the best in me. I never knew I could love someone the way I love you, Mae."

She looked at him with wide eyes. "Oh, Thomas," she breathed. "I have never loved a man, not ever. That gift has been reserved for you, my love. I will love you until I die."

Thomas had heard those words before, but not when they came from someone who meant something to him. He pulled her into his embrace again, holding her tightly, kissing her ear, her temple, and finally her lips. They weren't kisses of lust or passion, but those of true and deeper emotion.

Her kisses were imprinted into his very soul.

"Remember that," he whispered. "Remember that when I return to Wark because my father has ordered me to marry Adelaide. I cannot tell you my devastation with this, but it cannot be helped. For now, my mother is going to keep you and the children here at Northwood until my father can travel. Then, she tells me that she is going to take you back to Castle Questing. She does not want you returning to Edenside until the walls can be reinforced and a proper gate built. I promise I will come and see you at Questing as soon as I am able, but know that it may take some time. I must return Edmund's body back to Kyloe Castle and I must become familiar with my earldom."

Maitland was holding to him tightly, but she was nodding her head. "I know, my love," she said. "Take all the time you need. You know where I will be."

His embrace tightened and he lifted her off the floor, holding her against his body and feeling her warmth. "God, I don't want to leave you," he whispered. "Every day we are apart will feel like an eternity."

"I know," she said, squeezing him before loosening her grip and sliding down to the floor. "Things are not ideal. They are not even good. But I know you love me, and you know that I love you. There is hope in that, Thomas, whatever the future may bring us."

He didn't want to tell her what he hoped it would bring – an annulment of his marriage to Adelaide once Patrick arrested her for the murder of two young men. He didn't want to dare give her hope because if it didn't happen and he was forced to remain married to that horror of a woman, then he didn't want Maitland to be disappointed. Already, he was planning the life he would live with her, marriage or no.

Cupping her face between his two big hands, he kissed her one last time.

"The future is bright as far as I am concerned," he said. "I have never been this happy, in spite of everything, and it is all because of you. You and those seven little waifs and that goat cheese you make. It's such a beautiful, simple life and I want to be part of it."

Maitland smiled, holding up her hand and he saw the ring he'd given her. "You already are," she whispered. "Now, I must return and help your mother before those children get that entire chamber wet. I like your mother, Thomas. She is a wonderful woman."

He returned her smile. "And she likes you a great deal," he said. Then, his smile faded somewhat. "I will try to say farewell before I leave for Wark on the morrow, but if I do not, then let this be my farewell for now. You have my love and my heart, Maitland de Ryes Bowlin. Never forget it."

"I will not."

He winked at her as he started to move away, but then he paused. "Just a mention," he said, "but Des is not too happy about the situation."

"You told him?"

"I had to."

Maitland frowned. "I love my brother, but he worries like an old woman."

Thomas grinned. "Do not tell him that. He will think I told you to."

She started to laugh, blowing him a kiss as he moved down the corridor and reached the stairwell. He blew one in return before disappearing down the stairs.

Maitland stood there a moment, basking in the glow of their encounter, thinking on what they would both be facing from now on. She'd told Thomas when she met him that she would never carry on with a married man and until this moment, she'd kept that vow. As he'd pointed out, he wasn't married, though they both knew that was a technicality. Once a man was betrothed, in the eyes of the church, he was indeed married, but neither one of them had brought that up. It was easier to pretend otherwise. But soon, they wouldn't be able to pretend at all and she struggled against the sorrow that provoked. She knew very well it was a contract marriage and that Thomas hated the sight of Adelaide, but that didn't change facts that the woman would be his wife. Maitland would have his love, but Adelaide would have his name.

She wondered how that would play out in the years to come.

Maitland wondered if she would have to defend herself from a jealous Lady de Wolfe in the days or years to come. Not that she cared. Or, at least, she didn't at this moment. But only the future would tell if the love she and Thomas were building could withstand the test of time – and the pressures of their complex situation.

She fervently hoped so.

CHAPTER TWENTY-FOUR

Two days later

I T WAS HIS wedding feast.

At least, it was a meal and it was taking place after the marriage mass to Adelaide, but that was all Thomas could say for it. It wasn't a happy event, by any means.

It was hell.

His parents hadn't come. William was still recovering from his head injury and Jordan remained with him at Northwood Castle because he needed constant tending. That was the excuse, anyway. Scott, Troy, and Patrick had come to Wark to observe the nuptials, but Blayth had returned to Castle Questing because William couldn't travel and he wanted his second-in-command back at Questing. No one was happy about this wedding except the bride, who had been released after five days in the vault by Thomas, who stiffly informed her that he'd brought Lady Teviot's priest from Northwood Castle to perform the mass immediately.

The man was Scots and spoke in a heavy Scots accent, completely insulting Adelaide, who looked down upon those from north of the border. She'd waited for this moment for so long, however, that she didn't turn down the offer of Lady Teviot's priest. She wanted to be married to the man who had locked her in the vault with her dead father and she wanted to be married to him now.

That was all she cared about.

With the help of Hilde, Adelaide bathed and dressed for the event, magnanimously telling Thomas that she forgave him for putting her in the vault. But Thomas didn't care; he also didn't bathe or change. He presented himself to Adelaide in the same clothing he had been wearing when he rescued Maitland, which was dirty and smelled awful. Somehow, he just couldn't take it off because she had touched it. He wanted to keep it against his body. He didn't even know what he was going to do when it came time to consummate the marriage. Perhaps if he got drunk enough, he might be able to get through it.

So, he started drinking before the mass. He was significantly tipsy when the priest started the ceremony at the door to the great hall and then moved everyone inside to complete the service.

While Desmond remained outside on the walls, Scott, Troy, and Patrick went inside and stood with Thomas, passing him cups of wine, and the man literally drank his way through the entire service. Adelaide noticed and she was greatly upset by it, but the more she frowned and shook her head at him, the more he drank. At one point, Scott, Troy, and Patrick had their own cups. So towards the end of the prayers, all four of them were drinking.

It was an unhappy moment of unity.

Thomas was more miserable than he'd ever been in his life. He cursed himself for being stupid enough to agree to marry Adelaide, for being stupid enough to agree with his father. But then in the same breath, he knew he was doing what needed to be done. He longed for Maitland in the worst way, closing his eyes as the priest intoned prayers in Latin and imagining that it was Maitland standing beside him.

Then he'd open his eyes and see Adelaide. And he felt like his world was crashing in. Maitland was still at Northwood Castle with the children, so he knew they were all safe and warm and fed, and being spoiled by Jordan and even Caria, who had taken a liking to little

Dyana. In truth, they were quite inseparable. It had done Thomas' heart good to see that, but the mere fact that he wasn't with Maitland made him feel alone as he'd never felt in his life.

Mercifully, the mass concluded and the priest finished the ceremony by giving Thomas a "kiss of peace", always bestowed upon the groom, and the groom was expected to pass the kiss on to his bride. When Thomas looked at Adelaide, who was gazing at him quite expectantly, it took every ounce of effort he had to lean forward and kiss her on the cheek.

And with that, Thomas de Wolfe became the Earl of Northumbria.

He also became a man with no patience and no courtesy for his wife. He turned to assume his place at the feasting table, leaving Adelaide simply standing there, but Scott and Troy shook their heads at him, forcing him to reconsider his rude behavior. The situation was bad enough without him acting like a complete jackass. Turning to Adelaide, who was already upset about the drinking and the lack of a kiss to her mouth, Thomas held out an elbow to her, which she snatched. With her claws digging into him, Thomas led her over to the dais for the wedding feast.

Food and drink were immediately brought forth, and minstrels from Kyloe, who had come those months ago when Adelaide came to Wark because she liked music when she ate, began to play. It was all rather warm and festive, and would have been quite pleasant had the groom actually been happy about the marriage. He declined food but not the drink, and as the evening wore on, the drunker he became.

"Tommy," Scott leaned in to his brother when he saw him empty a third pitcher of wine. "Passing out from too much drink will only delay the inevitable. Mayhap you should slow down and have something to eat."

Thomas looked at his brother, his head bobbing and weaving ever so slightly. "I rescued her only to leave her," he muttered. "She is all I ever wanted, Scott. Only her."

Scott was tipsy but he wasn't drunk like his brother. He held up a hand so the man would lower his voice, as Adelaide was sitting on the other side of him.

"I know," Scott said quietly. "I am deeply sorry for you, you know that. But you married Adelaide for a purpose. Keep to that purpose, Thomas."

Thomas cocked a dark eyebrow. "Keep to that purpose," he muttered. "I *have* kept to that purpose at the expense of my own happiness. Is Papa proud of me now? Are *you* proud of me now?"

"Aye," Troy put in, speaking for all of them. "Of course we are proud of you. I told you – we always have been."

Thomas looked at them, his three older brothers, men he loved deeply. "I am now the Earl of Northumbria," he said with a hint of irony in his tone. "I could take my army and wipe out everything in Northumberland. I could march it into Scotland and take control of the borders, or I could march it down to York and claim all of York as mine. Did you know that?"

"I know that," Troy replied softly.

Thomas threw up his hands. "I have so much power but I do not have the power to marry the woman I love," he said. Then, he shook his head and turned for his half-empty cup. "You do not understand. None of you do. You all love your wives. You cannot know my misery."

By now, Adelaide was listening carefully. She was watching drunken Thomas lament his love life, becoming more enraged and jealous by the moment. She knew he didn't like her; she'd always known. But now, his guard was down, smashed by too much drink, and she was coming to hear something she'd never heard before. *I do not have the power to marry the woman I love.* She happened to catch Scott's eye.

"Who is he speaking of?" she demanded. "Who is this woman he speaks of?"

Scott shook his head, hoping they didn't have the start of an enormous problem on their hands as the bride came to discover her husband was in love with someone else. Adelaide was unpredictable enough without that added trouble.

"It is nothing, Lady de Wolfe," he said calmly. "He has simply had…"

Thomas cut him off. "Don't you dare call her Lady de Wolfe," he snarled. "She is not worthy of the name and I'll not hear it from your lips, do you hear?"

Adelaide shot to her feet, taking a swing at the back of Thomas' head. "I *am* Lady de Wolfe," she barked. "It is you who are not worthy of the Northumbria name. I do not know what I was thinking when I told my father to seek this betrothal!"

The slap to the head enraged Thomas. He bolted to his feet as well, standing a good foot taller than Adelaide as he gazed down at her, his nostrils flaring with rage. Suddenly, he didn't look so very drunk.

"What *were* you thinking, Adelaide?" he asked her, his face looming very close to hers. "Why *did* you ask your father to seek mine and offer a betrothal? Weren't you already betrothed at the time?"

Adelaide's eyes widened and her features paled. She swayed back, away from him, and a flicker of horror crossed her features. Her jaw ticked as if she very much wanted to say something, but the urge passed. The urge to strike out at him left her. Instead, she took a step back.

"You are mad," she said. "You do not know what you are speaking of."

"I know more than you think I do."

To Adelaide, that was a threat. Those knowing words filled her heart with rage and terror, with jealousy and disgust. Something in his eyes told her that he did, indeed, know more than she thought he did. Perhaps he even knew everything. Even if he did, that didn't matter now.

They were married.

She backed away from him, moving around the chair she'd been sitting in.

"I am going to my chamber," she said. "You will join me there shortly. Do you understand? And no more drink. I will not take a drunkard to my bed."

She didn't wait for him to answer. As Adelaide quit the hall, moving through the smoke and the celebrating mass of soldiers, Thomas and his brothers watched her go. Thomas could hear Scott grunting unhappily.

"Tommy, if that woman has killed the two men before you, you are tempting fate by provoking her like that," he said. "Must Troy and Atty and I go with you to your marital bed and protect you from your murderess wife now that she thinks you know about her killing tendencies?"

Thomas looked at his brother. "The only thing I fear in my marital bed is coupling with a woman that I detest," he said. "Other than that, there is nothing to fear."

Scott sighed heavily. "You must be careful, Tommy, please. She could be up there right now poisoning your wine."

"I will not drink any wine."

"Then she could be hiding a dagger under the pillow."

"I do not intend to take the woman on her back. I'll bend her over the bed and take her from behind, like a dog. That way, I will not have to look at her face."

He was confident, as he usually was. Scott and Troy and Patrick exchanged glances, for certainly, nothing would convince Thomas to be cautious about his wedding night. The drink may have loosened him enough to perform his husbandly duties, but it also took away his sense of self-protection. Thomas had spent the past six months with Adelaide, insulting the woman, hating her, and detesting the coming marriage. Now that he'd finally married her, to Thomas, the marriage bed was simply a necessary evil and he had absolutely no fear of it.

The older brothers hoped that wouldn't be his undoing.

"Very well, Tommy," Scott said. "Let us drink to your wedding night and pray you live through it."

Thomas lifted a cup to that. Even as he drained it and spoke of returning to Northwood Castle as soon as he could, Scott and Troy and

Patrick were making plans of their own. Perhaps they wouldn't invade Thomas' marital chamber simply to ensure that his new wife wouldn't slit his throat, but that didn't mean they couldn't follow him up there and linger in the corridor outside.

Something told them not to stray far from Thomas this night.

ADELAIDE WAS ALREADY in a state when she reached her chamber and threw open the door. Hilde was in the room, having stoked the fire and prepared the marital bed with freshly washed linens. She'd sprinkled lavender buds between the linens and was in the process of lighting several banks of fat, yellow tapers when Adelaide burst in.

The woman was dressed in a beautiful pale green silk that she'd had specially made for the wedding. Green symbolized love and Adelaide had hoped the color would somehow inspire Thomas, but he didn't seem to notice and if he did, he didn't say anything. Frustrated, she moved straight to the bed and began ripping the adornment out of her hair.

"Damn him," she said angrily. "All of this – everything I did – went unnoticed and unappreciated and now I know why!"

She was raging, a very bad sign as far as Hilde was concerned. She was over by the bedside, lighting the last bank of candles to give the room a soft, warm glow.

"What has happened, Lady de Wolfe?" she asked timidly.

Adelaide froze when she heard the woman address her by her new title. She stared at Hilde a moment before breaking into a humorless smile.

"Lady de Wolfe," she muttered. "It sounds horrid. I should make him take the de Vauden name. That is the name of the earldom, after all. Or mayhap I shall not let him have the earldom, after all."

A hint of warning went off in Hilde's head because she knew what had become of the two men who had preceded Sir Thomas. Those deaths had been preceded by a mood much like the one Adelaide was displaying now. The first betrothed had been a fine young man from the Horncliffe family. He had been kind to Adelaide but she'd quickly grown bored of him. He wasn't handsome enough or powerful enough. Rather than buy her way out of the contract, she simply decided to get rid of him. He'd met his end by being pushed down a flight of stairs, buried in the storage vault of Kyloe.

The second young man, blond and dashing Cabot de Berck, would have made a good earl but he'd suffered a bout with poison when Adelaide had returned from the trip where she'd first lain eyes on Thomas de Wolfe. It had taken poor Cabot two days to succumb to the poison Adelaide had used, and his body had been buried next to young Horncliffe.

And now, Thomas was displeasing Adelaide as well.

Another body in the vault.

"He is your husband, my lady." The old nurse tried to gently force the woman to see reason. "You have married him and he is the earl. This is what you wanted, was it not?"

Adelaide eyed the woman before resuming pulling the adornment from her hair, more slowly now.

"I did," she said. "He is handsome and powerful. I deserve a handsome and powerful husband. But he has been mean and cruel and inattentive, and now I know why. He is in love with another woman!"

Hilde finished lighting the last candle and move around the end of the bed. "How can you know that, my lady?"

Adelaide looked at her and the old woman recognized that look of utter fury. "Because he said so!" she snapped. "He just said so at our wedding feast! Can you imagine? The groom at his own wedding feast speaks of his love for another woman! It was bad enough that he locked me in the vault while he was away. He tossed me away like an animal. Well, I will not stand for it any longer. He has humiliated me for the last time."

Hilde knew what that meant. Fine, strong Thomas de Wolfe was not long for this world. She hustled over to her charge and began helping her remove the adornment from her hair, combs and pins that had been shoved into an elaborate style. But Adelaide was upset, and agitated, and when Hilde pulled on a comb too hard, Adelaide swung around and hit her, hard, on the side of the head. She hit her twice more until the woman fell down, hands over her head to prevent Adelaide from doing any real damage.

"You useless old fool," Adelaide hissed. "You are worthless to me, do you hear? One of these days it is going to be your own fault when I kill you. You are going to do something to displease me and it will be your fault!"

Hilde's hands came away from her head but there was blood on her left hand where she'd touched her ear. Adelaide's violent beating had made her bleed and as she looked at the blood on her hand, she realized there was something symbolic there.

Blood on her hands.

Aye, she knew about the two young men and she hadn't done anything about it. She had been terrified to. Now, Thomas de Wolfe's life was on the line, as well as her own. Adelaide as much as said so. She'd been afraid of Adelaide for so long that the paralyzing fear had crippled her into inaction but, at this moment, she realized that if she didn't act, Thomas would meet his death and so would she.

She couldn't let that happen.

It was finally time to take a stand.

"Get up," Adelaide snapped. "Get off the floor and help me dress. Bring me the blue shift, the one I had made for this night."

Hilde stood up on unsteady feet and shuffled over to the wardrobe. Opening the elaborately carved panels, she could see a variety of possessions at the bottom of it; satchels, mirrors, and a small assortment of beautiful daggers that Edmund had purchased for his daughter. She always traveled with them and that was what she used to cut her arms when the mood struck her.

As Hilde looked at them, an idea occurred to her, a thought of self-preservation that was born of fear. She grabbed the blue sleeping shift, the one that was sheer and delicate, and also one of the larger daggers.

Quickly, she returned to Adelaide.

"You have worked hard to marry Sir Thomas," she said, her voice trembling with fear and age, but she said it so forcefully that the trembling could have been construed as excitement. "He is finally your husband now and instead of punishing him for loving another, you must make him love you. You must *make* him appreciate you, my lady."

Adelaide was dubious. "How am I to do that if he loves another woman?" she asked. "I think I know who it is. Do remember the nun who visited Wark not long ago? The one who was going to Edenside? He showed her great attention. I would be willing to wager it is her!"

Hilde shook her head. She placed the blue shift upon the bed and held up the dagger to Adelaide.

"Do what you do best," she said encouragingly. "Bring your blood forth and tell Sir Thomas that you wish to die. He always comes when you do this, does he not? It has always brought him to you in the past. What better to spur a husband's regret and desire on his wedding night but the sight of his wife bathed in blood? He shall be sorry he was ever so cruel to you."

Adelaide eyed the dagger, her anger at Thomas diverted by Hilde's suggestion. Her mind was easily swayed, especially when it came to the dramatics she was so capable of.

"Do you think so?" she asked. "You do not think I should be a *tempestarii* again?"

The old woman shook her head. "Nay, my lady," she said. "No more *tempestarii*, no more fertility amulet. Be defenseless and near death. Lay down upon the bed and cut your arms, and I will summon Sir Thomas to come to you to save you. He must love a wife who would love him so much that she would die for that love."

It was a thin premise, but Hilde knew her charge well. She knew that Adelaide was always willing to cut her arms or pretend to be deathly ill if it would gain her what she wanted. In this case, it was Thomas' attention. The old woman was successfully diverting Adelaide's anger away from death and revenge and towards the very thing she took pleasure in – putting on an act for others. She had done it for her father her entire life, and for others to bend them to her will. This was nothing new. It was what she lived for.

Only this time, Hilde was going to help.

"Go, now," the old woman said. "Lay upon the bed. Shall I help you cut your arms? I shall find the best place."

Adelaide was swept up in the suggestion, agreeing to it because it was something she did so regularly. "Do not cut over a scar," she said. "It will hurt too much. Find clean flesh."

"I will, my lady."

"And you will run and tell him that I am dying?"

"Of course I will. Right away."

Adelaide lay down upon the lavender-sprinkled bed in a pose that looked very tragic but very innocent. When she was comfortable, Hilde had her hold out both hands close together with her palms up, making the tender undersides of both arms exposed. With the very sharp, and somewhat large dagger in-hand, Hilde lifted the blade.

"Are you ready, my lady?"

Adelaide nodded. "Be quick. And not too deep."

Hilde didn't reply. Instead, she swung into action. Taking the dagger, she sliced the blade across both of Adelaide's tender wrists, so deep that it was like she was carving into a side of beef. Adelaide screamed as Hilde cut so deeply that she nearly cut off Adelaide's right hand. Blood spurted, gushing all over Adelaide's green silk dress, all over her neck, and down her arms.

There was blood everywhere.

Adelaide lowered her damaged arms as Hilde moved away from the bed, rushing over to the door, still holding on to that bloodied dagger. Adelaide's extreme blood loss was so much, so quickly, that by the time Adelaide put her feet on the floor in an attempt to rise from the bed, she immediately fell to the floor, bleeding all over the stone. Her pale face turned to her old nurse, her eyes wide with accusation.

"What did you do?" she cried. "What did you do to me?"

Hilde was surprisingly unemotional. For a woman who had lived in fear her entire life, the sight of her charge bleeding to death didn't upset her in the least. In fact, there was something quite cathartic about it but she maintained a grip on the dagger in case Adelaide suddenly stood up and charged her.

She would defend herself.

"I did what needed to be done, my lady," she said in her heavy Germanic accent. Then, she shook her head in a gesture of sorrow and disgust. "You were going to kill Sir Thomas just as you killed those other young men. Fine young men that you threw away like rubbish. And me... you see me as rubbish, too. I will not let you throw me away, not when I have spent a lifetime being abused by you. What I did needed to be done."

Adelaide collapsed onto the floor as the puddle underneath her widened. It was clear that she wasn't long for this world.

"You... old bitch," she hissed. "What have you... done?"

With that, she made an odd noise that sounded like choking, but there was no more breath going into her lungs. She twitched a couple of times, her body going through death throes, before finally falling still with her sightless eyes wide open.

Hilde stood there a moment, holding that razor-sharp dagger, until she was sure Adelaide would rise no more. Then, she calmly walked over to her and put the dagger in her hand, making it look as if Adelaide had cut herself again, only this time, she had succeeded in cutting too deeply.

And that was how Thomas found her.

CHAPTER TWENTY-FIVE

Northwood Castle

I T WAS DAWN.

The mists were rising above the fields into a clear sky, signaling the start of a bright new day. But for Maitland, it was the first day of the rest of her life with a man who was married to someone else.

She hadn't slept all night, knowing that Thomas was touching Adelaide in the most intimate way. Even if he hated every second of it, he was still touching her as a husband touches a wife because it was required of him. Touches that were meant for Maitland were given over to a woman Thomas hated.

In truth, she wasn't sure who she was more upset for – herself or Thomas. And perhaps she was feeling just a little bit weak because when they'd spoken of their love for each other three days ago, she'd felt strong and fortified by it. But time and distance had caused her to doubt her resolve to love a man who could never give her his name. That name belonged to another.

It would never be hers.

She struggled to come to terms with it, not to linger on what could have been. At least she still had her children to keep her occupied, and their love was unconditional.

It brought her small comfort.

In the large bower at Northwood that Lady de Wolfe had put her in, Maitland looked around to her sleeping charges and to one who wasn't her charge at all. Caria was very attached to little Dyana, so the two of them slept in one small bed together while the other children slept in several other small beds that had been brought in for them.

Nice, comfortable beds with mattresses stuffed with feathers. Artus actually had his own bed and, even now, he was sprawled out over the top of it because he wasn't used to sleeping with a coverlet. He normally slept with nothing at all over him, so comfort like this was foreign to him.

Maitland smiled at Artus and his resistance to a coverlet as she stood by a big lancet window, watching the sun rise. She missed Thomas; she missed everything about him. Even though she knew this was the life, and love, she agreed to, as he'd never kept anything from her, still, it was a very lonely existence.

She was going to have to get used to it.

A breeze was picking up as the sun began to rise, rippling the silver-green grass of the fields beyond Northwood Castle, a truly massive bastion that literally sat right on the border between England and Scotland. Since Lady de Wolfe didn't want Maitland or the children returning to Edenside until it could be fortified, for now, this was to be their home. Maitland had met Lady Teviot, a very nice older woman who was most kind to the children, and she'd met Lady Ellsrod, too, a very tall woman with blonde hair and a somewhat stern manner about her.

But everyone seemed to be very pleasant, and the children were even visited by William and Paris yesterday as William began to take a few slow and short walks around the upper floor. William seemed to be healing very quickly from his injury, which put all of Northwood at ease. It was clear that William de Wolfe was important to Northwood, and Northwood to him. They were all intertwined from decades of service and alliances. Maitland envied that. She'd always hoped to be part of something strong and honorable like the House of de Wolfe, but it simply wasn't meant to be.

She was to be part of Edenside and that would have to be enough.

Maitland was just turning away from the window when she heard the sentries on the wall give up the cry. It was a call that moved along the wall, from man to man, until it reached the gatehouse. Curious, she peered from the window and could see men moving around the gatehouse, quickly, and the man-gate in the portcullis opening. It was clear that someone was approaching, though she couldn't see anything from her angle. But soon enough, the man-gate closed and the portcullis began to lift. And she saw, very clearly, when Thomas and several other men charged through the gatehouse.

Startled, Maitland's instinct was to run down to the bailey and greet him, but she didn't act on it. She stopped herself, as difficult as it was, knowing that Thomas would come to see her if he could. For him to have traveled from Wark to Northwood in the early morning hours must be important, indeed, so she nervously paced the floor for a few moments before she found a chair and perched on the end of it. She wondered what could be so crucial that Thomas had come. Perhaps it wasn't anything at all. Perhaps he'd only come to see to his father's health.

Perhaps he'd only come to tell the man about his wedding.

As she waited anxiously, Artus woke up, rubbing his eyes and declaring he was hungry. Maitland didn't move. She shushed him and told him to go back to sleep, but he wouldn't. He lay there and stared at the ceiling, his feet on the pillows as he wondered aloud when he was going to have some food. All he wanted was a little bread, he told her, but she told him to be quiet again. The others were still asleep and she knew Artus could wait a little while. Besides... she couldn't move.

Thomas had come.

Just as Maitland didn't think she could wait another moment for Thomas to make an appearance, there was a soft knock at the door. She jumped up from the chair and hurried to it, lifting the bolt and slowly opening the panel. The first face she saw was Thomas, standing in the corridor with his brothers and his mother, and finally Desmond. Desmond looked pale and weary. In fact, Thomas did, too, and she looked at him with great concern.

"Thomas!" she gasped. "Whatever is the matter?"

Thomas seemed to be breathing heavily; from exertion, or excitement, she couldn't tell. But his eyes were fixed on her.

"Something has happened, Mae," he said. "I must speak to you."

Maitland blinked in surprise. "Of course," she said softly, coming out into the corridor and shutting the door behind her. "The children are still sleeping. Has something happened?"

Thomas nodded, looking to Desmond with an expression that silently prompted the man. Desmond reluctantly stepped forward.

"Aye," he said, looking to Thomas, to Lady Jordan, and finally to Scott, Troy, and Patrick, who had ridden to Northwood with their younger brother at this ungodly hour. He finally sighed, heavily. "Mae, Adelaide de Vauden is dead. She killed herself on her wedding night."

Maitland's eyes widened and her hands flew to her mouth. "Dead?" she gasped. "My God... she *killed* herself?"

Desmond nodded. She could see the disbelief in his expression, still, as if he didn't quite believe what he was telling her. "The woman has been cutting herself since she came to Wark those months ago, and long before that, even," he said. "She did it for attention, but last night, she cut too deep and ended up killing herself. Her old nurse told us that she saw her do it."

Maitland's hand was still over her mouth as she looked to Thomas. "Are you well, Thomas?" she asked. "She did not hurt you, too, did she?"

Thomas shook his head, which was a feat in itself considering how much he'd had to drink the night before. Everything hurt, but that didn't matter. He'd never faced a more important moment in his life.

"Nay," he said. "Mae, I am genuinely trying not to be insensitive about Adelaide's death. The woman had problems... many problems, according to her nurse, but she was an evil woman. Nothing can excuse the things she has done to others and, mayhap someday, I will tell you all of it. But right now, I do not wish to speak on it. I do not want to bring that evil into this place or into this conversation. Adelaide will now be buried with her father, which is fitting considering he helped perpetuate her wickedness. But all that aside, I had to come to tell you what had happened. It could not wait."

Maitland nodded, looking at everyone standing alongside Thomas, including her brother. But her focus returned to Thomas. "You are the Earl of Northumbria now?" she asked.

He nodded. "Aye," he said. "Northumbria is mine."

She smiled faintly. "That is a very proud thing, Thomas," she said. "You will make a fine earl."

He returned her smile. God, all he wanted to do was smile at her, but this was such a delicate situation. Adelaide had killed herself and, as he'd told Maitland, he didn't want to be insensitive about it. Adelaide may have treated others with disdain, but Thomas didn't want to fall into that category. He wanted to do what was right, to show respect and compassion in the situation. But the truth was that nearly the moment he realized Adelaide had killed herself, all he could think of was marrying Maitland. He was blinded to almost any other thought.

"Thank you," he said after a moment. "But I wanted to speak with you about... Mae, I am not sure how else to say this, so I shall simply come out with it. You have seen me treat Adelaide with less than kindness and I told you once that I did not want you to think I treat all women that way. I do not, and I have brought my mother and my brothers here to vouch for my character. They will tell you of the man they know. I want you to know that in spite of what you saw with Adelaide, I am a man of good character."

Maitland's smile grew. "I know that," she said. "I have known that from the start. I saw how abominable Adelaide was, the poor woman. You were reacting to the way she treated you."

Thomas sighed heavily, one of relief. "Thank you," he said sincerely. "I want to make sure you understand that because, since you have no father, I have asked your brother for your hand in marriage."

Maitland's eyebrows lifted in shock as she looked to Desmond, who was looking at her with a reluctant smile on his lips.

"He did," Desmond confirmed. "But before I give you my answer, you should know that when he first confessed his feelings to me, I told him to stay away from you. I told him that you deserved more than simply being a courtesan to an earl. But when you and the children were abducted, I saw a side to Thomas I've never seen before, Mae. I saw a man who ceased to think only of himself and become a man who was concerned only for you. I suppose... I suppose that, in that moment, I saw how much you meant to him. I would have never believed it coming from Thomas de Wolfe, but it is the truth. I do believe he loves you."

A smile spread across Maitland's face. "And?"

"And I gave him my permission to marry you."

Tears sprang to Maitland's eyes as she looked at Thomas, who had an expression of such hope and joy on his face that it was the brightest thing she had ever seen. Reaching out, he grasped her hand, the one wearing the ring that he'd given her, and took a knee as he gazed up into her beautiful face.

"I am not a perfect man, Maitland," he said hoarsely. "I have always been the wild colt of the de Wolfe pack, but you make me want to be a better man and I swear that I will love you, as much as any man has ever loved a woman, for the rest of my life. You and those foundlings are mine, and ever will be, and I will do my best to be worthy of you all if you will have me."

Maitland chuckled at his sweet words as tears spilled down her cheeks. All she could manage was a nod and Thomas grinned at her as she cupped his face, bending down to kiss him. He wrapped his big arms around her, holding her tightly as around them, the older de Wolfe brothers began to clap. It was a joyful noise, from joyful men, who had finally seen their little brother grow up. Standing next to them, all Jordan could do was beam at her formerly irresponsible, reckless son.

He had become a man.

The noise awoke the children, and the door flew open as little ones began to swarm in the corridor. Thomas found himself mobbed by Caria and Dyana. He was separated from Maitland, but only briefly, as he picked up two little girls, one in each arm. But he wasn't distressed. Looking at the woman he loved, at the woman who would soon become his wife, it was a moment he had dreamed of but never truly believed would happen.

But it had.

At that moment, Thomas knew he'd found what he'd been searching for. Family, love, and a woman of his own... that was all he could ever want for. The knight who brought the storms with him had found the peace he'd been searching for.

Thomas de Wolfe finally found his corner of heaven.

CȜ THE END ȣ

Children of Thomas and Maitland
Artus
Nora
Phin
Marybelle
Renard & Roland
Dyana
Alexander
Cabot
Matthew
Wade
Tacey
Morgana
(William de Wolfe lived long enough to see
his first two grandsons born, Alexander and Cabot)

ABOUT KATHRYN LE VEQUE

Medieval Just Got Real.

KATHRYN LE VEQUE is a USA TODAY Bestselling author, an Amazon All-Star author, and a #1 bestselling, award-winning, multi-published author in Medieval Historical Romance and Historical Fiction. She has been featured in the NEW YORK TIMES and on USA TODAY's HEA blog. In March 2015, Kathryn was the featured cover story for the March issue of InD'Tale Magazine, the premier Indie author magazine. She was also a quadruple nominee (a record!) for the prestigious RONE awards for 2015.

Kathryn's Medieval Romance novels have been called 'detailed', 'highly romantic', and 'character-rich'. She crafts great adventures of love, battles, passion, and romance in the High Middle Ages. More than that, she writes for both women AND men – an unusual crossover for a romance author – and Kathryn has many male readers who enjoy her stories because of the male perspective, the action, and the adventure.

On October 29, 2015, Amazon launched Kathryn's Kindle Worlds Fan Fiction site WORLD OF DE WOLFE PACK. Please visit Kindle Worlds for Kathryn Le Veque's World of de Wolfe Pack and find many action-packed adventures written by some of the top authors in their genre using Kathryn's characters from the de Wolfe Pack series. As Kindle World's FIRST Historical Romance fan fiction world, Kathryn Le Veque's World of de Wolfe Pack will contain all of the great story-telling you have come to expect.

Kathryn loves to hear from her readers. Please find Kathryn on Facebook at Kathryn Le Veque, Author, or join her on Twitter @kathrynleveque, and don't forget to visit her website and sign up for her blog at www.kathrynleveque.com.

Please follow Kathryn on Bookbub for the latest releases and sales: bookbub.com/authors/kathryn-le-veque.

53972547R00236

Made in the USA
Columbia, SC
23 March 2019